Reborn

Jessica Miller

DEDICATION

This book is dedicated to my Dad and my Mom. We may not always agree on things, but I wouldn't be where I am if it weren't for the both of you.

ACKNOWLEDGMENTS

First and foremost I would to thank my friends and family for their ongoing support. Thank you to Tiffany for always being the first one to buy my books the second they're released. Thank you to Jenny D, Carrie, Jill, Missi, Shanna, Tara and Rose for your encouragement and endless excitement when I talk about a new book. Your kind words and support are forever in my heart. You give me the strength to keep going and never stop reaching for the stars.

Reborn
A Wanderers novel
2013

CHAPTER ONE

The sun was hot. It glistened off the beads of sweat that trickled down my skin. I sat up, staring out into the vast ocean before me. My skin was tingling. I basked in the glory of it all, soaking up as much of the scenery as I could.

I reached into my beach bag and pulled out suntan lotion. I gradually applied the lotion to my legs, face, and arms. "Want some help with that?" he asked, flashing me his cocky smile. I smiled back and handed him the bottle. He sat behind me and very delicately applied the cream to my shoulders and back. I relaxed, enjoying the feel of his hands on me. His touch was something that I never got tired of.

When he stopped, I had a feeling of disappointment. That quickly changed when he wrapped his arms around my waist. I leaned back into him and rested my head on his chest, feeling content. "I wish we could stay here forever," I said as I dug my toes in the sand.

"I know, but we can't," Tristan said solemnly.

"Why not? Why can't we?" I asked, desperate to stay here forever. I turned to him, my eyes pleading for an explanation as to why he would want to leave this paradise.

He rubbed his thumb over my pouty lip before he replaced it with a gentle kiss. "Because we can't," he sighed, knowing how soon this would end. I moved in closer, wanting to feel his soft lips again. "I love you," he whispered. I pulled back and smiled, looking into his beautiful blue eyes. I opened my mouth to tell him I loved him too, but before I had the chance, everything disappeared. My whole world went dark and all I could see was black. I blinked a few times trying to adjust my eyes to my current surroundings. When I opened them, the only thing I saw was a plain, white ceiling above me. The

1

same plain, white ceiling I've been staring at for the past month and a half.

I sighed, kicking off the covers. Ginger grumbled, not happy about being buried by the blanket. "Sorry girl," I said, patting her head. I looked at the clock on my night stand. It was nine a.m. My eyes moved over to the pictures sitting next to my alarm clock. Pictures of friends I would never see again. Loved ones that were taken away from me because of who I was. I hastily wiped away the tears from my cheek and took down all the pictures, stuffing them in a drawer. I crawled back in to bed and pulled the covers up over my head.

Ginger nudged me with her nose, whimpering in my ear. I drew the covers back to glare at her. She crooked her head to the side, staring at me with her big brown eyes. I tried tugging the covers back up over my head but she just pawed at them and kept whimpering. "What do you want?" I snapped. Ginger lied back down, laying her head on her paws, giving me an, *'I'm sorry'* look. The look on her face was enough to make me feel bad for snapping. All she wanted was a little attention.

I exhaled, patting the spot next to me. She slowly scooted her way closer. I scratched behind her ears, which caused her to roll over so I could scratch her belly. "I'm sorry for snapping. You're probably hungry, aren't you?" Ginger jumped up and licked my face. "I'll take that as a yes."

I forced myself out of bed and headed down stairs to the kitchen where I found Danni and my mom. The room grew silent the moment I stepped foot onto the cold tile floor. "Good morning sweetheart, you hungry?" my mom asked as she quickly swiped a sponge over the counter, trying to appear busy.

"No. I just came down to feed Ginger," I replied. She nodded and went back to pretending to clean. It would have been more believable if our maid wasn't standing right next to her. I was too tired to care. So I let her continue with her act. My mom could pretend all she wanted. It wasn't going to change the pain I felt inside, eating away at my chest. She's been like this since they brought me home. It's not just her. Everyone's been walking on eggshells around me ever since I've returned. I assumed they were afraid if they said or did anything that would upset me I'd fall into a deep state of depression. It didn't matter what they said or did. I was already gone. I guess you could say I was thankful for the peace and quiet. No one bothered me and I didn't bother them. Everyone just left me alone to wallow in my own misery.

I fed Ginger, and then I dragged my feet back up the stairs to my room.

Returning home was hard. I knew once I came back that meant what happened was real. I would have to accept that Josie and Tristan really were gone and were never coming back. They were now just two more names on a list of people I loved that Jack had taken away from me. Jack, the rogue vampire who killed people I cared about just to get my powers. Powers that I never knew existed until my parents were forced to tell me the truth of what I was, a half-human half-vampire princess. I had to admit the part about being a half-vampire was pretty cool, but when you add a tiara on top of that, no thank you.

I didn't want any of this. If I could take it all back and just be human I would. The worst part of it all is that I remember that night back in Vermont as if it were yesterday. The fight between Cadence and Tristan that caused her to lose her life. The fight between Jack and Tristan and then Jack and I. All these memories were permanently planted in my head and stuck on instant replay.

I spent the first few weeks blaming my parents. I argued that if they would have told me who I was from the beginning, all of this could have been prevented. I would have known Cadence and Jack were rogues. I would have never befriended him or joined that stupid sorority. I would have done a lot of things differently and I would have known how to protect myself. They swore to me up and down that knowing the truth wouldn't have mattered. It would have just put me in potential risk of more danger. The only thing they managed to convince me of was that this was all my fault. It was my own stupidity for being naive. If I hadn't been so closed off, Tristan and I could have had something more. He would still be here and I would still be with him.

Tristan.

My heart wept every time I thought of him. There wasn't a single day when he didn't cross my mind. I'm not going to lie, in the beginning, our relationship was pretty rocky. I guess the best way to describe it would be that our relationship was a one way street and I was running the wrong way. I loved him. I loved him more than I ever loved anyone. Now he was gone, ripped from this world way too soon.

I was told his memorial service was private, family only, which I was happy to hear. I didn't think I would have been able to handle it.

Josie's funeral was hard enough. I couldn't recall much from that day, but the little bits and pieces I did remember I wanted to forget.

I remember standing by her grave thinking, *"today is the day I bury my best friend and today is the day I watch Josie's little brother say goodbye to his sister."*

After the service, her parents invited everyone to come by the house. I hid in the shadows, away from everyone. I spent very little time engaging with people. The rare moments when I wasn't numb, I would wander around aimlessly. At one point, I wandered all the way down to the end of the hall to Jake's bedroom. I found him alone, on his bed, with his head hung low.

I had slowly made my way into his room and sat down next to him on his bed. "You know Josie loved you very much," I said, hoping in some way that that might comfort him. He nodded, almost robotic. "Here, I have something for you." I reached behind me, in my purse, where I was holding Jake's favorite stuffed penguin that he let Josie borrow.

"I don't want him. You can have him," he said with tears in his eyes, making my heart break.

"Why not," I asked. "I thought he was your favorite?"

"He was...but not anymore."

"How come?"

"He was supposed to keep Josie safe, but he didn't," he said, bowing his head. It took everything I had not to break down and cry.

I couldn't bear to see him so upset. So I came up with a small white lie to make him feel better. "Well, you see Jake, he did keep her safe. When they were together. But a friend was looking after him for Josie that night so he was keeping someone else safe," I said, holding my breath and hoping he bought it.

"Really?" he sat up.

"Really," I said, holding the penguin out to him.

He hesitated for a minute, then took the penguin, and held him tightly in his arms. I wrapped my arms around both of them. "Ella?"

"Yes Jake?"

"Will you still come over and see me?"

"Of course I will," I said, giving him a kiss on top of his head. After that we both just sat there for a while, taking comfort in each other, in silence.

When I reached my room I climbed back into bed only to discover I had a few texts. One of them was from Dixon telling me he would be in the area and we should get together. I ignored it not wanting to see anybody. The other text was from Billy, Tristan's best friend.

In Scotland. Nothing yet.

I deleted the texts and turned off my phone, not wanting to be disturbed. I lied back down and stared up at the plain, white ceiling. Reading Billy's text took me back to when I was still in Vermont. I had to stay until my dad finished cleaning up the mess Cadence and Jack left behind. It was a rough couple of weeks, but I lasted by concentrating on helping Billy get better.

Billy had survived the attack against Jack leaving him hospitalized for a few weeks. I visited him every day I could until I had to return home. And every day he swore to me that as soon as he was well he was going to seek revenge on Jack for what he did to Tristan and Josie. He told me he would not rest until he killed him. I begged him not to, but there was no convincing him otherwise.

On the last day, before I had to return home, I went to visit Billy one more time. When I got to his room, I was too late. He was already gone. I saw him at Josie's funeral. He was standing in the back of the crowd, but by the time I got the chance to go talk to him, he disappeared. That was the last I saw him. I would get letters or a text every now and then letting me know of his progress. From what I could tell he wasn't any closer to finding Jack than my father and his crew was.

I haven't seen or talked to anyone since Josie's funeral. The McNaughton's decided to take some time off and get away. My dad told them to take all the time they needed and not to worry. Xander would help him with the business until Mr. McNaughton was ready to come back to work.

Since returning, I basically spent every day in my room. I closed myself off from the world outside. My parents tried to get me to go to counseling again, but I refused. No amount of talking was going to change what happened. In less than a year I had lost my boyfriend, Kyle, my best friend, and the first guy I ever truly loved to a crazy vampire who was still on the loose. I find out I'm half-human half-vampire with powers that I didn't even know how to use. My family was part of the vampire royal court and I'm supposed to take over for my dad in just a few years.

Yes, today was just another day in the life of Ella McCallister.

I was starting to believe I was a curse, doomed to have anyone in my presence harmed. I thought about leaving and getting away for a while, but I couldn't even if I wanted to. I was on house arrest according to my dad. I wasn't allowed to go anywhere without at least five guardians. He claimed it was just a precaution until they caught Jack. I had a feeling this wasn't something that was going to change, even if they caught Jack.

All these memories were making my chest hurt. I closed my eyes tight, hoping to fall back asleep so I could dream of Tristan. Seeing him in my dreams was better than nothing at all. It helped the days go by a little easier knowing that when I closed my eyes I might see him. Unfortunately, right when I was about to fall back asleep there was a knock on my door.

"Ella?" It was Jasa.

I sat up, cursing to myself. "Come in," I said, trying to be polite.

Jasa was my brother, Xander's, girlfriend. We met briefly before I left for school. After everything that had happened, my dad asked Xander to move back in temporarily. He said having him nearby would be easier for the business, but a part of me knew it was because of me. The doctors told them having family around would be the best thing for me, but clearly they didn't know my family very well. It wasn't long after Xander moved back that Jasa started hanging around more. More than I cared for, but Xander seemed to really like her so I thought I'd be nice.

"I'm not disturbing you am I?" she asked, popping her head in the door.

Yes.

"No, what's up?"

"Well, as you know, Christmas is only about two weeks away."

"Really, I hadn't noticed," I admitted. Lately all the days just seemed to blend together.

Jasa sat down on the bed next to me. Her long blonde hair was pulled back into a sleek ponytail. She had on dark blue jeans and a light colored sweater that complemented her pale complexion. "I was wondering if you would like to go shopping with me?" she asked.

"Sorry, I'm not in the mood."

"I understand," she said, fidgeting with her sweater. I knew there was more. So I sat patiently and waited. "It's just I'm having a hard time finding a present for Xander and I thought maybe you could help me." The last thing I wanted to do was go shopping, but she had a way of making me feel bad for saying no. She was nothing but nice to me since I returned. "I'm not going to force you to do anything you don't want to." She stood up thinking my silence meant no. "I'll just leave you alone then," she said, walking away.

"No...wait," I sighed, giving in. "I'll go."

"You sure? You don't have to if you don't want to."

"No, it's fine. I should probably get my shopping done. Just give me a few minutes to get ready."

"Take all the time you need. I'll be downstairs when you're ready," she said smiling at me and closing the door behind her.

I originally planned on having Danni do my shopping for me so I wouldn't have to, but it was probably better that I did it myself. I forced myself out of bed and into the shower.

*

Jamila

Downstairs in the kitchen, Jasa informed Jamila that Ella had agreed to go shopping with her. "Oh Jasa, thank you. You have no idea how much I appreciate you getting her out of the house," Jamila said.

"It's no problem. I've been meaning to find an excuse to spend more time with her. I think this could be the perfect opportunity to get to know her better."

"I should probably warn you, I don't think she'll be in the mood to talk much," Danni chimed in.

"Give her some time. She'll open up," Jamila hoped. "She has been through a lot. I just don't know what to do to help her." She shook her head, worried for her daughter.

"Jamila, Ella's a strong girl. You know she'll get through this. She just needs time to heal," Danni said, placing a kind hand on Jamila's shoulder.

"Thank you Danni. I'm so glad you're here. Ella really responds to you best. I don't know what I'd do without you," she said, hugging Danni tightly.

"I'll always be here," Danni told her as she shot a look to Jasa. Jamila knew there was tension between the two girls, but right now wasn't the time to deal with that issue. Not when her daughter was in so much pain. Ella was her first priority.

"You're more than welcome to join us," Jasa said, inviting Danni along.

"Thank you, but I have too much work to do," Danni politely

declined, getting back to work.

Ella

I stepped out of the shower, wiping the fog from the mirror. I stared at my reflection. After receiving my powers my appearance has altered slightly. My skin was clearer than it has ever been and looked as smooth as silk. My teeth were whiter and my hair was silky, shiny, and a little longer, almost half way down my back. Even my eyes deepened in color. While I always categorized my eyes as green, they had a habit of changing. One day they looked green, some days yellow, and others a mixture of both, making them look hazel. If you looked close enough you could even see a few brown dots around the irises. My mom used to tell me my eyes reminded her of a child with a playful nature because they were always changing – whatever that meant.

Another startling new feature was the electric blue streak that showed up in my hair after I had received my powers. It was about two inches wide and sat on the right side just behind my ear. It flowed from the roots all the way down to the ends. I tried everything I could to get rid of it, aside from cutting it. I dyed it, bleached it, but nothing worked. I was stuck with it. And now from all the dye my hair was black like a raven. I didn't mind the black hair, but it did cause the blue streak to stand out more. I got used to the blue after a while. For the most part I could hide it if I wanted to, but I never went anywhere so it didn't matter.

I quickly dried my hair and pulled it into a low ponytail on the side. I slipped into a pair of jeans and a long sleeved shirt. I threw on a hat, zipped up my boots, and grabbed my purse on my way downstairs to meet Jasa.

I found her in the kitchen talking to my mom. "I'm ready," I told her.

"You girls have fun," my mom said. She gave me a hug and a kiss before we left – one of many since I've been home.

"You need us to pick up anything while we're out?" Jasa asked.

"No thank you," she said, smiling sweetly. We made our way

outside to the car where there were guardians waiting for us, making me regret going.

When we reached the mall, I was overwhelmed with the all the people out shopping. I should have expected this. It was two weeks before Christmas as Jasa had pointed out. I felt uncomfortable with the way people stared at us as we walked through the stores. No doubt from being flanked by guardians. I overheard a few people whispering, wondering if we were celebrities, or someone important enough to be so heavily guarded. I tried my best to ignore them all.

I was not in the mood to shop and I was having a hard time acting like it. Jasa didn't push me to talk and I appreciated her for that. She would ask my opinion every now and then, but all I gave her was a nod or a one word response. After a while she stopped asking. About an hour into our shopping, Jasa asked if I wanted to grab something to eat. I agreed and followed her to the food court. I ordered a fruit salad not feeling very hungry. I barely ate much lately so I just more or less picked at my food.

"I'm sorry about your friend Josie," Jasa said after a few minutes of silence. Of all the topics she could have picked, she chose this one. Honestly, anything would have been better, even talking about something as lame as the weather. "I can't imagine what you're going through."

"No, you can't," I said curtly, annoyed that she would bring it up.

"I didn't mean...I just I..." she said, stumbling over her words.

"Look, I know you're just trying to help, but I'd rather not talk about it." Jasa nodded and went back to eating her salad. The awkward silence that followed made me feel guilty for snapping. I knew she was just trying to be polite. I had no doubt she was nervous just being around me without the added drama, but this was not something I wanted to talk about, especially not with a stranger. Regardless of my feelings I still felt inclined to apologize. "I'm sorry," I said. Jasa peered up from her salad. "Everyone tries to get me to talk about it. They think that if I discuss what happened I'm going to magically be okay. But it won't change the fact that my friends are dead because of me."

"You think it's your fault?" she asked, slightly surprised.

"Of course it is. Jack killed them to get to me," I said before I mentally slapped myself in the head. No wonder Jasa looked so confused. She didn't know the real reason Jack was after me. Like everyone else she believed Jack was just some jealous kid who snapped and went on a killing spree taking out anyone who hurt him mentally or physically. Well that was the story my dad and his people spun to keep our existence a secret. I needed to be more careful when I spoke around humans. Another thing I would have to learn to get used to.

Before I could correct myself Jasa spoke up. "I don't think your friends would want you to believe that. I think they'd want you to know that they loved you and wouldn't want you to blame yourself for something you couldn't control. Most people would want you to celebrate their lives instead of mourning their deaths."

She had a point. I could just hear Josie now. *"Seriously Ella, get a grip. This boo-hoo look is not attractive and frowning that much is going to give you wrinkles*." I smiled slightly at the thought of Josie lecturing me. "Maybe you should start a journal?" Jasa suggested, distracting me from my thoughts. "Since you don't want to talk to anyone, maybe writing your feelings down will help clear your head."

"Maybe," I shrugged.

We finished our lunch and then continued shopping. I told Jasa to get Xander anything from the Apple store and she would be good. She got him the latest IPad and I let her know it was a good choice. I even managed to get all my Christmas presents checked off my list including a few items for myself. One of those items was a journal. I took Jasa's suggestion and thought it might help me if I wrote down my feelings. As lame as I thought it was, I figured it wouldn't hurt to give it a shot. What did I have to lose?

When we got home, I carried all my stuff upstairs to my room where I found my mom, snooping. "Mom, what are you doing?" I asked suspiciously.

She turned around, startled. "Oh, honey, I didn't hear you come in. I was just putting away your laundry," she said, closing the top drawer of my dresser.

"Where's Danni?" She was the one who usually dropped off my laundry. I preferred that because I knew she wouldn't snoop, unlike my mom. I didn't keep clothes in the top drawer of my dresser and I'm pretty sure my mom knew that.

"I sent her on some errands," she replied, avoiding the fact that I just busted her.

Since I had nothing to hide, I ignored her, and sat on my bed. I learned it was my parents who hid things, not me. I unsnapped my watch and placed it on the nightstand noticing my pictures were back. I sighed and lay back on the bed knowing that was my mom's doing. After placing my sweaters in the wrong draw, she came over, and sat next to me on the bed. "How was shopping?" she asked.

"It was fine."

"Wanna show me what you got?" She leaned back on her elbow while I sat up and grabbed my bags, dumping the stuff on my bed. Most of my bags consisted of hooded sweatshirts, jeans, and plain tops. My mom sifted through my purchases. She tried to hide her disappointment when she saw all the plain, basic items I bought, but I knew there was worry behind her smile. She was used to me wearing bright, sparkly tops, but lately I wasn't into anything bright and sparkly. "What else did you buy?" she asked, reaching for the other bags.

I quickly pulled them away from her. "That, you can't see," I said, tucking the bags under the bed that contained her presents. She smiled and leaned back on the bed. "I got some make-up, perfume, and lotions too." I dumped out the cosmetics and spread everything out.

"Anything I'll like?" she asked, searching through the pile.

"Maybe," I shrugged.

She frowned at all the dark and neutral colored shadows I bought. She was used to seeing me in pinks and purples. Again something I was not in the mood for. "Danni's going to bring Hadley over later and we're going to bake some cookies. You wanna help us?" she asked, changing the subject.

"Maybe," I said, lying back on the bed.

"You know, helping me bake cookies for Christmas used to be your favorite thing."

"I know," I sighed.

"Ella honey?" she said warily. "I know this year has been rough for you."

"That's an understatement."

"I just want you to know we're here for you. Whatever you need."

"I know mom."

"I wish I could tell you things will get better over time, but that's up to you. The only person who's going to help you heal is yourself. I will be here for you every step of the way, but you have to find it within yourself."

I stared at the ceiling fighting back the tears. My mom pulled me to her and hugged me tightly. I laid my head on her shoulder and let the tears fall. She just squeezed me tighter. "Oh mom, I miss them so much," I wept.

"I know you do," she said, gently stroking my hair.

"Will it ever stop hurting?"

I felt an intake of breath on her chest. "Eventually," she exhaled. "It's okay to miss them and its okay to cry, but I don't think they would want you to be sad. They'd want you to cherish the time you've spent together and move on, because Ella, you have to remember you're still here. Even though they're gone, you have to try to go on living."

"But I can't live without them."

"Maybe it feels that way now, but soon you'll see that you can." I wiped the tears from my face and sat up. "Will you do me a favor?" I nodded and she stood up from the bed, hand held out for me. "Come take a little trip with me."

"Where?" I asked.

"Just trust your mother," she smiled.

I took her hand, allowing her to pull me off the bed and out of the room. When we got downstairs she paused. "Wait here a minute." She walked out to the kitchen, spoke a few words to the guardians, then grabbed her purse and keys, heading for the door. She spoke a few more words to the guardians outside and they stepped aside letting us pass.

"No guardians?" I asked her as we hopped in the car.

"Not today," she said, squeezing my hand before putting the car in drive. Once we got off the main road it didn't take me long to figure out where we were going. My mom pulled into the gates of the cemetery and drove up the hill. She put the car in park and turned to face me. "Want me to go with you?" she asked.

"No," I said, letting out a breath. I placed my hand on the handle of the door, pausing to take another breath. I lifted the lever, stepped out of the car, and walked over to Josie's grave. I knelt down and sat Indian style in front of her tombstone. At first I just stared at the giant, granite rock that represented what was left of my friend. I picked at the blades of grass, wondering what I should say. I wanted to tell her I missed her, I'm sorry this happened to her, and if I could I would trade places with her in a heartbeat. I wanted to tell her no one will ever replace her and I'll never find a friend as great as her.

I placed my hand on the ground and spread my fingers wide. I closed my eyes and cleared my head so I could say goodbye to my friend. As I sat there, I started to feel a warm tingling in my hand. The warmth made its way up my arm and through my whole body, spreading like wildfire. It was like the sun was warming me from the inside out. It was soothing, like a gentle caress of a summer breeze. The heat tickled my skin and made me smile. It was like Josie was here with me, wrapping her arms around me in a comforting hug. A tear escaped my eye and slid down my cheek, splashing on my hand. I looked down at the tear and watched it shimmer in the light like a sparkly diamond. It dissolved making my lips twitch into a slight smile.

"I love you too Josie," I whispered. I closed my eyes, releasing some of my pain and anger. Coming here today and having to face this, accept the truth. It helped give me what I needed to move on. I'm not saying I'm miraculously healed, but part of me is getting there. When I was ready, I stood up, and walked back to the car. Once inside, my mom turned to me with a questioning look. "Thank you," I said, giving her a kiss on the cheek. Before I could pull away she hugged me, placing a hand ever so lightly on my cheek. She smiled, a smile so sweet and loving it could brighten anyone's day.

Once we got back my dad instantly castigated my mom for leaving the house without any guardians. I was going to step in and say something, but I knew my mom could handle herself. Instead I went up to my room and fell down on my bed. I spotted the pictures on my nightstand and instantly started to feel that warming sensation again. The one I felt not so long ago at Josie's grave. I sat up and decided it was time I got outside. It wasn't the most glamorous outing, but anything was better than lying around and sulking, staring at the same plain, white ceiling for the next who knows how many hours.

It had gotten considerably warmer since this morning and I thought I'd take advantage while I could. I got up and grabbed my bathing suit out of my dresser and got changed. I grabbed my new journal on the way out, only to stop when I passed my mirror. I decided to throw on a pair of shorts and t-shirt over my bathing suit. I knew eventually they'd find out what I did, but not sure I was quite ready to bare it all, just yet.

*

Liam paced back and forth in his home office. His face was red and stressed and his eyes were filled with anger. "Jamila, honestly, do you not care about this family's safety?"

"How could you ask me that? Of course I do," she replied, aggravated that he would even ask that.

"Then why did you and Ella leave the house without any guardians?" he spat back.

"Because I care more about our daughter's sanity. She needs to be able to breathe and that's hard to do surrounded by guardians twenty-four seven."

"It's for her protection. She has been targeted and attacked, something that should have never happened in the first place. We should have never let her go to school so far away. We should have sent guardians with her from the beginning," he rambled. He went through every possible scenario he thought that could have prevented this tragedy, but they both knew nothing would have changed the outcome.

"Liam, you know we can't protect her all the time, unfortunately. She's growing up and needs to experience things on her own. I don't think keeping her here or having her guarded all the time would have changed things." Liam sighed, knowing she was right. "You need to realize that right now Ella is the one suffering more than she should be."

"I'm doing the best I can," he snapped. Liam hated the thought of his daughter having to endure what she did this past year. If he could have prevented it in any way he would have. He thought he had. He thought he was doing the right thing by not telling her what she really was, but now he's slowly learning maybe that wasn't the best idea. He scrubbed a hand down his face. If only he had been there, he could have stopped it.

Jamila stood up, closing the distance between them. "You being there wouldn't have stopped it. We've already proven that. You can't blame yourself." Liam turned to face his wife wondering how she always knew what he was thinking. "I know you Liam. So I will always know what you're thinking," she said, giving him a small smile. "Outer wounds heal. Inside is where she's hurting the most. She needs time and suffocating her won't help."

"I know," he said, bowing his head, feeling defeated. He looked at his wife, her beautiful face, her gorgeous green eyes, just like their daughters, her gracious smile. She was the picture of perfection and always had the ability to calm him when he needed it the most. He took her in his arms and inhaled her sweet scent, letting out a breath and instantly calming. "Just tell me what to do," he said.

"Just be patient," Jamila smiled, kissing her husband on the lips.

CHAPTER TWO

December 10

It's been over a month and today is the first day I feel...I feel less pain. I feel a little more like myself as opposed to someone trapped inside an empty shell. The pain I felt after losing Josie and Tristan was too unbearable. After everything that happened, I thought I needed something to help me ease the pain, a way to release some of the pressure. So I decided the only way I knew how to do that was to inflict pain on myself. I know now that my decision may not have been the best idea, but what's done is done, I can't change it now. I can say I don't have any regrets though.

I sat back and pushed up my sunglasses.

I remember the first day it happened, when I made the decision to ease my pain. It was one day while we were heading back from the hospital after visiting Billy. On the drive back to the hotel we had passed a tattoo shop. I asked Gabe to pull over. "Miss Ella, I don't think this is wise," Gabe said.

"I didn't recall asking for your opinion. Now pull over," I demanded. Gabe did as I asked and followed closely behind me as we entered the tattoo shop. I ignored all the stares I got from the people in the waiting room and proceeded to look around at all the different designs.

A short, bald, heavy set man, covered from head to toe in tattoos came up to me. "Can I help you?" he asked in a deep voice.

I straightened myself out, put on a brave face, and said, "Yes, I would like a tattoo."

He gave me a funny look, but obliged. "Alright, how about you pick some pretty thing off the wall and let me know what you decided."

I never took my eyes off of him. "I know what I want," I said firm.

He turned his head to Gabe, than back to me, and smiled creepily. "Let me guess, your boyfriend's name inside a heart."

I turned to Gabe and laughed. Gabe just looked uncomfortable. Once I was able to contain my laughter, I gave Gabe an apologetic look and turned back to the tattoo guy. "No, I'm leaving it up to you." He looked me up and down brows creased. To give him a little more incentive, I threw a couple hundred dollar bills on the counter in front of him. He eyed the money then signaled for me to follow him in the back. Gabe kept tight on my tail reminding me how much of a bad idea he thought this was. I ignored him and took a seat in the chair as the tattoo artist had directed me to.

"How big and where do you want it?"

I thought it over for a minute. "My back and as big as you can make it." I took off my shirt giving him free range to do whatever he wanted. I knew I was taking a risk by letting him choose the design. I could end up with two naked ladies on my back, but at the moment I didn't care. I sat in the chair trying not to let my nerves get the best of me. It was hard to listen to the buzzing sound coming from the other rooms. The longer I waited, the more I wanted to jump out of the chair, but I stayed strong.

"Do you want a test shot?" he asked.

"No, just do it," I said so I wouldn't back out.

"This may hurt a little."

"That's the plan," I said to myself. I closed my eyes ready to take on the pain and boy did it hurt, a lot. Each drag of the needle felt like a hot razor on my skin. The pain I felt from the tattoo needle didn't release the hurt I felt inside like I thought it would, but it still distracted me, at least for the time being. When he was done, he handed me a mirror to take a look at his work. He had covered my entire lower back with intricate swirls around a purple butterfly leading its way up to two brightly colored flowers.

It was perfect.

I turned to him and asked what had made him decide to do the design. He scratched his head saying he wasn't sure. He said he just started drawing and this was the outcome. He said he felt like it was if someone was guiding him. I shrugged and threw another hundred at him telling him I'd be back. Gabe gave me a wary look as we left the shop. I knew he didn't like the fact that I told them I would be back. When we got in the car I reminded him it would not be wise to tell my parents about our little detour. He nodded in agreement knowing he'd be in more trouble for taking me.

I stopped by one more time before I left Vermont. I had gotten two more tattoos on my stomach and had become addicted to the pain.

Once I got home, I figured out how to sneak out of the house undetected. I continued to get inked feeding the addiction for the pain. I kept most of them hidden the best I could. My lower back was covered as was my upper back and shoulders. I had four across my stomach and one that stretched from the top of my breast all the way down my ribs and back up the side. I also gotten one on my foot and thigh and every time I got a new one I would tell them the same thing. "I'm an open canvas, do what you want." And each time after they were done I would ask them what made them decide on what to do. They all said the same thing. It just came to them, as if someone was guiding them on what to draw.

I think a big part of why I went the tattoo route was because it wasn't something I would normally do, but lately I didn't feel much like myself so doing something out of the ordinary seemed like a good idea.

Mom and dad don't know about my little addiction, but they are about to find out soon enough. I keep myself covered most of the time so they have yet to see them, but being in my bathing suit is another story. There's no hiding them then. I didn't care. I was prepared for the storm that was about to erupt and was willing to take the consequences for it, or so I hope. Maybe I'll just join a convent. Yeah, that would be pretty funny to see - a vampire nun - ha. Well hopefully after they find out they'll be happy to know I'm done with the tattoo thing. After visiting Josie's grave today, I no longer feel the need to inflict pain on myself. I feel that part of me has healed and someday I'll find a way to heal the rest of myself. Until then I'll have to find a way of releasing my pain without inflicting more.

I put my journal aside and lay back against the chair. I lay there trying to think of a good way to break the news of my new body art to my parents. I knew deep down there was no way to do it. Just then, my mom came out and sat in the chair beside me. The tattoo on my thigh was peeking out of the bottom of my shorts and caught her attention. "What's this?" she asked, pulling up the side of my shorts. "Oh Ella, a tattoo?"

I guess the cat's out of the bag now.

Her eyes shifted down my leg where she spotted the one on my foot. I'm surprised she didn't see that one first. "Please tell me those are the only ones you have?" she asked, her face expressionless.

"Well," I said. I guess I might as well get it over with. I stood up and took my shirt and shorts off. She gaped at me as I spun around to show her. I couldn't tell if it was a good or bad reaction.

"Why?" she gasped.

Okay, we're going to go with bad.

I shrugged. I couldn't tell her the real reason, afraid she might have me committed. "Please tell me this is just a phase."

"You don't have to worry mom. I promise I'm done. It was just a phase," I said, sitting back down.

She let out a sigh of relief and looked over my tattoos again. "They are...nice. I just wish there was less of them." I rolled my eyes. I should be happy that's the only reaction I got. "How about we just keep this between you and me? At least until I can find an easy way to break it to your father."

"What are you two trying to butter me up for?" my dad joked coming up behind us.

So much for breaking it to him gently.

I stood up from the chair and faced him. "Please tell me this is another side effect from your powers, like your hair?" I shook my head no. "What the hell is wrong with you?"

"Liam."

"No. This is not something she can weasel her way out of or something that can just be overlooked."

"What are you going to do ground me? Send me to my room? Because that would be a real change from the past month, and I'm eighteen. I don't need your permission," I snapped, not in the mood to hear a lecture from him. He had a lot of nerve coming down on me considering all the things he's hidden from me over the years.

"You are royalty and royals do not have tattoos," he said with a distasteful look on his face.

"Well I'm a royal who does so deal with it. It's the twenty first century dad. I highly doubt that there isn't a royal with at least one tattoo. And if that's your only argument then you just lost."

"Don't get smart with me young lady."

"Why am I next in line anyways? Why not Xander?"

"He was, but he declined," my dad said, biting back his tongue, and showing me there was more to it then he was letting on. Obviously more secrets he was keeping from me.

I crossed my arms, annoyed. "And that's okay? He can but I can't? What about Dean?" My dad choked on a laugh. Even I knew that was a foolish question. Dean would end up having five wives and deal with his problems by getting drunk.

"You will take over for me when the time comes. End of discussion."

"That's not fair! I thought you said I had a choice!" I stomped my foot ready to throw a temper tantrum. I looked to my mom for help, but her lips were pressed into a tight line.

"You did, until you started this...ridiculousness. Mutilating your body. For what?"

"Artistic expression," I said, narrowing my eyes at him.

"From now on you will do as I say. You no longer have any more privileges."

"How is that any different from before?" I said, crossing my arms again.

"Ella, don't make this worse," my mom said. I glared at her for just sitting there and not defending me.

"All your expenses are cut off and you are not to leave this house, ever."

"Like I said, how is that any different?" I challenged my dad to come up with something better. I knew I was pushing my luck and would probably regret it, but I'd be damned if I was going to back down.

"You are going to that school on the east coast," he said with a smirk, knowing he got me.

"What school?"

"That special school that deals with our kind."

"What, no way! You can't be serious?" Crap. I went too far.

"Dead serious," he said, smiling satisfied.

"Just because I got a few tattoos?" I had a feeling that wasn't the real reason but he was just using it as an excuse to send me there.

"Who took you to get these tattoos?" he asked, avoiding my question.

"No one," I said, which was the truth.

"Don't lie to me. You cannot leave this house without any guardians," he said, not believing me.

"Yeah, well, maybe you should hire some new ones because it was pretty easy for me to sneak out undetected." And it was, except when Gabe was here. He caught me a few times and refused to tag along saying, *'he wouldn't be part of my self-destructive behavior and that if I didn't get back inside he would tell my dad.'* But when Gabe was busy on some errand, I had no problem sneaking pass the guardians that replaced him.

"Ella, you are being reckless and it's putting you in danger. This is a perfect example of why you should go to this school. You need to learn how to control your emotions."

"Yeah, because you do it so well," I spat back.

He noted my sarcastic tone with a glare. "Ella our powers are connected to our emotions and without proper control you could hurt someone or yourself and I can't allow that to happen. You are going to that school end of discussion."

"Liam, don't you think you're being –"

"No negotiations," he said, cutting my mom off and turning to leave.

I huffed, plopping down on the chair. "I'll talk to him honey. I think he just needs some time to cool off," my mom said, kissing my forehead before she took off. I sat there, pouting. I really got myself in deep now.

"How's it going?" Xander asked, taking mom's seat. I pulled my sunglasses down and gave him an, *'are you serious'* look. "Um, yeah, I heard." I frowned at him. "Give him time. He'll come around. He just needs to cool off."

"That's what mom said, but I don't think it will be that easy this time."

"How did you expect him to react?" he asked, looking at me like I should have known better.

I just shrugged. "I'm still alive. I guess I could look at it as better than I expected," I admitted, getting a chuckle from Xander.

"You have to admit. The tattoo thing is a little out of sorts, even for you."

"I know, I just..." I didn't know how to explain it to Xander. I knew I could tell him the truth and he wouldn't judge me or think I was crazy, but I just didn't think he'd understand.

"Looking for a way to deal with the pain? To relieve some of the pressure?" he guessed.

I nodded slowly. "What are you a mind reader or something?" I asked jokingly.

"No, but I get it Ella. Trust me. I do." He lifted up the back of his shirt to revel a tattoo he had on his shoulder – A Celtic cross. I never knew he had that, but what drew my attention wasn't the tattoo. It was the scars beneath it that had me wondering.

"When did you get that?"

"A few years ago. After dad told me I was supposed to take his place on the royal court. I didn't take the news so well."

"Yeah, well, you declined and now I have to take over, thanks."

"It wasn't as easy as you think. It took a while for him to accept the fact that I didn't want to take his place."

"Obviously you survived. Again, thanks."

"I see I'm going about this the wrong way. I wanna help you Ella –"

"You wanna help me?" I interrupted. "Then tell dad you changed your mind and you will take over."

"It's not that easy."

"Sure it is. Hey dad, I changed my mind. I want to take over your spot on the royal court. See. Simple."

"Ella, that's not what I mean," he groaned, frustrated. "The decision for me to not accept my seat on the court was mutual."

"What are you talking about?" I asked, thinking he was bullshitting me. No way would our dad let him off that easy.

"I didn't decline at first. I wanted to take the responsibility, but it became too much. Dad was on me every day and introducing me to all kinds of people. I had to be perfect all the time."

"Gee, thanks for the pep talk."

"Would you just let me finish before you make a smart ass comment," he said, glaring at me like our father does. I nodded, allowing him to continue. "I'm not perfect," I opened my mouth to retort, but he made me close it with just a look. "I couldn't take the pressure. So I started to do bad things to relieve some of the stress I was feeling."

"The scars?" I asked. He gave a barely noticeable nod. "Not to sound like a moron, but, umm...how'd you reach back there?"

"Dean."

"Wait, Dean did that?" He gave another slight nod. "He did it willingly?" I heard about brothers bonding but this was some kind of sick and twisted brotherly love I did not want to be a part of.

"No, he refused. He said I was disturbed and he wouldn't be

pulled into my weird, twisted game."

"Then how…"

"I compelled him. He didn't know he was doing it."

"Oh," was all I could manage at the moment. I had a million questions I wanted to ask but didn't know how.

Xander must have sensed it because he started to explain. "I thought having someone else do it wouldn't be as bad as me doing it to myself. I had him mark up my shoulder so it wasn't visible to me. I thought if I couldn't see it, I wouldn't have to admit how crazy I was."

"I don't think you're crazy," I said, trying to make him feel better.

"See, you're not the only one who's messed up," he said, a smile starting to creep at the corner of his lips.

"Shut up," I said, pushing him and making him laugh.

"Well, well, well. So it's true. The precious Ella finally rebels. Good girl gone bad," Dean said as he joined us by the pool.

"Shut up Dean," Xander said in unison.

"I'd just like to thank you for taking the attention off of me for once."

"You're welcome," I said sarcastically.

"Wow li'l sis, when you go for it you really go for it," Dean said, coming up from behind the chair, catching full view of my tattoos. "I take back all the previous remarks I have ever said about you." I just rolled my eyes as he sat on the end of my chair. "So what's with all the ink? You going to start hanging out at biker bars and start dating some guy named Bubba?"

"Shut up," I said, trying to hide my smile. "And that is such a horrible stereo type."

Dean looked at me, his face all serious now. "I get it Ella. Even if you don't believe me. I get it," he said with sincerity.

"Yeah Ella, you're never alone. We want you to know that. We're here for you know matter what," Xander said, squeezing next to me on my chair and putting an arm over my shoulder.

"Xander's right. We'll always be here for you. Even if you go all butch, buy a Harley, and start dating chicks," Dean smiled. I kicked him and he just laughed. "Seriously though, whenever, whatever, we got your back."

"Thanks guys," I smiled, feeling all warm and fuzzy inside. I knew my brothers loved me, but it was still nice to hear it. "Alright, enough of this mushy stuff or I might actually start to believe you guys like me," I teased.

"You're our baby sis, of course we like you. Besides, who else would we have to blame stuff on and torture?" Dean smirked.

"Oh, I see how it is," I said. Dean and Xander just laughed. "Like the time you broke mom's favorite crystal vase and blamed it on me." Xander looked away guilty. I turned to Dean. "Or how about the time you took dad's vintage Mustang for a joyride, scratched the fender, and blamed it on me." Dean didn't seem to feel any remorse.

"That was you?" Xander said and Dean nodded. "Man, I remember that. I thought for sure they were going to ship Ella away," he chuckled.

"Yeah, thanks for that," I said, kicking Dean again. "For all the crap you guys blamed on me. You should be nicer considering the fact that I haven't blown your cover...yet."

"Hey, what else are little sisters for?" Xander laughed. I narrowed my eyes at him and pushed him off the chair.

He quickly recovered and lifted me from the chair. I squealed as he carried me over to the pool. "If you don't put me down I'll tell mom and dad about the party you had while they were out of town."

"Go ahead, I don't care." I had a feeling he wouldn't since it was over seven years ago. They couldn't really punish him anymore.

"Whoa, wait a minute," Dean interrupted, thinking Xander didn't care because they would blame Dean and not him. "You should tell them about the time I caught him on their bed with Debbie Klinger."

"Hey, whose side are you on?" Xander complained.

"Okay eew, I didn't need to know that and Debbie Klinger, really?"

Xander just shrugged. "She knows too much." Xander and Dean exchanged looks.

"Alexander James, if you don't put me down right this second I'll...I'll..."

"You'll what?" he asked, knowing I had nothing. Crap. I yelped and struggled to get free, but Xander was stronger. He threw me into the pool like I weighed nothing. Dean tried to push Xander in, but when Xander lost his balance he grabbed onto Dean taking him with him and making a huge splash when they hit the water.

*

Jamila gazed out the window of her husband's home office. She watched her children rough house in the pool. She smiled brightly as warmth of joy filled her chest. She loved when her children were together and getting along. Even though they were adults now, she still thought of them as her babies, her precious angels that she couldn't live without.

Liam came up behind her, calmer than he was a few moments ago. She had spoken to him about controlling his anger with their daughter, which resulted in a very heated discussion. "Liam, look at our children. I want you to see how happy they are. Despite what you may think you have not failed them. They are everything we expected them to be and more."

Liam slipped his arms around Jamila's waist. "Yes, they can be quite wonderful at times." She elbowed him playfully in the ribs. He chuckled. "I believe they are who they are because of you."

Jamila turned to his smiling face. "We both had a hand in raising our children. We try our best but we're not perfect. Therefore we cannot blame our children for the same mistakes we have made. We can only hope to do better for them and try to guide them in the right direction, but they're going to make mistakes." Liam sighed not wanting to admit how right she was. "And we're going to have to let them or they'll never learn. Liam, you also need to stop being so hard on them." He eyed her warily. "Yes, I'm not happy about Ella's tattoos either, but maybe next time instead of blowing up, talk to her."

"I'll try," he said, letting out a slow breath.

"Besides, she is her father's daughter," Jamila chuckled.

"I do not have any tattoos," he scoffed.

"Yes but her rebellion and attitude she gets from you." She poked a finger teasingly at his chest before her face turned serious again. "I do agree with you on her going to that school. I think it would be wise to have someone else help her."

"You actually agree with me?" He tried to act surprised.

Jamila laughed lightly. "Yes, some things I do agree with you on...some." Liam chuckled and hugged her tighter as they continued to watch their children.

CHAPTER THREE

After I took a beating from my brothers in the pool, I decided I had enough and went inside to change. I dried off the best I could, put on some warmer clothes, and then headed back downstairs to grab a snack in the kitchen where my mom and dad cornered me. "Ella, come sit. We need to talk," my mom said with a kind voice. It didn't matter how she sugar coated it. I had a feeling this wasn't going to be something I liked.

"Talk or yell," I said, sitting down at the table, and narrowing my eyes at my dad.

"That depends," he said, scowling back.

"Liam," my mom warned.

He took a deep breath before he continued. "I've made it clear I am not happy about the tattoos but I can," he paused to take another breath. "Over look this...behavior, if you're willing to come to a compromise."

"A compromise, yeah right. Your compromises usually consist of do what you say and that's it."

I could see the big vein in his head start to bulge as he clenched his fist by his side. A sign that he was about to blow a gasket. I sat and waited for the yelling to begin, but it never did. My mom reached across the table and cupped his hand. The tension in his face relaxed as he unclenched his fist, and wiggled his fingers allowing the circulation to flow again. "Alright, can we please manage to have a conversation without someone making smartass comments or losing their temper?" My mom asked, looking back and forth between the both of us. We nodded.

"Okay, first off," my dad begun. "I'm sorry. I may have

overreacted a little." I opened my mouth to comment but my mom gave me a warning look not to. "Your mother and I were talking and both of us agree you should attend that special school in January."

"What's the compromise?" I asked impatiently.

"You're no longer grounded," he said like this should make me jump for joy.

"You're kidding right? Clearly you need to look up the difference between being grounded and held prisoner." This is what they were offering me? This had to be a joke.

"There's more," my mom said, urging my dad to continue before this turned ugly.

"If you agree to go to this school, you'll be free."

"Free?" I said, looking at them confused.

"Yes, no guardians, no hounding you twenty-four seven, and when you finish school it will be your choice if you want to take over for me on the royal court."

I looked at my mom and then back at dad knowing they haven't gotten to the fine print yet. "What's the catch?"

"No catch. School for your freedom," he said.

"So you're telling me if I go to this special school you'll leave me alone? No guardians and no royal court?" They both nodded. "Okay, I'm sorry, I'm not buying it. You've kept me trapped in this house and I can't leave without being flanked by guardians. What's the sudden change? Did you catch Jack?" I sat up hopeful.

"No honey, I'm sorry. We're still looking for him," my mom said with sympathy and worry in her voice.

"You do not need to worry about him. He will be caught," my dad said, his temper flaring at the mention of Jack.

"Well then who's going to take my place on the royal court if I say no?"

"Xander is willing to reclaim his place as my heir."

"Wait, what?" I said, not believing what I just heard.

"He approached me earlier and told me he was willing to try again so you didn't have to."

I couldn't believe he would do that for me. I sat back in my chair, shocked that Xander would make such a rash decision like that. Especially after what he had told me about how it took a real toll on him. My dad got right back to the discussion, not giving me much time to let it sink in what Xander had done. "The school is well protected with its own guardians and Gabe will be there as well."

"I thought you said no guardians?" I knew there was a catch.

"Gabe will be working with the other guardians and helping out with the training process of new ones. He will not be a bother to you unless you need him. I thought maybe having someone familiar there would help make you feel more comfortable."

Having Gabe there might not be a bad thing, I thought.

"And speaking of having someone familiar with you," my mom paused, and I held my breath. "Dean will be there too."

"Dean, why does he have to be there?"

"Because that is where he goes to school."

"What? The school is in Rhode island?"

"Yes," my dad said like it was no big deal.

I slammed my head down on the table. A new school I could handle. I could even deal with Gabe being there, but Dean? This felt like torture. "What's my other option?" I mumbled into my arms.

"There is no other option," my dad said slightly aggravated. I knew he was holding back.

I met his aggravated stare with one of my own. "That's not much of a compromise."

"It's more than fair. You can choose to go on your own or we can force you and you'll be back to being grounded, guardians and everything," my dad said, not really giving me much of a choice, which is pretty much what I expected from the moment I sat down.

None of my options seemed fair. It's not like I didn't love my brother, I did. I just loved him more from a distance. There was only so much time spent with Dean I could tolerate. I put my head in my hands and sighed not in the mood to argue anymore. "Fine, I'll take the first option."

"Great," my mom cheered giddily, standing up. "Now, help me get everything ready to start baking cookies. Danni and Hadley should be here soon."

We spent the next four hours baking cookies. By the time we were done, I was cookied out. I went upstairs and got ready for bed. As soon as my head hit the pillow I was out.

The next thing I knew I was in a garden. I looked down and saw I was wearing a white, strapless sundress. My feet were bare. I wiggled my toes in the soft grass as I looked around at my surroundings. The garden was exquisite. It was filled with all types of flowers, everything from pansies, wild roses, violets, forget-me-nots and so on.

I walked a little ways toward a gate. I bent down to smell one of the flowers. I closed my eyes and inhaled deeply, letting the petals tickle my nose. A light breeze caressed my shoulder and I smiled. "Legend states that fairies can hear bluebells chiming. When they gather around the flower they become mischievous and enchant the area so that any human who wanders among them becomes trapped," a familiar voice said. He wrapped his arms around my waist and rested his head on my shoulder making my body tingle.

"Fairies?" I giggled. "Does their enchantment work on us, vampires?" I teased smoothing my arms over his. He just chuckled and turned me around to face him. He was wearing a white button down shirt and khakis. He was also barefoot and looking as handsome as ever. "Where are we?" I asked.

"My grandmother's garden, in Ireland," he said, gently brushing my hair off my shoulder, sending shivers down my entire body. He started to kiss my shoulder, working his way up to my neck. I tilted my head to the side and when I looked down I didn't see the tattoo on my foot. Strange, I thought. Then I remembered I didn't have any of them in any of the other dreams either. I scratched my head confused and decided to not put too much thought into it, considering it was a dream.

Tristan, sensing my distraction, lifted my chin to meet his eyes. "What's wrong?"

"Nothing," I smiled, grazing my hand against his cheek.

He closed his eyes and I could hear his heart racing. "I lo –"

I put my finger to his lips stopping him. "Shh, don't say it."

"Why not," he pouted.

"Because after every time you say it, I wake up, and I'm not ready to leave yet." I put my arms around his neck and stared into his beautiful blue eyes. I pulled him closer and kissed those wonderful lips I loved and missed so much.

He pulled back way too soon. "Come with me," he said, holding his hand out.

"Where are we going?" I asked, following him.

"For a walk," he smiled, making me melt. It didn't matter where he led me. I would follow him to the end of the earth if he asked.

We walked hand in hand along the stones steps that lined garden. I let my hand fan out allowing my fingertips to brush lightly against the soft petals of the flowers. The garden was in full bloom complete with the night blooming flowers, Jasmine, and several others that weren't even in season. I wanted to ask how that was possible but I didn't want to ruin the moment with silly questions.

Instead, I leaned into him, laying my head on his shoulder, admiring the beauty of it all. I was so happy I danced my way down the lighted path. Tristan smiled at me and twirled me around. I've never seen him so content. I never wanted this feeling to fade.

Our Journey ended when we rested by a small pond. I walked over to where the grass met the water and stuck my toe in to test the temperature. I jumped back, when out of nowhere, a frog appeared, scaring me.

Tristan chuckled and caught me before I fell. "Rogue vampires you can handle, but you're afraid of frogs?" he questioned, raising a brow.

"No," I said, slightly embarrassed. "I'm not afraid of frogs, it just...I wasn't expecting it."

"Un-huh," he said teasingly. I pinched him and he grabbed my arms holding them behind my back, and then he kissed me.

When he pulled away I lay my head on his chest, sighing. "Did you ever notice how real this feels?"

"What do you mean?" he asked, running his fingers through my hair, making it hard for me to concentrate on anything else.

"This. All of this," I gestured around. I turned to him and placed my hand on his chest. "You."

"Ella, you're not making any sense," he said.

"How are we here? I've never been here before?"

"It's just a dream Ella. It's what our subconscious minds have created," he said, gently caressing my cheek.

"But you..." I shook my head. I couldn't bring myself to say it out loud. I looked away from him. I could feel the pain start to bubble up in my chest again. He was wrong. He wouldn't be able to dream this. He was no longer here.

"Hey, don't be sad," he said, lifting my chin to meet his eyes. "I'm right here. I'll always be here." He put his hand over my heart and pressed a soft kiss to my lips. I threw my arms around him, squeezing him so tight it hurt. Then I kissed him hard and fast, wanting to devour every part of him. "Hey, easy there love." He pulled back. "What's the rush?" he asked concerned.

"I just..." I didn't know what to say. I had a feeling this dream was about to end soon. I pressed my head to his chest, listening to his heart. I never thought the steady beat of his heart would sound so lovely to me, almost musical. "I don't ever want to let you go," I spoke into his chest as I tightly gripped his shirt, trying hard not to cry.

"I'm not going anywhere," he said, gently stroking my hair. I could no longer hold back the tears. I let them slip down my cheeks one by one. Tristan tucked a loose strand of hair behind my ear forcing me to look at him. He wiped the tears from my cheeks and kissed away the ones that fell upon my lips. "I love you," he whispered.

I woke up with a jolt.

I looked around the empty room and then, I started to cry. I cried myself to sleep.

All week when I slept, I waited in hopes of dreaming of him, but he never appeared. It wasn't until the night before Christmas when I found him again. I was lying on my side, on a blue checkered blanket. I was wearing a long, white, spaghetti strapped dress.

Okay seriously, what is with all the white?

I sat up to discover I was on a hill top. I gazed down at the bright lights of the city beneath me. The view was breath taking, but not as beautiful as what lied next to me. I turned to my left where Tristan was lying casually on his palms. He had on black slacks and a dark blue, button down shirt that brought out the color of his eyes. I instantly threw my arms around him. "Whoa, hey," he said, trying to catch his balance.

"I thought I'd never see you again," I said, holding on tightly.

"I told you I wasn't going anywhere."

"It's been over two weeks since I've seen you last," I said panicked, still holding on.

"Is that all?" he chuckled.

I untangled my arms to look at him. "It's too long."

He cupped the sides of my face. "You're right. Any amount of time spent away from you is too long," he said, gently pressing his lips to mine. I sighed and lay back on the blanket. Tristan leaned on his elbow, gazing lovingly at me while I stared up at the bright, starry sky.

He surprised me with a bouquet of forget-me-nots. "They're beautiful," I smiled.

"You're beautiful," he said, brushing my hair off my shoulder. He pulled one of the flowers from the bouquet and started to softly caress my skin with it. Tristan dragged the flower across my hand, working his way up my arm, over my shoulder, and across my chest. I bit my lip, blushing. The feel of the soft, silky petals against my skin were giving me chills. He continued by sweeping the flower down my nose, cheek and breasts. He then replaced the flower with his lips, giving me goose bumps.

Tristan carefully pushed down the strap of my dress, kissing the exposed skin. Sliding his other hand behind my neck, he guided me down gently onto the blanket beneath us. Then he climbed on top of me and found his way to my lips. One hand was tangled in my hair while the other glided up my thigh, pushing up my dress. My heart was racing and my skin was getting hotter with every touch. I slipped my fingers through his hair, pulling him closer to me. He kissed me passionately, pressing his body against mine. I moaned at the pressure of his weight on top of me. My entire flesh was covered in goose bumps. I brushed a hand across the bare skin of his lower back. He let out a moan himself at the gesture.

I had to pull away to catch my breath. "Tristan I —"

"Yes," he breathed.

"I..." was back in my room.

"Son of a bitch!"

"I wouldn't go that far, but mom does have her moments."

"Dean?" I sat up, rubbing my eyes. He was leaning in the doorway. "What do you want?" I grumbled.

"Ho, Ho, Ho," he said, holding out a small wrapped box.

"This couldn't wait?" I asked, annoyed and pissed that I woke up from my dream right when things were getting good, but of course, isn't that what always happens?

Dean, taking it upon himself to enter without my permission, came over and sat down on my bed. "Open it," he said, handing me the present.

"What is it?" I asked a little frightened.

"Just open it," he said rolling his eyes.

I tore into the present and opened up the box. Inside was a men's silver watch. The face of the watch was encrusted with diamonds and had a purple heart dangling from the band. I looked at Dean confused. Why in the world would he give me something like this? Before I could open my mouth he said, "Turn it over." On the underside were the initials T.W.M. "The watch was Tristan's and the heart charm —"

"Josie's," I finished for him. I recognized it almost right away. When we were little Josie and I got charm bracelets and we picked out a charm for each other. I picked out the heart for Josie and she got me a shamrock. "How'd you?" I asked, wondering how he got these things. I remember losing my bracelet years ago and thought

Josie had lost hers too.

"A little finessing and my natural charm," he smiled proud.

"You didn't steal these did you?" I asked cautiously. Dean was many things, but I never pictured him to be a thief. With Dean though, you could never be too sure.

"Come on, give me some credit here," he said insulted. "I thought maybe you would like to have something of theirs to keep with you so I asked Tristan's and Josie's parents if there was something of theirs to give you." He pointed to the watch. "This is what Tristan's mom gave me and Jade told me I could look around Josie's room and pick what I wanted. I remember when you guys got these bracelets and how upset you were when you lost yours. So I knew this would be the perfect thing of hers for you to have. I couldn't find the bracelet itself, but this was lying on top of her jewelry box."

"Thank you Dean. It's perfect," I said, embracing him in a hug.

"You wanna go downstairs and sneak a peek at our presents?" he asked with a sly grin.

"Dean, I'm not five. I don't need to peek at my presents."

"What if I told you there was a really big present downstairs with your name on it?" he said, trying to entice me. I contemplated for less than a second before I was off my bed, grabbing my slippers and sweater, and heading downstairs with him.

We tiptoed down the steps careful not to wake anyone. I stopped by the kitchen first to help myself to the left over cookies and a large glass of milk. Then I joined Dean in the living room where he was already shaking gifts to see if he could guess what was inside. "What are you two up to?" I jumped, almost spilling my milk.

When I turned around I was surprised to see Xander standing behind me. I thought for sure it was our dad by the sound of his voice. Xander laughed when he saw my face. He was the only one who could imitate our Dad's voice. "That wasn't funny," I said, narrowing my eyes at him as he stole a cookie from my plate.

"Here to guess your presents too?" Dean asked Xander.

"Grow up you guys," he said rolling his eyes.

Dean looked around the pile of presents for one with Xander's name on it. "Hmm, I wonder what this is," he said, lightly shaking the box. "Could it be that new IPad you were hoping for?"

"Give me that," Xander said, taking the gift. Dean and I laughed knowing Xander couldn't resist.

Our little guessing game didn't last long. Mom busted us. "What are you kids doing?" she asked with her hands on her hips.

"It was Ella's idea," Dean and Xander said in unison.

"Hey!" I scoffed at them.

Mom just laughed and took a seat next to me. "Boys, I know better," she said, stealing a cookie. "You're supposed to be a good influence on your sister," she chastised. I stuck out my tongue at them when she bent over to take a sip of my milk. "I saw that Ella."

"Saw what?" I acted all innocent.

She just shook her head. "I guess since it is tradition, you each can open one present now, but I get to pick which one," mom said, getting up and searching through the presents. Every year on Christmas Eve our parents would let us open one present, but we were never allowed to pick which one.

Mom handed Xander and Dean their presents then handed me mine before sitting back down. Inside the small box she gifted me was a heart shaped locket. "It's a family heirloom," my mom said. It opened up like an accordion showing three pictures on each side. My mom leaned in close. "This picture here," she pointed to the one in the middle. "Is your great, great grandparents." The picture next to it was one of my dad and mom holding me as a baby and the other one was of Xander, Dean, and me when I was two. I flipped it over and in the middle of the other side was a picture of my mom and dad on their wedding day, one of my grandma Bea and me and one of Josie and I. "I added this one," she said, pointing to the picture of Josie and me.

"It's beautiful. Thank you mom." My mom helped me clasp the locket around my neck. It fell low on my chest so that when I looked down I could see it.

My mom pointed to the locket. "Now you'll always have us with you. Always close to your heart," she smiled. I gave her a warming hug, sat back, and lay my head on her shoulder while I watched Xander and Dean open their presents. They also received family heirlooms. Xander got our great grandfather's cufflinks and Dean got his watch.

Afterwards, we all settled into the couch, and had a fight over which Christmas movie we were going to watch. Xander and Dean wanted to watch a Christmas story, but mom and I wanted to watch National Lampoon's Christmas vacation, which was a classic if I do say so myself. Of course mom and I won. I cuddled up to my mom as we watched our favorite Christmas movie.

My dad woke me up early the next morning. "Good morning," he said softly, careful not to wake everyone else up. He cautiously stepped over Dean who had made his way to the floor during the night. I pulled up my feet giving my dad room to have a seat on the couch.

"Morning dad," I said, just now realizing my mom was up as well when my dad handed her a cup of coffee.

"Merry Christmas," he said, handing me a mug of hot chocolate. Clearly he still thought of me as his little girl.

"Merry Christmas Dad," I said, leaning my head on his shoulder. He flinched slightly before he relaxed and threw an arm over me. My dad and I hadn't been very affectionate lately so I wasn't surprised by his reaction, but no matter what happened he was still my dad and I still loved him.

When the boys woke up, my mom made us breakfast, and then afterwards we opened up all our presents. When we finished, I went upstairs to shower and get ready for an early dinner. The McNaughton's had finally returned home and were going to join us for dinner along with Danni and Hadley.

For dinner I decided to wear the new sweater dress my mom had gotten me. It was cream colored with short sleeves and a cowl neck. I paired it with my new tan, knee high boots and locket. I tried taming my hair the best I could by pulling it half up. When I was finished battling with my hair, I went downstairs to find the McNaughton's had already arrived. Jake took off on a running start and jumped into my arms. I picked him up and hugged him tight not realizing how much I missed him. "Merry Christmas Jake."

"Merry Christmas Ella. I missed you," he said, causing a small tug at my heart strings.

"I missed you too," I replied, squeezing him one more time before I put him down. Jake pulled me over to his parents and I greeted each of them with a hug.

"You look beautiful, as usual," Mrs. McNaughton said. I thanked her before Josie's dad asked how I was.

"Better," I smiled weakly. Seeing them here without Josie was weird to me. I reminded myself to stay strong and not lose it in front of them.

"I just wanted to let you know I talked to Josie and she's happy where she is," Josie's mom, Jade, smiled.

"You talked to her?" I asked, wondering if Jade already had a few before she got here.

"Yes. My psychic Jacinda —"

"Jade." Mr. McNaughton interrupted. There was an undertone to his voice that warned his wife not to continue with this conversation, but she ignored him by waving him off and pulling me aside. Jade went into this whole story about her and her psychic having a breakthrough and breaking the barriers between the worlds.

She truly has lost it.

I guess everyone grieves in their own way.

Dean distracted Jade with a drink and I mouthed the words *"thank you"* in reply. Dean and I then took Jake into the living room so he could open his presents we had bought him. Xander got him a new baseball mitt and cap while Dean and I each got him a new video game. I got him one of latest baseball games while Dean got him some zombie killing one. I yelled at Dean and told him that wasn't an appropriate game for a six year old, but of course he could have cared less.

Shortly after, Danni and Hadley arrived and joined us in the living room. As soon as Jake spotted Hadley he froze. You could almost see the glow around her as she sashayed her way over to me in her cute, puffy, Christmas dress. I picked her up, pulling her onto my lap. "Merry Christmas Ella!" she cheered, throwing her tiny arms around me.

"Merry Christmas Hadley. What kind of goodies did Santa bring you?" She listed all the things she got as Jake stared at her in awe.

"Boom!" Dean yelled. "I just took you down Jakey."

"I think his interest is on something else," I giggled. "Jake, you remember Hadley." He barely moved. He just watched her like he was mesmerized.

"Oh man Jakey boy, I think we need to have a chat," Dean said, catching on. I just rolled my eyes.

"D-do you wanna p-play?" Jake stuttered, offering Hadley a remote and stealing Dean's. I laughed making Dean narrow his eyes at me.

"We so need to talk about the bros before hoes code," Dean said, feeling rejected.

"How about we play a different game, one where you don't get points for dismembering body parts." I searched through the other games until I found one we could all play. "How about Just Dance. Girls versus boys?"

"You're on. Come on Jake, we'll show these girls how it's done,"

Dean challenged.

Eventually everyone else joined us in the living room and in the game. We kept to girls versus boys. It was the most fun I had in a long time and of course the girls won.

CHAPTER FOUR

After the game we all gathered around the table for dinner. We bowed our heads as my mom led us by saying grace. "Amen," everyone said. I was just about to dig in when Xander stood up. "Before we eat, I'd like to make an announcement," Xander said, grabbing everyone's attention. "Last night," he paused and looked at Jasa. "I asked Jasa to marry me and she said yes."

My jaw dropped as I looked around the room at everyone's expression. Dean nearly choked on his wine while Danni looked horrified not believing what she just heard. Everyone else cheered happily. I didn't know what to think. I managed to get out congrats just as my mom and dad welcomed Jasa to the family.

Dean and I exchanged looks. Apparently he was as surprised as I was at Xander's announcement. I looked back at Danni who forced out a smile and congrats through gritted teeth. I was definitely going to have to pull her aside later and find out what was going on there, but first I'd talk to Xander. This was so unlike him. They haven't even been dating that long and Xander never made rash decisions like this. I remember it took him a week to pick out his outfit he was going to wear for his graduation which I thought was ridiculous because you wouldn't even see it under his cap and gown.

Not wanting to destroy everyone else's joyful mood, I plastered on a smile and pretended everything was fine. Danni pretty much stayed silent throughout the rest of dinner while my mom spent most of the time discussing wedding plans with Jasa. Every now and then I would catch Danni and Xander exchange looks, making me wonder even more what was going on there.

Once we were finished, the boys retreated to the den to smoke cigars and celebrate while Jade, my mom, and Jasa continued to talk wedding stuff. My fake smile was making my face hurt so I opted to take Jake and Hadley into the living room to play some video games. After Jake and Hadley were settled, I went back into the kitchen to help Danni clean up. "Okay, so what's up?" I asked Danni.

"What?" she said, acting like nothing was wrong.

"Don't act like you don't know. I saw your face when Xander announced he and Jasa were getting married," I said, challenging her to lie to me again.

"Ella don't be silly. I'm happy for them," she replied, downing her glass of wine.

I took the glass from her and hid the bottle, then I made her face me. "Danni, seriously, you looked like someone just stabbed you in the heart. What's going on?"

"Danni, what are you doing?" my mom asked, interrupting before I could get some answers out of her. "It's Christmas, come sit down with us. Today is your day off." My mom tried to pull Danni out of the kitchen thinking she was in there cleaning up, but I knew she was in there to hide.

Taking the hint as a good distraction, Danni picked up one of the sponges, and started to clean the dishes. "I don't mind."

"Well I do," my mom said, stopping her. "Come on." She tried to pull Danni back into the dining room, but she wouldn't budge.

"I just remembered I told Hadley I'd take her for a walk and show her all the lights," Danni said.

"Nice save," I thought to myself.

"Oh my goodness. I had totally forgotten about that. Ella, why didn't you remind me?"

"Um, because I didn't think we would go considering..." I broke off not wanting to dampen the mood.

"Ella, it's Christmas and it's tradition. I'm sure even your father won't deny us this. Come on now. Go get the kids ready." I looked at my mom thinking she was nuts. No way would my dad let us go outside to look at Christmas lights we've seen a million times. "Be sure to dress warm. I heard there was a cold front coming in so put on a coat, gloves and scarf," she called over her shoulder. I looked back at Danni. She just shrugged, taking the opportunity to continue avoiding my questions by going into the living room to get Hadley ready.

I followed my mom into the den where I found my dad smiling happily. He embraced my mom in a hug and gave her a sweet kiss before they exited the den and walked back downstairs. I followed them clueless as to what was going on. "Ella, you should put a coat on, it's gotten quite chilly out," my dad said.

"Wait, what?" I said, looking at him befuddled.

"You want to go outside and see the lights, don't you?"

"Well yeah, but..." I bit my tongue realizing it was not wise to press my luck. Clearly my dad was in a good mood and my mouth, if not kept closed, would probably spoil that. So I did what he said and grabbed my coat. "I highly doubt I'll need this though. I mean come on, we live in California. It never snows let alone drops below sixty degrees." My mom stopped me at the door forcing me to wear a hat, scarf, and gloves. "Mom, really, I'm sweating in this stuff. There is no need −" I stopped short when she opened the door letting in a gust of cold air and...snow?

I gasped at all the feathery, light, white stuff that was drifting in from the outside. I ran passed everyone and out into the cold air. I lifted my head up to the sky and spread my arms wide, smiling. I spun and spun catching giant snowflakes on my tongue. I couldn't believe it. It wasn't the first time I saw snow, but it was the first time it snowed here, and on Christmas. I was brought back to reality by the sound of giggles coming from Jake and Hadley. I looked to see them smiling and playing in the several inches of snow that had accumulated on the ground. "It's snowin' Ella, it's snowin'!" Jake cheered, picking up piles and throwing them in the air.

"Can you believe it?" Danni said as surprised as I was.

"No, I can't," I said, unable to unscrew the smile from my face.

I was about to walk out into the street when my dad stopped me. "Let's not got ahead of ourselves here," he said, pulling me back. I looked at him funny before I noticed him motioning for guardians to stand on either side of the street. Of course, I should have known this was too good to be true. I sighed, trying my best not to let this ruin my good mood. Once flanked by guardians, my dad allowed us to continue on our way through the abandoned streets. I strolled aimlessly through the snow, not paying attention to where I was going and nearly ran into Gabe.

"Miss Ella, you should be more careful," he said, steadying me so I wouldn't fall.

"Gabe? What are you doing here? Shouldn't you be home having Christmas with your family?"

"Duty calls and as I can see I believe I arrived in the nick of time," he winked.

I straightened myself out. "I can't believe my dad would have you work on Christmas, of all the rotten things to do."

Gabe shook his head. "I had the morning off as did the rest of the guardians who are here now. Besides, most of my family is long gone by now and those that are left live out of the country," he said like it was no big deal. I think even if his family was here Gabe would still put his Job first which made me kind of sad. "Do not be sad for me," he said, lifting my chin. "This was my choice to be here."

"But that's the part that makes it sad," I admitted. "I mean. Why would you rather work than be with your family?"

"You have not met my family. Those who have would know that they are sometimes considered more work than what I do here," he said, giving me a half smile. I had to give him one in return for that. As far as wacky families go I could understand.

"Well then, in that case, I'm glad you're here," I said, linking my arm through his so I wouldn't slip. We walked through the streets enjoying the decorative lights throughout the neighborhood.

I finally felt like I was at peace. That was until something cold, round, and wet whizzed by my head. I turned around in time to catch a snowball to the chest and Dean hiding behind a bush laughing. "Dean!" I yelled before I got pelted in the side by another. I turned to the left to see Xander wielding another weapon in his other hand ready to fire. "Grow up you guys!" I shouted. I turned back around to keep walking when one hit me in the back of the head. Mouth open, ready to bring hell, I turned around and stopped when I spotted the guilty party. "Dad, really, you would hit your own daughter?"

"That should teach you not to turn your back on your enemy," he said, smiling slyly.

"That's it." I bent down and retrieved my own weapons. Gabe moved out of the way and stood in front of my mom, Jasa, and Jade. He was just big enough to block all three of them from any oncoming snowballs. I took my first fire at Dean and then Xander. I saved the biggest snowball for my dad. I pulled my arm back and fired away. I hit him dead center in the middle of his forehead. I froze, anticipating the beating of my life.

I heard Dean snicker and looked over to see my mom trying to hide her smile. My dad wiped the cold, wet snow from his face. I waited for it, cringing. "You better run," he said, bending down and preparing to pelt me with snowballs. I shrieked and ran behind the nearest tree, dodging flying snowballs left and right. Danni joined me behind the tree with Hadley and Jake to help. The snowballs were flying faster than we could make them. I couldn't understand how the boys were able to collect them so quickly.

I pulled Jake aside, pointed out where Dean was hiding, and told him to stuff snow down his back. Not a minute later I heard a yelp and knew Jake had succeeded. "Jake, you traitor! I thought we were friends?" Dean grumbled, making me laugh.

I was cold, wet, and feeling numb. From the look on Danni's face I could tell she had enough as well. We bravely stepped out from behind the tree with our hands up showing we were unarmed. "Truce," I called out.

"Truce," Xander and my dad agreed.

I dusted off the remaining snow and joined my mom with Gabe where I knew it was safe, just in case.

We strolled down the street gazing at all the amazing light displays. Jake and Hadley ran ahead still playing in the snow with Danni not far behind them. Jasa and Xander lagged behind while the rest of us held up the middle. I eventually made my way up to Danni who Dean was closing in on. I'm sure so he could make a move on her. I pushed pass him receiving a dirty look and linked my arm with Danni's. "Oh, hey Ella," she said, snuggling closer to me for warmth.

"Can you believe this? I mean who would have thought it would snow in California?" I said, still amazed.

"I know. I'm just glad Hadley gets to experience all of this," she said as she watched her daughter play.

"Are you happy?" I asked.

"What?" she said, caught off guard by my question.

"Are you happy? I mean with the way your life turned out."

She let out a breath before she said, "Yes. Yes I am."

"Care to tell me why you avoided my questions in the kitchen earlier?"

"I don't know what you're talking about," she said.

"Oh come on Danni. You know exactly what I'm talking about," I said, giving her a playful nudge.

"Just drop it Ella."

"Danni seriously what's the —"

"I said drop it Ella," she snapped. I stopped. Danni unlinked her arm and walked ahead. "Come on Hadley. It's time to go back." I opened my mouth to stop her but decided to let it go. I caught Xander's face turn to concern as he watched them walk back to the house.

"Is everything okay?" he asked Danni.

"Yes, I just want to get Hadley back inside. She's not really dressed for this weather," Danni replied.

"Would you like us to walk back with you?" Xander asked, troubled.

Danni looked down at his hand that was twined together with Jasa's. "No, I'll be fine," she said, taking off in a hurry. My dad signaled for one of the guardians to follow them back. I looked forward to catch Jake with a sad look on his face. No doubt from his new girlfriend heading back inside. Considering I couldn't feel my toes anymore, I thought it wise to head back inside as well. I told Jake I would take him back to play with Hadley. I let my parents know I was heading back to the house with Jake to warm up. Gabe and two other guardians followed with us which I thought was a little ridiculous since we were only about a half a mile from our house.

Once inside, I took off my boots and hung my coat in the closet. I found Hadley on the couch next to Danni, who was clutching a half empty glass with a half empty bottle on the table. "Danni I'm sorry," I said.

"Ella it's fine," she slurred a little bit. "It's no big deal. I overreacted." She picked up the bottle and refilled her half empty glass.

"Danni, maybe you should —" She glared at me and I stopped myself from finishing my sentence. Instead I just sat down next to her while Jake and Hadley played video games.

Everyone else returned about a half hour later. My dad lit up the fireplace as everyone else settled in to warm up. "Ella dear, will you be a doll and go downstairs to retrieve another bottle of wine?" my mom asked. Between Jade and the way Danni was downing the bottle I'd probably say it be safer if I just brought up a case.

I returned with two bottles. I felt if I brought up any more I might be encouraging bad behavior. I handed both bottles to my mom while she collected more glasses from the hutch. She allowed me one small glass and I accepted kindly knowing tonight might be a rough night.

For the rest of the evening, my mom couldn't stop talking about wedding stuff and from the look on Danni's face I knew she was feeling uncomfortable, but why I still didn't know. Danni managed to hide her feelings by drinking most of the wine. To help save her from what would be a killer hangover tomorrow, I corked the bottles, and put them away. If Danni didn't finish them I knew Jade would and neither of them needed that. After I put the bottles away and out of reach, I went to check on Jake and Hadley who had retreated to the family room to play.

I found them both asleep on the couch. They looked so sweet and innocent I didn't want to disturb them. I pulled one of the blankets from the chest and laid it across them gently. A few seconds later, Danni entered the room to check on Hadley. "I think you might have a wedding of your own to plan soon," I whispered with a giggle.

Danni stood behind the couch staring down at her daughter. She kissed her forehead before turning to me and said, "Ella, she's only five."

"They look so peaceful. I'd hate to wake them," Jade said, startling us.

"If you want Jake can spend the night and I can bring him home tomorrow?" I suggested, hating to break these two up.

"Thank you Ella. That would be wonderful," Jade said, squeezing my shoulder. We let them sleep where they were and made our way back to the living room where we said goodnight to Jade and Gabriel. Afterwards, I made my way to the kitchen to help my mom clean up. When we were done, we went back into the living to watch a movie. My dad was already relaxing in his favorite chair and talking to Xander.

After I sat down and got comfy, I noticed someone was missing. "Hey Xander where's Jasa?"

"She had an early flight tomorrow so she's staying at the hotel." When I looked at him confused, his response was "Work." And he didn't seem happy about it. I shrugged and sat back to relax.

I felt a soft hand on my shoulder and turned back to see Danni leaning over the couch. "Hey, I think I'm going to head home," she said.

"Uh, Danni, no offense, but I don't think you should drive. Why don't you just stay here? There's plenty of room." I could tell she wanted to argue but knew in the end it would be wiser for her to just stay here. "I even have some pajamas you can borrow," I told her. She and Xander exchanged a quick look before I got up and took her to my bedroom so she could change.

Once upstairs, I dug through my draws to find something that would fit her petite figure. "Here," I said, handing her an old pair of pajamas that were a little snug on me. "These should fit. They might be a little big but it's probably better than what my mom can offer."

"Thanks. I'm sure they're fine," Danni said, taking them and placing them on her lap.

"Are you okay?" I asked, noticing her distant look.

"Huh, oh, yeah...fine," she said, getting up. "I'll go change in the bathroom." She closed the bathroom door behind her while I lied back on my bed and waited.

When she emerged from the bathroom I noticed how the clothes hung loosely on her tiny frame. "Sorry they're so big. If you want I can –"

"Ella, they are fine, and they're not that big, really," she said, thinking I was getting down on myself for my size. I never had a problem not being what society's idea of skinny was. I always liked my curves and made the most of them, but after receiving my powers, I swear my boobs and butt grew a size which made me feel a little self-conscious. "Is something bothering you?" she asked.

"No, I mean well yes." I stood up. "Look at these things," I said, pulling my dress back to show the size of my new breasts. "And this." I turned around to point out my butt. "Seriously, I didn't even think it was possible for these things to get any bigger."

"Ella, there is nothing wrong with the way you look. You are perfectly fine with who you are."

"I know," I sighed.

"Did somebody say something because if so I will totally kick their ass," she said, puffing her chest.

I laughed. "No." She narrowed her eyes at me for laughing at her. "And when have you known me to care what people think?"

"True," she admitted. "So what's really bothering you then?"

"I don't know. I mean, I love my body, but I'd also love it if my boobs and butt were a little smaller," I said, looking at them in the mirror.

"I'm not gonna lie, you do have a mean ba-dunk-a-dunk," she giggled.

"It's not funny!" I cried, trying to push it down.

She managed to stop laughing long enough to be serious. "Ella, your body is still growing. It's only natural that certain...things would get bigger."

"Yeah, but how much?" I said, turning in the mirror. "I swear if my boobs get any bigger I'll fall over."

"Oh stop it, they're not that big," she said.

"Jealous?" I teased.

"Shut up," she snapped, crossing her arms over her barely there chest. "Maybe." I laughed, joining her on the bed.

"You two decent?" Dean called after he knocked on the door.

"Yes," I replied.

He opened the door and stepped into the room. "I got you a present," he said handing a medium sized bag to Danni. "You can open it later." He winked and walked out of the room.

"I'm afraid to look," Danni confessed. She opened up the bag slowly and instantly started to crack up when she saw what was inside.

"What is it?" I asked almost afraid to know. She pulled the contents out of the bag to reveal sexy, black lingerie. "Oh, my, God," I said, jaw dropped. "I can't believe he did that. That is so inappropriate."

"I think it's sweet," she said, putting it back in the bag.

"Whoa, okay, how drunk are you and are you feeling well?" I put the back of my hand to her forehead.

"I'm fine." She slapped my hand away, and then sighed, putting her head in her hands.

"Okay seriously Danni, what gives? You haven't been yourself ever since Xander announced his engagement to Jasa and don't say to mind my own business."

She fell back on the bed. "Ella, you have no idea what you're asking me."

"Danni, whatever it is, you can tell me."

She let out a long, deep breath before she sat back up. "Okay, everything I'm about to tell you, you have to promise me, promise me Ella that it doesn't leave this room."

The look on her face told me this was something serious and something she didn't like to talk about. "Of course Danni, you can trust me," I said, squeezing her hand for encouragement.

She gave me a weak smile before she started to rub her hands up and down her legs nervously. She ran a shaky hand through her hair. "I could really use a drink right now," she said, jumping up and pacing the room.

"Okay one, I think you had enough, and two, it can't be that bad."

Danni stopped and turned to look at me. I would be lying if I said I wasn't a little frightened. "Xander and I use to date in high school. I thought he was the one, but I was wrong and here we are today," she said in a rush.

"Okay, Whoa! First, when did you and Xander date and how did I not know this? And second, could you be anymore vague? I mean really Danni. I want to know everything and I want the truth." She started pacing again. "And can you stop pacing you're making me sick."

"Sorry," she said, finally coming to a stop. "Okay," she pulled at her hair. "Well the reason you didn't know was because nobody did.

Xander and I kept our relationship a secret because your parents didn't exactly approve of me."

I started laughing hysterically. "Yeah, right." I found it hard to believe that my parents wouldn't approve of Danni.

Her expression said it was no joke. "When I was younger, I wasn't exactly…" she paused looking for the right word. "I guess the way to put it is I kinda followed my own rules." She smiled as if the memory was not that long ago. "I was a very different person back then. Someone your parents would not want Xander to date."

"Whose idea was it to keep it a secret?" I asked curious.

"Mine," she said with slight regret. She let out a breath before she continued. "Xander and I were in love, or so I thought. After I got pregnant, things got…complicated."

"Wait," I said, putting the pieces together. "Is Hadley Xander's?" She nodded slowly. "Oh my God! Oh my God! This is huge! Does Xander know?" I stood up, unable to contain my excitement.

"No and you can't tell him. Promise me Ella, promise me you won't tell him," she pleaded.

"I promise I won't, but…I think he should know," I said, sinking back down on the bed.

"I know," she said, joining me. "It's just complicated."

"Well, how about you make it uncomplicated?"

"It's not that easy."

"Does anyone else know?"

"Your parents do."

"Whoa, what? They know and they haven't said anything?" I tried to wrap my mind around why they would keep this a secret.

"Obviously this wasn't something we planned and we were so young. Not to mention it was right around the time Xander found out he was supposed to take over for your father on the royal court."

"You know?" I asked shocked. She nodded. "God, am I always the last one to find everything out." Danni laughed at my little ramble. "And this doesn't freak you out knowing that we're…vampires," I whispered.

She pulled back and looked at me wide eyed. "Why, you're not going to bite me are you?"

"Eew no," I said, making her laugh.

"No Ella, it doesn't freak me out. I guess you can say I always believed there were other things out there." She shrugged like it was no big deal.

I shook my head. "Okay, let's get back to the topic at hand. Why did Xander taking over for my father have anything to do with it?"

"Like I said, we were very young and having a baby would have ruined Xander's opportunity to take over." I opened my mouth to comment but she continued. "When I first found out I was pregnant, Xander was going through a lot so I confided in your mom first. She and your dad convinced me not to tell Xander. They said it would ruin his future. I convinced myself they were right. So I told Xander I cheated on him and was pregnant with the other person's baby."

"Oh Danni, I'm so sorry. I can't believe they made you do that. They are such assholes."

"No they are not." I looked at her like she was crazy. "Ella, you have to see it from their perspective. I mean can you imagine some strange girl you never met showing up at your house and telling you they were pregnant with your son's baby?"

"Yeah, I see your point," I said, imagining the horrified look on my mom's face when Danni told her.

"I didn't have to listen to them, but I did. They were right. Xander had...has a bright future ahead of him and a baby would have destroyed that. The only thing I regret is letting him go."

"What do you mean?"

"After I told him I was pregnant with someone else's baby, Xander still wanted to be with me, but I couldn't. I couldn't face him every day and lie to his face. At first it was hard, but over time it got easier."

Her confession made me think of Tristan and I wondered that if over time, losing him would get easier. Then it made me think. "You came back though, why?"

"Your mom. She felt guilty and didn't want Hadley to grow up without a family."

"That's why they bought you a house and gave you a job." She nodded even though it wasn't a question.

"And help out with Hadley," she added.

"You still love him, don't you?" I asked, even though I already knew the answer. Danni bowed her head unable to form words to describe what she was feeling. "Danni I'm so sorry. I can't imagine how you must feel right now," I said, taking her hand. "And you have to know Xander would have done the right thing if he knew. He wouldn't have let you go."

"I know," she said with a sad smile. Not knowing what else to say, I wrapped my arms around her and gave a tight squeeze. She hugged me back and I could tell she was trying really hard not to cry.

"Am I interrupting?" Xander asked, stepping inside my room. Danni pulled back and hastily wiped away the few tears that managed to escape.

"No, what's up?" I asked.

"If you don't mind, I'd like to talk to Danni, privately," he said, looking straight at her.

"Umm," I looked at Danni. She shook her head letting me know it was okay. "Yeah, I'll be downstairs." I left the room, closing the door behind me. But I didn't go downstairs. Instead, I pressed my ear close to the door. At first I heard nothing. I leaned in closer, thinking they just didn't start yet.

Still nothing.

What were they doing, whispering?

Suddenly the door swung open and there was a very annoyed Xander standing on the other side.

Crap, I was busted.

"Goodbye Ella," Xander said, standing by the door, waiting and watching until I went downstairs. When I got to the bottom of the steps, I heard him shut the door. I contemplated about going back and trying to listen again, but he would just probably catch me, again. I wondered if this new school would teach us how to be stealthy. I shrugged it off and decided to check on Hadley and Jake. They were still sound asleep wrapped in each other's arms. I brushed aside Hadley's hair and gave her a soft kiss on the forehead. I can't believe I have a niece. I didn't know why I hadn't seen the similarities before. She had Xander's green eyes and that thick, dark hair. Dean was the only one in the family who had brown eyes. I always wondered if they made a mistake at the hospital. It would explain a lot.

I gazed over them one more time before I headed into the kitchen and helped myself to some of the leftover cake from desert. I felt a cool breeze and noticed the back door was slightly ajar. I went to close it when I spotted my mom outside on the deck wrapped up in a blanket. I grabbed my coat, an extra fork, and joined her outside. "Ella, what are you doing out here, it's too cold. You should go back inside."

"It's not that bad." It had warmed up considerably since this morning. "What are you doing out here?"

"It's a nice night. I wanted to enjoy it," she said, poking at the logs in the fire pit. The smoke and ash stirred, sending waves of embers swirling in the air as the fire spread and grew, warming the area around us. My mom sat back and lifted the blanket so I could join her in the cocoon. It had stopped snowing a few hours ago and already started to melt as if it was never here in the first place. I snuggled up closer to my mom for warmth and then handed her a fork. "Are Jake and Hadley still sleeping?" she asked, taking the fork graciously and helping herself to some cake.

"Yes," I said.

She paused for minute and looked at me. "Is something bothering you?"

"No," I lied.

"Ella, I am your mother. You cannot lie to me. Besides, your aura tells me otherwise."

"My what?" I said, giving her a sideways glance.

"Your aura, I can see it. It gives me a feel for your emotions although it's not always accurate."

"You can see auras?"

"Well, it's more like colors. That's part of my power and I'm also very intuitive," she smiled.

"That would explain a lot."

She laughed. "Well, I would like to think most of it was basic mother intuition, but my powers do help."

"Is that what my power is?"

"Maybe, we will find out. I have a feeling you're going to surprise us," she winked taking another big bite of cake.

"What else can you do?"

"I can manipulate emotions."

"How so?" I asked intrigued.

"When someone is angry, I can calm them down or when someone is upset, I can take away their sadness."

"Is that what you did to me?" She looked away not wanting to answer. "It's okay mom. I understand why you would do it. If it was you I would have done the same thing."

"Ella, most of it was you. I only took away a little bit to make it easier for you to heal, but the rest of it was you. You did it all on your own."

I leaned on her shoulder. I knew she was telling the truth. This was definitely something my mom would not lie to me about. "Is that why you're always able to calm dad?"

"Mostly. He would say it's me and not my powers that calm him. "I rolled my eyes and she laughed. "Ella, when you fall in love, you'll understand." I think I already did. I did love Tristan, I still do. "Now honey, what's really bothering you?"

"If you're so intuitive, then why don't you tell me?" I challenged.

She gave me her annoyed mother look before taking a deep breath, closing her eyes, and concentrating. "You know," she said, letting out a breath. "You know Hadley is Xander's."

I stared at her in astonishment. "Wow, you really are good."

She laughed. "No. Just a good listener." I looked at her funny. "I overheard you and Danni talking."

"Mom, that's eavesdropping and not very nice," I scowled.

"You're one to talk," she countered.

"I have no idea what you are talking about?" I said, trying to play the innocent.

"Uh-huh," she smiled and tried to take another piece of cake, but I pulled it away.

"Wait, how often do you spy?"

"I wasn't spying Ella. I could feel Danni's emotions. They were very strong so I opened myself up to understand what was going on and that's when I heard what you were talking about."

"You don't do that all the time do you?" I wondered how many private conversations she listened in on without me knowing.

"Ella no. Like I said, when emotions are that strong, I get pulled in. I never invade anyone's privacy unless I feel it's necessary."

"And exactly how many times did you feel it necessary?" I teased, still holding the cake away.

"Would you stop it Ella?" she said. "Look at me and tell me you really believe I would do that." I studied her. If she could really read auras and emotions then she'd already know my answer, which for the most part I believed she wouldn't intentionally invade someone's privacy.

She hit me. "Ow! What was that for?" I complained, rubbing my leg.

"I know what you were thinking," she said, narrowing her eyes at me. I couldn't help but crack a smile. "Now give me that cake."

"Get your own," I said, turning and holding the plate away from her.

"Ella, do not disobey your mother." She pulled me around and swiped the cake from my hands. "Hey!" I shouted. "Maybe if you learn to share," she said.

"Fine," I grumbled.

Her teasing smile turned serious. "Ella, you do understand that you cannot tell Xander about Hadley or anyone for that matter."

"Yeah, I do," I sighed. "It just sucks."

"The important thing is Hadley and Danni are safe and will stay that way as long as no one knows."

"Are they in danger?" I asked worried.

"No, but it is just better this way."

I relaxed back into the chair and let her finish the rest of the cake. There was no reason to dwell on the Hadley Xander issue so I moved on. I wanted to know more about her powers. "So when you say you feel emotions, does that mean you feel everyone's all the time?"

"Yes and no. I learned how to control it. People I'm closer to and care about I feel their emotions the strongest."

"So you experience what their feeling?"

"Yes, so when you hurt I hurt," she said softly.

"I'm sorry."

"For what dear?"

"That you have to feel what I do."

"Ella, don't ever be sorry for feeling the way you do. Yes it makes me sad to know how badly you are hurting, but it also helps me to understand better what you're going through."

"I guess," I said.

"Ella, I love you no matter what and I never want you to hold anything back, okay?" I nodded slowly and laid there with her for a while, taking comfort in the fact that maybe she did understand how I was feeling and sad because she had to feel it with me.

CHAPTER FIVE

In the morning, I made Jake and Hadley breakfast. Danni was still sleeping when they woke up and I didn't want to disturb her. I could only imagine how she was feeling so I decided to let her sleep in. She deserved a day off.

When Hadley and Jake were done eating, I let them play for a while before I took Jake home. He didn't want to leave Hadley which I thought was cute. It reminded me of when Kyle and I first met. He told me he never wanted to be away from me and would always protect me from danger. This was followed by him running around the yard with a plastic shield and sword chasing Xander and Dean. Dean was the dragon and Xander was the evil king. The things we did and said when we were five. I laughed to myself at the memory as I waited for Jake to say goodbye to Hadley.

"You know Jake, you only live a few houses down. If you want you can come and play with Hadley again." His eyes lit up and I could tell I just made his day. He hugged my leg and waved goodbye to Hadley. Once I saw Jake was safely inside, Hadley and I walked back to the house to find Danni awake and already in the kitchen cleaning.

"Mommy!" Hadley yelled, running into Danni's arms.

"Morning baby, did you eat?"

"Ella made us breakfast!" she cheered.

"Not so loud honey. Mommy has a headache," Danni cringed.

I had a hard time hiding my smile. "Come on Hadley. Why don't we go play while mommy relaxes a little?" Danni whispered, "thank you," and got back to work. I found Dean in the living room and he volunteered to keep an eye on Hadley for me so I could go back into the kitchen to help Danni. "Why don't you eat something and I'll clean up," I told her.

"I'm afraid to eat," she said honestly.

"Well, that's what you get for downing glass after glass of wine last night," I teased.

She just rolled her eyes. "What's Hadley doing?"

"She's playing with Dean. She convinced him to play Barbies with her."

"You're kidding?" she said, not believing what she just heard.

"Nope," I laughed. "It really is a sight to be seen." Danni laughed and continued to clean. I got up and grabbed her hand to stop her. "Danni, sit down, I got this," I said, taking over for her.

"If you keep doing my job for me I won't have one anymore," she said as she sat down with a cup of coffee. She sipped it cautiously while resting her head on her hand.

"Please, I can guarantee you could be the worst maid ever and my parents still wouldn't fire you." She gave me a look saying, "don't make me regret telling you about Hadley." I held up my hands in defense. "I'm just saying, regardless."

The kitchen was messier than I expected. I gave up half way through and Danni laughed at my pitiful attempt to help. She shooed me away once she finished her cup of coffee and I headed back into the living room to check on Hadley. She was still playing Barbies with Dean. I thought quickly and pulled out my phone to take a picture. The flash surprised him. Dean whipped his head around and glared at me. "What are you doing?" he asked, annoyed.

"Blackmail," I smiled, waving my phone.

"Ella, if you don't delete that picture I'll..."

"You'll what?" I teased.

"Dean!" Hadley yelled annoyed that he wasn't paying attention to her.

"Have fun," I sang and walked upstairs laughing.

"I'll get you for this later," he yelled aggravating Hadley again. I could hear her giving him a lecture for not listening to her, which made my day. When I reached my room I fell down on my bed, assessing the mess my Christmas presents made as they lay scattered around the room. I put my arms over my face and decided I would deal with the mess later and take a nap instead. My nap was interrupted by Dean barging into my room. He tried to compel me to delete the picture.

"It won't work. You can't compel me," I said with a smug smile.

"What are you talking about," he squinted, still trying. "I've done this before," he admitted to my surprise.

"Yeah, thanks for that by the way," I glared. "But for your information we learned I cannot be compelled."

"Why not?" he asked frustrated. I shrugged. He still tried even after I told him he couldn't. I continued to sit there, amused at his attempt. I gave him credit for his effort and laughed when he got mad and failed. After he started to break out into a sweat he finally gave up and left.

We discovered after Tristan tried to compel me and I later remembered, something wasn't right. My dad decided to do a few tests which revealed that I could not be compelled. I also learned it was the reason for all my headaches and black outs when I was younger. My brothers had compelled me when we were little when they didn't want to get in trouble for something they did. I never understood my lost time or headaches until now. This would also explain why no doctor could ever find anything wrong with me. Now knowing the truth, I had planned to get my brothers back for what they did to me. I was also happy they couldn't do it anymore.

Since I could no longer sleep. I decided to clean up my room. Once I was done, I sat down at my computer desk and stared at the brochures my mom had left about the school I was going to attend in January. There were several different pamphlets including a map, all the different courses they offered and some other information they offered about the school. I moved my mouse on the computer and waited for the screen to come to life. I typed in the name of the school to do a little research on my own. I got very few results as the searches came up. I was beginning to discover that this school was more private than what it listed.

Since finding no new information on the computer, I shut it down and picked up the brochures to look over on my bed. I knew I would begin after their winter break ended sometime near the middle of January. My mom told me I only had a week left to choose my classes so everything would be organized and ready when I arrived. I flipped through the course book to see what they had to offer. Most of what I found was stuff I never heard of. For instance, Vampire History 101, Spells and Castings levels 1-5, and the list went on. I knew most of my classes would be chosen for me. Being a first year student it was a prerequisite to take certain classes. I had very few choices of electives, most of which were sports, which I did not play. Thankfully they did have an art class and my only other option that I would be interested in would be dance. I checked both boxes and slipped the paper in the envelope.

I gave the paper to my mom and she said she would fax it to the school so they could get my schedule together for me. I still wasn't looking forward to this, but at least I might be able to figure out what my powers are and how to use them. It really did suck having powers that you didn't know what they did. My mom told me that sometimes even after you receive your powers you don't always automatically get the full effect of them right away. She said they build over time.

Time was all I had lately.

Everyone was going to a party at The Hilton tonight for the New Year celebration. I opted to stay home with Danni and the kids. I wasn't so much in the celebrating mood.

After playing all the day with Jake and Hadley, I decided to take a short nap knowing if I didn't I wouldn't make it till twelve. It was a little cool in the house so I searched my closet for a sweater. As I dug through my closet I came across the black dress Josie and Dixon made me buy back in Vermont. I ran my fingers over the shiny black fabric. I hugged it close to my chest and I swear I could hear the songs playing from that night. I squeezed my eyes tight and promised myself I wouldn't cry. I took a deep breath, letting it out slowly. I knew there was something I had to do. Something I've been putting off for too long.

I needed to let go of Tristan.

Holding onto something that didn't exist anymore wasn't healthy. I knew I needed to start the New Year fresh. I closed the closet door and lay down on my bed. It only took a few minutes before I fell asleep.

I was in the restaurant at the hotel we stayed at in Vermont. The one where I finally gave my heart to Tristan. The restaurant was empty. I was standing in the middle of the dance floor alone, and I was wearing the black dress. I looked around the empty space scared I wouldn't find him.

I felt him before I saw him. I turned back around and spotted Tristan sitting casually in a chair by our table. He was wearing a suit and his hair was its normal messy style. He was the picture of perfection and every bit as handsome the day I met him. The sight of him made what I had to do that much harder. I forced a smile and walked over to where he was sitting. He stood up when I approached, kissed my hand, and surprised me with a bouquet of wild flowers.

"Thank you," I said softly, afraid my voice would betray me. He took one of the flowers from the arrangement and placed it in my hair. Holding out his arm for me, he led me to the dance floor. We danced as if we never stopped dancing that night. I closed my eyes, resting my head on his chest, savoring the moment. I listened to his heart and it hurt more than I could have imagined. I would never hear this again. I pulled back before I lost all of my nerve. I placed my hands on either side of his face. I tried to take in as much of him as I could; his hair, his skin, his cool, minty scent, his smile, and his intoxicatingly dark blue eyes. I absorbed the feeling of his arms around me, the feeling I get when he touches me, when he's around. I took it all.

I dropped my hands to his chest and looked up into his eyes. "Tristan?" my voice cracked. He met my eyes, smiled, and kissed my lips tenderly. "Tristan, I have to go." My voice was weak and it was getting harder to speak. I pushed myself and tried again. "I have to go. I have to move on."

"Ella, what are you talking about?"

"You aren't real. This isn't real. This is all just a fantasy I've created to keep you with me, but I can't do it anymore. I can't keep torturing myself like this. I have to let you go."

"Ella?" There was pain in his eyes. He reached up to touch my face, but I stopped him, holding his hand in mine. I had to do this before it was too late, before I changed my mind.

The aching in my chest was building. I started to cry. Standing on my tip toes, I kissed his wonderful lips one last time, lingering longer than I should have. "Goodbye Tristan," I whispered, closing my eyes. The clock signaled it was midnight. I closed my eyes. When I was brave enough to open them, Tristan was gone.

I was alone.

The only thing that let me know he was here was the bouquet of flowers lying on the floor in front of me. I picked them up and hugged them close to my chest. When I opened my eyes I was back in my room. "Ella! Ella!" Hadley and Jake yelled. "Happy New Year!" they cheered, jumping up and down on my bed causing, ginger to grumble and get down.

"Sorry Ella, they're fast little buggers," Danni said, trying to catch her breath.

The sound of fireworks outside caught Jake's attention. "Fireworks! Can we watch?"

"Just take Ginger with you. I'll be out in a second." Ginger lay on the floor not happy with my request to go outside with the kids. "Go on girl, go." She reluctantly got up and followed them out.

"Everything okay Ella?" Danni asked.

"Yeah, just give me a minute," I said, swinging my legs over the side of the bed. She hesitated in the doorway for a moment. I knew she could tell something wasn't right, but she also knew I would come to her when I was ready. She left me alone to hash out my issues before I joined them outside. I got up off the bed and took a deep breath. I managed to compose myself enough to go outside and watch the fireworks. I found Danni with the kids over by the fire pit that was already ablaze. All four of us cuddled together on one of the larger chairs and watched the explosion of beautiful, multicolored lights.

When they were over, I gave Jake and Hadley some sparklers to play with. "Ella, what's in your hair?" Danni asked, looking at me funny. She reached up and pulled out a purple violet. I examined the flower in her hand. *How the?* I had no idea how that got there or where it came from.

I took the flower from Danni twirling it between my fingers. Crazier things have happened I thought and shrugged it off. "Ella, come play with us," Hadley squealed, running over to us. Her eyes went straight to the violet in my hand. "Pretty," she said, touching the petals with her tiny fingertips. I tucked the flower behind her ear. "How do I look mommy?"

Danni squeezed her cheeks and kissed her nose. "Beautiful baby." Hadley giggled and took my hand pulling me off of the chair.

"Xander!" Jake yelled. "Come play with us!"

"You're home early," I said as he joined us on the lawn.

"Jasa has an early flight tomorrow," he replied.

"Where's she going?" I asked curiously.

"New York. Her firm has a big case they're working on and she has to be there," he said a little saddened about not being able to spend the whole night with her.

"Xander come on!" Hadley and Jake complained, tugging on his arms impatiently.

"Okay, okay," he laughed and allowed them to pull him along. We lit a few more sparklers and watched as they danced around in the grass with bright, smiling faces.

"Fly me Xander fly me!" Hadley cried. He picked her up in the air and spun her around. She giggled happily and I could see the longing in his eyes, wishing that she was his. I wanted to burst forth and tell him she was. He no longer had to wish because it was true. But it was not my secret to tell. So instead I bit my tongue and stood back.

"Alright Hadley, it's time for bed," Danni told her as she stood up and joined us.

"I'm not tired," Hadley complained.

"I know but it's late," Danni said through a yawn.

"Will you read me a story?" Hadley begged with her big green eyes.

"Yes," Danni caved. There wasn't anything that little girl couldn't get her mom to do.

"And Xander too!" Danni looked slightly uncomfortable.

"I don't mind," Xander said. If I didn't know any better, I could swear Xander still had feelings for Danni.

I watched them walk in to the house before I turned to Jake and told him it was time for bed too.

It only took a week for the school to get back to me with my schedule. My first class wasn't until ten in the morning making this school a little more appealing. I looked over the schedule they had sent me.

Vampire history 101 10:00 - 11:00 room 232
Spells and casting 11:15 - 12:15 room 333
Lunch 12:30 - 2:00
Chemistry beginner 2:15 - 3:15 room 124
Power control beginner 3:30 - 4:30 room 208
Self-defense 5:00 - 6:00 gymnasium

And that was just Monday. Tuesday was a whole different schedule.

Royal politics/economics 8:00 - 10:00 room 239

And the little appeal the school had was now gone.

Art 10:15 - 11:15 room 393
Dance 11:30 - 12:30 studio
Lunch 1:00 - 2:00

My schedule alternated like this every other day. At least the days I had to get up early I got done earlier so I tried to look at it on a positive note. I didn't use to mind getting up early, but after experiencing the joys of sleeping in on a regular basis I was kind of spoiled.

I slipped my schedule in my desk and walked over to my bed where I picked up my journal.

Jan. 7

I'm really starting to get nervous. I have no idea

what to expect. Not only am I starting a new school, again, but I won't know anyone and Dean doesn't count. I have no idea what the people will be like. It's not like when I started school in the fall. I had Josie with me then, it was easier, and I was more than willing to meet new people, but now, after everything that happened? I wasn't willing to make new friends and risk putting them in danger. Plus this entire school will be filled with people like me. Vampires, half-breeds, witches...I wonder if there are any others out there? Like werewolves? Angels? Hey if there are vampires and I'm living proof there is, why not other folk lore creatures?

I pondered that thought for a moment.

Maybe starting somewhere new again would be a good thing. I'm sure I won't be the only new student? I hope. A new place where no one knows me...doesn't know what happened. I could literally start fresh. Oh who am I kidding? I can't do this___

"Ella, what's the matter?" my mom asked, coming into my room, uninvited.

"Huh? Oh, nothing," I said, putting my journal aside.

"Ella, something's bothering you," she said, making her way over to me.

"I'm fine," I said a little annoyed.

"Ella, your emotions are practically screaming at me. I felt you all the way downstairs."

"Oh, right. I forgot you're an empath," I sighed. That's the name for people like my mom with her kind of powers. It was one of the many things I looked up after she told me.

"Now, care to tell me what's wrong?"

"You can't figure it out?" I said, snippier than I intended to.

"No," she said, ignoring my attitude. "Your emotions are all jumbled. Let me –"

"No! Stay back. I can do this myself." I knew she planned to calm me with her powers, but I didn't want an easy fix.

"I have no doubt you can, but Ella, please. Not just for your sake, but mine as well. You're a jumbled mess right now and it's killing me."

"Can't you just block it?"

"Not when they're this strong," she said, covering her ears as if the voices were too loud.

"Sorry," I said, feeling bad. I forgot she could feel everything I could when our emotions run high. She sat next to me on the bed, placing her hand over mine. I instantly felt warmth and a soothing, calm feeling. "Thank you," I said, letting out a breath.

"Wanna tell me what's bothering you?"

"I'm just really nervous about this new school. I thought maybe I could start over, but I'm scared."

"It's normal to be scared Ella, but you can't let it get the best of you. Besides, Dean will be there, and he'll help you." My head shot up. "I'll make sure he helps you out. What else is bothering you?"

"I'm afraid I'm never going to be able to trust anyone again. I'm also afraid I'm going to be so paranoid that I'll think everyone is out to get me."

"Oh, honey," she wrapped her arms around me. "It's normal to feel that way."

I snapped, no longer feeling the calming effects of her powers. "Stop saying it's normal!" I stood up. "Everything about me is far from normal!" My mom had a stunned look on her face, not sure what to do.

"What is all this shouting about?" my dad asked, joining the party.

"This is all your fault!" I yelled, pushing past him.

"Let her go," I heard my mom say as I stomped down the stairs. I didn't know where I was going and I really didn't have many options either. I couldn't leave the house without any guardians and all I wanted was to be left alone. I was feeling trapped, like my head was going to explode. I walked out back and screamed at the top of my lungs.

"Feel better?" Dean asked, shaking a finger in his ear.

"Sorry, didn't see you there...and no, I don't." I thought letting it out would help but all it did was make my throat sore.

Dean stood up from his chair, drink in hand, "Alright, we're going out. Go get dressed," he said, making me do a double take.

"What? And I am dressed," I said, crossing my arms, annoyed.

"You need to put something slutty on if we're going to pass you for twenty-one, well, you could pass on your own considering you look like you're thirty, but then you'd still stick out like a sore thumb," he said, pushing me into the house. I opened my mouth to retort, but I was too stunned to form words. "Just trust me," he winked. "Go," he said, shoving me up the steps.

I managed to close my mouth and walk up the stairs to my room. I didn't completely trust Dean, but I thought I'd go along for at least entertainment value. I searched through my closet trying to find something *'slutty'*, which was hard because everything I owned now was hoodies and jeans. Not to mention even before most of my clothes, I guess you could say, were more conservative. Josie was always yelling at me.

I reached in to the back of my closet and found my only mini skirt and a lace tube top. I pulled out the lace tube top. I've never seen it before and wondered how the hell it got in there? Regardless, it would have to do. I grabbed Josie's favorite black boots from the bottom of the closet and got dressed. I then rimmed my eyes with black eyeliner for a more dramatic effect. I wasn't too worried about looking older. Dean was right. I was always told I looked older for my age. My mom used to say it was because of the way I carried myself and what gave away my true age was my eyes – my dad said it was my lack of maturity, *whatever*. My Grandma Bea told me it was because I had a warrior's spirit inside of me. The spirit masked my appearance to make me look older and wiser to fool my enemies. I liked Grandma's reasoning the best.

I didn't mind looking older, it came in handy sometimes. For example, like tonight.

When I was done, I met Dean downstairs where he was waiting with Xander and Gabe. "That's your idea of slutty?" Dean mocked.

"Sorry, I left my pasties and G-string at the dry cleaners."

"It's fine," Xander butted in before the bickering started.

"Where are we going anyways?" I asked.

"You'll see," Dean said, leading me to the car.

"Does dad know about this because if not I do not want to get in trouble for this," I stopped and paused, not wanting to pursue this any further without confirmation.

"Yes dad knows," Dean said rolling his eyes. "Why do you think Gabe is with us?" I didn't ask any more questions. I was just glad to get out of the house.

They ended up taking me to some dive bar in the not so nice part of town. "Seriously, this is where you guys bring me?" I was afraid to touch anything for fear of getting hepatitis.

"It's not about the place. It's about the company you keep," Xander smiled.

"Yeah, well, that's questionable too."

CHAPTER SIX

We sat in the back near the billiards tables. Dean ordered us a round of drinks and shots. "Here," he said, handing me a shot.

"I don't know? What is it?" I asked apprehensive.

"Just take it," he said rolling his eyes.

I reluctantly took the shot. "Oh god, what was that?" I cringed as my throat burned with a horrific after taste.

Xander and Dean laughed. I think I even caught Gabe smile. I glared at them thinking how not funny that was. "Whiskey," Dean replied to my question. "It will put some hair on your chest," he said, patting my back.

"Don't worry, you'll get used to it," Xander said. That was not something I wanted to get used to. "Come on, let's play some pool."

"I'm not very good," I told him. I only played one other time and that was when Tristan *tried* to teach me and failed miserably.

"I'll teach you," Xander said. We walked over to the pool tables, but they were all taken. "We got next game," Xander told one of the guys that were playing and put some quarters down on the table.

"I don't think so. Why don't you and the little kiddies go play some video games?" The guy laughed, throwing the quarters back at Xander.

"Come on Xander, you can teach me another time," I said, trying to pull him away, but he wouldn't budge.

Instead he just walked right up to the guy and got in his face. Gabe instantly tensed up and stood by me ready to take me out in case this got ugly. "I said we got next game," Xander repeated, more stern. The guy laughed again and bent down to take his shot.

Dean put his hand on the ball. The guy stood up ready to knock him out. "Better yet, you're done. We'll take it from here," Dean said, making the guy's eyes go wide. "And the next game is on you." The guy just stood there, staring at Dean dazed. Two seconds later, the guy put quarters on the table and walked away. His friend's stared at him like he was nuts. Gabe relaxed a little when he walked away.

"Dean, how did you?" He turned to me and winked. It took a moment before it registered. *Son of a bitch, he compelled him.*

"Nifty little trick, isn't it," Xander whispered. I just shook my head as Xander racked the balls. "Dean, you break."

Xander tried to explain to me how to line up the cue ball with the one I wanted to hit. He told me that normally you're supposed to call your shots but since I was a beginner and we were playing for fun he wouldn't make me. I played very well. Dean said it was beginners luck and Xander said I was a natural. Even Gabe relaxed enough to play a few games. Xander suggested I play someone for money. "I hope you have money to lose because I'm not that good," I said.

"No worries, we'll play teams," he said. "Besides, I have faith in you," he smiled.

"I know the perfect person to," Dean said before he walked away. He came back with another round of drinks and shots. "Here, you're going to need this." He handed me the shot. I didn't hesitate this time. "Hey you!" Dean called over his shoulder. "Wanna play?" he asked the guy who we took the table from earlier.

"Dean, what are you doing?" I said, grabbing his arm.

"Further humiliation," he smiled.

"For who him or me?" He ignored me.

"What's the bet?" the guy asked.

"A hundred a ball," Dean said with a cocky smile.

"Dean!" He was taking too much faith in me being able to win. I was definitely not willing to risk that.

Sensing my hesitation he said, "Ella don't worry. You got this." He turned back to the guy "You against her."

"Wait, I thought we were playing teams?" I asked a little panicked now.

"Next one. Trust me Ella. You can take him." I wasn't so sure. I swiped Dean's shot from his hand and threw it back, letting the liquid burn my throat. "Relax," he said.

"You breaking sweetheart?" the guy asked with a smug smile.

Dean whispered so low in my ear that only I could hear him. "Tell him to break. You'll have a better advantage that way."

I looked the guy dead in the eye before I said, "No, you break."

He smiled, exposing the giant gap between his yellow teeth. I tried not to shudder. Xander pulled me aside to give me some quick pointers, but I was too nervous to listen. When my turn was up

Xander told me to call my shots, which made me even more nervous.

I didn't know how I did it, but I won. I had a feeling somehow Xander and Dean were behind it. I had no know idea what their powers were, but something in my gut told me they played a part in me winning. The guy looked truly embarrassed to be beaten by a girl. I smirked at him as I walked over to collect my winnings. "Pay up," I said, holding out my hand. He had to ask his buddies for some extra cash to cover what he lost.

Once I had all the money, I told the boys next round was on me. I made Xander come with me to order the drinks so he could help me carry everything. On our way back to the table some jerk felt the need to interject.

"Hey sweetheart, here's a dollar. Why don't you come over here and shake that ass for me," the creep shouted. I ignored the lewd comment and kept walking as Xander shoved me along.

We spent most of the night playing pool and drinking. Dean ended up getting these shots called car bombs. "You do this and you're officially in the boys club," Dean said. I dropped my shot in the beer like he told me and downed the drink before they even started. "Damn Ella, welcome to the boys club," Dean and Xander cheered, clanking their glasses together.

After a few more car bombs, I could barely see straight. Xander and Dean seemed to be in the same predicament. We tried horribly to play pool but gave up after realizing none of us could even hold a stick straight. I pulled Xander over to an open area and made it a dance floor. Dean followed, pushing us aside, insisting he had the best moves. It was the most ridiculous thing I've ever seen. "That's what you call dancing?" I laughed.

"Like you could do better?" he challenged.

I shoved him out of the way and did the best I could without falling over. "Damn girl, shake it!" The creep from earlier called. "Oh, come on honey, don't stop. I was enjoying the show." I ignored him again and started to move closer to Xander but the creep jumped up and grabbed me. "Dance with me sugar." Dean, Xander, and Gabe instantly rushed over to me. "Whoa! Relax guys I was just having some fun." He let me go and put his hands up defensively.

The boys backed down and I turned to walk away again when the creep smacked me on my backside. Gabe was about to strike when Xander stopped him. "Wait, she can handle this guy," he told Gabe. Feeling confident, I turned around and fixed the creep with a scowl. He smiled wide, exposing his summer teeth (some of them are there some of them aren't). He also had the worst comb over I have ever seen. I smiled back my sweetest smile and swung.

Unfortunately, I missed. My coordination was off just a bit.

I swung so hard I spun around and lost my balance. Gabe caught me before I did a face plant on the floor. "Miss Ella, I don't think it's wise for you to engage with this character."

"I got this," I said, turning back around and facing the creep who was now laughing at me for my failed attempt.

"Wanna try again," he taunted. "I like it rough." He bent down closer to me. "I'll give you a free shot. Go ahead, hit me right here." He pointed to his cheek, laughing. I did not like being antagonized and this guy was really pissing me off. He straightened himself out and turned his back, ready to walk away. I tapped him on the shoulder and he pivoted to face me. I could feel the boys getting ready. I signaled with my finger for the creep to come closer. He smiled that toothless smile as I put my hands on his shoulders, more or less for leverage.

I looked him in the eye, smiled, and then slammed my knee into his groin. He fell to the ground crying out in pain. Xander and Dean were surprised and proud at the same time even though I know they cringed a little at my low blow. Gabe had a big smile on his face nodding his head in approval. I dusted off my hands and smiled, proud of myself.

"Bitch!" the creep yelled, lunging for me. I yelped as Gabe yanked me out of the way and shoved the guy to the ground. The creep bounced back quickly and made a pathetic attempt to take on Gabe. He hit him in the jaw and it was like watching a rubber ball bounce off a brick wall. I think it would have to take a bulldozer to take down Gabe.

The creep shook his hand out like he broke it. He looked stunned. Clearly he had thought he packed enough power in that punch to knock him out. The creep's friends noticed the failed attempt and felt the need to join in. Xander and Dean came to stand beside Gabe and before I knew it chaos broke out. "Ella, get out of here!" they yelled.

I couldn't move though. People were getting thrown left and right. Some guy jumped in front of me and grabbed my arm. I shrieked and reached for a bottle on the bar, smashing it over his head. I've seen people do this in the movies a million times and thought it would work, but all it did was stun him for a second.

He looked at me grinning as blood dripped from his forehead.

"Ella!" Dean yelled throwing me a pool stick before he was socked in the face. I caught it and cracked the guy on the side of the neck with it. He barely flinched. I hit him again and again and again. "Why...Won't...You...Just...Fall...Down!" I yelled.

Frustrated and out of breath, I grabbed a beer mug off the bar – this was definitely heavier than a beer bottle. I nailed him right on the side of his head. He stumbled and fell down. "It's about damn time!"

"Nicely done," Dean said, coming up next to me. "Come on, let's get out of here." He started pulling me out as I yelled for Xander and Gabe. In the process of our escape, some big, brooding, bald man knocked Dean into me so hard I fell on my butt.

"That's it!" I stood up and brushed myself off. The guy that pushed Dean now had him in a headlock and Xander and Gabe were too busy fending off the other goons to help intercept. Having enough of this debauchery, I picked up a chair and bashed it over the back of the guy who had Dean. The chair shattered into pieces upon impact. He dropped like a fly releasing Dean. Dean looked at me wide eyed before I started to push him out the door. Gabe and Xander fought their way out as we ran to the car. Gabe hoped in the driver seat and peeled out before I even had my door closed.

Once we got enough distance from the bar and knew we were all safe, Xander started to laugh and then Dean joined him. "What is so funny?" I asked, not finding the humor in this.

"Who would have thought our li'l sis was a scrapper?" Dean said, laughing harder.

"Hey, I saved your butt!" I said, still not thinking this was funny.

"You definitely are a McCallister," Xander joked ruffling my hair.

"Yeah have fun using that as an excuse to explain this to mom," I told him. At the moment I wasn't so crazy about going home.

"I'm just glad you didn't puke," Dean said.

"I thought you were going to when that guy hit you in the stomach," I said, teasing Dean.

None of us wanted to go home and face mom and dad. I felt even worse for Gabe. I was pretty sure he would be in more trouble than the rest of us.

After the adrenaline rush wore off, I was slapped in the face with the contents of everything I drank tonight. I knew if I wasn't careful this could turn ugly. Xander and Dean had to help me out of the car so I wouldn't fall. I could barely stand up straight and was wondering how Xander and Dean had an easier time holding themselves up when they drank more than I did.

The three of us managed to make it to the door unscathed. We had told Gabe we would take the brunt of the abuse from our parents and make up some lie so he wouldn't get in trouble. But Gabe being the honorable man he is said he would follow this through and take whatever punishment that was coming to him.

So now all four of us stood by the door, not wanting to go inside and face the wrath of our father. Just as I was about to open the door, Dean retched forward and started puking in the bushes. "How long were you holding that in?" Xander laughed.

"Ever since that guy punched me in the gut," he said, wiping his mouth. He threw his arm over my shoulder no longer able to stand on his own.

"Ew gross, you have puke breath," I squealed. I tried to push him away but ended up tripping over my own feet. Luckily for me Xander caught me before I hit the ground and just as our dad opened the front door. We froze. Dean not able to hold his liquor anymore, keeled over and puked in the bush again, making our father's eyes grow wide with rage. Xander and I started to bust up laughing.

"Enough," my dad growled. The anger in his voice was enough to shut us up real quick. Xander helped me stand up straight while mom came out to see what all the fuss was about. "Oh Dean, not in my rose bushes," she complained.

"Sorry mom," he said embarrassed.

"Get. IN. The house. NOW!" my dad demanded. We grabbed Dean and leaned on each other as we made our way into the house. "Kitchen!" We tried to compose ourselves the best we could. "Sit!" my dad said, pacing back and forth, eyeing us all. I had to keep my head down because every time I would look at Xander or Dean I wanted to laugh. Gabe was the only one of us who decided to stay standing. He stood with his hands crossed in front of him ready to accept his punishment. My dad barely even gave him a glance.

It felt like hours before my dad had finally decided to speak. He would open his mouth, close it, and then shake his head several times before he finally said, "Why?" He shook his head again. "No, I don't want to know," he said, changing his mind. "What would possess the three of you to act like this? I expect this from you two," he pointed at me and Dean. I scoffed. "But Xander," he shook his head again, ashamed. "You told me you just wanted to get her out of the house for a little. Not take her out drinking. This is not acceptable." He scrubbed a hand down his face and turned on me.

"If I wasn't already sending you away I –"

"Oh relax dad," I interrupted, not in the mood for a lecture.

His head spun slowly to meet my gaze. He eyed me suspiciously. "Are you drunk?"

"No," hiccup. "I am not," hiccup. Dean and Xander could no longer contain their laughter and started to crack up. My mom looked more embarrassed than anyone hiding her face in her hands.

"You think this is funny?" my dad yelled.

"Oh Liam please, don't act like you were a perfect angel at their age," my mom said, standing up for us.

"Jamila this is different. I've never acted this recklessly. Look at them they're belligerent. So far gone that they get themselves into a bar fight," he said angrily.

"How do you know it was a bar fight and we weren't attacked?" I asked a little defensively. Xander and Dean shook their heads at me to shut up. I looked at them confused.

"Alright, we're not going to get anywhere with this tonight," my mom said. "Gabe, thank you for bringing them home. Your service is done for the night," she said, dismissing him. He nodded his head and left without a word. She turned to my dad next. "Liam, you are too angry right now and they are too drunk," she scowled at us. "I think those bruises and the hangover they'll feel tomorrow will be punishment enough."

"Oh, they'll be punished alright," my dad grinned. "And now I have all night to think of the perfect punishment," he chuckled.

We were no longer laughing.

My dad walked away with an evil smile on his face and we all feared for what we'd be in for tomorrow. "You two, look at you. Go clean yourselves up and stop bleeding on my table," my mom said, feeling no sympathy for us.

I sighed and got up to get some paper towels and ice for my brothers. Danni walked in just then and stopped when she saw us. "What the hell happened to you guys?" she asked, running over to Xander and inspecting his cuts.

"We took Ella out," Dean smiled. Danni rolled her eyes before bringing her attention back to Xander.

"We need to get you guys cleaned up," she said. I handed her the paper towels I had gotten. She stood up and headed over to the sink to wet some of them, retrieved the first aid kit from the cupboard, and then returned to Xander to address his wounds. She gently wiped the blood from Xander's face as he stared into her eyes noting how he still cared deeply for her. I hated knowing what I did and not able to do anything or say anything about it. It was obvious these two still loved each other.

"Hey! I'm hurt over here to you know?" Dean whined.

"Awe, poor baby. You want me to fix your boo-boo for you?" I teased. He glared at me. I ignored his glare and reached up to check out the cut above his eyebrow. I felt a strange pulsing, almost a tingling sensation. Out of nowhere, my hand started to glow.

Dean flinched. "What the hell was that?"

"I don't know?" I said just as surprised as he was. I stared at my hand. The tingling was gone and so was the glow making me think I almost imagined it.

"Do it again," Xander said.

"I don't know what I did?" I said honestly.

"Put your hand over his cut." I did as he requested and watched as my hand began to glow again. There was a silvery blue color that reached from my wrist to the tips of my fingers. I quickly pulled it back afraid of what might happen. I tucked my hand in my lap and looked back up at Dean. The cut on his brow had appeared to look smaller. I blinked not believing my eyes.

"What happened? What did you do?" Dean asked panicked. He got up to look for a mirror.

I looked at Xander not sure what was going on. "I think you're a healer Ella," Xander said smiling. I looked at my hand again. "Here, try it on the cut on my arm."

"Wait, shouldn't you clean it first?" Danni asked.

"No, it should be fine," Xander said, brushing it off.

"Just clean it first to be safe," I said. He rolled his eyes, but let Danni clean it anyways. She wiped off all the dried blood and dirt. "Thank you." I took a breath and prepared myself. I wasn't sure how exactly this worked so I concentrated on his cut and willed it to heal. I placed my hand just above his arm and watched as the cut magically disappeared. "Ah!" I jumped up almost knocking my chair over.

"Well done sis," Xander smiled proudly.

"What I miss?" Dean asked, coming back with a hand held mirror.

"Watch," I said, holding my hand up to his eyebrow. He held up the mirror and watched as my hand slowly began to glow. He flinched slightly but relaxed when he noticed the cut was disappearing.

"I'll be damned," he said, examining himself out in the mirror. I smiled not able to stop staring at my hand.

"What is going on down here?" my dad asked, coming back into the kitchen with my mom trailing not far behind.

"Which one of you is it?" my mom asked, pointing an accusing a finger at each of us. She fixed her eyes on me. "I can feel the magic." She tightened her belt on her robe and looked back at the boys.

"Go ahead Ella, show them," Xander encouraged. All eyes turned on me making me feel nervous. I pushed out a breath and concentrated as I had done before. I reached up and gently placed my hand over the black eye that had been forming on Dean's left. There was only a faint glow this time. I tried harder but only managed to take down some of the swelling. My shoulders sank, discouraged. I didn't understand why it wasn't working now? Was I doing something wrong?

Noticing my disappointment, my mom came over and rested a hand on my shoulder. "It's the alcohol," she said. "It lessons your powers."

"Oh," was all I could manage.

"Wait, I have an idea," my dad said, walking into the kitchen. He returned with a knife and dragged it across his forearm slicing it open.

"Oh my god, what are you doing?" I cried, jumping up, and throwing my hands over his bleeding arm. The power flowed through me stronger than before closing up the cut on his arm. There was still a faint pink line, but he and I both knew it would heal quickly on its own. My dad swung his arms around me and picked me up off the ground. "My daughter's a healer," he said, smiling proudly.

"But not a very good one," I said as he put me down.

"Don't get discouraged. You just got your powers and they're still growing. Give it time. They will get stronger," my mom smiled at me.

"Don't you think it's a little weird that Ella's a healer?" Dean asked.

"How so?" I said annoyed. He would be the one to rain on my parade.

"Nobody else in the family is. Your power usually comes from your bloodline," he said.

I looked at my mom and dad. "Normally yes, but we're learning that Ella is special," my dad said, still smiling proudly.

"She's special alright," Dean muttered. I smacked him on the arm.

"Like I said before, I have a feeling you're going to surprise us all," my mom said, kissing me on top of my head.

"So that's my power. I'm a healer," I said a little disappointed. I was kind of hoping it might be something cool, like throwing fire or something like that. My dad chuckled to himself and I pulled back to look at him. "What's so funny?"

"Only witches possess the power to throw fire."

"How did you?" I asked, scratching my head.

"I can read thoughts," he said.

"What!?! That is so...so..."

"I can only do it when I'm in contact with the person and that's how I knew what you were thinking."

"Oh."

"I can also talk inside someone's mind and put thoughts there."

"Really?" I asked intrigued.

He nodded. *"It can be very useful sometimes,"* he winked.

I stared, stunned. No one else seemed to hear him but me. "Wait, did you just?" He laughed. "Interesting," I said stroking my chin. "Do you have to be touching the person to do that too?"

"No, but it is easier," he said.

"That's cool," I thought to myself.

"Indeed it is."

"Hey," I said, pulling myself away from him.

"Now remember, if you lie to me, I will know," he said, looking down at me. It was almost as if he was testing me. If he was, I wasn't going to chance it. I kept my mouth shut and my head clear, which was hard to do with everything that happened.

"Liam," my mom chastised. "Don't scare Ella. Honey remember, he can only get in your head if you let him."

"Jamila."

"Oh stop it," she laughed and hugged him tight.

"Okay, so I know what mom and dad can do. What about you two?" I asked Xander and Dean.

"I can project thoughts like dad," Dean said.

I turned to Xander next. "I can move things."

"Like telekinesis?" He nodded and demonstrated by moving the flower vase across the table. "I knew it! That's how I won the game, isn't it?" He didn't confirm nor deny it, but I knew.

"What game?" my mom asked.

Dean and Xander shook their heads at me. "Umm..."

Crap.

"Pool," my dad said simply.

"How, I thought you had to –"

He cut me off. "I know my boys. Who you think taught Xander?" he said with a slight gleam in his eye.

"You took Ella to a pool hall?" my mom said aghast. Dean and Xander looked away guilty, not wanting to answer her.

"Come on Jamila," my dad said, pulling her away. He no longer seemed to be too upset about our little outing. "We'll discuss their punishment in the morning."

Crap. Crap. Crap.

After they left I turned back to Xander. "Okay if our powers come from our bloodline, then how come you can move things?"

"Our grandfather could and I can also read auras like mom."

"So no one in our family could heal?" I asked, again, hating being the outcast.

"No," Xander said softly, sensing my frustration.

I ran a hand through my hair and let out a breath. I put the thought behind me telling myself no, I was not an outcast. I was special, one of a kind like my mom said. "Do you want me to heal that for you?' I asked Xander.

"You can tomorrow, when you're stronger. Just rest for tonight."

I agreed with him on the rest part. It was definitely a long day and night and sleep was what I needed. I thanked them both for trying to help by taking me out and then Dean and I left Danni and Xander alone in the kitchen. I went straight up to my room, washed off all of my make-up, and crashed on my bed. I learned so much tonight and my mind was reeling with all this new information. I had a hard time shutting it off. I took out my journal and wrote down what I knew. It didn't take me long to fall asleep after that.

Reborn

CHAPTER SEVEN

I had two more days until I left for school and most of it was spent cleaning and gardening. My dad had given the workers the week off putting Xander, Dean, and I in charge of their duties as per our punishment. I also believe he gave us ten times more work than he normally did the workers. I could tell Danni was really enjoying watching us do all her work while she sat back and played with Hadley. I even caught her laughing a few times and even tried to get Xander to wear an apron. He glared at her which just made her laugh even harder.

I tried arguing about the punishment. I pleaded not guilty, saying they had taken me against my will, but of course they didn't buy it. I think this was just my dad's way of getting back at me for my tattoos. I had to admit my Dad was a lot harder on Xander and Dean for the fact that they had taken his only, under aged daughter to some scummy bar and got into a bar fight. So I guess I couldn't complain...much. My mom even got her own revenge by making us go to her garden club meetings and taking away our cell phones. She said it was punishment for gambling. I didn't mind the garden club, but I knew it was torture on the boys, especially Dean since he didn't have a phone. Xander was the only one allowed to keep his phone because of work. I could have cared less. I had no one to call me anyways.

By the end of the week I was exhausted, sore, and in desperate need of a manicure. My dad let me off the hook early because I had to pack for school. Usually this was something I would have done earlier, but I really wasn't looking forward to going so I tried pushing it off as long as I could. There were a lot of things I didn't do the same any more.

Dean had warned me not to worry about packing too many

clothes since they had a uniform, which I was not happy about. The only upside to it was not having to worry about deciding what to wear every day. I was told that the school to the outside world was thought of as a very prestigious, private college. I guess uniforms would be suiting to keep up with façade – although I never heard of a college where you had to wear uniforms.

The school was a four year school depending on how well you developed. After you finished your prerequisite courses you could switch to any course you wanted to take – that is if you passed. I knew my dad was hoping that I would continue to stay on at this school even after I finished the required courses. I told him I wasn't making any promises, but would consider taking on some extra courses to see how I liked it. I figured if I kept myself busy in school work I wouldn't have to worry about other things like making friends or trying to fit in.

After mentally driving myself crazy with what to pack, I finally decided to pack just the essentials; hoodies, jeans, and pajamas. I also packed a few basic shirts, minimal make-up, and Josie's favorite black boots. I didn't really need anything else.

Thursday morning, I dragged myself out of bed and got ready to leave for my new life at my new school. My mom had made a huge breakfast spread and packed some snacks for Dean and I to take with us, making me feel like I was five and going on a field trip. "Don't forget your winter coat," Dean reminded me.

Crap, I forgot.

I quickly ran upstairs and opened my closet, realizing the only winter coats I had were from Tristan. I sighed and grabbed my puffy vest instead. I did not want to take something with me that would remind me of him. I still wore the star necklace he gave me, but that's only because it was the one thing I couldn't bear to give up.

I headed back down the stairs telling myself the vest would have to do until we got to Rhode Island where I could buy a jacket. My mom tried to calm me before I left, but I knew it wouldn't last long. My nerves were a wreck and getting worse by the minute. I allowed her to do what she does to give her some peace of mind. We left shortly after we said our goodbyes and piled in the car.

When we arrived in Rhode Island, we had a car waiting for us to take us to the school. First year students weren't allowed to leave campus without written consent and from what Dean had told me that was usually only in case of an emergency. So unfortunately there was no need to have my car sent here. One more thing I didn't like about this school. Being confined inside the school's walls and not being able to leave made it feel more like a prison than a school. They claimed it was for our safety, but I say it's so they can control us better.

I asked the driver to stop at one of the local shops so I could find a winter jacket. We had an hour drive before we would reach the school and this vest was not warm enough for the cold winters here. I found a basic black coat that fell just above the knee. I also got gloves, a scarf, and hat. On the drive there, Dean tried to explain a few things to me about the school, but I was too busy being distracted by the scenery to pay attention to him.

The school was located a few miles away from all civilization. They claimed it was for privacy and to help keep us from getting distracted – from what, I don't know. From what I saw there wasn't much to do around here. There were only a few mom and pop shops, one restaurant and one diner. I think there was a theatre, but couldn't even be sure if it was open. The place looked so rundown I wouldn't be surprised if it was condemned. I sighed at the lack of life that seemed to be present here.

The car turned down a long stretch of road that was lined with trees. The deeper we got the denser the woods became. It was hard to imagine how anyone could ever find this place. There was no sign when we turned onto the snow covered road, if you could call it that. I imagined that is was just a path made of rock and dirt from the way the car shook back and forth. As we continued down the bumpy road my eyes wandered out the window, gazing upon all the bare trees. Icicles hung from the branches, weighing down the weaker ones, causing them to scream with anticipation of breaking free. Snow covered most of the land creating a white blanket across the ground. I was glad I took Dean's suggestion and picked up a pair of snow boots, although I hadn't expected to bust them out so soon. I wasn't keen on losing my feet to frostbite so I made sure I got some heavy duty ones.

"We're here," Dean said, catching my attention. "Welcome to Hamilton Hill." I tore my eyes away from the scenery and focused straight ahead on the long, winding driveway. As we approached the school, I glanced at the perimeter. It was lined with a dark gray stone wall that reached to what looked to be about eight feet high, reminding me more of a prison than a school.

The car paused in front of a large, black iron gate. A security guard approached the vehicle. The driver rolled down his window and handed him some papers. The guard looked them over, handed them back, and then opened the gate to let us through. I noticed a security camera on both sides of the gate and monitors in the guard tower. Two guards stood in the tiny tower watching over the monitors. I assumed they were vamps. They were huge like Gabe and not someone you would want to mess with.

As we drove up another long, winding road, I noticed more guardians perched at different spots all over the premise. Reason number three I felt like I was heading into solitary confinement instead of school. "What's with all the muscle?" I asked Dean.

"For extra protection," he said. "Although, there's a lot more than usual."

I sighed. I knew he wouldn't admit it but I'm sure our dad had something to do with the extra guardians.

The school stood at the top of a hill and it was massive. The pictures in the brochures did not do it justice. The school was made up of dark gray stone similar to the wall that lined the perimeter. The building looked very old, but well kept. It was like something out of a history book...it's castle like feel. The school seemed to stretch about a half a mile long and looked as tall as the sky. There was a bell tower to the right and a watch tower on the left. I couldn't even imagine what the rest of it looked like.

Dean told me he would help me settle in then I was on my own. He was even nice enough to help me out with my luggage – of course he picked out the lightest ones. He only had one small bag because most of his stuff was already here. I threw a bag over each shoulder and slid out the handle on my extra-large suitcase, dragging it behind me. I had to lean forward or else the weight of the bags would have toppled me over. I had only packed two bags but my mom insisted it wasn't enough and decided to finish packing for me. I was afraid to see what she packed.

Dean kept yelling at me to hurry up. I glared at him as he easily made his way up the steps with his bag and the two small ones he offered to carry for me. "Jerk," I mumbled to myself. I adjusted the bags and continued on my way, checking out the sights as I did. I guess I wasn't paying attention, because something or should I say, someone, slammed into my shoulder causing me to stumble backwards.

"Watch it!" the girl sneered. Her and her group of friends laughed as they walked past, leaving me in the cold snow.

Great, just perfect.

I lay on my bags, on the ground for a moment, like a turtle stuck on its back. The air shifted, a shadow casted over top of me. My eyelids fluttered open to see a pair of piercing blue eyes staring back at me. I flinched. My heart sputtered out of control, making it hard for me to catch my breath. I thought for a second I was dreaming, that was until he spoke. "You okay?" he asked with an Irish accent, offering a hand to help me up.

"Yeah," I said, brushing the snow off my jeans which had now soaked through, making my wet butt freeze. I stood there, mesmerized by the familiarity of his eyes. His long, black, wavy hair was teetering close to his eyelashes, threatening to hide those beautiful blues. He gazed back at me intensely for a mere second before the spell was broken.

"Roman!" I heard a girl shriek. The boy gave me a half smile before he jogged away to rejoin his friends.

Dean turned around to see what the holdup was. "Seriously Ella, quit dawdling. We didn't even make it inside yet and you're taking a break?" he complained.

I narrowed my eyes at him. "What! Me! She ran into me and I fell and the bitch didn't say she was sorry."

"What are you babbling about?" he asked, looking at me like I was nuts.

"That girl," I said, pointing in the direction of which they were walking.

"Were you watching where you were going?" he asked like it was my fault.

"That's beside the point," I growled.

Dean helped me pick my stuff up off the ground and I handed him one of my bigger bags as I shivered from my cold, wet jeans. "You're off to a good start of making friends," Dean said, laughing.

"I'm not here to make friends," I replied, making him frown.

"Well, that bitch that you ran into is Mackenzie Hilliard. She could make you or break you."

I looked back over my shoulder at her and her group of friends. The boy who had helped me was peering back at me. The bitch who had given me the sore butt elbowed him, making him turn back around. He threw his arm over her shoulder without another glance. "Ella?" Dean called.

"Who's that guy?" I asked Dean.

He looked up. "That's Roman Ashby. He's one of the good guys. Not a psycho, I promise." I gave him one more glance before I followed Dean inside. There was something about that guy. I felt it when we touched. Almost like a small shock from static electricity. I couldn't put my finger on it but something told me I would be seeing a lot of him.

Dean took me to the office where I had to sign in as a new student and get the room number of where I would be staying. The office looked like a fancy Doctor's waiting room. Chairs lined the giant glass windows, magazine racks hung on the walls, gray filing cabinets, and dark brown shelves lined with books. I was thankful for the short break while they put my information in the system. The secretary handed me an envelope with the school rules and regulations along with my schedule and room number. I picked up my things while juggling the paperwork in my hand and followed Dean out of the office. He told me after he took me to my room I was on my own. I learned from the brochure that girls and guys didn't live on the same level. I guess this was another one of their ways to keep us from getting *'distracted'*. I was even surprised they had us in the same building.

My room was on the fifth floor and there were no elevators. So we had to trudge up the five flights of stairs to get there. I barely made it to the third floor before I had to take a break. Not that I couldn't handle the steps, it was just a lot harder when carrying about fifty pounds of luggage.

Dean rolled his eyes at me, called me pathetic, and took my heaviest bag. When we finally reached my floor, we figured out that my room was at the end of the hall. I dragged my luggage behind me and kept my head down. There were a few students here and there gossiping about - I assumed - their holiday break. About everyone we passed said hi to Dean or gave him a high five. All the girls swooned as he walked past saying their hellos. *"Hi Dean," "Hey Dean,"*

"Welcome back," "I've missed you."

"Megan, Sherry, Kylie." He smiled and winked at every single one of them. It took everything I had not to gag. I shouldn't have expected anything less. Of course Dean would know everyone, and by everyone, I mean all the girls.

When we reached my room he handed me my bags. "Alright, you think you can handle it from here?" I rolled my eyes. "My room is the next floor down, 407. So if you need anything just come find me, but knock first." He winked and gave me a light punch on the arm. "I'll come get you for dinner later," he called over his shoulder as he jogged down the hall. "Ladies," he said, throwing his arms over two blonds who started to giggle. I rolled my eyes and turned to unlock my door with the key they had given me at the office.

I opened the door to my new room and carried in all my stuff. The room was fairly large, bigger than my dorm in Vermont. Inside were two full size beds, two nightstands, two chest sets, and two small closets. The bed closest to the window was already taken and decorated with what looked like very expensive, designer fabrics.

I looked around the room. I didn't see anyone else so I assumed my roommate was off mingling somewhere. I was nervous about meeting her. This time I wouldn't be lucky enough to get someone I knew.

In my investigation of the rest of the room I discovered we had our own bathroom. The bathroom wasn't very big and most of it was taken up by my roommate. "It could be worse," I shrugged, closing the door. On the empty bed there were two brown boxes with my name on them. After further digging, I learned they were my books and uniform. The uniforms reminded me of a catholic high school. There was a few pair of black slacks, navy blue and black V-neck sweaters, and of course the dreaded plaid skirt. It wasn't as bad as I pictured. The majority of the skirt was black with thin blue and green stripes. There was also a few button down shirts; black, white, and light blue. At the very bottom was gym clothes, knee high socks, and a pair of regulatory shoes. "This sucks," I huffed, sagging down on the bed. I was beginning to feel like I was in some reform school where everyone was a drone.

I took a deep breath and tried not to let it get the best of me. I was contemplating taking a tour of the school, but I remembered the brochure saying they would do that during orientation. Instead I decided to unpack my stuff to pass time until dinner and change out of my wet jeans so I wouldn't catch pneumonia.

It took me only about thirty minutes to unpack my things – so much for killing time. I thought I'd take a tour of the school despite them giving us one later. I figured I could venture more on my own this way. I grabbed my IPod, pulled up the hood on my sweatshirt, and set out to tour the school. I took the steps two at a time down to the first floor. I didn't bother to check out the other floors, I figured they were all the same plain, brown tile floors, beige walls, and the same wooden doors that all the rooms had.

When I reached the bottom, I pushed open the cool metal door receiving a frigid blast of air to my face. I flinched at first not used to this cooler climate. I braved the cold, cranked up my tunes, and headed down the small shoveled path. There was a large building to my right, which I learned from the map I studied on the way over here, held the classrooms. Another building not far to my left was the teachers' dormitory followed by the gymnasium, auditorium, and dining hall. In the distance was another building. I assumed it was another set of dorms since it wasn't listed or marked.

Fighting the bitter chill, I continued with a light stride, absorbing everything I could. The grounds were fairly large and in the middle of everything stood a three tied fountain. There were several tables with chairs and benches spread throughout the garden. Giant oaks lined the school's massive barrier. I scooted carefully across the snow, taking in the different structures and agriculture. I had apparently reached the end of my tour when I stumbled upon what looked like an entrance to a maze. "Cool," I said to myself. There were two angel statues on either side followed by wooden benches that sat in front of the towering hedges. I thought it odd to have a maze like this at a school.

I moved closer, letting my curiosity get the best of me. I took a step forward ready to check it out when someone grabbed my arm. I instantly tensed and turned around ready to strike. My attempt was cut short when the person blocked my punch. "Gabe?"

"Sorry Miss Ella. I didn't mean to startle you. I called your name. But when you didn't answer me I thought something was wrong," he said.

I took out my headphones showing him why I didn't respond. "I was just going to check out this maze," I said.

"I know. That's why I stopped you. With this weather, it's not a good idea to go exploring. It's tricky in there and I wouldn't want you to get lost."

I looked back inside the maze. He was probably right. With this snow and ice it would be hard to walk through, not to mention I had no idea how big this maze was or where it led to. If I couldn't find my way out I might freeze to death. "Thanks Gabe. I'm really glad you're here," I smiled at him. At least then Dean wouldn't be the only one I knew.

"What are you doing out here all by yourself?" he asked. "Why isn't Dean with you?"

I gave him an, *'are you serious'* look. Even he had to know that was a dumb question, but by the expression on his face I would guess not. "I'm meeting up with him for dinner. Didn't want him cramping my style," I said, getting Gabe to crack a small smile. Most of the time Gabe was in serious guardian mode but every now and then I could get him to relax and get a smile out of him.

"Understood," he nodded. "You should head back inside. It's getting dark and that's when the real chill sets in. I'll walk you back."

I mumbled thanks as we headed back to the dorms. Gabe had left earlier than we did. He had more on his plate with helping out and everything so he wanted to get a jump start. In a way I was glad Gabe was here. Even though the school had its own guardians, I felt better knowing Gabe was close by. Before we parted ways, Gabe told me he would have his cell phone on him at all times and if I ever needed him don't hesitate to call. I waved goodbye and shot back up to my room to wait for Dean to come get me for dinner.

I walked into an empty room. If this was any indication that my roommate wouldn't be around much I think I might like her. Happy to have the room to myself for the meantime, I did a little spying. I wanted to get a feel for what my roommate was like. You know, just making sure she wasn't some crazy vamp out to get my powers.

I didn't find much except for a bunch of stinky, expensive perfumes, a lot of Mac cosmetics, and a few style magazines. I stopped my snooping and sat down on my bed. I wasn't sure what time dinner was, so I laid back on the bed, and listened to my music until Dean came and got me.

I ended up falling asleep and by the time I woke it was almost seven. I cursed at myself and checked my phone. I had two missed calls and one text from Dean asking where I was and why I wasn't picking up my phone. He also said he was leaving without me but would save me a seat if I ever decided to join him. That was over an hour ago. I called him to see where he was at. He said he was still in the dining hall and would wait for me.

I grabbed a couple bucks from my purse, slipped them in my back pocket, and made my way to the dining hall. Dean gave me simple instructions on where it was. It wasn't that hard to find, I probably could have found my way here on my own.

I opened the doors to the dining hall and stepped inside to a fairly crowded room. I half expected it to be empty by now. The room looked like any other lunch room I've been in. Black and white tiled floors, round and square tables spread out everywhere and filled with students. Over to my left were large glass windows that showed an outside patio filled with benches and tables covered with umbrellas. I'm guessing the students would sit out there when it was warm.

I made my way into the line and searched my options, which wasn't much. There were a few cold sandwiches, veggie snacks, and basically nothing I would eat. "Out of the way freak," said Mackenzie, the girl who knocked me over earlier.

She bumped me so hard I almost fell face first into the coleslaw. I opened my mouth to come back with what was hopefully a witty retort when I was stopped short. "Let's just get through the first week without me having to come to your rescue all the time," Dean said, pulling me to the other side where there was a whole different option of foods.

"That is the second time that bitch –"

"Ella, I'm trying to help you out here the best I can. Now just shut up and trust me," Dean said, but he didn't speak the words out loud. He said them inside my head so only I could hear. I knew his power was to project thoughts, but knowing and having him actually do it was still a shock to me. He rolled his eyes and pulled me through the line. I learned there were two different sections, one for cold food and one for hot. This side had tacos and I was more than thrilled.

I stuffed the shells with meat, leaving out all the lettuce and stuff, because, you know, that just leaves less room for the gooey good stuff. I grabbed an icy tea and followed Dean out to a table. He gestured to the seat next to him and even pulled out the chair for me. I'm pretty sure he was just showing off for the girls at the table.

I pulled my hood down and got a few startled glances from the people around me. I didn't understand what they were staring at and was starting to feel uncomfortable. *"Your blue streak,"* Dean said in my head. *"You were quite the topic of conversation earlier."*

"Why?" I asked out loud, causing everyone to look at me. I forgot I was the only one who heard what Dean said.

"I'll tell you later," he replied, rolling his eyes. "Ella this is Sienna and Cameron," he said, pointing to a petite blond across the table and a slightly taller brunette. They both smiled politely and gave a quick wave. "And this is Reagan, Blake, and Austin," he gestured to the other side.

The three boys looked like a bunch of preppy, stuck up fraternity boys. I just put on my best fake smile and pretended to be nice. "Really Dean, since when did you volunteer to be a guide for the handicapped?" Mackenzie snickered. She sat down at the table across from me followed by two blonds flanking her side. I glared at her. I wanted to leap across the table and scratch her pretty brown eyes out. Seriously, what was this chick's problem?

"Come on Mackenzie, you know I never volunteer for anything," Dean said, flashing his cocky smile. "And this is Ella, my sister," he continued in a cold tone, making it clear not to mess with me or you would have to deal with him. Everyone at the table took another collective stare. Looking at me as if they now understood why Dean was hanging out with someone like me.

"Sister?" Mackenzie smirked, looking me over.

"Well, not everyone in the family can be as good looking as me," Dean said, getting a laugh from the table. I just ignored him and started to eat my dinner. As soon as I sunk my teeth into my taco, Roman Ashby sat down right in front of me. I was taken aback by his beauty. It was easier to see him now without the sun glaring in my eyes. He ran a hand through his wavy black hair making it puff and stick out slightly to the side. His strong facial features made him look more like a man than a boy, and his eyes. His eyes were like a deep dark pool of ocean water. When I looked into them I felt like I was getting swept away. There was something about this boy, his hair, his eyes, his strong facial features. He reminded me a lot of Tristan. I quickly looked away feeling a pang in my chest at the thought of him. Afraid I might lose it in front of everyone, I kept my eyes down, and took a breath. When I managed to get a grip, I looked back up to see Roman's eyes looking back into mine. I understood why I thought I saw Tristan earlier when he helped me up. Their similarities were uncanny, but then again lately every guy with dark hair and blues eyes reminded me of Tristan.

I must have not realized I was staring until Dean told me to *'stop staring'*. When I came to, I saw Roman had a weird, uncomfortable look on his face and Mackenzie was scowling at me. I quickly put my head back down, embarrassed that I was staring like that – adding more to my weirdness factor. "Ugh! How can you eat that?" Mackenzie asked giving me a look of disgust.

"You mean...tacos?" I asked, unsure if I heard her right.

"It's so fattening and piggish," she cringed. Not caring what Dean had said to me earlier, I thought I'd make it a point to let her know she couldn't get to me. I took a big bite out of my taco, causing juice to spill over the side. I wiped off the grease that slipped down my chin and then licked it off my fingers. Mackenzie and her two friends gave me revolted looks. I got a laugh from Dean and Roman which pissed Mackenzie off even more. "Come on girls, let's go. I'm suddenly not hungry anymore," Mackenzie said, standing up from the table. "Roman," she turned her eyes on him.

"I just sat down," he said. Mackenzie glared at him with her hands on her hips. Roman sighed, swiped his sandwich and drink, and left with her.

Cameron moved over to sit in the seat next to me. "Don't let her bother you," she said.

"Yeah, we're just waiting for the doctors to invent a surgery to remove the stick from her ass," Sienna smiled sweetly. I smiled back thinking I might actually start to like these girls.

"So, you're Dean's sister, lucky you," Cameron smirked.

"What's that supposed to mean?" Dean asked, pretending to be offended.

Cameron laughed. "Oh come on Dean, you know I love you," she said, blowing him a kiss.

"Hey," Austin complained.

"I love you too baby," Cameron told Austin.

"This is your first day?" Sienna asked. I nodded. "What do you think so far?"

"I haven't really done much to gather an opinion yet," I said honestly.

"Dean, you didn't show her around?"

"Hey, she's a big girl, she can handle her own," Dean said defensively.

"I'll give you a tour Ella," Blake offered and winked at me which made it look more creepy than coy.

"You're not going anywhere near my sister," Dean declared.

"What?" Blake said all innocent. Dean threw a roll at him causing Blake to chuck one back.

"Ignore the Neanderthals," Cameron said. "If you want Sienna and I will show you around."

"Thanks, but you don't have to do that," I politely declined.

"We insist," Sienna smiled.

"Go, you'll like them and they're nothing like Mackenzie," Dean said in my head. *"You can trust them."* I turned to him and he nudged me, encouraging me to go. "Okay, yeah, thanks," I said.

"So what's with the blue streak?" Cameron asked abruptly.

"Cameron!" Sienna scolded.

"What? Oh come on, like you weren't thinking the same thing?"

Sienna just looked down, a little uncomfortable.

"It's okay," I said. "Honestly, I don't know. It just kind of showed up after I got my powers."

"I think it's neat," Sienna said, making me feel a little better about it.

We finished up our dinner and then Sienna and Cameron took me on a tour of the school. They said I'd do this again at orientation, but was better to have someone who had been here show you around. I learned the ins and outs of the school and the premise, including my tour guides.

Sienna was a petite blond with very soft facial features and naturally rosy cheeks. Her hair was chin length with Shirley Temple curls. She had a crush on Reagan, but he was currently dating one of Mackenzie's friends. According to Cameron he was only dating her because she put out, which made him a total dick and Sienna should look elsewhere.

Cameron was the opposite of Sienna. She was tall with straight brown hair, steel gray eyes, and caramel colored skin. She seemed to be straight forward and laid back while Sienna tended to be more over-eager and always hyper. The girls had also told me not to believe everything I read in the brochures. They said a lot of stuff was glamorized to entice people to come here.

"Awesome," I thought.

They also told me students ages here ranged from thirteen to thirty, but the majority was sixteen to twenty-five. Surprised at the stretch in age, Cameron explained that some blossom late and the school didn't want to discourage anyone from coming because of their age. I had remembered reading something similar to that in one of the pamphlets. This also explained why we had to wear uniforms. Because of the big age range, they said it was to help tell the difference between students and teachers.

Cameron also said that they have a program for rogues who want to go straight and for those who were born into this and abandoned, leaving them helpless. Sometimes that's how I felt.

After the tour, the girls dropped me off at my room and told me about a party the dorm was having tonight and insisted that I come. They wouldn't take no for an answer. I told them I would check it out. Cameron took my phone to punch in her number then she handed it back and told me to text her later. I waved goodbye to the girls and headed into my room, happy to have met some normal people.

CHAPTER EIGHT

When I opened the door to my room I got a big surprise.

Roman was lying on the bed closest to the window. I stepped back out and checked the room number on the door to make sure I was in the right room. Yep, room 510, my room. "What are you doing here?" I asked.

Before he could answer, Mackenzie stepped out of the bathroom. "What the hell are you doing in my room freak!" she screeched.

"This is your room? You're kidding, right?" This had to be some kind of joke. Yep, someone was playing a joke on me. The world couldn't be that cruel.

"Does it look like I'm kidding?" she said, glaring at me with her arms crossed.

Just my luck.

I pinched the bridge of my nose feeling a headache coming on. *Seriously, why am I being punished? Haven't I suffered enough?* "Lucky me, I'm your new roommate," I said sarcastically.

"Like hell you are. I'm not rooming with you," she spat.

She looked me up and down like I had some incurable disease that she could possibly catch. I rolled my eyes at her. "Look, I'm not any happier about this then you are –"

"Please," she cut me off. "Anyone would kill to room with me," she said, like I should feel privileged just being in her presence. I never thought I would meet someone more conceited than Dean, but she definitely takes the cake. "I'm going to the head master right now to fix this," she finished. The look on her face said she would plow down anyone who got in her way.

"Kenzie, relax, deal with it later," Roman whined. "Besides, headmaster Callahan won't be back until tomorrow," Roman said, reaching for her and making me want to cringe.

She stopped glaring at me long enough to let Roman pull her down on top of him so he could kiss her. "Do you mind?" Mackenzie sneered.

"You want me to leave?" I asked annoyed.

"Yes," she said, like it should have been the obvious answer.

"This is my room too. You can't kick me out just so you can make out with your boyfriend." The last thing I wanted to see was these two get it on, but this was my room too.

Roman sat up. "You're more than welcome to stay and watch. I'm not really one for an audience, but I might make an exception this time," he said, flashing me a cocky smile, once again reminding me of Tristan. Mackenzie glared at him, pushing him back down. I didn't even respond. I just turned around and left. I hadn't even been here twenty-four hours and already I hated it here. I thought about texting Cameron, but then changed my mind. I decided I needed to be alone for a little and clear my head. I zipped up my vest and flipped up my hood, bracing myself for the cold.

I had no particular destination in mind, so I just walked. I found myself by the fountain. The one I saw earlier today when I decided to tour the grounds myself. It was a lot larger than I originally thought. I had to crane my neck to get the full view. The fountain itself you could tell was old with all it's wear and tear. There were a few cracks in the foundation with some pieces missing. Dirt was busting through the holes with ivy creeping its way up and trying to take over. No one caring enough to keep up with its maintenance. I sighed at the crumpling fountain. Somehow I could sympathize with it.

I dusted off a spot on one of the benches and took a seat. I pulled up my legs and turned on my IPod, tuning out the rest of the world. I tried to relax and forget about all the negative things about this place, which only lasted about a second. I knew someone was there before I even opened my eyes. I could also sense they were harmless. I let out a breath and looked up. I blinked back in surprise. Standing in front of me was a very handsome, tall man with short, dark brown hair and hazel eyes. He looked too old to be a student and too young to be a teacher, but then again there was a large age range so who knew.

"I'm not disturbing you, am I?" he asked kindly. I took out my head phones and shook my head. "You mind?" he gestured to the bench, taking a seat next to me. "Any particular reason you're out here by yourself?"

"I wasn't in the mood to watch my roommate make a porno with her boyfriend," I replied.

His eyes widened a bit at first, but then they smiled when he chuckled. "I see. Who's your roommate?" he asked curiously.

"Mackenzie Hilliard," I said. Just saying her name left a bitter taste in my mouth.

"I take it you two are getting along well then," he smiled mockingly. I rolled my eyes. "You're new here, aren't you?"

"Gee, what tipped you off?" I said, keeping with the sarcastic tone.

He gave another subtle laugh. "Not one for small talk?"

"Sorry, been a long day."

"Things not what you expected?" he pried.

"I don't know. I guess I don't really know what to expect. Then again, it's only the first day and I have the roommate from hell who kicked me out so she could make out with her boyfriend. I can't say I was expecting that."

"Well, as you mentioned, it is only the first day. Give it time. It will get better," he smiled, making his eyes reflect a light green color.

I quickly turned away, feeling my cheeks get hot. "If it's so great what are you doing out here?"

"I like to come out here and clear my head," he admitted.

"It seems like a good place to do that," I said, tugging down the sleeves of my shirt, trying to fight the chill.

"It is, but I wouldn't stay out here too long. It can get pretty chilly at night."

"What are you, my keeper?" I said with a little more attitude than I intended. I'm sure he was only trying to be nice, but I was tired of people deciding for me what would be in my best interest.

"You going to the party tonight?" he asked, ignoring my comment.

I sighed, picking at my nails. "I guess, what else is there to do?" He didn't answer, confirming I didn't have many other options. "I assume you're going?"

"Nah, not my thing," he said nonchalantly.

I raised a brow at him. "Not your thing?" He totally looked like the type to be guzzling beer at a party. He had that whole preppy frat boy look to him.

When he didn't clarify I thought maybe I insulted him. "Well, it was nice chatting with you. Enjoy your party, but not too much," he smiled, getting up. I was about to tell him I was sorry if I upset him, but before I even got the chance he was gone. I looked around, but he was nowhere in sight. *Huh, weird?* I turned back around scratching my head. I looked over my shoulder wondering how he disappeared so quickly like that. I shrugged it off, putting my ear buds back in. I had to keep reminding myself this was a school for the supernatural, anything was possible.

"Ella." I sat up. *"Ella."* I looked around swearing I heard someone call my name. *"Ella, take out your head phones and turn around."* It was Dean. He was talking in my head again. I tugged on my ear bud strings and turned around to see Dean, Cameron, and Austin coming up behind me. "Hey guys," I said, standing up.

"What are you doing out here? Cameron asked.

"Avoiding my roommate," I said, tucking away my IPod.

"She can't be that bad," Dean said, thinking I was overreacting.

"Who's your roommate?" Cameron asked.

"Mackenzie."

"Ooh," they all said with sympathetic looks. "Well cheer up, because we're going to a party," Cameron said, jumping over the bench and linking her arm in mine. "But you need to change first."

I looked at my outfit wondering what was wrong with it. Cameron tugged on my arm. "I can't. Mackenzie kicked me out so her and her boyfriend could make bastard babies."

"Ah yes, Roman and Mackenzie, the most tragic love story of all," Austin said.

"Tragic?" I asked.

"Tragic in the way that the relationship coincides in the first place," Cameron said, confusing me. "Roman and Mackenzie are complete opposites. While Roman is an all-around standup guy, Mackenzie is an evil hag from hell. I still insist she put a spell on him. That would explain the only reason he fell for her."

"She's not that bad. Did you ever think he actually likes her and that maybe he sees something in her that nobody else does?" Austin said, making Cameron glare at him.

"If you like her so much maybe you should date her," Cameron replied.

"Oh come on babe," Austin said, pulling Cameron closer and whispering sweet nothings into her ear, making her giggle. She blushed and then pushed him away, pretending to be mad again.

"I think he's with her because she puts out," Dean said.

"You would," I said, looking at him disgusted. "If you hate her so much than why are you friend's with her?" I asked.

Austin laughed while Cameron rolled her eyes. "She's my stepsister," Cameron replied. "It's clear my dad was in some tragic accident altering his perception and making him blind."

I tried to hide my smile. I was happy to know I wasn't the only one who had to suffer. Maybe I could ask Cameron for some tips on how she survived. "Oh, I thought being her roommate was bad. I can't imagine being related to her."

"Trust me, as far as I am concerned nothing is legally binding. I give it a year at the most," she said. "Come on, we'll go with you to make sure the wicked witch doesn't give you any problems." She took my hand and led the way across the snowy grass back to the dorms.

I opened the door to my room to have Mackenzie snap at me again. "Hello, knock much?" Mackenzie said as she quickly adjusted her shirt.

"Not on the door to my own room," I countered.

"It won't be your room for long," she sneered.

"Chill out Mac," Cameron said, barging in the room behind me with Dean and Austin on her tail.

"I told you not to call me that," Mackenzie said, scowling at Cameron.

Cameron ignored her as she plopped down on my bed. Dean and Austin walked over to Roman, said what's up, and made themselves comfortable on the bed causing Mackenzie to stomp off into the bathroom. Roman rolled his eyes and got up to knock on the bathroom door. "Kenzie…"

"Let her go," Cameron said. Roman knocked again. Mackenzie finally came out of the bathroom and turned to glare at me, again, then stomped out of the room. "Have fun," Cameron sang as Roman took off after her.

"He sure does go out of his way for her," I said.

"She puts out," Austin said simply. I tried to ignore the bile that was rising in my throat as I looked through my clothes for something to wear.

"Why can't I just wear what I have on?" I whined.

"Because this is a party Ella, not a hike through the woods," Cameron said, eyeing me up and down. I ignored her jab about my outfit and continued to look for something to wear. Everything I brought was pretty much the same as what I had on. I didn't even want to go to this party, but I knew they wouldn't leave me alone unless I did.

I decided on a long sleeve shirt with jeans and Josie's boots. I didn't care to deal with the stress of my blue streak so I pulled up my hair and tried to hide it. From what my parents had told me, no one had ever heard of someone's appearance altering like this after receiving their powers. So I stuck out like a sore thumb. And why not, let's just add another thing to the list of reasons why people think I'm weird.

"So what's the big deal about this party anyways?" I asked, coming out of the bathroom. The disappointed look on Cameron's face said she wished I would have kept my hair down. She told me earlier that she liked my streak and said I should embrace it.

"It's the party of all parties," Dean said. Although I'm sure he would have said that about any party.

"It's kinda like a welcome back party," Cameron said.

"More like check out the new meat," Austin smiled.

"Perfect," I thought.

"He's just kidding," Cameron said, throwing a pillow at him. I grabbed my phone as we headed out the door and downstairs to the first floor. I started to wonder where this party was when they took a quick right down a hall, leading to a door that read *Basement* above it. Austin knocked on the door with some kind of secret knock.

After a moment, the door opened and we were led down a flight of stairs. What kind of party was this, and why was it in the basement? It seemed kind of creepy to me to have a party in a dark, damp, dirty basement, but then again it could be worse.

CHAPTER NINE

Okay, so this was definitely not like any basement I have ever seen. There were hardwood floors covered by a few throw rugs. The walls were painted in bright colors and looked like some of the students had added their own special touch. They had twined twinkling lights around the few poles that stuck out and hung outdoor Christmas lights along the ceiling. The couches and chairs looked like they were donated from the goodwill along with lawn chairs and folding tables. Overall it was the perfect place to have a party and not at all what I had expected.

On the one wall there was a mural of a garden – which looked vaguely familiar – and on another was a forest with witches huddled around a cauldron, wolves hidden in the trees with – if I had to guess – vampires standing next to them, all of their eyes glowing bright. Interesting choice of art, but then, this is a school for the supernatural.

In one corner kids were playing beer pong and in another they were playing flip cups. Some were just standing around socializing, flirting, and some were dancing. All in all it was like one of the many parties we had back in Vermont at the sorority house.

"So what's with the secret knock?" I asked Dean.

"Have to weed out the uglies somehow," he smiled.

"You're such a dick," I groaned. He just laughed and took off to go talk to some girls. Austin spotted some of his friends and dragged Cameron with him, leaving me to fend for myself.

Fantastic.

I glanced around the room, hoping maybe I would find some nonalcoholic beverages. I spotted a plastic tub against the far wall and thought I'd take my chances. Half the ice was melted and whatever was in there was sitting on the bottom. I pushed my sleeve up and stuck my hand in. The freezing cold water was a shock at first and took everything I had not to pull my hand out right away. When I finally got a hold of a can, I pulled it out to discover it was a beer. I set it aside, stuck my hand back in, and tried again, and again. Everything I found was a beer.

"Fishing for gold?" Roman asked, startling me. I stood up, wiping my arm on my pants, and then pulled down my sleeve. He was leaning casually against the wall, wearing dark blue jeans and the stereo typical, tight, black T-shirt.

"No. I was looking for soda," I said.

"Soda's over there," he replied, pointing to a corner in the back.

"Thanks," I mumbled.

"I'm Roman," he said, extending a hand.

"Ella," I said, feeling a little guarded.

"You're new here."

"Yeah."

"Welcome to Hamilton Hill," he smiled kindly.

When he didn't offer up anymore conversation I said, "Soda over there?"

"Yeah," he smiled. I made my way over in the direction he pointed. I could feel him watching me. I looked over my shoulder and confirmed my suspicion. I couldn't get rid of this strange feeling that I knew him. I knew I never met him before but when he was around I felt a strange connection to him. Maybe it was his eyes or his hair or the fact that I'm still in love with my dead boyfriend and any guy with dark blue eyes and black hair reminds me of him. This wasn't healthy. I was supposed to have let him go, but I knew in my heart there'd always be a small part of him that remained there. I took a breath, relinquishing all thoughts of Tristan.

I didn't see any plastic tubs in the corner Roman had pointed to. I stepped through the arch way and found a freezer. I opened it up figuring this was what he was talking about. What I found was not soda. "What the...?" I picked up one of the blood filled bags that was inside the freezer.

"What are you doing?" Mackenzie said, startling me.

I spun around dropping the bag. "I was looking for a soda," I said quickly, hoping she didn't spot the bag I just dropped by her feet.

"Clearly," she said, picking up the bag and waving it in front of me. Not in the mood to deal with her, I ignored her and pushed past her on my way back out into the party. "Hey, Ella," Mackenzie called. "You forgot something."

I turned to face her as she threw the bag at me. I caught it as it exploded in my hands, blood squirting all over my shirt and face. "Oops," Mackenzie giggled, receiving a few laughs from the kids nearby. She walked by me smiling wickedly while I stood there shell shocked. I had to bite my lip to keep from crying. No way was I going to let this bitch get to me.

Cameron and Sienna caught wind of what happened and came rushing over. "I'll go get some wet paper towels," Sienna said, hurrying off.

Cameron picked up the now empty bag and threw it in the trash. "What happened?" she asked.

"Mackenzie," I said, grinding my teeth.

"I couldn't find any," Sienna said apologetically.

"Let's take her to the bathroom," Cameron suggested, noticing I was about to lose it. They led me to the bathroom so I could get myself cleaned up. Unfortunately, there was a line, forcing us to wait. I got more and more agitated as we waited because I couldn't touch anything for risk of spreading the mess.

"If I would have known you were such a messy eater I would have offered you a bib," Roman joked.

"I'm glad I was able to amuse you," I glared, whispering 'prick' under my breath.

He narrowed his eyes at me clearing hearing me. "It was just a joke," he said defensively.

"Yeah thanks, ha-ha so funny I forgot to laugh." I squared my shoulders, proving to him that he and his girlfriend's little prank was no bother to me and I would not be bullied easily.

"Whatever," he growled, walking past us. So much for him being one of the good guys.

"What a dick," I thought, biting my lip again to keep from crying. I wasn't usually the type to cry when I was upset. It was more when I was so angry I couldn't control it and I hated that. I wasn't going to allow that to happen now. I took a breath and looked up at the lights so I could blink away my tears. Cameron, noticing my expression, banged on the door to the bathroom. "Hurry up in there," she shouted. "If it wasn't working for you when you left your room it's not going to work for you now."

Some short, chubby, brunette stepped out of the bathroom and gave Cameron a nasty look. "Finally," Cameron said, not caring about the girl's feelings. She pushed the girl aside and dragged Sienna and I into the cramped space that was the bathroom. I ran my hands under the faucet and splashed some cool water on my face. I wiped off the rest of the blood with wet paper towels.

"Good as new," Sienna smiled optimistically. I looked down at my blood soaked shirt and her smile faded. "Well, almost?"

Someone knocked on the door. "In a minute!" Cameron yelled. The person's response was to bang on the door. Cameron pounded her fist back. "Use the other bathroom," she grunted and turned back around to face me rolling her eyes at the distraction.

Feeling at a loss, I was about to tell them I was just going to go back to my room when Cameron said, "Take off your shirt."

I looked at her thinking she couldn't be serious, but the look on her face told me she was dead serious. "Okay, but then I would be naked and I don't think that would help."

"It might help your reputation though," Sienna giggled. I shook my head letting her know she wasn't helping.

Cameron sighed. "Just trust me. Give me your shirt," she said, holding out her hand.

I thought what the hell. I had nothing left to lose, well, except maybe my pants. I took off my shirt and handed it to Cameron. Before I could ask what her plan was both girls stared at me with wide eyes. "What?" I asked self-consciously.

"I just...never seen someone our age with tattoos, well with that many, I mean..." Sienna stammered.

"Is this another side effect from your powers?" Cameron asked, gawking at me curiously.

"No. I was just...bored," I joked. I crossed my fingers hoping they would leave it at that. It was best excuse I could come up with on short notice. I didn't know these girls well enough to let them in on the truth.

"I would have guessed you did it to piss off your parents. I mean, that's what I would have done," Cameron shrugged, giving me a good excuse for the future. I made a mental note to keep that one in mind.

Both girls managed to drag their eyes away to concentrate on the matter at hand. Cameron handed the shirt to Sienna. "Do a glamour spell on it," she said.

"Oh, I don't know. I've only done it once before and I'm not very good at it," Sienna said sheepishly.

"A glamour spell?" I asked, completely clueless.

"Sienna's a witch and a good one. She's better than she gives herself credit for," Cameron said, nudging Sienna and trying to encourage her.

"I'll try, but I'm going to warn you, the last time I tried this I turned my pants into a cat."

"Wait, what?" I said as she took the shirt.

"I was going for a leopard print skirt," she clarified as if that made it all better. Not knowing what else to say I just nodded as she gripped the shirt tight and closed her eyes to concentrate. I stood there hoping this would work. There wasn't much room left in this tiny bathroom for her to accidentally conjure something else.

While we waited, I turned to Cameron, and asked, "So what's the deal with Roman?" I had a hard time believing he was one of the good guys after the stunt he pulled. I needed to know what the real deal was so hopefully I could put this mess behind me.

"Roman's actually a good guy," she said. I've been hearing that a lot, but have yet to be convinced. "He helped save me from a disastrous relationship and introduced me to Austin. I owe him a lot. His only downfall is that he's dating Mackenzie," Cameron moaned. "Besides that everyone pretty much loves him, including the teachers. He gets along with everyone, gets good grades, and never causes any trouble."

"Okay I'm done," Sienna said, handing me the shirt.

I almost didn't take it, it seemed way too easy. "Um, the blood is gone, but so is the part of the shirt the blood was on," I said, sticking my hand through a giant whole in the front.

She took the shirt back and sighed. "Let me try again." She closed her eyes once more.

"So what's the sudden interest in Roman? Does someone have a crush?" Cameron asked, wiggling her brows.

"No!" I said. "I just think some people aren't always who they seem to be." I knew this for a fact. I decided to leave out the part about him being the one who put me in this whole predicament in the first place. I didn't want to hear any excuses on his defense.

"Okay, how about now?" Sienna asked hopeful.

This time she got it right. "That's awesome, how'd you do that?" She just shrugged her shoulders like it was nothing. I was kind of surprised at how easy it was. I thought maybe she'd say a spell or there'd be some kind of smoke or lights flashing, but no. I was realizing there was a lot I had to learn.

"See, I told you you could do it," Cameron said, praising her.

"*Why* is there a cooler full of blood bags?" I asked as I put my shirt back on.

"Hello, Ella, we do go to a school with a bunch of vampires," Sienna said laughing.

Too embarrassed to mention that I didn't know anything about our kind, I just brushed it off. "Right," I said, laughing with her as we headed back out to the party. Cameron promised me she wouldn't leave my side for the rest of the night.

"Staying out of trouble I hope?" Dean projected. I craned my neck in search of him. I found him over on one of the couches with his arm around some redhead. I gave him an exaggerated smile and he went back to entertaining his guest. I really disliked this one way mind speak thing. I didn't think it was fair he could talk in my head when I couldn't talk back.

"Here you go," Sienna said, handing me a soda.

"It's not going to explode is it?" I asked a little frightened.

"No. I handpicked it myself so you should be safe," she smiled. "You want some snacks?"

"No, thank you."

"She just wants an excuse to go talk to that cute guy over there by the snack table," Cameron groaned.

"Really, what guy?" I asked interested, anything to take the attention off of me for a while. Sienna pointed over in the direction of the guy she was swooning over. "The guy with the Mohawk in the red polo shirt?" I asked, thinking that Mohawk looked vaguely familiar.

"Is there something wrong with him?" Sienna asked, noticing my odd expression.

"No," I shook my head. "It's just...there's something familiar about him." I looked over my shoulder at him. I disregarded my feeling and turned back to Sienna. "Why don't you go talk to him?"

"Oh, I can't," she said, blushing shyly.

"Do I have to do everything?" Cameron said, dragging Sienna over to the guy.

"Oh my God. Oh my God," she shrieked, trying to pull away.

Not wanting to be left behind, I caught up to them and tried to calm Sienna before we approached the mystery stranger. Cameron marched right up to him and tapped him on the shoulder. Sienna was so nervous her palms were sweating. I had to wipe my hand on my pants. When the mystery man turned around I almost fell over. I spotted his red streak before I even saw his face. I did the whole girly thing and squealed excitedly – like girls did when they hadn't seen someone in a while. I didn't give him any time to react, instantly throwing my arms around him, almost knocking him over. I pulled back enough to get a good look and make sure my eyes weren't playing tricks on me.

"Ella?"

"Oh, Dixon," I cried, jumping on him. He laughed, shuffling back a bit from my attack. I was never so happy to see him. "What are you doing here? Are you a vampire?" I asked in a soft whisper, even though it was no secret there about what we were.

"No, I'm a warlock," he said, like I should have known.

"A warlock?" I scrunched my nose.

"It's the male version of a witch. And you're a vampire," he said, matter of fact.

"How'd you know?"

"Your smell," he smiled. I sniffed my shirt and he shook his head laughing. "No honey. You give off a distinct aroma that lets me know what you are. It's not a bad smell, trust me, you smell quite delicious," he said, winking at me. I blushed and turned my head.

Cameron cleared her throat. "I take it you two know each other?"

"Oh, sorry," I said, finally hopping down off of Dixon. "Cameron, Sienna, this is Dixon."

Dixon bowed, kissing both their hands and making Sienna blush. "Oh, a fellow witch. How do you do?" Dixon smiled. He then turned on me. "You know, you also have the smell of a witch on you," he said looking me over. "You weren't making out with one were you?" he asked with a disapproving look on his face. There was nothing more that Dixon loved than good gossip.

"No," I said, elbowing him. "Long story short Sienna had to do a glamour spell on my shirt."

He scrunched his brow at me suspiciously but let it go. "You know I should be mad at you for not returning my calls," he said with his hands on his hips.

"Yeah, I'm sorry about that. I just...I wasn't really talking to anyone and –"

He cut me off by crushing me in a bear hug. "I know," he said softly, knowing this was a sensitive subject. "But I'm not just anyone," he reminded me. After everything that happened Dixon was the one person who was there for me to help me cope with everything. He picked me up when I couldn't myself and let me be when he knew I needed to do things on my own. I owed him a lot.

"Okay, enough of the reunion," Cameron said, pushing me out of the way and linking her arm with Dixon's. "So Dixon, who does your hair?" she asked, pulling him away and into the crowd.

The girls instantly fell in love with Dixon, as do most people.

Cameron was the one who spotted Dixon's interest right away and had to tell poor Sienna the bad news. I knew she was disappointed to find out that he admired the male figure more than she would have liked, but she put on a smile still enjoying his company.

After running into Dixon I was able to relax a bit, making Mackenzie's little stunt a distant memory in my mind. We spent the next hour gossiping with Dixon, learning things about people here I never wanted to know. The girls hung onto his every word impressed that in the small amount of time that he was here he was able to discover the juiciest gossip.

Sometime during the end of the night Austin had whisked Cameron away for some 'alone time' while Sienna joined some of her other witch friends. Dean had left earlier in the night with the redhead he was hanging out with, but made sure to throw me a few brotherly words of advice. I ignored every single comment. Dixon and I spent the rest of the evening catching up and when the party started to die out Dixon offered to walk me back to my room.

On the way back I filled Dixon in on all the letters and texts Billy had sent me. Including his latest one where he felt he was getting closer to finding Jack. That's what most of them said, but I didn't feel he was any closer than from when he started. His last tip had him bouncing around Europe.

Dixon told me all about how he found out he was a warlock and came to the school. We ended up taking a walk instead of going back to our rooms and sat by the fountain to catch up. We talked for over an hour. We talked until I could no longer feel my toes.

After Dixon dropped me off at my room we agreed to meet for lunch tomorrow. I gave him a hug and kiss goodbye, then sighed, not wanting to deal with Mackenzie, but luckily she wasn't there. Happy to have the room to myself for the moment, I changed into my pajamas, and slipped underneath the covers.

I woke up sometime in the middle of the night. I could feel someone watching me. I sat up, spying someone standing at the foot of my bed.

I froze, surprised at who it was.

I rubbed my eyes thinking I was dreaming. "K-Kyle?" I stuttered.

His eyes met mine for a moment. He opened his mouth to say something, but all too soon he was gone. I blinked a few times. I must have been dreaming. I ran my fingers through my hair and looked over at Mackenzie sound asleep in her bed. I rubbed my chest and lay back down. There was a pain inside; one that wouldn't go away. I closed my eyes tight, praying that I would be able to fall back asleep.

CHAPTER TEN

When I woke up in the morning, Mackenzie was sitting on the edge of her bed, staring at me. "Can I help you?" I asked groggily.

"Get up. We're going to the headmaster to get this whole room situation dealt with," she said, crossing and uncrossing her petite legs. I sighed and threw off the covers, stepping out of bed. "That's what you slept in?" she criticized.

I looked down at my pajamas thinking, *"What the hell was wrong with them?"* I had on a long sleeve shirt and flannel pajama pants. I looked back up at Mackenzie who was giving me a look like I just stepped out of a discount outlet store and I should be embarrassed to be caught wearing this. I ignored her sneer and got dressed. I didn't sleep well last night and was not in the mood to deal with her snotty remarks.

We headed down to the headmaster's office in silence. She kept at least two feet in front of me the whole way – I didn't mind. When we entered the office, Mackenzie walked straight up to the secretary and demanded to see the headmaster that instant. The woman behind the desk was tiny, with thin red hair that was pulled back into a tight, braided bun. Her pale face was covered with freckles and she wore turquoise, turtle shell glasses that hung just barely on the bridge of her long nose. She had a few wrinkles around her eyes, indicating she was maybe in her fifties.

For a tiny person she had a tough exterior that demonstrated she didn't tolerate impatient children. "Miss Hilliard, please have a seat and I will let you know if Mr. Callahan is available to see you."

Mackenzie huffed and sat two seats away from me, letting us know she wasn't happy about having to wait. Thankfully it wasn't much longer before the secretary told us we could go in. Mackenzie jumped up and flew to the door before I even had the chance to blink. I rolled my eyes and pushed myself out of the chair to join her in the office. I followed Mackenzie's lead and took a seat in one of the chairs across from the desk. I imagined this office would have belonged to some old, stuffy Professor, but to my surprise it had a young feel to it. There was an autographed Dave Mathews poster on the wall, along with a few ink blots, and college degrees with a recent graduation date, a few Japanese ferns along the window sill, a dream catcher hanging on the wall, and tons of Pop art – everything from Abstract to Surrealism.

The headmaster stepped out of what appeared to be a bathroom, disposing paper towels in a trash can before having a seat behind his desk. My jaw dropped at the sight of the young man sitting before me. "Miss Hilliard, Miss McCallister, how can I help you?"

I managed to close my mouth when Mackenzie started to talk. "Mr. Callahan, there seems to be some kind of mistake with our room situation. I was told from the beginning I would be allowed my own room. So you can see as to why I was surprised to find out that I suddenly had a roommate," she said in her sweetest voice.

"Miss Hilliard, I don't know how you managed to not have a roommate until now, but I can assure you this was not a mistake," he said affirmatively.

"Can't you just give her another room?" she asked, trying to hold onto her sugary sweet attitude.

"We have limited space as it is. Everyone has a roommate. No exceptions," he said.

"Can't we switch roommates then?" she pleaded, trying anyway possible to get rid of me.

"That wouldn't be fair to the other students who have already settled into their rooms."

"But," she yelped. All her kindness from earlier gone.

"I'm sorry Miss Hilliard but there is nothing I can do. I suggest you brush up on your socializing skills."

Mackenzie stood up and stormed out of the room.

"Is there something else I can help you with, Miss McCallister?" he asked, looking at me for the first time since I arrived in his office.

"So, you're the headmaster...and you didn't care to share this with me last night because?"

He met my eyes and smiled. "Would you have been so honest if you knew I was the headmaster?"

"Yes." I lied. "You're kind of young to be a headmaster."

"I'm filling in for my father until he is well," he said. When I met his eyes I felt a small flutter in my stomach and shifted uncomfortably in my chair. "Anything else?"

"No," I shook my head, standing up to leave. "You're sure there's nothing you can do about the roommate situation?" I asked, hoping that there might be a slight chance of a miracle.

"Sorry, I wish I could. Unfortunately you're just going to have to deal with the roommate you were given."

"Great," I muttered to myself.

On the walk back to my room I thought about Mr. Callahan. It was strange to see him all dressed up in a suit. Last night he seemed so laid back. And why was he there at the fountain? I remember Roman saying he wasn't supposed to be back until today? I waved off the thought as I reentered my room.

Mackenzie was pacing back and forth angrily. It was obvious she was used to getting her way and when she didn't things got ugly. Instead of making matters worse, I thought I'd try to make peace. Seeing that we were stuck with each other there was no reason we couldn't try to be civil. I was even willing to look past her little stunt from last night, be the bigger person. "Look Mackenzie, neither of us is happy about rooming together. So instead of being angry with each other for something we can't control, why don't we try to find a way to be civil?"

She turned and faced me, letting out a harsh laugh. "Okay fine, here are the rules. Touch any of my things and die. I need an hour every morning in the bathroom to get ready with no interruptions." I couldn't imagine what she did for that hour to get ready. By the looks of her split ends I would have to say she flat irons her hair to death and plasters on way more makeup than necessary. I shrugged, letting her have the hour. If she needed to do all that to feel better about herself then so be it. All I needed was ten minutes in the shower and I was good.

"Also, none of your lame friends are allowed to hang out here. I don't want their weirdness near my stuff and getting their cooties all over and this is just for now. I will get back to you with a list of official rules. Now you can leave," she said, dismissing me.

"Excuse me?"

"I need to be alone when I meditate."

"Where the hell am I supposed to go?"

"Not my problem," she said, sitting on her bed with her legs crossed and eyes closed. She waved me off like I was some cat she was shooing away. I bit my tongue, grabbed my IPod, and slammed the door behind me. Clearly she was one of those kids who never understood the meaning of share time in preschool - there was always one.

Not knowing where to go, I pondered on what to do. I thought about paying Dean a visit, but it was early and I knew he would still be sleeping. Lost in thought, I felt my stomach growl at me in protest so I decided to check and see if the dining hall was open and serving breakfast.

To my luck it was. The dining hall wasn't crowded and I was happy for that. I grabbed a tray and stuffed it high with scrambled eggs, toast, and bacon. Then I picked a seat in the corner and put in my ear buds while I dug into my breakfast. I contemplated about making a list of rules myself, but then again what could I possibly make a rule? I didn't really care about much, just as long as she left me alone.

While I continued to eat my breakfast, I got the strangest feeling that I was being watched. I put down my fork and scanned the room for the person with prying eyes. I spotted Roman not far off in the opposite corner from me. When I met his gaze his eyes quickly dropped down to his plate, embarrassed at being caught staring. I glared, going back to my eggs. He had a lot of nerve. I didn't know what his problem was with me and after that little prank he and his girlfriend played on me, I didn't care. I wasn't worried about trying to fit in here. I just wanted to make it through the semester without someone trying to kill me.

I bit off a piece of toast and almost choked on it when I saw Roman pull out the chair in front of me. "Hey," he said.

"Can I help you?"

He ran his hands through his hair. I could sense he was feeling uneasy and having trouble forming words to speak. I narrowed my gaze not in the mood for him first thing in the morning. "I wanted to..." he paused and took a breath. "I wanted to apologize for last night." Clearly apologizing wasn't something he did very often. "It really was just a joke and I had no idea Kenzie was going to follow you and try to pull something like that."

"I find that hard to believe," I scowled.

"Hey, I'm trying to be nice. I said I was sorry. What else do you want?"

"I want you to leave me alone," I said, thinking his apology was a joke.

"Fine," he snapped, getting up and leaving.

The last thing I needed was another enemy, but I wasn't going to tolerate people making an ass out of me for their own personal entertainment. He was dating Mackenzie after all. I'm sure it would just be a matter of time before she convinced him to jump on the 'I hate Ella' band wagon. Although I didn't expect I'd be the one to help him jump aboard so quickly. But what's done is done. It was probably better off this way anyways since I got a strange vibe every time he was around.

No longer hungry, I pushed my tray aside, and leaned back against the wall closing my eyes. "Your food is going to get cold," Mr. Callahan said, taking a seat across from me.

"I lost my appetite," I said, sitting up.

"May I?" he gestured to the tray. I shook my head and pushed it toward him.

"So, Mr. Callahan, what brings you down here to slum with the students?"

"Aidan, Mr. Callahan is my father," he said. "And it wasn't that long ago that I was student here myself."

"Reminiscing about the good old days?" I teased.

"I'm only twenty-five you know."

"How come you're eating here? Don't the teachers have their own lounge?"

"We do, but I find it to be a little stuffy," he winked, making my stomach do flip flops.

I self-consciously wrapped my arms around my waist. "Do you always hang out with the students?"

"Only with the ones I find interesting," he said with a sly smile. If I didn't know any better I would say he was flirting with me, but I knew I was wrong because he was a teacher. This was probably just his way of being nice to help make us feel more comfortable around him. Oddly, it was having the opposite effect on me.

I looked away, feeling my cheeks start to flush with heat. I bashfully tucked a piece of hair behind my ear and then held my hands tightly in my lap. Of all the students here I wondered why he had chosen me. "So what's so interesting about me?" I asked, flirting right back. I instantly clamped my mouth shut, not believing that I just said that out loud. I had no idea where this sudden courage had come from.

He didn't even blink an eye. "You're new here, so was I, once. I know what it's like. I thought maybe I could help you out."

I rested my arms on the table and leaned in closely. "And how exactly are you going to do that?" I challenged, giving him a flirtatious smile.

He smiled right back and said, "I could show you the ropes. Let you know what your teachers expect of you and what not to do to piss them off. Help keep you out of trouble."

"Sorry, but apparently trouble is my middle name."

Whoa, did I just say that?

Where was this stuff coming from?

He laughed at my cheesy joke bringing my attention back to him. For a minute I thought he was going to reach across the table and hold my hand. *I wish he would.* The thought was gone as quick as it came when Mackenzie showed up. "Mr. Callahan, have you changed your mind about our earlier discussion?" Mackenzie asked, interrupting us and breaking the spell. I think this was the first time ever I was happy to see her.

Aidan leaned back casually in his chair. "Sorry Miss Hilliard, but the situation still stands as is." He turned to me and smiled. "Besides, I think it's great that you and Ella are rooming together. I think the both of you could teach each other a few things. You never know, you might even have a few things in common."

Mackenzie choked on a laugh.

"Well if you'll excuse me ladies, I have to get back to my office," he paused. "And Ella, that offer's still good if you're interested."

"I'll let you know," I said. He waved goodbye and took off. The more distance I got from him the clearer my head was on what had just happened. Did I really just flirt with a teacher? And did he...flirt back? I felt the presence of evil and looked up to see Mackenzie was still standing there. She was watching Mr. Callahan. She turned to me, her scowl turning into a devilish grin. I could only imagine what was going on in her head.

"You and Mr. Callahan seem chummy," she said with a smirk.

"Um, Aidan was just welcoming me to the school," I said skeptically, careful of how much info I divulged.

"Aidan? So you two are on a first name basis?"

"It's not like that." I knew what she was getting at.

"Sure it isn't," she cooed.

"Look, Mackenzie, it's not what you think –"

She put up her hand to stop me. "Whatever, I don't care. I just came here to give you my list of rules." She threw the paper at me and flipped her long, blond hair as she spun around.

I sighed and picked up the paper. I was almost afraid to look at the list. It wasn't as bad as I expected. Most of it was what she had already covered earlier. Don't touch her stuff blah, blah, blah. Basically stay out of her way. She even listed the days and times when she would require 'alone time', whatever that meant. I folded up the paper and stuck it in my back pocket. Then I headed outside to take a walk.

I found an outside track surrounded by bleachers and a field on the inside. I wandered over to the empty track and out into the field. I lied down in the snow covered grass and stared up at the sky. I closed my eyes and let the cool air burn my lungs as I inhaled deeply. The first thing to cross my vision was Aidan. His bright, hazel eyes flashed through my mind along with his light brown, wavy hair, and dimples when he smiled. He had a way of making me feel funny when I was around him, but in a good way. And when he left, it was like a string was pulled, letting the air out of a balloon, and when all the air was gone I had a sudden sense of clarity. I didn't understand it. How can someone I just met make me all of sudden feel a certain way around them and then when they're gone it was as if those feelings never existed, leaving a cloudy feel in my head.

I lied there, going over possible solutions as to what was happening, but the more I tried the more confused I got. There was a sudden drop in the temperature, like a cloud had shifted over the sun. Someone kicked me, making me grunt in agitation. I opened my eyes shielding them with my hand to see the giant cloud was Roman. "What are you stalking me now?" I sat up.

"No," he glared. "I was out here for a run and I saw you lying in the grass. I came over to make sure you weren't dead," he said.

"Thanks for your concern, but as you can see I'm fine," I said, giving him a sarcastic smile.

"Next time I'll be sure to let you freeze," he said, jogging off. I was just making friends left and right. I sighed and headed back inside.

I met up with Dixon for lunch as promised and spent the rest of the day with him, Cameron, and Sienna. The remainder of the night I spent in my room. Thankfully Mackenzie didn't bother me and I didn't bother her.

On Monday morning new students had to meet in the auditorium for orientation an hour before classes. There were only about twenty new students and most of them were half asleep. Dixon saved me a seat next to him. We sat and listened to one of the teachers go on about the rules of the school, the dress code, and so forth. Pretty standard stuff, most of what they went over was covered in the brochure and as far as the tour went, well, that consisted of them handing us a map and letting us find everything out on our own. I never did take Aidan up on his offer to show me the ropes. After the looks Mackenzie was giving us, I didn't want to take the chance of her starting rumors.

They let us out early for our *"tour"* of the school. Since I've already pretty much knew my way around and Dixon could have cared less, we decided to stop and grab some coffee before our first class. We exchanged schedules and discovered we had one class together – chemistry. That was it. I sighed and finished my coffee. I said goodbye to Dixon as we parted ways for our first class of the day.

My first class was vampire history. Since there weren't a lot of new students they put us in the regular classes with everyone else, having to start where they left off, and leaving me with a lot of catching up to do.

I found a seat near the back, settled in, and took out a paper and pen. I hated the fact we had to wear these stupid uniforms. Dixon also vocalized his distaste as well and tried everything in his power to add some flair that wouldn't get him sent back to his room to change. I adjusted the sleeves of my shirt and wrote the date in the corner of my notepad.

I tapped my pen repetitiously, counting down the minutes until class started. The rest of my classmates slowly started to file in and of course, amongst those students was Roman and Mackenzie. She glared at me as the two of them took a seat in the back corner not far from me. Not a moment later the teacher arrived, closing the door behind him and shutting out any students who didn't make it in time. "For those of you that are new, my name is Mr. Grant and I will let you know I only have two rules. Don't interrupt me in the middle of a lecture and make sure you are through that door," he pointed. "Before I am or you will not be allowed in my class. Got it, good," the teacher said, automatically getting into the lesson.

I was completely lost. Maybe if I wasn't so distracted by my teacher's bulging biceps I could pay better attention. He was fairly large. My guess would be that he was a full vampire. He had light blond hair, dark gray eyes, and his clothes looked like they were about to burst at the seams. I tried to follow along the best I could but every now and then the hairs on the back of my neck would start to stand. I looked over my shoulder. Roman was staring at me. When I caught him, he shifted in his seat and leaned closer to Mackenzie. She just clutched him tighter, glaring at me. I ignored both of them.

After class, Mr. Grant called me up to his desk to give me all the work I needed to catch up on. He told me I had until the end of the week. He said that should be enough time for me to finish everything. Yeah, one week to catch up on months' work of assignments and lessons, sure, no problem. I threw my loaded up messenger bag over my shoulder and headed to my next class – spells and casting.

When I arrived, I found out – to my unfortunate luck – Roman was in this class as well. I was barely in a seat when the teacher begun. "Okay class, today we are going to pick partners, but before you get too excited they'll be picked at random." There were a few sounds of disappointment from the students. "I want everyone on the right to put their names on a piece of paper and throw it into the empty can on my desk."

Everyone had done as the teacher asked. After she collected the last name, she stood up, and walked over to a freckled face kid holding out the can for him to pick a name. He reached in, opened the piece of paper, and read off the name. She did this with every table. When she reached my table, I reached in and retrieved one of the tiny folded slips of paper. When I opened it up I wanted to kick myself. *Why am I being tortured?*

The teacher stood there, tucking a piece of her black as night hair behind her ear, waiting patiently for me to respond. I gritted my teeth and read the name out loud. "Roman Ashby."

There were a few chuckles from the other students, making me want to sink in my seat. The look on Roman's face said he wasn't any happier about this partnership than I was.

"Alright students, get together with your new partners."

Roman stood up, dragging his backpack behind him, and then slammed it on the desk between us, creating a barrier. "I'm going to give you some time to get to know your partners while I make up the seating chart and yes this is where you will be sitting the rest of the year," the teacher announced.

Just perfect.

The rest of the class chatted amongst themselves while Roman and I sat in silence. This partnership was going to be a difficult one if neither of us was going to talk. I didn't want to spend the rest of the year with a partner who despised me so I decided to swallow my pride – again – and make nice with Roman. "Obviously we got off on the wrong foot, so maybe we should try this again," I said, hoping to smooth things over.

Roman just looked at me, like I was setting him up for a trap. "I think maybe you hit your head harder than you thought." I looked at him completely lost. He sat in his seat, giving me a sideways glance. I waited for another quip, but the only thing he delivered was a half-smile. "Alright, I'm willing to give you a second chance. I feel you at least deserve it." I opened my mouth to comment but thought it wise not to.

"How about we start over...Hi, I'm Roman," he said, extending a hand.

"Ella, new girl," I said, shaking his hand.

"Well, new girl Ella, I believe this is a good start to a new found friendship," he smiled, making me blush. I self-consciously tucked a piece of hair behind my ear exposing my blue streak. Roman caught a glimpse of it and shifted uncomfortably in his seat, making me feel like shit. It's not like the streak was a snake ready to strike out and bite him.

I was about to say something when Ms. Kraft brought our attention back to the front of the class. "Okay, now, you and your partner are going to have an assignment to complete. I want you to create your own spell and demonstrate it for the class." Some of the students got excited about this, me, not so much. "There will be some exclusion and you cannot get help from the witches and yes I will know," she smiled. "I've made up a list of subjects you can use to create a spell from."

She handed out a piece of paper to each table. "And Roman, since Ella is new I will give you two some extra time to complete the project." I smiled thankfully at her as she turned around to dismiss the class. Roman stuffed the project list in his backpack and took off without another word. I was puzzled to his sudden mood change. Was he so freaked out by my blue streak that he changed his mind and no longer wanted to play nice? Before I let my head explode with a million why questions, I packed up my stuff, and got ready to head to my next class. But before I could escape, Ms. Kraft stopped me, and handed me a mile high stack of books and some assignments she wanted me to do to get caught up. She told me not to worry and that she had faith in me that I would be able to breeze through the listed work. At least one of us was confident.

Next on my schedule was lunch and my stomach was never so happy. I was supposed to meet Dixon outside the dining hall. I text him to let him know I might be a few minutes late because of all the books I had to drop off at my room. I managed to make it out of the school and to the courtyard without dropping anything. I thought for sure with the way all the students were sprinting by me I would have done a face plant on the floor.

After only three pit stops, I made it to my dorm and up the steps to my floor. "Ella!" I spun my head at the sound of my name, taking my eyes off where I was going, and tripped up the last step. My books and papers went flying and I lay face first on cold tile floor. "Seriously Ella, could you be any more uncoordinated?" Dean said, helping peel my face off the floor.

"Well maybe if you didn't scare me like that," I said annoyed. He just shook his head and helped me pick up my books while I picked up my papers and what was left of my dignity. Dean went to hand me my books when I shot him a nasty look. "Don't be a dick." He rolled his eyes and carried them the rest of the way down the hall. I collected all of my papers and had a few out of reach when all of a sudden they blew right to me. I moved back a little, stunned. I slowly reached out to pick them up.

Nothing.

I shrugged it off and stuffed them in my bag. Dean had dropped one of my books on his way not noticing. I walked down the hall ready to pick it up when it slid across the floor and stopped right at my feet. "Dean!" I shrieked.

He turned around so fast he almost dropped all the books. "What's wrong?"

"The books...they're moving...on their own," I said, thinking how crazy that sounded now that I said it out loud.

"What the hell are you talking about?" He looked at me like I was nuts.

"You dropped one of my books and then all of sudden it was at my feet."

"Are you taking drugs?" he asked in a stern brotherly tone.

"What, no! Just forget it." I picked up the book and met him at the door, unlocking it so I could let us in. He dumped all of my books on my bed and waited to walk me to lunch.

After lunch I had chemistry with Dixon, then powers beginners, and self-defense. Dixon and I walked to class together catching each other up on how our morning went. Luckily in chemistry we got to sit where we wanted and pick the partners we wanted. Of course it was a given that Dixon and I were partners. At first I didn't understand why we had to take chemistry; I mean I already took it in high school. They explained this was a different kind of chemistry. This was where we learned how to mix potions.

The class flew by without a hitch. We spent most of the time learning the rules of the class and what would be covered this semester. My next class, powers beginners, was all new students. Since it was something that needed more attention it was better to have a smaller class. Being that it was our first day, we just went around the room and introduced ourselves and our powers. I was the center of attention when I revealed I was a healer. Apparently this was not a common power. Another item on the list of why I was an outcast.

Once the gawking stopped, they continued around the room. There were only about ten students total in the class. After the introductions the teacher let us talk amongst ourselves for a little. A short, curvy girl with thick, black framed glasses sat next to me. "Hi, I'm Riley," she said softly.

"Ella."

"I like your blue streak," she said, adjusting the yellow headband she wore in her mousy brown hair.

"Thanks."

"Where are you from?"

"California."

"Wow, I always wanted to go there. Is it just like you see in the movies?"

"Sure."

"Do you always talk in one word phrases?"

"Sorry, lately I've been sticking my foot in my mouth so I figured the less I talk the better."

"Gotcha. I've done that lots of times. It's probably because I tend to ramble on and don't know when to shut up."

The teacher called the class to attention forcing Riley to be quiet and face forward. We spent the rest of class learning about what to expect over the next couple of months and the next class he said we would work on our breathing techniques. He also handed out a ton of paper work and two large books about the history of vampire powers. With all the books and paper work they've been giving me I'd need a wagon to cart all this stuff around.

Once class was over, Riley automatically picked up the conversation. I didn't mind. I knew being new it wasn't always easy to make friends so I thought I would give her a chance. "So where you off to next?" she asked.

"Self-defense."

"Me too, mind if I walk with you?" she asked sheepishly.

"No."

"So what do you think about the school so far? I was so excited when I found out I was coming here. I knew since I was born I was a vampire so it was no surprise about the school, but to come to a place with people like you where you didn't have to hide what you are..." she went on and on. She talked all the way to the gym. I learned she had five siblings; three brothers, two sisters, and her parents had another on the way making this one lucky number seven as she called it. I thought having two older brothers was enough, but man I couldn't imagine having three brothers plus two sisters. I also learned she was from Ohio so the cold weather didn't bother her. They had three dogs, two cats, and a huge aquarium tank filled with exotic fish. Her favorite color was yellow and favorite music was pop. She told me her favorite TV show, movie, and even the type of car she wishes to buy in the future. She told me all of this in the short time it took us to walk to the gym. I half expected her to be out of breath at how fast she was talking. Not to mention her having to walk twice as fast to keep up with the stride of my long legs.

I didn't mind her chatter – too much. It helped keep me distracted and frankly she was kind of nice. I could tell despite her jabber jaw that she was shy and didn't make friends easily. I didn't know why, but in a way I felt sort of protective of her. It was strange this feeling I got, but I knew I couldn't ignore it. I made a call to keep a close eye on her even though I somehow knew that wouldn't be an issue. I could tell she was the type to get easily attached.

We headed into the gym locker room to change and since I didn't have my own lock, Riley offered to share hers with me. Rambling on about always being prepared and you could always count on her. Apparently the one thing I couldn't count on her for was shutting up anytime soon. "So what kind of self-defense do you think they're going to teach us?' she asked.

"I'm not sure, but I guess we're about to find out," I said as we joined the rest of our classmates on the bleachers.

Two very large teachers in track pants and sweatshirts made their way out into the middle of the gym. The male teacher looked like he was over seven feet tall with short, light brown hair. He was big enough to be a pro wrestler and if his size wasn't intimidating enough the serious scowl on his face would make anyone want to back down.

The female teacher had dark blond hair that was pulled back into a tight bun. Her face showed signs of wear and tear, probably from spending a lot of time in the sun. She was only about a foot shorter than the male teacher, but looked like she was built like a brick house. Her expression wasn't any less frightening than the male teacher's. I would definitely not want to bump into these two in a dark alley.

The male teacher blew his whistle quieting the class. "For those of you who are new I'm Mr. Miller and this is Mrs. Daniels. Now everybody up and let's start stretching."

After we all climbed down the bleachers and onto the gym floor I noticed Dean was in this class and so was Roman.

The teachers led us through a series of stretches then made us do ten laps around the gym. By my second lap I caught up to Dean who was lagging pathetically behind. "You should lay off the booze, maybe than you wouldn't get so winded," I teased.

"Whatever, I could beat you. I just don't want to show off," he said.

"Pick up the pace!" Mr. Miller yelled.

"Yeah come on McCallister, my grandmother can run faster than you," Roman said to Dean.

"The only running your grandmother does is to the local Dunkin Doughnuts," Dean laughed. Roman pushed Dean into the wall causing me to almost run into them. Annoyed with their goofing around, I rolled my eyes, and picked up the pace, passing them.

Roman caught up to me by the fifth lap. "If you're as slow as your brother this will be an easy race to finish," he said with a taunting smile.

"I wasn't aware this was a race?"

"Care to make it one?"

"What do I get if I win?" I asked.

"Who says you're going to win?" he smiled, picking up the pace.

I pushed a little harder and caught up to him. "Are you always like this?" I asked and he looked at me confused. "Confident?"

"Just offering some friendly competition," he said, pushing himself in front of me again.

Friendly competition my ass.

I picked up the pace, passing him, and then it began. We raced each other for the last few laps. I even passed Riley and teased her about being a slow poke. She responded with a slow wheeze. "Are you okay?" I asked her.

"Asthma," she replied.

"Giving up already?" Roman said, keeping stride with us.

I looked over at Riley and she waved me away. "I was just slowing down to give you a chance to catch up," I said, hoping he hadn't noticed how out of breath I was. I was not a runner, but I could manage a few laps around a gym. It wouldn't have been so bad if I hadn't pushed myself to race Roman who was clearly in better shape than I was, but I needed to shut him up.

We kept pace with each other as we came up on the last lap. We were neck and neck until I passed Riley again. She looked worse than before. Her face was bright red and she was gasping for air. Roman flew by me when I stopped to check on Riley. She was walking and had her hand on the wall for balance.

"No stopping," Mr. Miller yelled.

"Riley, you don't look so good," I said concerned.

"I'll be...fine...I just...need...to..." her eyes rolled into the back of her head and I caught her before she hit the floor.

"Mr. Miller Mrs. Daniels!" I called.

Both of them came rushing over. "What happened?" Mrs. Daniels asked.

"She has asthma," I said.

The rest of the class came over to see what was going on. "Everyone back up! She needs air!" Mr. Miller shouted. "Does she have an inhaler?"

"Riley, where's your inhaler?"

"Locker," she whispered.

I hauled ass into the girls' locker room, but it never occurred to me that I didn't know the combination to the lock. "Shit!" I shouted as I tried number after number but was coming up empty.

"Move," Roman said, pushing me out of the way. He put his hand on the lock and bent it back and forth until it broke.

I stared at him eyes wide. "How'd you?"

"Ask questions later," he said, pointing to the locker.

I tore through Riley's backpack and found her inhaler inside the small pocket. "Got it," I said as we ran back out into the gym. I handed Riley her inhaler. She reached for it with a shaky hand and took two puffs. Her breathing started to come back slowly as they gently helped her up.

"Take her to the nurse's office," Mrs. Daniels said.

"I'm okay," Riley breathed.

"Just to make sure you should go to the nurse's office," Mr. Miller said. I started to walk with her when Mr. Miller yelled at me. "Where do you think you're going?" he asked.

"I was helping her to the nurse's office," I said.

"It's only down the hall. She'll be fine getting there on her own." I looked at Riley and she told me she would be okay so I headed back over to the rest of the class. Mr. Miller had two students set up mats on the gym floor and frankly I was a little worried as to what he would have us do next.

As we waited for them to finish setting up, I bit my nails wondering about Riley, hoping she was okay. I was too distracted worrying about Riley that I didn't even hear the teacher call my name. "Earth to Miss McCallister," he grunted, looking up from his clipboard. His eyes scanned the bleachers for the disobedient child.

"Ella pay attention!" Dean squawked in my head.

"Yes," I stuttered, receiving snickers from my classmates.

"Front and center," Mr. Miller demanded.

I nervously walked down the bleachers and stood in front of all the students next to the teacher feeling very small. "Today we're going to go over our defense moves. Want to make sure you didn't completely fry your brains while you were on vacation and forget everything we taught you."

Great, how am I supposed to go over something I didn't even learn? "Um, excuse me, but I just started and I don't know anything," I said.

"Don't worry about it, you'll be fine. Instinct will kick in," Mr. Miller said, not making me feel any better.

"Ashby!" Mr. Miller called signaling for Roman to join us on the mats.

Oh fan-freakin-tastic.

"Alright Ashby, let's see what you remember," Mr. Miller said, then turned to me. "McCallister, strike."

"Excuse me?" I asked, making sure I heard him right.

"You heard me, attack him."

"Like, hit him?"

This earned me more laughs from my classmates and an impatient teacher growing more impatient. "Yes, hit him," he said.

I looked at Roman who was smiling smugly and enjoying every minute of this. I was about to ask the teacher that maybe he should choose someone else to demonstrate, but the look on his face told me if I didn't he might demonstrate on me. Sighing, I took a deep breath, and swung at Roman. He waved off my punch like he was swatting away a fly. "That was pathetic. Do it again and put some weight behind it," Mr. Miller shouted, making my cheeks turn red. I tried again, harder this time. "That's good, but I know you can do better," he said.

"Stand shoulder width apart and bend your knees," Mrs. Daniels instructed me while demonstrating.

I followed her lead. I pulled my arm back and swung, putting weight behind it like Mr. Miller had told me. Not satisfied. I swung again and again. Roman blocked every punch with ease like this was boring him. He kept a smile on his face the whole time mocking me. "Is that all you got?" Roman taunted.

Not amused, I tried harder. I was starting to get winded which made him taunt me even more. "Mr. Miller, this really isn't fair you know. She's just a girl."

Now that really pissed me off. All that frustration and anger that was building up I put into my swing. The look on Roman's face as my fist made contact with his eye was priceless. I knocked him to the ground, surprising myself as well as Roman and the teachers. "Well Mr. Ashby, I believe next time you'll think before you speak," Mr. Miller chuckled, helping him up. Roman glared at me as he held his hand to his eye. "Seeing as Mr. Ashby can't remember some basic moves I think we need a review."

Everyone groaned as we made our way back to join our classmates. "Spread out," Mrs. Daniels shouted. They demonstrated basic blocking moves then had us fan out and partner off to practice. I didn't know anyone so Dean volunteered to be my partner. Although I think he just picked me because he knew I wouldn't hit as hard as everyone else.

We spent the next hour learning how to punch properly and then block those punches. I was glad this was my last class of the day. By the time we were done I was sweating like a pig, tired, and starving. I hopped in the shower in the girls' locker room then went to check on Riley.

When I arrived in the nurse's office, Riley was still there and lying down on one of the beds. "Riley?"

"Oh, hey Ella," she said, sitting up, and looking much better than she did about an hour ago.

"How are you doing?" I asked, carefully sitting on the edge of the bed.

"Oh, I'm fine. The nurse made me stay, but good as new," she said cheery as ever.

"Good, I'm glad...Do you mind if I ask what happened?"

"Oh, it's no biggie. I just get winded easily because of my

asthma. Not supposed to push that hard. I guess I just over did it," she shrugged.

"Maybe you should ask −"

She cut me off before I could finish. "No, I don't want any special treatment. That's why I never said anything in the first place. I know if they think I can't keep up because of my condition then I'll constantly be asked to sit out on things and...and well I just don't want to do that. I know I just have to be more careful, that's all," she said smiling.

I could tell there was more to this story, but I didn't want to pry. "Well, I brought your stuff," I said, setting her bag down on the end of the bed.

"Thanks, how'd you get the lock open?"

"I can answer that," Roman said, peeking his head around the curtain.

"What happened to your eye?" Riley asked, automatically noticing the bruise that had developed.

I looked down, picking at my nails. Roman wouldn't even look at me. "An accident. Wasn't paying attention," was all he said. I didn't blame him. I wouldn't want to admit what really happened either. "I had to break your lock to get the locker open. Sorry, I'll buy you a new one."

"Oh, that's okay," Riley blushed.

"I just wanted to come by and see if you were okay and get some ice for my eye," he said, glaring at me from his good eye.

"Thank you. That was very nice of you," Riley said.

"Yeah well...I guess I'll see you." Roman said to Riley and ignoring me.

I quickly chased after him. "Roman wait." He stopped and turned to face me with his arms crossed. "I'm sorry. It was an accident. You know that, right?"

He let out a breath. "I know. I guess I sort of deserved it. I was being a jerk."

"Yeah, you were," I agreed. He raised a brow at me. "Well you were."

"That's...fair, I guess," he choked out. "Call it even?"

"I think I can manage that," I said, giving him a slight smile. Not knowing what else to say I stood there, shuffling my feet.

"I'll see ya around," Roman said, making a quick getaway. I

wondered about his abrupt departure before I remembered I left Riley hanging. I walked back in to let her know I would wait outside while she changed out of her gym clothes. I invited her to sit with me at dinner. I thought I'd introduce her to the group and help her feel more welcome.

Everyone was already at the usual table. "Hey guys, this is Riley," I said, taking a seat.

Dixon, the gentleman he was, pulled out a chair for her as everyone introduced themselves.

I dug into my dinner, starved. I paused, mid-bite when the table went silent, and looked up to see Roman take a seat with Mackenzie. They all stared at Roman waiting for an explanation. "Dude, what happened to your eye?" Blake asked, having no patience.

"Accident. Wasn't paying attention," was all he said.

So accident was his story and he was sticking to it. I didn't bother to correct him. I'm sure he was embarrassed enough as it was. After Roman's explanation, the table went back to their normal conversations, and digging into their dinners. Riley took this opportunity to introduce herself to Mackenzie before I had a chance to warn her. "Hi, I'm Riley."

Mackenzie gave her a, 'why are you talking' to me look and then turned her back to her. "Since when did this turn into the rejects table," Mackenzie said.

"Why do you always have to be such a bitch," Cameron snapped.

"Because someone has to fill in for your mom," Mackenzie smirked.

Cameron's face turned bright red and I half expected her to bitch slap her, but she kept her cool and held herself back.

I spent the rest of dinner trying to help Riley feel included. Thankfully Cameron, Dixon, and Sienna did a good job of making her feel welcome. Mackenzie glared at us the whole time whispering snide comments to her bitch friends and laughing. I ignored her like I always did knowing this was something she wasn't going to stop doing anytime soon.

CHAPTER ELEVEN

I woke up dreading the day ahead. I had royal politics and economics – bore – then art and dance. I counted down the minutes until art and dance knowing I would at least like those classes. Cameron was in my first class and saved me a seat next to her. I was glad for the companion. If I didn't have Cameron to throw me an elbow every now and then I would have fallen asleep from the incredibly boring lecture. I was forced to take this class as part of my compromise to my dad. He reminded me every day before I left that I was a royal and needed to learn how to act like one. I also decided this was one secret I was going to keep to myself. As far as I knew no one knew and even Dean was keeping our royal status under wraps.

After two hours of listening to the teacher go on and on about the importance of good leadership, I was never so happy to have art next. My fingers were itching to paint. To my unlucky surprise we had to study a specific artist first before we were allowed to paint, making this another long, drawn out class.

I wasn't looking forward to dance anymore, afraid we'd have to study the history of dancers before we did anything. Thankfully that wasn't the case. Sienna was in this class and let me know before it started that we indeed did dance. For once I wasn't scared jumping in where everyone left off. Back in high school I was head cheerleader and on the dance team. Not to mention all the dance classes my mom had stuck me in. I was dancing since I was five so today I was grateful for the training. We did a hip hop routine which was a nice change from my lyrical training. I ended up really liking this class and was looking forward to the next one.

After class, Sienna walked with me back to the dorms to change for lunch. On our way there I spotted a large dog with light brown hair running along the perimeter of the school. I couldn't tell what kind of dog it was considering his size was bigger than any dog I've ever seen. He had a fierce look in his eye as he ran and that frightened me.

"Um Sienna, I don't mean to frighten you, but there is a very large dog running freely over by the wall," I said, slightly panicked.

She stopped and looked over in the direction of my stare. "Oh, that's just Mr. Miller," she said nonchalantly.

"Excuse me?"

"Mr. Miller, he's a werewolf."

"There are werewolves?" I asked, scratching my head.

"Of course there are. Geez Ella, have you been hiding under a rock or something?" she laughed.

Or something. If there are witches and vampires why not werewolves? "So are there students here that are wolves?"

"Yep."

"Do they bite?"

My question caused her to laugh so hard she snorted. "Only if provoked," she winked. I turned my attention back to Mr. Miller and watched as his massive paws pounded the ground while he ran. "Ella, come on," Sienna shouted.

After lunch I went back to my room and decided to work on the tons of extra work I had to catch up on. I only had about an hour before Mackenzie came back and kicked me out for her *'alone time'*. I still didn't know what she did during this time and frankly I didn't want to know. I thought it be wise to head out before she came back to avoid a possible argument of my neglecting her rules. I grabbed what I could and headed to the library.

I picked a table near the back where I wouldn't be disturbed and cracked open my vampire history book. I had a report due by Friday on how the existence of our kind came about. From what I've learned so far most of us had come from Eastern Europe as in parts of Romania, Russia, others Greece, Italy, and Spain. According to the history book it was believed that a person became a vampire because of a birth defect, unnatural death, or conception on certain days. These were just some of the beliefs of the people who couldn't explain what we were.

There were many myths and stories about vampires, but there was one that stuck with me. An ancient vampire named Lasairian. He was amongst the first of the royals, the one who actually created the vampire court. He believed we could live civilly with the humans. Blend in and work together. Vampire society in the beginning was chaotic. Vamps killed without remorse leaving messy trails behind. Mobs were formed to hunt down the killers and take revenge on the loved ones they had lost. Lasairian was a different kind of vampire. He saw great things in the future for our kind but knew we needed a leader, someone who could show us a better way to live.

They say he wandered all night in search of vampires who were worthy to join him on his journey causing death and destruction to those who dared to challenge him. In his search of those who he would deem worthy he stumbled across a large beast who we know today as the werewolf. This beast had come to his rescue one night while fighting several vampires who thought the idea of a royal court setting rule over our kind was a bad idea. They did not want to be ruled so they fought to take him down in hopes that his ideas would not be passed on.

After the beast had helped him take down the rogue vampires he invited him to come along with him on his journey. Thus starting the beginning of how the werewolves became the protectors of vampires. Now that was definitely interesting.

January 25

So far everything was going by smoothly. No more issues with Mackenzie, thankfully, and even Roman was starting to live up to his so said reputation. Although I still wonder if these random acts of kindness I catch are staged or for real. I have yet to determine which. My main accomplishment was that I survived the first two weeks. Now I just needed to get through next.

I managed to develop a normal routine of getting up, going to my classes, and hanging with my new friends. I actually had Mackenzie to thank for that last one. If it wasn't for her ridiculous schedule and Dixon convincing me to be more social, I probably would have hidden in my room. I was glad I got the time to hang with the group. It gave me the chance to get to know them and helped me to believe I could possibly start to trust people again. I even adopted Riley as my study partner and we helped each other catch up on all the work we missed the first half of the semester, well, most of it at least.

I was doodling in my journal when my phone buzzed in my pocket. I retrieved it to see who the text was from. It was Cameron asking me where I was. I replied, in the library at my normal location. I spent so much time there I was starting to leave a permanent indent in the chair.

"Hey Ella," Riley said, slightly startling me. She sat down in the seat across from me. "What you doing?"

"Hey Riley," I said, stretching my arms above my head. "I'm just working on a history report." I quickly slid my journal into my bag hoping she hadn't noticed how distracted I was. Riley was constantly lecturing me on not being more focused.

"I'm good with research, want some help?" she offered.

"No, I think I'm good, but thanks."

Riley sat there quietly, her eyes searching everywhere. I could tell there was something she wanted to ask me, but was too afraid to. Not able to concentrate anymore I thought I'd pick her brain. "Is there something you wanted to talk about?" I asked.

She looked down at her hands. "Well, there's this guy," she started.

"And..." I prompted her to go on.

"I kind of like him, but I don't think he even knows I exist."

"Did you talk to him?"

"Well...no. I'm not good at the whole talking to guys' thing," she said sheepishly.

"Maybe I could help you?" I suggested.

"Really?" Her light gray eyes lit up.

"I could try at least. So what does he look like?"

"Well he's tall, his hair is long, well not real long, kind of medium length I guess, and it's blond and curly, blue eyes. He's very athletic, well I guess he'd have to be, he is a wolf."

"Oh," I said.

"Oh? Is that bad?"

"No. I'm still new to this whole wolf thing," I admitted.

Now she was the one to say oh. "You don't know a lot about this stuff do you?"

"No. I only found out about my heritage this past year, long story," I said, hoping she wouldn't push for details. She was kind enough to drop it and go back to the subject of the boy she was crushing on. "So what's his name?" I asked.

"Who's name?" Cameron asked as her and Sienna joined us at the table.

"This boy Riley has a crush on," I said teasing her. She blushed and I could tell she wasn't comfortable talking about this with just anyone.

"Ooh boys, my favorite topic," Sienna said. She and Cameron stared at Riley waiting for her to reveal the mystery person's name. I could see in her eyes that Riley wasn't ready to blab to everyone about it so I quickly jumped in.

"We were just discussing how Riley could approach him," I said and she gave me a thankful smile.

"You could always ask him to the dance?" Sienna suggested.

"What dance?" I asked.

"That's not until the end of March and I'm sure she'd like to get with this guy before that," Cameron said. "How about a group date?"

"Oh, that would be good. You should ask him if he'd like to watch a movie or something and tell him it will be a group thing so he'll feel more relaxed," I proposed.

"Yeah, Austin and I can be there. We can use the social room. They have a giant big screen TV in there with surround sound," Cameron said.

"Will you be there to?" Riley asked me.

"Of course, I'll even invite Dixon," I smiled.

"I'll come too so that way it doesn't seem so couple-e, if that's okay?" Sienna asked.

"No that's great. The more the merrier," Riley smiled.

The three of them began to devise a plan on how Riley could ask him to watch a movie with her while making it not seem like a date. I drifted off somewhere in the middle of their scheming, distracted by the shimmery, bright light shining through the window. They were so into their conversation they didn't even notice that I got up from the table. I made my way over to the window and pressed my hand against the cold glass. I watched the sun slowly melt what was left of the snow.

"Looking for a way to escape?" Aidan said, startling me.

I jumped, hitting my back against the wall. "Aidan, I mean Mr. Callahan," I stammered.

"I told you, you can call me Aidan and I didn't mean to scare you," he said, noticing my tense expression.

"You didn't, I was just..."

"Staring aimlessly out the window?"

"Something like that," I said, looking away.

"How's school going for you so far?"

"Good, I guess."

"Any problems with anyone?"

"With anyone besides Mackenzie...? No, no problems."

He smiled before his face turned serious. He took a step toward me, making my cheeks flush hot. "Listen Ella, I just wanted you to know I'm aware of your," he stopped and looked around, then leaned in real close and whispered, "Situation."

I pulled back feeling uncomfortable with his close proximity. "Excuse me? My situation?" I said, feeling no need to whisper.

"Yes. I know what happened back at your school in Vermont," he said sympathetically.

"Oh, that situation." I pushed off the wall and walked into the book stacks.

Aidan followed me. "I understand that it's a subject you don't like to discuss," he said, keeping with a soft tone. "But I just want you to know that if you ever need someone to talk to my door is always open."

I didn't know what to say. I distracted myself by checking out the books on the shelves. I was tired of people telling me *they're here for me if I need to talk*. I *didn't* want to talk. Why couldn't everyone understand that? Not wanting to continue with this conversation I turned to Aidan. "Look, I appreciate the offer, but I'm pretty much talked out," I said over my shoulder.

"I understand," he said, almost like he did. I stopped and gave him a quick glance. His hazel eyes caught mine and I felt a sudden flutter in my stomach. I looked away busying myself with the books on the shelves. I tried hard to concentrate on finding a book for my report.

"Was there something else?" I asked, when he didn't make a move to leave.

"Yes. I also wanted to let you know I talked to Mr. Miller."

"Talked to him about what, *'my situation'*?" Angry, I turned around to face him. How dare he talk to other teachers about me when he didn't even know anything about me?

"I didn't tell him anything he didn't already know," he said, holding his hands up in surrender. He took a small step forward like he was approaching a wild dog. I narrowed my eyes at him, letting him know that yes, I do bite. He took the hint and stopped where he was.

"What are you talking about?" I asked, crossing my arms.

"All of your teachers are aware of what happened," he explained.

"Great, isn't anything private anymore?" I said, slamming my hand against the shelf and knocking books over on the other side. I rolled my eyes and walked over to the other aisle to pick them up.

"It was your father who insisted that we be aware of it," Aidan said, following me.

"Of course it was," I sighed, bending down to pick up the books. Aidan helped me replace them back on the shelf. Our hands brushed and I felt a sudden rush of heat. I pulled back and stood up. "So what does Mr. Miller have to do with this?" I asked, trying to get back to the subject at hand.

"He told me how well you're doing in your self-defense classes," he said.

"You're kidding, right?" I thought for sure I was the worst.

"Well...after you started to get the hang of it," he smiled. "I also heard about the incident with Roman, but it was also your first day and these things happen."

"Uh, yeah, well..." I blushed, embarrassed, even though he deserved it for taunting me.

"Don't worry. I'm sure it was an accident," he winked.

"Yeah...accident," I said, looking away guiltily.

"Anyway," he continued. "Mr. Miller and I were talking and we believe you have the potential to progress really well in his class, with some extra help." Great, here came the kicker. "If you're willing to, Gabe said he wouldn't mind spending some extra time with you to help train you."

I laughed lightly to myself. Of course Gabe wouldn't mind. He probably felt like it was part of his duty. "Why are we required to take self-defense anyways?" I asked, curious.

He thought for a moment before he answered. "Self-defense is something everyone should know, supernatural or not, don't you think?"

"Yes, it is something that could be useful, but why *us*? I mean, wouldn't our powers be our best defense and aren't we stronger than most humans?"

"While yes our strength does surpass that of a human's, knowing how to properly defend yourself is something you should know. Just in case," he said, hinting at something that I wasn't quite getting. It was hard to pay attention to anything he said. Every time he smiled his dimples showed and his eyes gave a slight sparkle, distracting me from the importance of the conversation. He leaned in closer, resting one arm on the shelf.

"Are we preparing for war?" I joked. I caught a glimpse of something in his eye and I felt myself being drawn closer to him. I heard voices on the other side of the aisle and quickly spun away to cool my heated cheeks. "When will this training take place?" I asked.

"That would be up to you and Gabe. You two can work it out and I'm sure he will make it so it won't interfere with your studies."

"Oh, I'm not worried about that," I laughed.

"You have a nice laugh," he said, taking a step closer to me – so close our bodies were almost touching. "I meant what I said earlier. If you ever need to talk, about anything, my door is always open." He hit my chin with his finger, smiled a sweet smile, and then walked away leaving me breathless. My head was spinning. I grabbed onto the shelves from the sudden rush to balance myself.

A thump alerted me, reminding me we were still in the library and not alone. I slowly regained a steady breath and made my way down the aisle to a book that lied on the floor. I picked up the book, ready to place it back in its proper spot when I was taken aback from the pair of dark blues eyes that stared back at me from the other side.

Eyes so piercing they kept me rooted where I was, unable to look away. "Ella!" Riley called, breaking me from the spell. I turned to address her as she joined me. "What are you doing? We thought you disappeared. You were gone for so long," she laughed.

"I was?" I said, scratching my head. I didn't think it was that long that I was talking to Aidan. I shrugged and held up the book I was holding. "I was just putting this back," I said, returning it to the shelf. When I did, the eyes on the other side were no longer there.

"It took you that long to put back a book? You know maybe next time you should ask the librarian for help," she said, shaking her head.

"Yeah...right," I said, still staring at the now empty space in front of me.

"Ella, you okay?"

"Yeah...sorry..." I followed Riley back to the table where we collected our things and headed off to dinner. Riley was right, not only was I wandering around for over a half hour, but I also had just spent the past four hours in the library working on my report and not even realizing it. Leaving for dinner now was probably a good thing. I needed a break to refuel, plus some fresh air would be a nice change from the musty, old library.

Before we even reached the food line, Riley grabbed my arm in a panic. "Oh my god he's here," she said.

"Who's here?" I asked, totally forgetting about our earlier conversation.

"The boy I like," she whispered.

"Where?" I asked, my eyes perusing the cafeteria.

"Over there, he's sitting with his pack," she said, keeping her head down.

"His pack?" I questioned.

"Ella, we're really going to have to sit down and discuss the basics of our world. If I didn't know any better I'd think you were human."

I rolled my eyes even though she was right. There was a lot of basic knowledge that I still didn't know and should. "We'll worry about that later," I said. "So which one is he?"

"He's the one sitting next to Roman."

I looked at her baffled. "Roman's a werewolf?"

"No, he's a vampire. He just hangs out with those guys."

"You know, you know an awful lot for someone who just started," I said, eyeing her accusingly.

"It's easy to learn about people when others forget you exist," she said sullenly.

Sadly, I knew what she meant. "I'm sorry."

"It's not your fault. You were actually one of the first people to welcome me, so thank you," she said appreciatively.

I gave her a small smile before taking a look at the boy she was crushing on. "He's cute, you going to ask him?"

"I don't know. I don't think I can," she said shyly. I grabbed her arm and started to pull her to the table before she could chicken out. "Ella wait, I can't do this."

"Yes you can, trust me. I may not know about our kind but I do know a thing or two about boys and confidence is always a plus," I said, urging her on and giving her a slight push toward the table.

At first she just stood there, not saying anything. I think this was the first time Riley was ever rendered speechless. I gave her another push encouraging her, because if she didn't say something soon this would probably end badly. "J-Justin," she started. The whole table went silent and turned their attention to Riley, which I'm sure wasn't helping her nerves. I poked her in the ribs, giving her another slight push. "I was just wondering...if maybe y-you wanted to hang out and watch a movie."

He gave her the once over and I could tell she was starting to get self-conscious, afraid he might say no. "There will be other people there too," she said quickly.

"What about you sweat heart? Will you be there?" asked some guy – I didn't know – with a Justin Bieber haircut.

I was afraid to say yes. I didn't want him to think I was interested. "Don't waste your time with that one," Roman said. "She's into older guys, much older guys," he said, his brows pinched tight together. I glared at him, wondering what the hell he was talking about. He just smiled at me like he knew some secret I was keeping.

"And how would you know what type of guy I'm into?" I countered.

"I know enough," he said through gritted teeth.

I looked down into his dark blue eyes and something clicked. "It was you. In the library. You were watching me," I said, confronting him.

He sat up. Clearly indicating I was right, but he wouldn't admit it. "Look darling, this little crush you have on me was cute at first, but now it's just embarrassing. You're even making up stories," he said, leaning back casually in his chair. His cocky smile returning, encouraged by the laughter he received from his friends.

It took all I had not to hit him, again. "Wow, really?" I turned to his friends trying my best not to let my anger show. "So did he tell you how he really got that black eye or did he say it was an accident," I said, mocking him. I tried using my best Irish accent which sounded more like a bad attempt at a British one.

His friends looked at him then back at me. The smile on Roman's face started to falter. "Mr. *I'm too cool* got knocked out by a girl," I said, crossing my arms, confident that I put him in his place. I even got a few chuckles from his friends.

My confidence was short lived when Roman recovered quickly with his own witty retort. "Well," he said, spreading his arms. "What can I say, I like it rough." There were shocked and amused expressions amongst his friends. I could feel my cheeks start to burn bright red.

"Oh, come on love. I was just messin' with you, relax," he said, reaching for my hand, trying to smooth things over. I jerked away, repulsed. If this was an attempt at humor, I was not laughing. What had gotten into him all of a sudden? Was this part of his plan all along? Fake a truce with me to get me to believe he was the good guy everyone claimed he was just to get back at me for humiliating him the first day in self-defense. Was he really that self-conscious that he had to give himself an ego-boost by making fun of me?

I stomped off leaving poor Riley by herself at the table. I didn't even bother to eat. I went straight to my room, but when I got there the door was locked. Apparently I forgot this was one of the times when Mackenzie required her alone time. I was pissed off even more because I couldn't wallow in my own self-pity in my own room when I wanted. I pounded and kicked the door before I walked off.

I didn't even know where to go and I did not feel like talking to anyone. Despite Gabe warning me about the maze being tricky and quite possibly I would get lost and freeze to death, I didn't care. The one thing I wanted to do right now was get lost and that's exactly what I did.

Literally, I got lost in the maze.

I was so absent in my own thoughts I hadn't realized when I entered the maze let alone how far I had walked until I got turned around. I found a bench around one of the corners and took a seat. I knew I couldn't stay out here too long, but I had to clear my head so I could hopefully find my way back. I was still so mad at what happened at dinner that I had a hard time trying to relax long enough to think straight. Not to mention it was getting dark and the temperature was dropping. Great, so I really was going to freeze to death out here all because Roman felt the need to try out his comedic act on me.

I jumped at the feeling of my phone vibrating in my pocket. I took it out to answer it. "Ella, where are you and why weren't you at dinner?"

It was Dean.

"I wasn't very hungry," I said, not caring to explain. "And I'm uh...in the maze."

"What the hell are you doing in there?" He yelled so loud I had to hold the phone away.

"Exploring?"

"You need to get out of there before it gets too dark. Do you know how to find your way back out?"

"I think so," I said unsure.

Dean let out an exasperated sigh. "Just stay where you are. I'm going to send someone out there to find you." I said okay as I disconnected the phone call. I was hoping he would send someone who knew their way around or they'd find two frozen bodies out here.

I sat there for about twenty minutes, wondering what was taking so long. It was getting colder by the minute and the light was decreasing. I pulled my jacket tighter around me trying to fight off the increasing chill. I was about to give up and try to find my way out on my own when I heard a twig snap. I looked up to see a large wolf standing not five feet from me. Not knowing what to do, I just sat there, frozen.

The wolf took a few steps closer to me and I tried to stay still so I wouldn't frighten him. My cell phone buzzed in my pocket again and I carefully reached in to retrieve it. "Ella, follow him," Dean said.

"Who, the wolf?"

"Yes the wolf. God Ella, sometimes I swear you can be –"

"Watch it," I warned.

"Just follow him. I'll be waiting for you at the entrance," he said, hanging up the phone.

I put the phone back in my pocket and stood up. "So, I guess I'm supposed to follow you?"

The wolf swung his head to the side signaling for me to follow. I kept a few feet behind him still not sure about this whole wolf thing. I knew he was part human, but you still never knew, he was also part wild beast. He could turn on me at any moment and snap my pretty little head off. As if he could sense what I was thinking, he turned around and I swear he was smiling at me. I stopped and stood there for a moment, until he started to walk again. I thought I even heard him laughing at me.

"Stupid dog," I muttered. He turned around and growled. "Just kidding... good dog...nice dog." He smiled again and continued walking.

It took longer to get out than expected. I didn't realize how far I had gotten. I just kept walking until I needed a break. After a few more twists and turns we were finally out of this god forsaken maze. I looked at the wolf and asked, "Is this the part where I give you a treat for being a good dog?" He growled at me, again, before taking off.

I found Dean over by the wall hanging with Blake and Reagan. I knew I was going to get a lecture from Dean. "Hey guys, I'll catch up with you later. I need to talk to my sister real quick," Dean said, narrowing his eyes at me.

Before they took off Blake turned to me and said, "Hey Ella, I'll still give you that tour if you're interested?"

"Dude!" Dean yelled.

"Thanks, I'm good," I replied. They left without another word. I turned to Dean, "Look before you start your lecture –"

"I'm not going to lecture you or tell you how stupid it was to go in there by yourself." I rolled my eyes. "Ella, I'm serious, you could have gotten hurt and no one would have known. You could have gotten lost in there for days –"

"Okay, I get it."

"Do you? Because I don't think you do. You haven't even been here a month and already you're causing trouble. You're getting into fights, wandering off."

"What fight?" I asked. I didn't recall getting into any fights and if he was referring to that stunt with Roman, so not my fault.

"Ella, I can't keep bailing you out."

"Sorry that I'm such an inconvenience for you."

"I didn't say that," he growled, frustrated.

"Whatever, you don't have to. It's written all over your face."

"Ella, I'm just trying to help you out, keep you safe."

"Well don't do me any favors!"

"Fine, from now on you're on your own. Good luck with that," he said, stomping off.

Great, now Dean was pissed off at me. The one person here who I thought I could count on I officially pushed away. I seemed to be getting good at having people hate me. Not to mention Riley was probably mad at me for leaving her there on her own. I was just doing a bang up job.

CHAPTER TWELVE

"Hey, Mom."

"Ella, honey, how are you? It's so good to hear from you. How is everything?"

My mom wasn't exactly the person I wanted to talk to right now, but at the moment I was running out of options. "Everything's good," I told her. No reason to make her worry. It was easier to lie to my mom over the phone than in person with her being an empath and all.

"Good sweetheart, I'm glad. So, want to tell me about your new school?" she asked, hopeful.

"Actually, I was hoping to talk to Danni. Is she there?" I asked, avoiding her question about school.

"No sweetie. She's out running errands. Anything you want to talk to me about?" I could tell she was a little hurt about me wanting to talk to Danni instead of her, but with Danni it was easier. She never passed judgment and well, she wasn't my mother. There were just some things I couldn't talk to my mom about.

"Um, no, I just had a question to ask her, but it can wait," I said, slightly disappointed.

"Okay honey, I'll let her know you called...Anything else?"

"No. Tell everyone I said hi and give them my love."

"Sure thing sweetie, I will. I love you."

"I love you too mom," I said and hung up the phone. I knew it was hard for my mom to just end the conversation. I knew she was dying to ask me a million questions, but another part of the compromise we made was that she couldn't smother me. She had to allow me my freedom. So that's what she did even though I knew it was killing her.

Disappointed that I couldn't talk to Danni, I found myself at a loss. What could I do and where could I go to be alone? I thought about the library again, but that wasn't private enough. I decided I was going to my room and I was going to be alone. I was going to force Mackenzie out. If she could have alone time than I could do it too.

When I reached my room I was fortunate enough to not have to send Mackenzie out with force. She was already gone. With a sigh of relief I put on my pajamas, then my headphones, and climbed into bed wondering how many people I could alienate and piss off tomorrow.

I woke up early the next day so I decided to kill time by working on my history report. I grabbed a quick bite on the way and sat in the back of the library in my usual spot. I was only a half hour into my work and I wasn't getting very far. I even dozed off a little from all the boring reading I was doing. To get my brain working again, I got up, and searched for more books that would hopefully have some better resources.

I wandered through the stacks looking for just the right book when I heard someone giggle. But not just anyone, Josie. I stopped. I thought I was losing it. It wasn't possible. I shook my head and continued to look for a book when I heard it again. Her voice echoed in the stacks.

No way.

I let the craziness of the situation take over me and followed the sound of her laugh. It led me to the back of the library. It was so close I could almost touch it. I heard her behind me and I quickly turned around. I caught sight of her pale blond hair out of the corner of my eye. I ran after her, but every time I got in reaching distance she was gone.

"Josie?"

She kept taunting me with her laugh. Tired of spinning in circles I stopped, closed my eyes, and waited for her to come to me. I felt a presence behind me. I spun around and pinned her to the bookshelf. "What the hell freak! Have you lost your fucking mind?" Mackenzie squealed.

"Mackenzie, what are you doing? Why were you following me?"

"As if! I was here to check out a book, because you know, that's what people do in libraries," she said, clarifying as if I didn't understand the whole purpose. "Then you go all schizo on me," she spat. I stepped back and let her go, feeling embarrassed. She straightened out her shirt before taking off in a huff but not before slamming her shoulder into mine.

Oh what a perfect start to the morning. Just what I needed, another reason for Mackenzie to think I'm a freak. I sighed, running my fingers through my hair and checked my watch. I barely had enough time to make it back to my room and shower before my first class. I collected my things giving the aisles one last look before I left. Did I really hear Josie or was I just imagining things? For now I went with the latter. I didn't have the time to deliberate if I was crazy or not and still make it to class on time. I left it go and decided to figure it out later.

I took the quickest shower possible, changed, and left with my hair soaking wet. I didn't have time to dry it and didn't know what the penalty was for being late so I didn't risk it. I jogged all the way across campus, making it inside the class room just before Mr. Grant and saving myself from a lecture on tardiness. I slipped into my seat and pulled out my notes. "How embarrassing, I can't believe she actually walked outside looking like that," I heard Mackenzie say.

I turned to glare at her. "Stop staring at me freak," she said, glaring back. But the oddest thing when she said it was that her lips never moved. "Seriously, I will cut all of your hair off in your sleep if you don't stop staring at me." I quickly turned around in my seat. How the hell did she do that? Could she project thoughts like Dean? Yes, that was it. That was the most logical explanation.

"I really hope this rash clears up. My balls are on fire," said an unfamiliar male voice.

"Gross," I said out loud.

"Care to comment Miss McCallister?" asked Mr. Grant.

Crap.

"No, sorry," I said as he went back to his lecture.

Again I thought I heard Mackenzie talking, but I ignored it until I heard Roman's voice next. "For a crazy bitch, she's still pretty hot. I like a girl with curves unlike Kenzie's rail thin body. There's something different about this one and I intend to find out." I looked over my shoulder at him, narrowing my eyes. He shifted in his seat. Mackenzie saw us exchange looks and gave Roman the look of death. He sat back throwing his arm over her chair while she leaned into him and gave me a smug smile.

I faced forward again having enough of them and their mind

games. "Look at her sitting there. Her hair dripping wet. I bet she did that on purpose so I would envision her naked in the shower, lathering up her soaking wet body. I would definitely like to –"

"What did you just say?" I asked Roman. He looked at me like I was nuts.

"Miss McCallister, I will not tolerate being disrupted again. Are we clear?" Mr. Grant shouted, making me shrink down in my seat.

"Yes Mr. Grant," I said, embarrassed and confused. Why was I the only one getting yelled at when I wasn't the only one talking?

"I'm so tired of these kids not knowing what respect is," Mr. Grant said. I looked around the room but no one else seemed to notice he said something or they just didn't care.

I sat up straight in my chair, grabbed my pencil, and prepared to take notes. Then the voices started again. *"I'm so going to fail this test tomorrow," "I wish she would ask me out," "I hate my hair I wish it was smoother," "I wish boys would notice me," "I wish I was popular like Mackenzie."*

What the hell was going on? I kept hearing voices and no one's lips were moving and I seemed to be the only one who noticed. My ears started to ring and the voices got louder and more jumbled together. I couldn't stop it. I couldn't block them out. My head was pounding and the voices were screaming at me now. The pressure was so over whelming I couldn't take it anymore. "Shut up! Shut up! Shut up!" I screamed, covering my ears.

Everyone stopped what they were doing and turned to look at me causing the chatter to grow louder than before.

I stood up, eyes panicked. I'm sure I looked like a deer caught in headlights. My head started to spin and my vision went blurry.

All eyes were on me and I couldn't breathe.

I tried to steady myself but was unsuccessful. Before I knew it I was falling and falling fast.

When I opened my eyes I was staring up at the ceiling and lying down on a...bed? My vision and hearing was still a bit hazy and the bright fluorescent light hurt my eyes. I sat up and groaned from the pain the pressure in my head was causing. "Ella, you shouldn't get up."

"Dean, what's going on...what happened?" I asked confused.

"You fainted in class," he said, worry written all over his face.

"How'd I get here?"

"Roman," he said. "After you hit your head, he picked you up and carried you here. That's what the nurse told me. Do you remember what happened?" I was afraid to tell him that I was hearing voices. Last time I checked they committed people for that. "Ella, you can tell me, whatever it is?" He said with kindness.

I might as well tell him. Maybe if they committed me, I would actually get some peace and quiet; it might not be that bad. I spied around the room for intruding ears. When I felt it was safe I lowered my voice and said, "I heard voices."

He sat back and looked at me funny. *"She really has truly lost it,"* he thought.

"I'm not crazy," I said annoyed.

"I didn't say that," he said.

"No? Sorry, how about this, *'she really has truly lost it',*" I mocked.

The look of surprise on his face told me I was right. "Wait, you heard what I was thinking?"

"That's what I'm trying to say. I was hearing what everyone was thinking. I just didn't know it at first. I thought everyone was talking out loud until I realized I was the only one who could hear them. Then all of it started to get jumbled together and my ears were ringing. It was so loud I couldn't take it anymore. I guess that's when I passed out," I said, sitting back in the bed. I could only imagine how crazy I sounded.

"So what does this mean? Is this...is this a new power or something?" Dean looked me over rubbing his chin, concentrating. "I know what you're thinking," I said. "And I'm not going to use this new power, if that's what it is, to your benefit."

He frowned and sat back as the nurse walked in. "How is the patient feeling?" she asked, bending over to check my pulse.

"Dean! Gross!" I cringed.

"Stay out of my head," he said, narrowing his eyes at me.

"I would if I could, trust me. Your head is the last place I want to be." I shuddered at the memory of his last thought toward the nurse. I hope all guys didn't think that way. Who am I kidding, of course they did.

"How's your head feeling?" the nurse asked, ignoring our banter.

"I have a headache, but the pressure's not as bad as before."

"Well, you do have a small bump on your head so I'm going to give you some pills to help with the swelling and the headaches."

I reached up and felt the small bandage that was placed above my left eyebrow. You know for being a powerful healer you'd think I'd be able to heal myself, but no, it doesn't work that way.

The nurse wanted me to rest for the next couple of hours and told me I should skip the rest of my classes. I was more than happy to get a free pass, but I had to argue to be able to rest in my room. She wanted me to stay in the infirmary, afraid there might be too many distractions at the dorms. After a little convincing of why it would be better for me to rest in my own room she finally agreed on one condition. "As long as you let Dean walk you back to make sure you get there okay," she said. I agreed and he helped me off the bed and out of the infirmary.

Once we were outside and out of earshot I asked Dean, "So what do you think this means and remember, I'll know if you're lying."

"I think that it's a new power. You know dad can read minds."

"Yes but only when in contact with someone. I wasn't touching anyone and I heard everyone."

"Our powers advance with every generation. So maybe you got the new and improved version," he shrugged.

I started walking again, but Dean stayed put. I turned around to see what the holdup was. He had an odd expression on his face. I couldn't quite make out what he was thinking. It was almost as if he was trying to block me from his head. "What are you doing?" I asked.

He squinted slightly, concentrating. He kind of looked like he was constipated. "Can you hear what I'm thinking?" he asked.

"No, it's all kind of jumbled. Sounds like static. How are you doing that?"

"They just taught us how to put up a wall to block mind readers."

"Do you think it works both ways? Like is there a way I can block everyone out?" I asked hopeful.

"Why would you want to do that? You just received probably one of the best powers ever. You can hear what other people are thinking."

"It's not as great as you think it is. I could barely decipher who was saying what. My ears were ringing and the pressure in my head. This is one power I would gladly give up."

"Don't be so quick to dismiss it. It's still new to you and you don't know how to control your powers yet so of course everything is going to be hectic at first. You just got this power today and each one comes with a price, but only when you first receive them," he said, trying to convince me not to give up just yet.

"Why don't I know any of this? Why am I only finding this out now? Oh, yeah, because everyone thought it would be better if they hid it from me," I huffed.

"Look, I know you're pissed at dad because you think he lied to you but he was protecting you. He was protecting all of us."

"Not you too," I said, getting ready to take off.

Dean grabbed my arm, stopping me. "Ella, just please, listen. I know you think you were the only one that didn't know but it's not true. Neither Xander nor I had any idea until we turned eighteen. Dad sent you here so you can find out who you are the same way we did."

"I thought uncle Bobby taught you?"

"Well, he did, or should I say he tried. Uncle Bobby's an alcoholic. He was drunk most of the time and one month with him was not going to tell me much. The only reason dad allowed me to go was because I fought him tooth and nail about it. I felt the same way you did when I first found out and a visit to Uncle Bobby was my only alternative."

"How come I didn't have that option?" I asked a little annoyed.

He laughed. "Trust me, you didn't want that option. You are much better off being here."

"Well, until I can figure out how to get a handle on this new power I think I'm going to have to hide in a cave," I sighed.

"Not if I can help it. I have an idea, come on," he said, heading back into the school.

Curious, I followed him. "So, I have to ask," I said as we headed up to the third floor. "Why did you come to the infirmary?"

"They called me out of class and told me you fainted."

"Yeah, but you didn't have to come. I mean, after last night I would have expected you not to," I admitted, embarrassed by my behavior.

He stopped, almost knocking me down the steps. "Ella, you're my sister. Regardless of what happened I care about you and I hate to see you hurt," he said sincerely.

"That's funny because you hurt me all the time."

"That's different. I'm your brother. I'm allowed to," he winked.

"So that's why you're such a jerk to me because you're allowed to be?"

"Hey, what else are big brothers for," he smiled. "Ella, we fight all the time, it's normal, but when it comes down to it no matter what, we're family first. So no matter how much you piss me off, I'll still be there when you need me."

"No matter how much _I_ piss _you_ off," I said, annoyed as we continued our way onto the third floor and down the hall. We stopped in front of Ms. Kraft's room, the spells and castings teacher. "What are we doing here?"

"You'll see," he said as he lifted his hand to knock.

"Come in," Ms. Kraft called. "Dean, Ella, to what do I owe the pleasure?"

"We're not disturbing you are we?" Dean asked kindly.

"No, no please, have a seat. What can I help you with?"

Dean and I took a seat in the desks across from her. Not knowing what Dean was up to I allowed him to speak first. "Well, we believe Ella has developed a new power today."

"Ella that's wonderful," Ms. Kraft said cheerfully. "What is your new power?"

"Um...mind reader," I said, unsure of the correct terminology.

"Oh, I see. You're here to see if I can temporarily bind your power," she said more as a statement than question.

"That's what we were hoping," Dean said.

She got up from her desk and went to the back of the classroom. She ran her finger along the bindings of the books she had on the shelves until she found the one she was looking for. Then flipped through the pages until she found the spell she desired. "Here," she said, taking a seat next to me. "Give me your hand."

I held out my hand and she sandwiched it in between hers. Then she closed her eyes. Her lips moved soundlessly as she incanted the spell. I watched intently as she cast a spell over me to help control my new power. She whispered a few more incantations, then took a deep breath, and let it out. "Okay, now we just need to make sure it worked," she said.

"Well, I can't tell what you're thinking or Dean," I said, looking over my shoulder at him. "So it must have worked."

"You won't be able to read my mind. All teachers already have theirs blocked and Dean I can tell is trying to block his."

"But how come I could hear Mr. Grant's?" I asked confused.

"Because you were just receiving this power so it allowed you to hear everyone. That's why it probably felt so overpowering."

"It was like my head was going to explode. I was hearing everyone at once and then the ringing in my ears and the pressure. It was just too much," I said, cringing at the memory.

She placed a hand tenderly on mine. "I understand," she said kindly. "Unfortunately when you receive a new power it hits you all at once, it's magnified ten times."

"Yep, that's kind of what it felt like," I said, recalling something when I first received my powers. "So is that why when I originally got my powers my senses were magnified, but now not so much." I remember being able to hear and see for miles but now it was like I had regular human senses.

"Yes, when a vampire first receives their powers all their senses are heightened temporarily to prepare your body for what it's about to endure."

"Why does it go away then?"

"That is because your body wasn't meant to take on that much power all at once. Over time as you grow so do your powers. They come gradually so you can handle it better."

I nodded, understanding. The door opened and in walked Mr. Cormac, the chemistry teacher. "You called?" he asked, stepping inside the door. I didn't remember her calling him.

I looked to Ms. Kraft for an explanation and she noticed my confusion. "Mr. Cormac is a warlock. We don't have to call on the telephone," she winked at me. "We can sense each other and communicate through the elements."

"The elements?" I said, scratching my head.

"Don't worry, you will learn about that later," she smiled. "But for now, we need to see if the spell worked." She turned to address Mr. Cormac. "You are currently tutoring a few students at the moment, yes?" He nodded in agreement. "Do you think we could let Ella into the classroom for a minute to see if the spell worked?"

"Of course," he said, smiling back at her. If I didn't know any better, the way these two were looking at each other I could swear there was something going on. I was thankful for the moment that I couldn't read their minds. I shuddered at the thought.

Mr. Cormac guided me to his room and told me to walk to the

back and pretend I was borrowing a book. He also said to linger for a moment to make sure. I did what he said and walked to the back of the classroom. I stood there pretending to look for a book and listened carefully. *"Do you hear anything?"* Dean asked. I hated that he could get in my head but I couldn't talk back in his.

I rolled my eyes and ignored his question obviously because I couldn't answer back. A few more minutes later and I heard Mr. Cormac say, *"I think you're okay. It's been long enough. You should have heard something by now."* I turned to see he was still standing by his desk. How the hell did he? *"The elements,"* he said smiling. Of course, I rolled my eyes again and left the room.

When I got back to Ms. Kraft's room I asked her if there was a spell to block out someone who could project thoughts. Dean glared at me while she gave me a soft laugh. "Ella dear, even though now it might seem as a..." she paused, choosing her next words carefully. "Inconvenience, I'm sure in the future it will be helpful."

"But how come I can't send messages back?"

"Because that is not your power. It may seem unfair, but this is how you will learn to communicate better and what a better person to try that with than your own brother."

Dean and I looked at each other. Neither of us cared to learn how to communicate better with each other.

We thanked Ms. Kraft for her help and Dean walked me back to my room. "What are you going to do now that you have the rest of the day off?" Dean asked.

"I'm going to enjoy my alone time," I smiled. "And thanks Dean...for everything."

"No prob'," he said, ruffling my hair.

I swatted his hand away. "Hey, careful there, my head still hurts you know," I said, gently touching the bandage. He laughed and left, heading off down the hall. I shut the door behind me and laid down on my bed happy to have the rest of the day off and to myself.

I closed my eyes and tried not to think about the fact that I totally flipped out in class and everyone probably now thinks I'm crazy. Or the fact that I still haven't had the chance to apologize to Riley and not to mention the strange impure thoughts Roman was having about me. All this mind babble was making my head hurt. I got up and went to the bathroom to take the pills the nurse gave me. It didn't take long for them to kick in and before I knew it I was resting peacefully.

CHAPTER THIRTEEN

I knew I was dreaming when I found myself in the school's maze again. This time I had found my way to the middle where there was a large square fountain and a statue of a goddess in the center. I didn't know which goddess it was, but she was captured beautifully. I noticed I was wearing the angel costume I had worn last Halloween, which made me a little nervous.

I walked over to the fountain and sat on the edge. I skimmed my finger over the top of the warm water and watched it swirl in mini whirlpools below me. "Ella!"

"Josie?" I sprung up from my seat. "Josie?"

"Ella, where are you?" she called.

"Josie I'm here. I'm right here!" I shouted. My eyes searched the area looking for her.

"Ella I'm over here," she said.

I followed the sound of her voice to the other side of a hedge. I spotted the black wings of her angel costume and ran to her. "Josie!"

She was gone.

"Catch me if you can!"

"Tristan?" This wasn't happening. "Tristan is that you?"

"Ella I'm over here. I need your help." This time it was Kyle's voice.

I felt like there was a dagger twisting in my heart. I ran back to the center of the maze. "Josie, Tristan, Kyle! Where are you guys?" I shouted.

"Chasing ghosts I see."

That voice. I knew that voice. It frightened me.

I turned around to face my worst nightmare. "Jack," I breathed.

"Ella, Ella, Ella. You can run, but you can't hide," he growled, leaping for me.

I sat up, screaming bloody murder.

"Christ almighty my fucking eardrums are bleeding," Mackenzie whined.

I couldn't catch my breath. I started to hyperventilate. I sat on the edge of my bed and put my head between my knees. To my surprise, Mackenzie handed me a paper bag and told me to breath into it. I had no idea where this sudden act of kindness came from, but I wasn't going to question it. Not now at least.

Once I was able to breathe normal and speak, I turned to Mackenzie and asked, "Why are you being so nice to me?"

She rolled her eyes. "Please, I just didn't want you to spaz out again or like die or something. I couldn't stay in a room that I knew someone died in and I particularly like this room," she said in her usual snooty tone.

I sighed, pulling my knees up to my chest. "I just had a bad dream, that's all," I said.

"I'm sorry if you misunderstood, but that was not an invitation for 'girl talk' or whatever."

I should have known better. This probably would have been a good time to see inside her head and know what she was really thinking, but then again, maybe not.

I went into the bathroom to change out of my uniform and into some jeans and a hoodie. We only had to wear our uniforms to class so as soon as class was over most of us students put on regular clothes. Since I was excused from my classes for the rest of the day I decided to change now.

I hadn't realized I slept through lunch and dinner wasn't being served for another hour or so. Each floor in the dorms had their own little snack area with drinks, sandwich type stuff, etc. I thought I'd grab a quick snack and head to the library to do some research on my powers.

I grabbed an apple and a bottle of water then took off for the library. It was quiet, but I still chose a table near the back. I took out my powers book and apple, taking a bite so loud it echoed through the library. I looked around to see if there was anyone nearby who heard it, but I didn't see anyone. I took another bite, but quieter this time. The Liberian stood in front of me and cleared her throat. When I looked up, she pointed to a sign that read no food or drink allowed in the library. I guess I wasn't as quiet as I thought. "It's only an apple," I said.

She pointed to the door. "Outside or in the trash," she said and proceeded to stand there until I made my decision.

I stifled an eye roll, walked outside and around the corner of the library. I leaned against the wall, in the cold, and tried to enjoy my apple. My enjoyment was cut short when a big puff of smoke drifted in my direction. I coughed and waved the smoke away from my face looking for the culprit. "I see they let you out of your cage," Roman said, foot and backside pressed against the far wall, cigarette in mouth.

I glared at him. "I'm not in the mood for you."

"Fancy a fag?" he asked, ignoring what I said and offering me a cigarette.

"No thank you. I'd rather drink Drano than touch one of those."

"Suit yourself," he said, moving closer to me.

"Do you mind?" I asked, annoyed. I pushed myself off the wall and crossed my arms. I was going to let him know I wasn't going to take any of his crap, especially after what he pulled at lunch the other day.

"Actually, I do. I was having a peaceful moment until you came out here," he said, blowing a puff of smoke right in my face.

"Me, what the hell did I do?"

"You're welcome by the way," he said, flicking ash off his cigarette.

"Excuse me?" I asked, wondering what the hell he thought I owed him for.

"You know, for saving your life."

"I wasn't aware my life was in any danger."

"You're a stubborn one, aren't ya?"

I stood there, my arms folded tight, annoyed at his cryptic conversation. He watched me like he was watching something interesting of the discovery channel. "I don't get you," I said, viewing the way he took a puff of his cigarette. "I mean what is it that you want from me?"

"A thank you would suffice."

"And what exactly am I thanking you for?"

"How about for not leaving you unconscious on the floor in history class?" he hinted at in a non-subtle way.

Oh, yeah, I forgot about that. Dean had told me when I woke up that Roman was the one who carried me to the nurse's office. "Thank you," I said.

"There, was that *that* hard?" he said flicking his cigarette. I narrowed my eyes at him. "So what happened anyway?" he asked, leaning his shoulder on the wall, crossing one foot over the other.

"That's none of your business," I said, squaring my shoulders. With him this close, I could see he was sporting a nasty bruise on his lip. "What happened to your mouth?" I asked. It looked like he had gotten into a fight.

"None of your business," he said with a slight smirk.

"Let me guess, got into a little argument with Mackenzie? Forgot the safety word?" I said, laughing to myself. His eyebrows shot up. "Accidently wrinkle her blouse by getting too handsy?"

"Jealous?" he asked, slightly amused.

"Ha!" I laughed. "Hardly. And you're one to talk." He looked at me puzzled. "What is it your so jealous about or should I say who?" I asked, remembering the feeling I got from him when I got my new power. On top of hearing everyone's thoughts I could also feel their emotions as well, but for some reason Roman's was the one who stood out.

"I don't get jealous, darling," he smiled.

I didn't have to read his mind to know he was lying. I could see it in his eyes. "You're so full of it. You know that. I know for a fact that you're jealous because when I –" I quickly clamped my mouth shut.

"When you what?" he asked curiously, taking a step closer.

"Nothing. I should go."

"No, Ella, wait," he said, reaching for me. When his fingers brushed my arm I felt a small shock. I turned around. My arm was pulsing from where his fingers brushed.

He stood there and stared at me for a moment, his dark blue eyes looking down on mine. He took a step closer, so close I could smell his cigarette cloaked breath. I mindlessly reached up toward his lip and my hand started to glow. "What the hell?" He flinched, taking a step back.

I quickly pulled my hand away, hiding it behind my back. "Sorry, I'm a healer. I don't know how to control it yet. It just kind of happens." He stood there watching me. "I could heal your lip for you, if you want?"

"No. I'm alright, thanks," he said and walked away.

What the frig?

I sighed and walked back into the library. I seriously did not understand him. He's nice to me one minute than nasty the next. He's so hot and cold. I really don't understand guys like I thought I did.

After my run in with Roman I had a hard time concentrating on my research so I gave up and went back to my room to drop off my books. Starving, I headed down to the dining hall for dinner. Today they were serving burgers and I couldn't wait to sink my teeth into one. I was drooling just at the thought of it. Of all the things here I thought the food they served was the only thing I liked so far.

I found Dixon, at what was becoming our normal table, and joined him. The look on his face when I sat down told me he had heard about my outburst in class. "I'm taking it you heard," I said. He didn't even want to look at me. "How bad is it?" I asked, knowing that if Dixon had found out already the rumors were flying.

"I heard you started screaming at everyone and then ran out of the classroom," he said.

A few girls I didn't know walked by whispering, pointing, and giggling. "That's not what happened," I said, stabbing a fork in my fries.

"You want to tell me what really happened?" Dixon asked sympathetically.

I took a deep breath and told him about my new power and the incident in class. "That would explain the bandage," he said, reminding me it was still there. "How cool is your new power though! Can you hear what I'm thinking now?" He scrunched his brows like he was trying to project thoughts into my head. I had to laugh a little at his expression.

"I can't hear what you're thinking. Dean had Ms. Kraft do a spell that basically put up a wall to block out everyone's thoughts until I can figure out how to use this power without it making me nuts."

"Oh," he said a little disappointed. More people walked by whispering and laughing at me. "Hey Britney, has that rash cleared up for you yet?" Dixon shouted at the group with a wicked smile. The girl looked mortified as she put her head down and rushed off, leaving her friends with new gossip to whisper about. I mouthed thank you to Dixon and he just fluttered his hands like it was no big deal.

"So word is you totally freaked out in class and attacked a desk," Cameron said, sitting down next to me. I looked at her wide eyed. "Don't worry. I don't care if you're crazy. I think it makes you more interesting," she smiled.

"Thanks, I guess, and I didn't attack a desk," I said, annoyed at how quickly rumors spun.

"Whatever," she shrugged. "I'm cool with it." I rolled my eyes and continued to eat my dinner.

No one else mentioned my incident from earlier and for that I was glad. I figured they either didn't care or were just being polite. Even Mackenzie kept her mouth shut, although, the smartass look on her face did have me worried. The only awkward moment was when I kept catching Roman staring at me. Even after I caught him he still didn't look away which just made me feel uncomfortable. Those two made me wish I could get a handle on my powers sooner. This new found power could be useful if it didn't kill me.

After I finished eating I decided to go find Gabe and talk to him about the extra training sessions Aidan wanted me to take. Then I was going to try and find Riley. She wasn't at dinner and I wanted to apologize to her for the other day.

I didn't know which room Gabe was in and students were not allowed to roam freely in the teachers' dorms, so I asked the woman at the front office if she could see if Gabe was in his room. She told me she would buzz him and see if he was available. I had a seat in one of the chairs and waited. She told me he wasn't in his room, but I could check the gym, he was usually there training. I thanked her and bundled up as I made my way outside.

The receptionist turned out to be right. Gabe was in the gym training someone. I couldn't see who it was that he was training. When Gabe saw me, he stopped what he was doing and came over to talk to me. "Miss Ella, how is everything? Are you okay?"

"Hey Gabe, yeah, I'm fine. I didn't mean to interrupt," I said, gesturing to the kid on the other side of the gym.

"You're not interrupting. I always have time for you." He turned back to the boy and shouted, "Roman, do a few laps until I'm done here."

"Wait, Roman as in Roman Ashby?" I asked.

"Yes. He asked if he could get a few extra training sessions and after what I heard happened in class I believe he could use them."

I snickered to myself. "What exactly did you hear?" I wanted to know if he knew the truth or just another made up story.

"Mr. Miller had told me that a new student had gotten the upper hand on him which surprised me because Roman is one of the top contenders in that class."

"Did he tell you who that student was?" I asked as Roman ran up to us.

"Come here to watch me or challenge me to a match?" Roman said cockily.

"If I remember correctly, a match with you isn't that much of a challenge," I said, making his smile turn into a scowl. Gabe catching on, started to laugh, then quickly covered it up with a cough.

"Roman, five laps outside," Gabe said. Roman glared at me one more time before he took off. Gabe turned back to me. "So, what can I do for you?" He gestured to the bleachers for us to have a seat.

"Mr. Callahan had approached me and suggested I talk to you about taking some extra training sessions," I told him.

"Ah, yes. I have talked to him and Mr. Miller and they both agree you have the potential. You just need some discipline. I'm willing to work with you, but I'm going to let you know that I will not take it easy on you. I will be as tough on you as I would be on any of my students and you must commit one hundred percent."

"I think I can manage," I said, hoping he was kidding about the part where he said he would be tough on me. Gabe told me he would let me rest for the week and that we could start our sessions on Monday. I thanked him and left the gym in search of Riley. It was getting late so I was hoping I could catch her in her room. I tried there first, but her roommate said she was at the library. So that's where I headed next.

I found her sitting at one of the computer tables in the far left corner. I walked over and had a seat in the empty chair next to her. "Hey Riley I —" She put up her finger for me to wait and started mumbling something about how she was almost finished finding something. I closed my mouth and waited patiently. When she was done, she turned to me with her hands folded neatly in her lap.

"Riley, I want to apologize about the other day. I'm so sorry about what happened, I –"

"No need. He said yes," she said, stopping my apology.

"He said yes?" I smiled, excited. Riley nodded, sporting a super grin of her own. "How? When?"

"Well, after you and Roman's little, whatever you want to call it, I didn't know what to say so I just left. Justin came and found me later and told me he'd love to and he even said he wouldn't mind if it was just the two of us," she said giddy.

"Oh my god, Riley, that's awesome. I'm so happy for you! So, you gonna go solo?"

"Oh no, no, no. I still need you guys there."

"Okay, no problem. We'll be there," I assured her and she relaxed. "I'm just glad you're not mad at me."

She looked at me funny. "Why would I be mad at you?"

"Well, I kind of left you to the wolves, no pun intended," I said and she giggled. "And then I hadn't seen you so I thought you were avoiding me."

"No, I've been very busy. What about you? You weren't in powers class today, how come?" I think she might be the only one who hadn't heard the rumors.

"Well, I kind of developed a new power during history class."

"Ella that's great!" she cheered, causing us to get shushed by the Liberian. She looked back to my sour face and lowered her voice. "Ella, why aren't you excited about it?"

"Because I kind of freaked out when it happened. I already have people staring at me because of my blue streak and after freaking out in class I'm now on the top of the list for weirdest person here. I came here hoping to blend in and get lost in the background, but the first month is not even over yet and already I've become the side attraction at the circus."

"Oh, Ella, I'm sorry you feel that way. Here I am all excited about Justin when you're truly hurting and having issues. I'm such a bad friend," she paused and looked at me shyly. "We are friends, right?" she asked, making sure she was using the correct term. "I mean, I like you and I'd like to be your friend. You were one of the first people to actually talk to me and the only one who has been nice to me..." she rambled on and on.

"Riley!" She stopped. Technically, as far as I was concerned, Riley was a friend. Even though we only just met, I knew she was for real.

She was someone who was honest and would be a true friend when you needed her. Not to mention the weird sensation I got to protect her. "Yes, we're friends. And don't worry about it. I always have issues, and I rather talk about you and Justin than my crazy day." I forced a smile and she went into how she has no idea what she's doing, or knows what to wear, or even what movie we should watch. I told her all she would have to worry about was showing up and the girls and I would take care of the rest. I was happy to know my mouth didn't ruin Riley's chance with Justin, but in my defense, Roman started it.

I hung with Riley in the library for a while and she caught me up on what I missed in class. They did breathing techniques like he mentioned on the first day. Oh, how I was disappointed I missed that. Riley noted my sarcasm and lectured me on how the importance of proper breathing is an essential part of having control over your powers. She sounded like she was quoting the teacher verbatim. She even demonstrated the techniques and made me practice them with her, which I did to make her happy.

When I got back to my room Mackenzie was asleep in her bed, thankfully. I changed into my pajamas and climbed into bed. I still didn't know how I managed to stay calm with everything that happened. It seemed like each day was something new and it felt like I was being tested on how well I could handle what they threw at me. If they kept this up this might be one test I fail. I didn't know how much more I could take. I didn't even know how I hadn't totally lost it already.

I woke up the next morning with a slight fear of what was going to happen. To my surprise today was the first normal day since I got here – with the exception of lunch and dinner. Once again, Roman was staring at me and this time Mackenzie caught him. She elbowed him in the ribs and stormed off. I was not looking forward to going back to our room later.

At the end of the day I spent a few hours in the library catching up on my work then retreated to my room for the night. When I got there Mackenzie was still awake. She gave me the silent treatment along with a few of her well-practiced scowls. Not a perfect day, but better and that was good enough for me. There was always tomorrow.

By Friday morning, I was happy it was almost the weekend. That happiness faded when I found Mackenzie standing at the end of my bed wearing her famous, *'I'm pissed off look'*. "Seriously Mackenzie, this whole watching me sleep thing is kind of creeping me out," I said, letting her know I could take on whatever she was about to throw at me.

"Please, I have to sleep with one eye open just to make sure you don't try anything funny," she spat. "I just want you to know, I know what you're up to, and it's not going to work."

"That's funny," I said, scratching my head. "I don't remember scheduling an evil plan against you? Care to fill me in?"

"Don't get smart. You know what I'm talking about," she said, crossing her arms tightly over her little but there chest.

"Clearly I don't. So why don't you just tell me what I did so we can get on with our day."

"Roman," she huffed.

"Roman," I scrunched my brow. "What about Roman?"

"Keep your freak infested paws off of him," she threatened with her hands on her hips.

I started to bust up laughing. "I'm so not interested in Roman. You have nothing to worry about," I said, getting up out of bed. I headed to the bathroom and locked the door behind me before she had a chance to say anything else.

The second I walked into my history class, everyone stopped talking. They all stared and whispered as I made my way to the back of class and sunk down in my seat. They continued to whisper and look over their shoulders at me until Mr. Grant called the class to order. "Alright class, the door is closed. That means quiet," Mr. Grant said.

"Yeah, we wouldn't want Ella to freak out again," Mackenzie said, getting a few chuckles from our classmates.

"That's enough," Mr. Grant yelled, silencing the class. The little bit of happy mood I had left was now completely gone. I was no longer looking forward to the weekend.

To make things more interesting, I forgot I had to sit next to Roman in my next class and we still hadn't talked about the spell we were supposed to come up with. It was a good thing Ms. Kraft had given us a few extra days, although, the way things were going that might not be enough.

After everyone settled into their seats, Ms. Kraft told us we could use today to finish our spells which were due at the end of class. That left Roman and I the rest of class to actually come up with something. With Roman though, you never knew which side of him would show up and I had a feeling getting this project done would not be easy.

While everyone else got together to work on their spells Roman turned to me and asked, "So why'd you wig out the other day in History?"

"You know what, I'd rather not talk about it and frankly, it's none of your business," I said, opening my book and pretending to look something up.

"I guess you want to figure out this whole spell thing on your own than, because unless you tell me, I'm inclined to just sit here and stare at the ceiling," he said, putting his hands behind his head and leaning back in his chair.

"Why do you even care?" I asked, feeling myself getting worked up and annoyed.

"Just curious," he said, still staring at the ceiling.

"Didn't you ever hear the expression curiosity killed the cat?"

He looked down and smiled at me. "I'll take my chances."

"You're really going to just sit there if I don't tell you what happened?"

"Yep," was all he said.

"Fine," I replied, not wanting to fail this project because I got stuck with an asshole partner. "I got a new power and it was a little overwhelming."

"A little overwhelming? You screamed and passed out hitting your head on a desk," he gestured to the now Smurf's band aid that replaced the white gauze. The Smurfs band aid was all Dixon's doing, despite my protest.

"Look, I told you what happened. Now, can we get started?"

"What power did you get?" he asked, not caring that I wasn't comfortable talking about this.

"I recall you saying I only had to tell you what happened and I believe that's what I did." I snapped, feeling my anger grow.

"I changed my mind," he said with a cocky smile, making me glare at him.

"Ella, how are you feeling today? You look well," Ms. Kraft said,

162

interrupting mine and Roman squabble.

"Better, thank you," I answered.

She leaned in close and lowered her voice so only I could hear. "Is the spell still holding up?"

"Yes, yes it is. Thank you again."

"Just so you know the spell is only temporary, but if you would like I could always cast it again," she offered, while resting a kind hand on my shoulder.

"Thank you," I smiled.

She stood up and turned to speak to both Roman and I. "How is the spell coming along?"

"We were just going over the final details," Roman said with his most charming smile.

"And what have you come up with so far?" Ms. Kraft asked curiously.

"It's a surprise," he said. I just smiled and went along with whatever he was saying. You could tell Ms. Kraft wasn't exactly buying his bullshit, but she left us go.

Once she made her way to the front, I turned to Roman and asked, "Do you even have a plan or you just making stuff up as you go?"

"What spell did she do for you?" he asked, indicating he had overheard the private conversation I had with Ms. Kraft.

"Why do you always avoid my questions?"

"Why do you always try to avoid mine?" he countered.

"Because the questions you ask are none of your business," I said with a scowl. Ms. Kraft excused the class, allowing me a small reprieve from Roman.

"Another time then," Roman said, standing up to leave.

"Wait, what about our project?"

"Meet me in the library after dinner," he said, walking out with the project list still in his backpack. The last thing I wanted to do was spend more time with Roman, but we needed to get this project done.

I didn't see Roman at dinner and wondered if we were still on to work on our project. Not wanting to take any chances, I went to the library, deciding that if he didn't show I'd do my own project.

Roman was stretched out at a table in the back eating a

sandwich. "You know, you're not supposed to eat in here. You'll get in trouble," I said as the Liberian came over and handed Roman a book, walking away without another word. "Now how come you didn't get reamed out for that?" I asked, peeved at the fact that she practically ripped me a new one for eating an apple, but didn't blink an eye at Roman.

"What can I say, maybe it's my charming personality?" he smirked.

"I highly doubt that," I frowned, taking a seat. I was ready to get this over with.

"So what's with the blue streak? You tryin' to start a new trend?" he asked, washing his sandwich down with a coke.

"How about we lay off the personal questions and just work on the project," I said in an effort to try and keep things easy.

"How about if I answer one of your questions? Will that make you feel better?"

"What would make me feel better is if we just worked on this project." I opened up my bag and pulled out my notebook.

Roman leaned forward in his chair, his dark, piercing blue eyes engaging mine. "Afraid I'm going to find out your deep, dark secrets?"

I met his gaze, moving closer. "If I were you I'd be more worried about me finding out yours," I warned.

He sat back with a slight disturbed look on his face. "I don't have any secrets," he said.

"Everyone has secrets," I said, knowing all too well. I would almost consider myself an expert on the category.

"Oh, yeah? And you think I'm going to give them up to you?" he said, resuming his normal cocky attitude.

I looked him dead in the eye, his smile breaking. "You don't have to tell me. There are other ways I can find out," I smirked, loving the feeling of making him squirm.

"What are you, like, a mind reader or something?" He joked nervously. When I didn't laugh back, Roman's smile fell. I could tell by the expression on his face he just answered his own question. "You are...that's why you freaked out the other day." I didn't confirm nor deny his suspicion. "Wait, you can't read my mind now can you?" he asked, looking uncomfortable. My guess would be that he was thinking impure thoughts again. He looked like his mom just caught him with a dirty magazine. I got an odd kind of excitement watching him out of his comfort zone.

I thought about seeing how long I could pretend I could read his mind before he realized I couldn't. But then I looked into his eyes and my stomach dropped. Those damn eyes were my weakness. "No, I can't," I said. "The spell Ms. Kraft did was to bind my power until I can figure out how to control it."

Roman just nodded and pushed over the list of spells we could choose from for our project. I guess he decided he didn't want to know any more about me. "I think we should do this one," he said, pointing to the one that read create a flame.

"You're kidding, right? Create a flame as in, like, light a match or rub two sticks together?"

"We're vampires not cavemen," he said, flashing his cocky smile.

"That's to be debated," I mumbled.

"What?" he asked, acting like he didn't hear me.

"Nothing…so care to elaborate on the whole making fire thing?"

The corner of his lip twitched, making his eyes sparkle. He pushed one of the books over to me. "You create a spell to use fire unlike witches who can just conjure it."

"Witches can conjure fire?" I asked, feeling perplexed.

"Some of the most powerful witches can conjure anything, but fire or anything from the elements is the easiest."

"Figures you'd pick something easy," I said, rolling my eyes.

"Actually, this is one of the harder spells."

"You just said –"

He shook his head. "I said conjuring the elements is easy for witches. We have to use spells and still don't come close to what they can do," he clarified.

"When you say the elements, you mean?"

"Earth, air, fire, water, and spirit. Everything we use in our spells comes from the help of these elements. Earth is a big one. We draw a lot of energy from the earth which is why it is so important that we give some back."

I nodded, understanding. Roman was the first person besides Riley who didn't treat me like some weirdo who didn't know anything about this stuff. Most of the students here knew about their heritage as I knew basically nothing. I appreciated him not looking down on me for not understanding something that seemed like a simple known fact. "Okay, so where do we start?" I asked, getting back to the project.

He gave me a half smile and opened up the book the Liberian gave him. "In here it explains how witches can conjure the element and other ways of how to come up with a spell to do it." His arm gently brushed mine, giving me a weird shock. I pulled my arm away quickly and from Roman's expression I'd say he felt it too. "Why don't you look through this book and I'll search this one," he said, flipping through the pages and refusing to look at me.

We sat silently researching the books for an hour before I decided I had enough of the awkwardness. "You never told me what your power is," I said, breaking the silence.

"That's because you never asked."

I fought the urge to roll my eyes. "Well, I'm asking now."

"If I answer than you have to answer one of my questions."

"Fine," I sighed, knowing no way around it.

He leaned back in his chair and waited a moment before he answered. "I can generate power." I just looked at him, waiting for the punch line. "Maybe if I show you," he said, standing up and looking around the area. He walked over to the wall and took down the clock that was hanging there. Then he came back over to the table and placed his hand on the side of the clock. The hands spun around as if he was changing the time.

"Am I supposed to be impressed?" I asked unenthusiastically.

"Fine, you want something bigger?" he said, walking back over to the wall. "You better hold onto your knickers." He smiled, placed his hand on the wall, and closed his eyes. I felt the floor shake and heard a crackling noise, and then the lights went out. "Impressed?" he asked.

"I'll be more impressed if you can turn the lights back on," I said a little panicked.

"What's the matter, afraid of the dark?" he teased.

"Okay, you had your fun. You can turn the lights back on now." He was right, I was afraid of the dark, but I wasn't going to admit that to him. I heard the crackling noise again and then the lights flickered and came back to life. Roman saw the petrified look on my face and came right over to the table and tried to peel my fingers off the back of the chair. I was gripping it so tight my fingers were turning white. "I'm sorry. If I really knew you were afraid of the dark I wouldn't have done that. Are you okay?"

"Yeah," I nodded, rubbing my hands. When I looked back up at him he was wearing an unreadable expression. "What, no witty insults about me being afraid of the dark?" I quipped.

"It's not funny," he said sincerely. "I can warm your hands for you? It might make them feel better." He didn't even give me a chance to answer him. He just took my hands and held them. I felt a slight tingling sensation then warmth. It was soothing and it felt nice. I looked up into his dark blue eyes and I thought I saw something familiar. I couldn't turn my eyes away. I felt trapped in his mesmerizing stare. Suddenly my hands got hot, very hot. I ripped them away from him. "Sorry, I didn't –"

"It's okay," I said. "Maybe we should just get back to the assignment."

"What made you so afraid of the dark?" he asked softly.

"I had too many close encounters with things that go bump in the night," I replied honestly.

"Understandable. What's with the blue streak?"

I dropped my pencil. "So we're back to the fifty questions now?" I asked, not surprised with the sudden change of subject. I think for once he was actually trying to be nice.

"Hey, I said you can ask me a question and I get to ask you one."

"Yes, but that was two questions. It's my turn to ask you one."

"Fine, go ahead," he said, leaning back in his chair.

"What's with the accent?"

"I'm Irish," he said proudly.

"Is it real or just a ploy to get girls?"

"Nope. You only get one. Now it's my turn."

"Fine. No, my blue streak is not a fashion trend. It was a side effect from my powers."

"That's kind of cool. Can I touch it?"

I crinkled my brow at him. "Um...sure?"

He carefully reached up and touched the blue in my hair. He had an awe expression on his face. I thought it would be funny to scare him so I jumped and said boo. He almost fell back out of his seat. I was laughing so hard my eyes started to water. "Ha-ha," he said his ego hurt. "I guess I deserve that for earlier."

His expression shifted. "What?" I asked, wondering if I had something on my face.

"You have a nice laugh."

"Thanks," I said blushing. "Okay, so, accent real or fake?" I asked, trying to distract myself and keep the conversation from turning awkward.

"Real, I was born in Ireland and moved here when I was twelve. Don't believe me? I can prove it to you."

"And how are you going to do that?" I asked, not in the mood for him to do another demonstration.

"You could bite me," he said, his voice shaky.

"What?" I said caught off guard.

"When you bite another –"

"Yeah, yeah, I know all that," I said, shocked that he would even suggest that.

"Have you ever bitten someone?"

"No," I snapped, turning back to my books.

"Ever have someone bite you?" he asked in a hushed voice, moving closer to me. I felt that electric pulse again and moved away from him. What kind of girl did he think I was?

"We're getting off track here," I said, shuffling through the pages and feeling the heat rise in my cheeks.

"Right, maybe we should take a break," he offered.

"Good idea."

"I'm going to go outside and have a smoke. You can join me if you want?" he smiled.

"I rather drink tar, but thanks," I said. "And why do you smoke anyways? I would think someone with such a stellar reputation wouldn't want to tarnish it."

"Maybe that's exactly why I do it," he said with a wink.

I got up to look for some books. I didn't even know what I was looking for. I walked through the stacks checking out all the different books when I saw a familiar face. I thought I was hallucinating. "Kyle?"

I closed my eyes and shook my head. When I opened them he was gone. *What the hell is going on?* I was starting to think that maybe being in the library alone was not a good idea. When I returned to the table I found Aidan searching through our papers. "Hey Mr. I mean Aidan."

"Hey Ella," he said a little startled. "Working on homework?" he asked, running his fingers over the books.

"A project," I said. "Is there something wrong?" I asked, wondering why he was here.

"No. Just wanted to see how you were doing?" he said with a half-smile.

"Do you check on all your students to see how they're doing?" I walked around him, getting a warm, fuzzy feeling. I touched my stomach to try and calm the erratic flip flops it was doing.

"Only the ones that I feel need to be checked on," he said, reaching for my hand.

I pulled away. "Do I have a ticking time bomb on my head or something?" I was annoyed at everyone thinking I was going to snap.

"No," he said defensively. "I just know how it can be being the new student and...different."

"How am I any different from anyone else?" I was tired of being considered the outsider when all I wanted was to be normal.

"Ella, that's not what I meant," he took a step closer to me. "It's just that I...I..."

I felt an odd pull to him. I closed the distance between us, placing a hand on his chest. I looked up into his eyes. "Aidan," I whispered when Roman came back into the room.

I jumped away as Aidan took a big step back. "If you need any help with your project I'll be more than happy to help," he told us.

"Thanks, but I think we got it," Roman said curtly, making me wonder what crawled up his butt.

"Well, if you need me I'll be in my office," Aidan told us, but I knew he was directing the comment at me. He gave me a sly smile before he left.

Roman sat down at the table angrily flipping through pages. He buried his head in the books and refused to look at me. "What's wrong with you?" I asked, perplexed by his sudden attitude change.

He didn't answer. Instead he slammed the books shut and stood up. "You know what, I think I'm done for the night." He stuffed all his papers in his backpack and took off.

"But what about our project?" I called too late. He was already gone. What the hell just happened? He was fine a few minutes ago and then when he came back and saw Aidan...that was it, it had to be Aidan, but why was Roman upset with Aidan? Not wanting to be in the library alone, I packed up my stuff and left.

The cool blast from the outside air gave me access to what just happened. For some reason I always felt an odd warming sensation from Aidan's nearness which also caused strange flutters in my stomach. Roman shocked me when our skin touched. This wasn't some static electricity either, this was something different. Two completely different guys causing two completely different reactions when in contact and even though I'm aware of all this I still have no idea what any of it means.

I zipped up my jacket, pulled up my hood, and tightened my scarf to help keep away the bitter cold. Instead of going back to my room I decided to go see Aidan in his office. With everything that was happening lately I did need someone to talk to and Aidan did say his door was always open if I needed to talk. Of the few people I could trust, I knew in my gut Aidan was one of them.

When I arrived at his office everything was quiet. I didn't see anyone around and assumed we must be the only two people here. But just in case I was wrong, I knocked on the door. "Ella, come in," he said.

"How'd you know it was me?" I asked, dropping my hood and loosening my scarf.

"Your smell. You have a distinct smell," he said, throwing me a sweet smile.

"Don't we all though?"

"Well, yes, but yours is different. That's how I knew you were at the library."

I didn't even think to ask how he knew I was there. "Is that bad?" This wasn't the first time someone had said this to me and I was starting to wonder if I stink.

"No," he laughed, like he knew what I was thinking. "It's actually a very nice smell, almost intoxicating."

"Oh," I blushed.

"So, what brings you down here?" he asked as he stuffed some files away in a cabinet.

"I was hoping maybe I could talk to you?" I was feeling a little sheepish. After saying it out loud I wasn't so sure this was a good idea.

"Sure, what would you like to talk about?"

"How much time do you have?" I said semi kidding.

He smiled and gestured for me to have a seat. He made himself comfortable in the chair adjacent to mine. I took off my jacket and scarf, draping them over the back of the chair before I took a seat. "What's on your mind?"

"I think I'm having a hard time adjusting to everything," I said, looking down at my over picked cuticles.

"That's understandable. No one expects you to be perfect, and it's a lot to take in at first. Just give it some time and you'll get there."

He sounded just like my mom. I fought the urge to roll my eyes. I took a breath, reminding myself he was just trying to help. "It's not just that. I mean, I don't want to sound like a whiny kid, but all the other students stare at me because I'm different. They gawk at the blue streak in my hair and not to mention all the recent whispers and stares from the rumors about what happened in my history class."

"They'll understand when they receive their powers," he said comfortingly.

"And I feel like I'm the only one who doesn't know anything about anything!" I snapped, letting it all out.

"Ella, it's okay," he said, placing his hand on top of mine. "And not everyone here knows everything. Some students are just as clueless as you are," he winked, letting me know he was teasing.

"Thanks," I laughed, feeling somewhat better. I started to get that fluttering feeling again. I self-consciously tucked a piece of hair behind my ear. I knew he was watching which just made my cheeks flush hot.

"I like your blue streak," he said, reaching up to stroke my hair. I felt a small shiver as his hand gently grazed my cheek. I looked up and our eyes locked. Before I could stop myself my lips were on his. I had no idea what came over me, but I just had the need to touch him, to kiss him, to feel his lips on mine. To my surprise he didn't pull away horrified or push me back. Instead he kissed me back.

His lips were sweet and tender, but his kiss was a hungry one encouraging me to engage with him more. I pushed him back on the chair and straddled his lap. I had never felt a desire like this before. I wanted to tear his clothes off the instant our lips met. He grabbed my hips and pulled me tighter to his body. I moaned with pleasure as I ran my fingers through his hair.

I couldn't seem to get enough of him. I knew this was wrong. I knew I shouldn't be doing this, but I couldn't seem to stop. It was like some strange force had pulled us together. Like magnets, unable to separate.

The urge became more pressing the more we kissed. Aidan pulled my shirt up over my head. His hot breath caressed my skin as his lips trailed down my neck and across my breasts. I tilted my head back engulfed in the pleasure. I grabbed his face, attacking his mouth as he thrust his hips into mine, causing us both to groan.

Aidan's lips glided back down to my neck. I felt a small prick and then a pinch as his teeth slid into my skin. "No stop!" I yelled and he quickly pulled away.

"I'm sorry. I didn't mean to. I thought…" he trailed off.

"I have to go," I said, suddenly embarrassed. I got up, grabbed my shirt, and slid it back on.

"Wait, Ella, you don't have to go." He touched my arm and I felt that same rush of desire I felt a few minutes ago.

I quickly pulled away before it was too late. "I'm sorry. I have to go. This was a mistake. I shouldn't have come here," I said as I rushed out the door. No further explanation. I ran down the hall, down the stairs. I ran until I reached the outside and then I stopped to catch my breath. I ran out of there so fast I forgot to grab my coat and scarf. I was freezing now, but I'd take the risk of walking back in the cold then going back to his office to get my things.

I covered my face with my hands. What the hell was wrong with me? "Ella!" I turned to catch Aidan running out the door.

"Aidan, I'm sorry. I don't know what happened, I…"

"It's okay," he said.

"No, it's not. That was very inappropriate and –"

He stopped me. "Ella," he said, softly wrapping my scarf around my neck and then helping me put my coat on. He gently grazed my cheek.

I grabbed his hand and held it out in front of me. "I have to go," I said, not able to face him at the moment. He didn't argue with me this time.

On my way back to my room I pondered what just happened. I still didn't understand any of it. One minute I was stressing out about school, the next I was straddling my teacher. My head was still spinning from the rush of his kiss. I touched my still tingling lips. *Damn it Ella.* I mentally cursed myself. My teenage hormones were screaming *YES!* While the small functioning part of my brain was whispering no. I quieted the screams by reminding myself that he was a teacher. This was a mistake and could not happen again. I did not need another complication in my life. Sighing, I pulled open the door to my dorms.

CHAPTER FOURTEEN

I rushed up the stairs in my dorm, battling the angel and devil on my shoulders. I threw open the door to my room, slamming it shut behind me before I could change my mind and turn around. I blinked in surprise. "What are you doing here?" I asked winded. Roman was the last person I expected to see after the way he stormed out of the library.

"I'm waiting for Mackenzie. She went to get us something to drink," he said, seeming in a better mood.

"Well, you guys can't stay here. This is my room too and I don't want to sit here while you two make out," I said snippy. I wasn't in the mood to deal with his multiple personalities and frankly I was tired of him being nice one minute then an asshole the next.

"What's your problem?" he asked, getting up.

"I'd just like to be able to come back to my room and not have to deal with you," I said, unwrapping my scarf, and tossing it on the bed along with my coat.

"What happened to your neck?"

I quickly put my hand over the little bit of blood that was dripping. I had forgotten about Aidan taking a bite. "Nothing, mind your own business," I snapped.

"It's kind of hard to when you just put it out there like that," he growled.

"What are you saying?"

"I think you know," he said accusingly. If I didn't know any better I'd say he was jealous considering our earlier conversation.

"You don't know anything about me," I said defensively.

"I know enough. I've seen your type before." He gave me a disgusted look and it took everything I had not to slug him.

"Get out!" I yelled, pushing him in the direction of the door. "You
174

are not welcome in here."

"It's not just your room." He stood there with his arms crossed, waiting for me to challenge him.

"Fine, when I'm here you're not welcome. So get out!" I shouted, tired of this banter. I had enough of Roman's mood swings for the day.

"Fine, I don't know why I even bother," he said, slamming the door behind him.

I took a breath to calm my nerves, then I went into the bathroom to check out my neck. It wasn't too bad, but I was definitely going to have to hide the marks until they healed. I cleaned off the little bit of blood that was left and opted for a skin colored band aid instead of the bright colorful ones Dixon had supplied me with. I pulled my hair over my shoulder to avoid any more questions from prying eyes.

I splashed some cold water on my face and stared at my reflection in the mirror. I couldn't get the argument with Roman out of my head. What was his deal? Why was he always in my business and why did he even care? I never met anyone who was so irritating. The worst part about all of this was that there was no way to avoid him. I had two classes with him and he was *'dating'* my roommate. *Why does everything have to be so difficult?*

When I opened the bathroom door, I found Mackenzie on the other side with her hands on hips and a scowl on her face. "This is my room too and you can't kick my boyfriend out," she hissed.

"Yes I can. It's ten o'clock and I want to go to sleep. If you don't like it then tough shit," I said, not in the mood for her right now.

"I'm going to Mr. Callahan right now and —"

"And what? Tell him that you're pissed because I kicked your boyfriend out and now you can't spread your herpes."

"I don't have herpes!" she scoffed.

"You know what, I don't care. I'm tired and want to go to sleep. So you can leave too. I'm now declaring this time as *MY* alone time," I said, climbing into bed forgetting I was still in my clothes, but didn't care because I was making a point.

"Gladly, you're pathetic. What kind of loser goes to bed at ten on a Friday anyways," she said stomping off. "And this isn't over. You will pay for this later."

I had no doubt about that.

After she left, I got up and changed into my pajamas. Then I turned off the lights, climbed back into bed, and pulled the covers up over my head.

I had the dream again where I was in the maze. I searched in and out, spinning around in circles, going around countless turns, and just like last time...nothing. It ended the same. With me face to face with Jack.

I tossed and turned all night. In between the nightmares with Jack I also dreamed about Aidan. I dreamed that we were together, intimately, and Roman had walked in on us ending the dream.

I woke up sometime in the morning. I wasn't clear on the time, but by the blinding light of the sun I would guess it was late morning. I looked around the room to discover I was alone. Relieved for the moment, I pulled back the covers, and stood, stretching my arms above my head. I then headed to the bathroom where I proceeded to take a nice, long, hot shower.

I let the water run for a while, allowing the steam to fill up the tiny room. I stood in the shower thinking about the dreams with Aidan. I thought about the way I felt in his arms, the way he kissed me, the extreme need and yearning to be with him. I stuck my head in the stream of water to try and wash away these feelings. This was wrong. He was a teacher and headmaster. A relationship with him could get him fired if anyone found out, but it might be worth it. No, no, I needed to stop. I needed to forget about him. He probably thought I was just some sex-crazed teenager and wanted nothing to do with me. I wouldn't be surprised if he tried to avoid me at all costs.

I sighed as I got out of the shower. I ringed the excess water out of my hair, wrapped a towel around my body, and stepped out of the bathroom only to jump back a foot. "Seriously...what the hell?" I said, glaring at Roman.

"Nice towel," he replied with a cocky smile.

"Get out!" I said, pointing to the door.

"Relax, I just came by to drop this off," he said, laying a note book on my bed. I narrowed my eyes and held my towel tighter against me as he eyed me up and down. "Cute tat," he said, looking at my foot as I self-consciously covered it up with my other foot. Before I had the chance to yell at him again to get out he took off.

I locked the door behind him and picked up the notebook he left on the bed. It was our project. Finished. Inside was a note that read:

I finished the spell, but don't worry I'll tell Ms. Kraft we both did equal work and I left detailed instructions on how I came up with the spell and how it works.

I looked through the notes and saw that's exactly what he did. I couldn't believe he did all that work by himself. Either he felt bad for leaving abruptly yesterday or he just can't stand to spend any more time with me than he has to. I assumed it was the latter and stuffed the notes in my backpack until I could look them over later.

I quickly dried my hair and pulled it into a low ponytail on the side to cover up the marks on my neck. Then I threw on some jeans and a sweater and was out the door. Cameron and Sienna weren't first year students and had permission to leave campus for a few hours. They went ahead and asked Mr. Callahan if Riley and I were allowed to go along with them. I wasn't there when they asked, but was told he said it was fine as long as we took Gabe with us.

We decided to take Riley shopping for an outfit for her to wear tonight. Riley came from a big family and got stuck with her sister's hand-me-downs. She told me they didn't have a lot of money, but they learned to get by with what they had and were happy with the little they got. So given the opportunity to help someone out I jumped at the chance. I told Riley this shopping trip was on me and I wouldn't take no for an answer. I knew she didn't want to seem to over excited, but I could see it in her eyes that she was ecstatic. She had told me people aren't normally nice to her like this and she wasn't sure how to act. I just told her to have fun and not to worry about anything.

I was glad to get off campus and into some normal civilization. Cameron had said there was a town about an hour and half away where they actually had some decent shops, unlike the dilapidated town I saw on my way here.

We met Gabe in the parking garage. I could tell he wasn't too happy about spending the day shopping with a bunch of girls, but he didn't complain. I was just about to hop in the car when Cameron bumped me on the shoulder. "What is Mr. Callahan doing here?" she asked.

I looked up and froze when I spotted him, unsure how to act or what to say. "It's a new rule this year. When any student leaves campus they must be accompanied by a teacher," Gabe said as he opened the door for Riley and Sienna. I wondered if this new rule had anything to do with me. I wouldn't put it past my father to do something like that.

"Morning ladies," Aidan greeted as he approached the vehicle.

"Morning Mr. Callahan. If you want you can sit in the back with me," Cameron purred.

He smiled politely at her and said, "Thank you, but I believe it will be better if I sit in the front."

"Your loss," Cameron said, shrugging her shoulders. I walked to the back to get in almost bumping into Aidan. We did an awkward dance around each other. I avoided looking directly at him. I rolled my eyes at my own stupidity and hopped into the back with Cameron.

Once on the road, Cameron and Sienna talked about all the shops they were going to hit and even convinced Riley to get her hair and makeup done. I zoned out shortly after that and ended spending most of the ride staring at the back of Aidan's head. I wondered what he was thinking – if he volunteered to come along or was forced to because no one else wanted to. I stared so long I knew every curve of his head. The way his hair laid nicely against his head, the small cowlick he had on the left. The way the sunlight hit it just right making it look like he had highlights.

"Ella?" Riley interrupted.

"Hmm?"

"I said what do you think?"

"About what?"

"Gee whiz Ella, you need to stop spending so much time in la-la land," Riley said rolling her eyes. "Justin asked if he could bring a friend and I wanted to know if I should say yes."

"That depends, is it a *girl-friend* or a *boy-friend*?" I asked.

"Hold on I'll ask," she said, opening her phone to text him back.

"NO!" Cameron and Sienna said at the same time. Riley looked at them confused.

"You don't want to seem jealous," Cameron stated.

"How would that make me jealous?"

"Just tell him it's fine," I said. After a lengthy debate whether or not she should tell Justin he could bring a friend, I tried my hardest to pay attention this time. I only lasted about five minutes before my mind wandered back to Aidan.

"So Ella, any guys on campus that tickle your fancy?" Cameron asked.

My eyes quickly gazed over Aidan before I replied, "No."

"Oh, come on. No one, not one?"

"Nope."

"What about Roman?"

"What about him?" I said, trying to keep my anger in check. Just the thought of him made my blood pressure rise.

"You don't think he's good looking? You have to at least admit that accent is super sexy. He's also the sweetest guy…"

I stopped her there. "Okay first, he's dating my roommate and your stepsister, which automatically gives him negative points."

"I know but I can tell it's not serious and I'd be more than happy to steer him in the right direction if a certain someone was interested," she hinted.

"Sorry to disappoint but I'm not your girl. That boy has more mood swings then a chick with PMS," I said.

"Okay, are we talking about the same guy?"

"Unfortunately yes," I said, biting my tongue.

"Well, that doesn't sound like the Roman I know," she said a little defensively.

"That's because the Roman you know and the one I know are two different people," I said a little bitterly.

Before Cameron could dispute it Sienna jumped in. "Well, you know what they say, boys always tease the ones they like," Sienna said, leaning over the seat. I rolled my eyes and went back to daydreaming about Aidan. Closing my eyes, I envisioned our last encounter together. The way his lips felt on mine, his hands moving all over my body, caressing every inch of my skin.

"I think she's drooling," Sienna giggled.

"Look at that smile on her face. I think she's having a sex dream," Cameron whispered.

"What?" I asked groggily.

"We're here," Riley said blushing.

"You've got a little something right there," Cameron said, pointing to my chin and laughing. I felt my face get hot as I wiped my mouth on my sleeve. I hadn't realized I had fallen asleep.

We all got out of the car and crossed the street to the mini strip mall. We hit store after store and in each one the girls threw clothes at Riley to try on. Cameron had her try tons of outfits that were kind of slutty and Sienna had her try on stuff that was cutesy and childlike, which worked for Sienna, but not Riley. I could tell Riley was getting frustrated so I stepped in to help her out. I found her a nice pair of jeans and a cute top that suited her. She cringed at the price, but I reminded her she didn't need to worry about it.

While the girls went and got their hair done, I went across the street to grab a coffee. I opted not to have my hair done. I didn't feel like answering questions about my weird blue streak. I also needed a break from Aidan. The more time I spent around him the more I wanted to jump on him and kiss him.

I went with a small coffee since my nerves were already on edge. "I got that," Aidan said from behind me, handing the cashier money. I stiffened, feeling my stomach flutter.

I took a calming breath before I turned around to face him. "Thank you," I said as he collected his change.

"No problem." He stuffed his wallet in his back pocket. "I wanted to talk to you, if that's okay?" He gestured to one of the tables by the window. I nodded and followed him over to one of the high top tables. I took a seat across from him, rubbing my hands nervously under the table as I waited for him to start the conversation. He didn't say anything right away and I was wondering if he wanted me to say something first.

"About last night," he started.

"I was out of line. I'm sorry. You don't have to worry. I promise it will never happen again," I spit out quickly, hoping to avoid the embarrassment of him trying to come up with an easy let down.

"Oh," he said.

I sat up. I wasn't expecting that. "Oh?" I echoed.

"Well, I was going to tell you I was out of line and I'm sorry, but..." he looked up into my eyes. "I don't regret it. I'm happy it happened," he smiled, making my heart beat double time.

I didn't know what to say. I was speechless.

"I know what you're thinking. You're a student and I'm a teacher and this shouldn't have happened. But it did and I'm not sorry about it. I like you Ella and I feel a certain way when I'm around you."

"Me too," I confessed.

Aidan grinned and reached under the table to hold my hand. The small sentiment made me blush and feel warm inside. "I know we couldn't have a normal relationship, but we could try?"

"How, no one could know about it? You'd get in trouble for dating a student."

"That's why it would be our little secret," he winked, squeezing my hand. "Let's just take it one step at a time."

"We should probably get back," I said. He squeezed my hand one more time before he let go. I couldn't believe he felt the same way I did. I still didn't understand why I had such a strong pull to him. I was just happy he felt the same way about me as I did him. I was also hoping that we could have a repeat of last night.

I quickly pulled Aidan aside before we stepped into the salon to meet the others. "So, when will we be able to be together?"

"Hmm, how about you stop by my office tonight and I think we can come up with something," he winked and gave me a quick kiss when no one was looking. I smiled sheepishly as he opened the door for me.

I sat with Aidan and Gabe in the lounge area while we waited for the girls to be finished. Five magazines later and several stolen glances from Aidan, the girls were done. They had straightened Riley's unruly hair and got rid of that headband she wears to try and control it. They replaced the headband with a small sparkly clip and the only makeup she wore was a light pink eye shadow with clear mascara and a soft pink lip-gloss which I thought was the perfect choice.

"Riley, you look amazing!"

"Really Ella, you like it?" she asked unsure.

"I love it!"

"Me too," she admitted. "But don't get used to it. There's no way I could do this myself."

"I can help you with that. Trust me. I know what it's like to have unruly hair," I smiled. "And I love that lip-gloss."

"Thanks, Gabe picked it out," she said.

I turned to Gabe eyes wide. He coughed uncomfortably. "I just simply suggested less is more," he said. I laughed which made Gabe turn red in the face.

"Don't worry, your secret is safe with me," I told him.

He leaned down smiling wickedly and whispered, "Don't forget we start training on Monday."

Crap.

I turned back to Riley and asked her, "Did you ask what lip-gloss they used so you can get some to take with you?"

"Sienna already got it for me," she said.

"And what about hair care products?"

"Oh I," she stammered.

"Well, you'll need stuff to keep up with the do. Excuse me?" I said to one of the stylist. "Can you please help her pick out some products and one of your best flat irons?"

"Oh, no Ella. You've done enough I can't," Riley protested.

"We'll make this one on me or should I say daddy," Cameron smiled, handing the cashier a credit card.

"You guys, thank you so much. I don't know how I could ever repay you."

"I have a history report coming up," Cameron said. Aidan cleared his throat reminding her that he was there. "Just kidding," she smiled and leaned in closer to Riley. "We'll talk later."

"What Cameron means is you don't owe us anything," I said, frowning at her. Cameron rolled her eyes and went back to charging things on her dad's account. "We are happy to help you out," I reassured Riley.

"Yeah, I love shopping for other people as much as I love shopping for myself," Sienna said.

Once we got back to the school I was in a much better mood. "Ella, would you please meet me in my office so we can go over your schedule?" Aidan said winking at me.

"Are you changing your schedule?" Cameron asked.

I drew a blank on how to answer. Aidan jumped in and answered for me. "No, we just want to see if we can fit in some extra classes she might be interested in taking," he said and I nodded. I said my goodbyes and quickly dropped off the few items I bought and then headed right over to Aidan's office. Since it was Saturday, the offices were empty. I knocked on the door lightly just before letting myself in, just in case. Aidan looked up from his desk at my entrance and smiled brightly as he told me to lock the door behind me.

"So, what exactly do you have planned?" I asked as I clicked the lock. Before I could even turn around he was behind me wrapping his arms around my waist. I sighed, feeling content and leaned back into him putting my arms over his.

"I've wanted to do this all day," he said, turning me around and kissing me. I slipped my arms around his neck and pulled him closer, savoring the kiss. He pulled back, took my hand in his, and led me over to the couch. I sat down on his lap and started to kiss him again.

It wasn't long before he pushed me down on the couch and climbed on top of me. My skin began to tingle as he slid his hand under my shirt. When he was kissing me, it was hard for me to keep my hands off of him. I didn't understand it. It was a different feeling, like nothing I felt with anyone else. I knew it wasn't love. I felt more of a need to just have him touch me and that need grew stronger every time I was with him. I started to unbutton his shirt while he kissed my neck. Once his shirt was off, it didn't take long for the rest of our clothes to follow. His hand slid down to my hips and he started to tug at my underwear. "Aidan...wait," I said breathless.

"You want to stop?" he asked.

"No," I said. And I didn't, which was the weird part. "I'm just...I'm...I'm a virgin," I confessed, a little embarrassed.

He flashed his dimples and gently tucked a piece of hair behind my ear, exposing the faded bite mark he left from last night. "It's okay, we can stop," he said, tracing the bite mark with his finger. "There are other things we can do."

"Except that," I said, pushing him away from me.

"What's wrong?" he asked concerned.

"It's just," I couldn't believe I was about to say this. "The last time someone bit me, it was to steal information from me."

"Oh, Ella, I had no idea."

"I'm surprised it wasn't in my file," I said sarcastically.

He chuckled softly and pulled me into him. "Ella, just having you here in my arms is good enough for me."

"Yeah, you say that now, but just wait."

He laughed again. "I will wait as long as you need."

"Now when you say a thing like that it makes it hard for me to resist you," I said, turning my head so I could nibble on his neck. I could see his pulse pounding and I could hear the flow of blood pumping in his veins. I started to lick my lips at the thought of sinking my teeth into his skin.

"Go ahead. It's okay. I know you want to," he said, his voice weak.

I pulled back. "I...I never. I wouldn't even know how?"

"It will just come to you naturally. Trust me," he said, tilting his head to the side.

"I don't know? What if I can't stop?"

"I trust you," he said, kissing my lips gently.

I wanted to, but I was nervous. I could feel it inside me, the ache for it, the thirst. I bent down and the sound of his blood flowing caused my fangs to appear. I could feel the draw of the blood calling to me. I was about to sink my teeth into his neck when there was a knock on the door. The tapping scared me. I flinched, accidently nicking his neck with my teeth. "Sorry," I said.

"Mr. Callahan?" The person on the other side of the door called.

"Who is that?"

"I don't know, but you have to hide," he said.

"What?"

"Do you have any other suggestions?"

"Yeah, don't answer it," I said, struggling to get my clothes back on.

"Who is it?" Aidan asked.

"Mr. Callahan, it's Roman. I'm here to drop off those papers you asked for."

"Right, just give me a second," he said, pushing me into the closet and throwing my clothes at me. I couldn't believe I was actually hiding out in the closet like some harlot. I prayed this didn't take too long. It suddenly got really hot. I started to fan myself. I felt like the walls were closing in on me and I couldn't breathe. Crap, this was not good.

I heard Aidan open the office door and let Roman in.

"What can I do for you?" Aidan asked.

"I just wanted to drop off these papers that you asked me to have Gabe sign about our extra training sessions."

"Right, I'll take those," he said, reaching for the papers.

I couldn't take it anymore. I felt like I was suffocating. I thought maybe if I could just get the door open a crack, let some air in, but when I did the door creaked. Roman turned his head toward the closet and I froze, holding my breath.

Aidan took the papers from Roman, distracting him. "Thanks Roman. Anything else I can help you with?"

"No," he said, turning his head back to the closet.

"Okay then. Sorry to hurry you along, but I'm kind of busy," Aidan said, pushing Roman out the door.

Roman turned back to Aidan. "What happened to your neck?"

"Huh?"

"Your neck. It's bleeding?"

"Oh, I cut myself shaving," Aidan said quickly. Not sure if Roman bought it or not, but he left. Aidan closed the door behind him and locked it. Then he opened the door to the closet and I leapt out gasping for air. "Are you claustrophobic?" he asked.

"I would guess so. Never been in a small confined space before," I said, trying to catch my breath. "That was close. We need to be more careful."

"We'll have to find another place to meet."

"Yeah, but where?" I asked, worried that we were kidding ourselves about finding a way to make this work.

"Don't worry, we'll figure this out," he said, cupping my face and pressing his lips to mine.

I had to force myself to pull away. "I have to watch a movie with my friends tonight, but afterwards we can meet, by the fountain? I can call you?"

"No need. I can see the fountain from my room. I'll watch and wait for you," he said, kissing me one last time before I left.

I couldn't stop smiling as I walked out of the teachers' dorms. My head was rushing from my time spent with Aidan. I was so out of it I didn't even notice Roman when I stepped outside. "Hey," he said.

I jumped back startled. "Christ Roman, stalk much?" I said, clutching my over beating heart. "What are you doing out here?"

"I was about to ask you the same thing," he said accusingly.

"Not that it's any of your business, but I had to talk to Mr. Callahan about my schedule."

"I was just there. I didn't see you."

"I went to talk to Gabe afterwards," I said, walking away. I didn't feel the need to justify my actions to him.

Roman reached out and grabbed my arm, stopping me. "You're lying!" he spat.

"Let go of me," I growled, struggling to pull my arm free. "You're hurting me!" I said, cringing at the tight grip he had on my arm. When he saw the scared look on my face he finally let go. I glared at him.

"He's just using you," he said, his voice pained.

"What are you talking about?" I asked, rubbing my sore arm.

"Mr. Callahan," he said like I should have known. "Once he gets you into bed he'll discard you."

"I don't know what you're talking about. There's nothing going on between me and Mr. Callahan," I spat defensively. Roman gripped my shoulders, getting in my face. There was an intense glow in his eyes. "Roman, you're scaring me," I said. His hands tightened just before he let go.

I stood there not knowing what to do or say.

I closed my eyes and tried to steady my erratic heart. By the time my pulse had slowed, Roman was gone. "What the hell?" I ran a shaky hand through my hair and walked back to the dorms. What a mess I had gotten myself into. I was messing around with a teacher and Roman, the last person I would want to know about it already has his suspicions. How did I even get myself into these situations?

When I finally got back to my room the door was locked. Not in the mood, I pounded and kicked the door. My run in with Roman had put me in a sour mood causing me to take it out on Mackenzie. "Mackenzie! Open the door!" She wouldn't answer which pissed me off even more. "Open! The door!" I yelled.

She swung the door open in a huff. "What the fuck is your problem?"

"My problem is that I'm stuck with you as a roommate."

"The feelings mutual," she said, slamming the door in my face.

I pushed the door back open and she glared at me. She had her friends Addyson and Madison with her. "What are you doing?"

"This is my room too. You can't keep me out of it."

"I gave you a schedule," she said, crossing her arms.

"You know what you can do with your schedule? You can take it and shove it up your ass!" All the girls gawked at me like they couldn't believe I was actually standing up to Mackenzie. Just to piss her off even more, I sat on my bed, took out a book, and pretended to read.

"You're just going to sit there?" she scoffed.

"Yep."

I knew Mackenzie was getting really pissed off, but tried not to let it show. She only lasted about five minutes before she gave up and stormed out with her friends. "Mission accomplished," I said to myself, smiling. Now that I had the room to myself I decided to get some studying done. I thought maybe now would be a good time to learn all the basic things I should know. So I pulled out my books and got to work.

CHAPTER FIFTEEN

The first thing I decided to look up was the whole drinking blood thing. After finding the freezer full of blood bags and the way I felt right before I was about to bite Aidan's neck, I needed to know what the deal was.

I flipped through my book until I came to a chapter that was titled blood lust. I started at the top of the page. It stated that over time we did need blood to survive but we weren't completely dependent on it. Full vampires did need to drink more blood regularly than half-breeds. I think I now knew what that secret storage locker in our wine cellar was. No wonder my dad always threatened a loss of limbs if we went anywhere near it. I shuddered at the thought.

I followed down the page and read more. Drinking blood was what helped strengthen our powers. Without it our powers could weaken or fade completely. Normally a vampire would not need to start consuming blood until a year after they had come into their powers. The blood lust was then at its highest because our powers were usually fully developed by this then.

My head was spinning from all this new information. "So, we do drink blood. Okay, gross." Although, I didn't think it was all that gross just a moment ago when I was about to bite Aidan's neck. I closed the book and put my head, taking a deep breath before I continued. I needed to know this. I couldn't keep being left in the dark about this. This was who I was. I had to face it. I was about to open the book back up when there was a knock on the door.

I reluctantly got up to answer it. "Hey, Ella."

"Hey Riley."

"I'm not bugging you am I?"

"No. I was just doing some research," I said.

"You want some help?" she offered.

If anyone could explain this to me it would be Riley. "Actually yes."

"Great," she said, excited to help. "What are you working on?"

"Well, I was trying to figure out about...us." She crinkled her brow at me. "Us as in vampires," I clarified.

"Ah, I see. So what have you learned so far?"

"I only got to the part about the blood lust."

She nodded, going right into study mode. "Well, I don't know everything, but I do know some things. So maybe we can learn together."

"That would be nice," I said smiling, happy to have some help.

"I can tell you you don't have to worry about the whole blood lust thing until later. That's something they teach us next year." I wanted to tell her she was wrong, but I still didn't understand why I felt this way and I couldn't tell her about Aidan.

Riley took the book from me and flipped through the pages. "How about we start here," she said, pointing to the part about our powers. We read the first few pages together, then went over them. We learned that not all vampires have powers, but those that didn't made up for it in other areas. For example, those without powers had better senses; sight, sound, and smell. They also possessed great strength and speed. Even though all vampires have heightened abilities the ones without special gifts are stronger.

We also learned that most of our powers came from our bloodline, but it has been found that sometimes a combination of different powers can create a whole new one. That would explain why I was the only one in my family who could heal. We read on to learn that full vampires are known for their strength and that was why most of them became guardians. It also talked about how each creature had their own distinct smell and over time we would learn how to tell each other apart. The more I read the more it went into things I already knew; how alcohol lessened our powers and lack of use could weaken them. Most of what Tristan had told me.

I sighed, a little frustrated. "Why don't we take a break here," Riley suggested. "Most of this we'll learn in history anyways."

"Good idea. I could use a break," I said, lying back on my bed.

"Is there something else bothering you Ella?" she asked quietly.

Yes I wanted to say, but I still thought I couldn't talk to Riley about it, not yet.

"You know you can talk to me about anything? I promise I won't tell anyone or judge."

"I know Riley, thanks, but I just don't think I'm ready to talk about it yet."

"I'm here for you whenever you're ready," she smiled.

"How about we get something to eat. I'm starving," I said, rubbing my grumbling belly.

"I don't know if I can eat. I'm too nervous about tonight."

"You should still eat something," I said, pulling her off the bed.

Riley picked at her food while I scarfed down three big slices of pizza. "Damn Ella you sure can put it away," Austin said as I started to stuff my face with fries. "Did they not feed you at home?"

"Uh, have you met Dean?" I said, washing my fries down with a coke. "Him plus our other brother Xander, I was fighting for scraps," I laughed.

"Dean is a pig. I've never seen anyone eat as much as he does, well, until I met you," Cameron joked. "Must be something in the water."

"What's with the triplet's?" Sienna asked, taking a seat.

"Triplet's?" I asked.

"Mackenzie, Addyson, and Madison. We call them the triplets because they're basically attached at the hip. Where you find one of them you'll find the other two," Reagan said, making Sienna blush.

"Aren't you dating one of them?" I asked him.

"Addyson, but just because I'm dating her it doesn't mean I always agree with what they do," he admitted to my surprise.

"What do you mean, what they do?"

"They're known for their evil plots to destroy people they don't like."

"And they look like they're up to some evil plotting right now," Cameron said eyeing them.

"They're definitely up to something. I could feel that they were channeling a lot of power," Sienna said worried.

"I feel bad for the person who pissed them off," Austin said.

"So, what would happen to so said person?" I gulped, having a pretty good idea who this person was. Everyone turned to look at me with wide eyes.

"Ella, what did you do?" Dean said annoyed.

"I didn't do anything," I said warily.

"Nice knowing ya," was Austin's reply.

"It can't be that bad, right?" No one dared to look at me or give me an answer, besides Dean whom I'm pretty sure thought he had to bail me out of another mess. I ignored his glare and looked over my shoulder at Mackenzie who had a sadistic look in her eye.

Great.

"Don't worry about them Ella. We won't let them do anything to you," Cameron said while Sienna and Dixon nodded their heads in agreement. I spared one more glance over my shoulder for Mackenzie. Then I went back to my dinner. Once I was finished, I went back to my room to change for the movie.

I met everyone in the social room on my floor. It turned out the friend Justin wanted to bring was the guy with the Justin Bieber Haircut.

Fantastic.

Riley Joined me, staying glued to my side. When Justin caught sight of her his jaw dropped. "Hi," she said shyly to Justin.

"You do something different?" he asked her.

"The girls and I went to the salon today. You don't like it?" she asked self-consciously.

"Oh god please say you like it, please say you like it," I thought to myself crossing my fingers.

"No I like it." He smiled, tucking a piece of her hair behind her ear, making her cheeks turn bright pink.

I cleared my throat. "Oh, yeah, Ella this is Justin," Riley said, introducing us.

"Hi," I greeted, extending my hand.

"We've already met," he said, confusing me. "I like Oreo's, you know, for next time." He gave me a smirk while he pulled Riley over to the couch to have a seat. It took me a moment to figure out what the hell he was talking about when all of sudden it hit me. *I'm such an ass.* I slapped myself on the forehead. Justin was the one who came and got me out of the maze.

I was just about to go over and apologize to him when his friend stepped in front of me. "Hi, I'm Kenny," he said, introducing himself to me.

"Ella," I said and walked away hoping he would get the hint that I'm not interested. "So what movie did you guys pick?" I asked Dixon.

"Well, it was a debate over a horror or a comedy, the horror won," Cameron said rolling her eyes.

Great, a horror movie. The last time I watched a horror film was when Jack attacked me. I was not up from reliving that.

I looked around at the seating arrangements and the only seat left was next to Kenny. He had a big grin on his face as he patted the seat next to him. I sighed and took the seat, leaning as far away from him as I could. He tried to put his arm around me, but one look let him know I wasn't having it. "Does anyone want something to drink?" I asked, getting up before Kenny tried to make another move. They all shouted their requests as I walked over to the fridge.

"Hey, Roman, we're about to watch a movie. Want to join us?" Austin asked him as he made his way over to the fridge.

I turned to face him and he looked right at me when he said, "No thanks. I'm good."

"Oh, come on, it's not that scary. I'm pretty sure you saw all Mackenzie's home movies. If you can sit through those and not run screaming this should be a piece of cake," Cameron joked.

Roman cracked a smiled but still declined. "Thanks, but it's a little crowded in here," he said, directing the comment at me. I ignored his jab and reached for the fridge the same time he did.

"Sorry, you go," I said, pulling back.

"No. You can go," he said, stepping back and waiting.

"Hey Ella, can you hit the lights while you're up?" Austin asked.

"Yeah," I said, but before I had the chance someone had beat me to it.

"Oh, good job," Dixon said. "We meant just the light in here not all the lights in the building," he quipped.

"Ha-ha very funny Roman. Turn them back on," I said annoyed.

"I didn't do that," he said.

I lowered my voice enough so the others wouldn't hear. "Look, I know you're mad at me, but enough is enough. Turn them back on."

"And I'm telling you I didn't do it. I wouldn't do that to you not after…" he trailed off. But I knew he was referring to the time in the library when he first demonstrated his power.

I sighed, running my fingers through my hair. "Can't you at least use your power to turn them back on?"

"I'm trying, but something's wrong," he said concerned.

Everyone else didn't seem to care and were entertaining

themselves by seeing who had the best evil laugh or who could make the scariest sounds. I rolled my eyes at their immaturity until I started to get a tightening in my stomach. I clenched my side knowing this feeling all too well. "Oh god," I whispered.

"Hey, Ella, don't worry. We'll fix it," Roman said, trying to make me feel better.

"No. No. No. It can't be?" I said, shaking my head.

"Ella, what's wrong?" Roman asked, reaching out for me.

"He's here. He found me." I was shaking and on the verge of hysterics. I knew he was here. I could sense him anywhere. I couldn't risk it happening again. I would not stand by and watch innocent people get slaughtered. "We have to go. We have to leave now," I said, pulling on Roman's arm.

"Ella, we're not going anywhere," he said, keeping me in my spot.

"What is going on?" Cameron asked, sensing my nervousness.

"We have to go. We have to get out of here now!" I yelled, hoping they would listen to me.

"Ella, I think it's better if we stay here," Dixon said.

"No we can't stay here."

"Ella, you're scaring me," Riley said.

"Why won't anyone listen to me?" I pleaded.

"I think we should get Dean," Sienna said.

"No wait," Justin said. "She's right. Someone else is here. I can smell them...it's different." I heard a ripping noise and then a low growl letting me know Justin had just switched to his wolf form. Then I heard it again and knew Kenny had changed as well.

Roman pushed me behind him protectively. "Stay here," he said.

"No, don't go." I grabbed on to him tight. Picking up on my fear he stayed right where he was. We all stayed put as Justin and Kenny made their way to the door to investigate. The only sound was the click of their claws on the linoleum floor. Not a second later Justin let out a growl and took off down the hall, Kenny not far behind him.

I couldn't take it anymore. I pushed past Roman and found my way to the door. I wasn't going to hide from him. "Ella, what are you doing?" Roman yelled, pulling me back into the room. I spun around defensively and Roman backed up surprised.

"Ella!" Dean yelled, coming into the room.

"Dean!" I ran over to him. Despite the lack of light I was able to make out where everything and everyone was. "Dean he's here he's really here."

"It's okay. I'm here now," he said, hugging me tight.

I cringed as the fire alarms went off, blaring loudly, and flashing bright red. "We have to go," I shouted over the sirens. Another alarm went off outside causing a slight case of panic.

"What the hell is going on?" Cameron asked.

"What are we supposed to do? The fire alarm is going off but so is the alarm for us to stay inside," Sienna asked confused as the rest of us.

Justin came back in the room in human form. "There's a breach in security. Someone got through the gates. We're all supposed to stay put until further notice," he said, joining Riley back on the couch.

We did as he said and stayed put and waited. No one said anything. The only thing you could hear was my pounding heart. A few minutes later the sirens stopped and the lights came back to life. "Everyone okay?" Dean asked.

I looked around at all my friend's faces full of mixed emotions. "Riley, your arm," Dixon said. He was the first to notice the long, exposed cuts that were oozing blood.

"Oh, it's okay...um...Justin accidently cut me when he transformed," she said softly.

"I'm so sorry. Why didn't you tell me?" Justin asked. He looked at her concerned that she was hurt more than she was letting on.

"It's no biggie. Really," she said smiling sweetly. I managed to pull myself away from Dean and walked over to Riley. I placed my hand over her cuts and healed her arm. Everyone looked at me with astonishment. Riley just smiled and said thank you. I stood up, took one look at her, and fainted.

When I opened my eyes the first thing I saw was his piercing, dark blue eyes, his messy black hair that I ached so badly to run my fingers through. He was cradling me in his arms. I thought I was dreaming. I smiled, looking deep into his eyes. I reached up to caress his face. "I missed you," I said. I pulled his lips to mine wanting the comfort of his kiss.

I heard a few collective gasps and then Dean clearing his throat. I pulled away and when my vision cleared, I realized I was kissing Roman not Tristan. I jumped up and pushed him away. Everyone was staring at me wide eyed. "What happened?" I asked startled.

"You fainted," Riley said. I turned back to Roman who was standing there with a stunned look on his face. My cheeks started to turn bright red with embarrassment from confusing Roman with my dead boyfriend Tristan. I didn't know how to explain it so I tried to pretend it didn't happen.

"Miss Ella," Gabe called, rushing into the room and saving me from having to explain myself. He always did have impeccable timing.

"Gabe, what's going on?"

"I'll explain it to you later. You and Dean are to come with me."

"But..." I looked at all my friends.

"All students are to report to their rooms. The school is on lock down," Gabe announced. When I still didn't budge, he leaned in closer, and whispered, "Ella, they will be fine. I promise."

"Ella, go ahead, it's okay," Cameron said, reading my worried expression.

"Miss Ella, please," Gabe pleaded, reaching for my hand. He led Dean and me outside where everything was chaotic. There were guardians and wolves running everywhere searching the perimeter. Gabe hurried us along, keeping us close to him. He took us to the teachers' dorms and upstairs to his room. "Stay here until I come and get you. There will be two guardians outside the door if you need anything," he told us before he took off.

I paced around the room before I decided to peek out the window to watch the mess. "I don't think you should stand by the window," Dean said.

"What does it matter? He already found me. It's just a matter of time before he comes for me."

"Ella, don't say that."

"It's true. This place was supposed to be like Fort Knox and he still found a way in. He's smarter than we think Dean." I turned back to the window. "Maybe I should just give myself up. Give him what he wants."

"Ella no. You are a McCallister and we do not give up. Not without a fight," he said with conviction.

I laughed. "When are you going to learn I'm not like the rest of the family? I'm different. I don't belong."

"I don't ever want to hear you say that. You belong to this family just as much as I do. Whether you like it or not you're stuck with us and we're not going to let you give up. Yes you're different, but you're different for a reason." He turned me making me face him. "I believe you are destined for greatness. We may not know what that destiny is yet, but I know if anyone can make a change it's you."

I sighed and gave him a hug. "Thanks Dean, I love you." I didn't exactly agree with his little speech, but at the moment I had no fight in me. There was no use in arguing with him. I let him think it was okay when really I wished I had the same self-confidence he did.

"I love you too," he said, pulling away. "Now care to explain to me what that kiss between you and Roman was about?" Clearly a change of subject was what he thought was best.

"Uh, yeah...well, I kind of thought he was Tristan," I said, biting my lip.

"You thought he was Tristan?"

"Yeah, I guess from all the stress my mind was playing tricks on me. So when I opened my eyes I thought I was seeing Tristan not Roman," I shrugged, not knowing another explanation.

"That makes sense. They do have some similarities. You just better hope Mackenzie doesn't find out. Jack will seem like a baby cub compared to her," he said, lying on the couch and turning on the TV like all of this was no big deal.

I was too restless to watch TV so I paced around the room until my legs gave in forcing me to lie down on the bed. I must have fallen asleep because when I opened my eyes I had a blanket over me and Gabe was lying on the couch instead of Dean. When I caught a glimpse of Gabe, I had to cover my mouth from laughing out loud. Gabe was twice the size of the small loveseat he was sleeping on. His one leg was dangling over the arm rest while the other was on the floor. I knew he had to be uncomfortable. I got up and decided to let him have his bed back.

"Gabe," I whispered, shaking him softly.

He opened his one eye, glanced at me, and then sprang into action. "What is it?"

"Relax, everything is fine. I just wanted to give you your bed back," I said, glad to know Gabe was always prepared.

"I'm fine," he said, rubbing his neck.

"Seriously Gabe?"

"I have to check in with the others anyways. I was just trying to get a couple minutes rest."

"What time is it?" I asked, not seeing a clock anywhere.

He looked out the window as if the sun would give him his answer. "I believe it's close to six."

"In the morning?" He nodded. "How long was I out?"

"I'm not sure. I checked in sometime after midnight and Dean said you had been asleep for a while."

"Where is Dean?"

"After things had settled down he was escorted back to his room. We didn't want to disturb you and thought you needed a good night's rest. So we let you be."

"Well, thank you. I appreciate that," I said, walking over to the window to look at the morning sun. I was grateful for the peaceful rest. It was the first I had in a long time. "So what happens now?"

"They're calling in more guardians to double security."

"Will that even make a difference? How did he get in in the first place?"

"We're still trying to figure that out," he said honestly. I knew it was hard for him to admit that. To him that meant he failed and didn't do his job, but I didn't believe that. "Miss Ella, you need not worry. I promise I will make sure nothing happens to you." Gabe was good at his job, but even on good days people made mistakes.

"I want you to know that the guardians they are sending are the best of the best. I can guarantee you, you will be safe with them."

"What about you? Will you still be my guardian?"

"Of course I will, but this way we'll have strength in numbers."

"You know, this is exactly what I didn't want." I sighed, wondering if this was how it was going to be until Jack was caught. "Can I go back to my room?"

"Yes, it's safe now. He won't try again. Not this soon," he said and offered to escort me back to my room.

"Can I go myself?" I asked. "You did say it was okay and the sun is up."

I knew he didn't want me to, but he let me go alone. I was glad because I didn't really plan on going to my room. I had to find Aidan, but I wasn't sure which room was his. I snuck down into the office to see if I could find out what room he was in. When I found the room number, I slipped back upstairs and down the hall to his room.

I wasn't sure if I should knock or not. I checked the door and it was unlocked. I let myself in. Aidan was asleep. After closer inspection I discovered he was wearing only his boxers. Man, did he have a nice body. I tiptoed my way over to the bed and sat down carefully next to him. I gently brushed a piece of hair off his forehead, causing him to stir. "Ella, is that you?"

"It's me," I smiled.

He pulled me into his arms. "I've been so worried about you. Are you okay? I couldn't get to you. They wouldn't even tell *me* where you were," he said, a little angry that my whereabouts were even kept secret from him.

"Don't worry. I'm fine. Better actually, now that I'm here with you." He slid his hand behind my neck and pulled me in for a kiss. I slipped under the covers and snuggled up next to him. "I can't stay long. Everyone will be up soon," I said.

"I know," he sighed, holding me a little tighter.

"But...while I'm here." I ran my hands up his chest and behind his neck pulling him in for another kiss.

Things had gotten so hot and heavy we hadn't realized how much time had passed until there was a knock on the door. We sat up abruptly and Aidan gave me that look again. "You are kidding me, right?" Not again. When he sat there not saying anything, I rolled my eyes, and grabbed my shirt up off the floor. "Does it have to be a closet again?"

"Under the bed," he said, rushing me.

This was getting ridiculous.

Once I got out of sight, Aidan opened the door. "Aidan, I hope I didn't wake you?" Ms. Kraft asked.

"No. What can I do for you Sylvia?"

"The guardians had informed me they want to call a faculty meeting to discuss what needs to be done."

"Why was I not told about this until now?" he asked. I could tell he hated how the rest of the faculty seemed to under mind him. I knew he thought because he was so young and just filling in for his dad most of them didn't take him seriously.

"I apologize. When I heard the news I told them I was on my way out and would let you know."

"It's not your fault Sylvia and I think it's a good idea. What time are we meeting?"

"In one hour in the auditorium," she replied.

"Thank you. I will see you then," Aidan told her and she departed.

"You can come out now," Aidan said.

I climbed out from underneath the bed. "How about next time you just don't answer the door," I said, tired of having to hide like I was the other woman.

"I'm sorry. I never said this would be easy," he smiled, pulling me into him.

"How long did she say you have?" I asked as I nibbled on his neck.

"An hour."

"I can think of a few things we can do in an hour."

"As much as it kills me to say no, we can't."

"Why not?" I pouted.

"Because the only thing that seems to stop us is when we're interrupted."

I sighed, pulling myself away. "You're right. I should go."

I walked over to the door and listened carefully to make sure no one was in the hall. When I knew it was clear I quickly made my way outside and back to my room. When I got there I found Roman asleep on the floor outside my door. I bent down and shook him gently. "Roman, wake up."

He blinked a few times before he looked up at me. "Oh, hey," he said, looking a little embarrassed. He got up and quickly ran his fingers through his hair.

"What are you doing out here? You and Mackenzie have a fight?"

"No, I was…I was waiting for you," he said, surprising me.

"Why were you waiting for me and why didn't you wait inside?"

"Mackenzie has this weird rule about me not spending the night and…" he paused looking uncomfortable with what he was going to say next. "I just wanted to make sure you were okay?" he said rubbing his neck.

"I'm fine…thanks."

"Good. I'm going to go then." He took off abruptly before I even had the chance to say anything else.

I didn't know what to think. Roman seemed to have multiple personalities and I never knew which one would show up or when. If I had to pick one, this would be the one I'd like to see more often.

When I stepped inside my room I could hear that Mackenzie was already in the shower. I quickly changed into clean clothes and left before she came out. Despite the events from last night, being with Aidan put me in a better mood, and I wasn't about to let Mackenzie ruin that.

I headed to the dining hall to grab some breakfast then I thought I'd hit the library and go over the project Roman and I had to hand in tomorrow. I headed to my normal table in the back and spread out my work. I started to look over the notes but had a hard time concentrating. I tried to blame it on the noisy couple hidden somewhere in the stacks, but the truth was I couldn't focus because of Roman. I couldn't get him out of my head. I still couldn't believe he slept outside my room on the cold, hard tile floor just to see if I was okay. Maybe Sienna was right. I shook my head. That was crazy. Roman didn't like me and I certainly didn't like him. I mean, what was there to like? He was arrogant, two faced, and dating Mackenzie – clearly proving he lacked any type of morals. Those intense, dark blue eyes had no effect on me, or that black, wavy hair, or sexy accent.

No. Not Sexy!

I buried my head in my hands. I was giving myself a headache. I tried once again to concentrate on the project. The project Roman did all on his own without me. Ugh! I shoved the papers away and put my head down on the table.

"Ella?"

I looked up. "Dean? I never thought I'd run into you in a library. What are you doing here and this early?"

"Just checking things out," he said as the giggling girl I heard earlier walked out, winking at Dean. I rolled my eyes. I should have known that would be the only reason Dean would set foot in a library. I'm just glad I didn't overhear anything I would regret later.

Dean pulled out a chair next to me and had a seat. "So how are you doing?" he asked.

"I'm fine."

"Ella, don't play coy with me."

"Really, Dean, I'm fine."

"You weren't fine last night. You know it's not good to suppress your emotions."

"Thank you Dr. Phil."

He narrowed his eyes at me, not appreciating my sarcasm. "Ella, I want you to be fine. I do. But pretending like nothing happened is not a good way to cope with things."

"What do you want me to do? Freak out? Because I could do that. I could rant and rave and hide in my room for the rest of my life, but what good is that going to do? It's not going to change the fact that Jack knows where I am and it's not going to stop him from coming after me."

"How do you even know it was him?" I knew he thought I was being paranoid.

"Because I know," I said, gripping my chair to try and calm myself. "Trust me when I say I know it was him."

"Okay, but I still need to know you're going to be okay and not go off the deep end." I stifled an eye roll. "Are you going to man up and explain to everyone what happened last night?"

"Yes I will be fine and no I'm not. I already embarrassed myself enough last night. It's none of their business so as far as I'm concerned nothing happened." He opened his mouth to argue but I stopped him. "Sorry if I would like to pretend for a moment that I have some kind of normal life."

"Ella, I hate to tell you, but your life is anything but normal and as soon as you start to realize that then maybe you can move on from this fantasy of trying to be normal," he said, leaving me.

I knew he was right, but it was so much easier to keep believing that maybe someday I could live a normal life. I also knew deep down that would never happen. Too much was expected of me. Sometimes I wished I could trade a life with someone else.

I spent the rest of the day in the library not wanting to face anyone and have to explain what happened last night. I wanted so badly to go see Aidan, but with everything going on I thought it best not to. I was also curious to know what happened at the faculty meeting, but that was something else that was going to have to wait.

CHAPTER SIXTEEN

I was woken up very early Monday morning by a knock on the door. I looked over to see Mackenzie still sleeping and not making a move. I got up to answer it to find Roman standing on the other side. "That's what you sleep in?" he said, giving me the once over.

Seriously, what the hell was wrong with flannel pajamas? "Roman, it's like five o'clock in the morning. What the hell do you want?"

"Gabe told me to come wake you for your training session," he said, leaning up against the door with his arms crossed.

"But it's five o'clock in the morning," I protested.

"I'm just the messenger," he shrugged. "You better change. This isn't summer camp," he smirked. I slammed the door in his face and went back to bed. I'm sorry, but no way was I getting up at five o'clock in the morning to work out. That was where I drew the line.

I was just about to fall back asleep when there was another knock on the door. I got up and swung it open in a huff. "Gabe, is there something wrong?" I asked, half expecting it to be Roman again.

"You're not ready," he said, narrowing his eyes at me.

"Yeah. We need to talk about this whole training session thing. I know I agreed to do it, but I did not agree to get up this early."

"Miss Ella, I have told you I take these sessions seriously and would treat you as I did any other student and you agreed to these terms. I would have thought after the other night you would be more than willing to get started."

"But..."

"But nothing. If you choose not to take this seriously then I'm sorry I have wasted your time and mine," he said, turning to walk away.

I stood there, shell shocked for minute, before I came to my senses and ran down the hall after him. "Gabe wait!" He stopped and turned around. "You're right. I'm sorry. Can we try this again?"

"You have five minutes to change. And dress warm, it's cold outside."

"We'll be outside?" I whined. Gabe crossed his arms, showing me he was not in the mood. I stifled an eye roll. "Where outside?" I asked.

"On the track. Where you'll find Roman," he replied.

"Roman?"

"Yes. In order to make time to train both of you Roman has offered to share his time so I could train you too."

"Oh," was all I said.

"Now go change and do ten laps around the track."

"Ten laps," I groaned. Gabe gave me a stern look and I put my arms up in surrender. "Okay, okay." I dragged my feet back to my room and grumbled to myself as I changed into warmer clothes. Then I grabbed my coat and hat along with my scarf and gloves and headed out to the track to meet Gabe and Roman.

When Gabe spotted me, he jogged over, and led me through a series of stretches. "Couldn't we have done this inside?" I complained, no longer able to feel my nose. Gabe let me know he didn't appreciate my commentary and for every time I would complain he would add an extra lap. I thought it wise to keep my mouth shut from now on.

Roman was done with his laps by the time I started and had already moved on to the next thing. Gabe actually ran the laps with me which was a nice surprise. I kind of think he only did to keep me going or in case I passed out, regardless, it was nice to have the company. When we were done, he had me join Roman on the bleachers and do sprints up and down the steps. Then he had us do another five laps. I thought my legs were going to fall off. I almost passed out in the grass when we did our after workout stretches.

On top of our training sessions we still had to take our regular self-defense classes. Gabe told me he wanted to meet with us twice a day every day before and after classes. I was ready to tell him this wasn't what I signed up for, but he was taking time out of his day to help me so I kept my mouth shut.

I spent a few extra minutes in the shower letting the heat sooth my aching muscles. Then I headed off to class. After this morning I was not looking forward to tonight's session.

At lunch no one said anything to me about Saturday night. I didn't know if they were afraid to bring it up or if Dean had warned them ahead of time not to. "We're going to hang out in the social room on my floor after class if you want to join us?" Cameron asked me.

"Sorry, I can't. I started training with Gabe today. He has me working out every day before and after classes," I said. She nodded and went back to talking to Austin.

"Okay, so what was with all the sirens Saturday? I had, like, a migraine all night because of them," Mackenzie complained as she sat down.

No one said anything. Instead they just looked down at their plates of half-eaten food. Mackenzie looked at everyone suspiciously and I wondered what was going on underneath that mass of over processed blond hair. "Why are all of you acting like you know something? Don't tell me you guys did something lame like try to sneak out of here or something," she laughed as Roman took a seat next to her. She leaned over and gave him a kiss on the cheek. He gave her a faint smile and me a quick glance before digging into his lunch.

"Okay, seriously, it's like invasion of the body snatchers. What gives?"

Mackenzie was not going to drop it and apparently no one else seemed to want to volunteer any information so I decided to. "Someone tried to break onto the campus," I said and everyone turned their attention to me.

Mackenzie looked intrigued. "Why would anyone want to break in here?"

They all kept their eyes on me as they waited for my response. "Because they were after me," I said, sighing. That was not how I wanted that to come out.

"You, please," she said with a dramatic head roll. "This is a joke right? Why would anyone risk the punishment to see you?"

I braced myself for the impact of my next statement. "He wasn't here for a friendly chat. He was here to kill me."

Everyone's jaw dropped to the floor, except for Mackenzie's. She kept her, *'I'm better than you'* attitude. "You want me to believe that someone actually cares enough to take the time to get rid of you?"

"Mackenzie," Roman scolded.

"What? What's so special about her that someone would want her dead," she spat.

"He wants my powers."

"All you can do is heal," she said snidely. "Seems like a waste of time to me."

"Regardless of what you think this is a serious matter," Cameron said. "Ella, why didn't you tell us any of this?"

"Because I was hoping I wouldn't have to. We thought with me coming here he wouldn't find me and I'd be safe."

"Great, so now there's a psycho on the loose around campus. I knew you were nothing but trouble the moment you got here," Mackenzie said.

"Lucky for us Ella's your roommate. Maybe he'll do us all a favor and take you instead," Cameron replied.

Mackenzie scowled at her and stood up. "Whatever, I'm done with you losers. This table is nothing but a bunch of freaks and fags." I stood up so fast I knocked my chair over, bringing attention to one of the guardians over in the corner. My fists were clenched by my side ready to strike when Dixon put a hand on my arm. I looked into his eyes. He pleaded for me to sit back down and let this go. I mentally counted to ten and let out a breath. Then I turned back to Mackenzie, glaring, while she stood there smiling. "Addy, Maddy," she said, storming off before she turned back around to address Roman.

"Roman?" I guess she expected him to follow her like Thing one and Thing two did. He didn't even turn to look at her. "Roman!" she screeched.

"No," he said.

"What did you say?" she asked even though she clearly heard him.

"I said no, Mackenzie. You can't treat people like shit and expect me to follow along. I'm not your little lap dog. You can't just call and expect me to obey your every command. That's not how this works," he said angrily.

"You rather stay here with these freaks?" she asked appalled.

"They're not freaks," he said, slamming his fist down on the table hard enough to make even me jump. "And yes, I am staying here, with my friends," Roman said, looking at me.

"If you don't come here this instant than we're over!"

"Then I guess we're over," Roman said, surprising us all, including Mackenzie. She stormed out of the cafeteria with her lackeys. Roman's eyes flashed over me before he went back to eating. I didn't know what to say so I just sat back down.

"Huh, what do ya know, miracles do happen," Cameron said, making Roman glare at her.

Everyone tried to go back to their normal conversation but you could tell there was a mix of emotions in the air. Dixon pulled me closer to him. "I wish you would have said something to me Ella. I was there, remember?"

Something inside me snapped. "No you weren't. You have no idea what really happened. You didn't find your best friend's body or have to watch innocent people die. So don't tell me you were there or you understand because if you were and did you would be scared shitless right now," I said, storming off, making things worse.

This was what I was hoping wouldn't happen. I wanted to avoid admitting I was scared and that my new friends might be in danger because of me. Everything that was happening right now was part of the reason I didn't want to befriend anyone. I didn't want to see anyone else get hurt. I just wanted this all to be over. I've lost so much already I didn't think I could handle it again.

When I got back to my room Mackenzie was there packing up her suitcases. "You're leaving?" I asked, suddenly feeling better.

"This is only temporary or at least until whoever's after you gets you. I'm not going to stay here and get murdered because of you. I'm staying with Maddy and Addy in their room," Mackenzie said, slamming her suitcase shut. I didn't say a word. I was not going to argue with her on this one. Despite my freak out at lunch, Mackenzie moving out gave me hope that there was some light at the end of the tunnel.

Since I left lunch early I had some extra time before my next class. So I decided to go see Aidan. I found him in his office, but had to wait because he was with another student. "Miss McCallister, Mr. Callahan can see you now," the secretary said.

I walked into his office and closed the door behind me. Then I ran over to Aidan and wrapped my arms around him, holding him tight before I pulled his lips down to mine. "Hey, hey, not here," he said, pulling back.

"Sorry, it's just so hard to keep my hands to myself when I'm around you," I confessed.

He smiled back at me. "I know what you mean, but we have to be careful." I sighed and sat down on the couch while he went back to his paper work on his desk. "Is this a business visit or you just here for pleasure?" he asked.

"Both," I smiled. "Mackenzie moved out."

He creased his brows and looked up. "What do you mean moved out?"

"She said she was going to stay with Addyson and Madison." I shrugged, not caring to elaborate. "Now that I have my own room maybe we can..."

"Nice try, but that would be too risky." I pouted and leaned back against the couch. "Is there something else?"

"Well, I was kind of wondering what happened at the faculty meeting?"

He let out a breath and sat down. "Not much. We just discussed the measures we're going to take to make sure the school is more secured."

"And how are they going to do that?"

"Ms. Kraft and a few other teachers are working on a stronger spell to block out unwanted guests. More guardians are coming and students are no longer allowed to leave campus. Ella, you are safe here. I won't let anything happen to you," he said, sitting next to me.

"No, I don't want you to get involved. In fact I need to stay away from you and you need to stay away from me. It's the only way I can keep you safe. I can't lose you too." I stood up to walk out, but he pulled me back down.

"I don't care. I'll take the risk. It will be worth it to be with you."

"Don't say that."

He reached up and cupped my face. I leaned into his hand wanting so badly to kiss him, but now was not the time or place. "Meet me tonight. In my room?" I told him I would when I thought it was safe for me to sneak out. Then I left and went to my next class.

For our next session, Gabe had us meet him in the weight room after we ran laps. We spent the next hour doing circuit training. When Gabe left to take a phone call Roman turned to me and asked, "What happened at your old school that has you so freaked?"

I set down my weight. "Nothing you need to worry about," I said, moving on to the next machine.

"If my life is in danger I think I have the right to know," he said, wiping the sweat from his brow.

"He only goes after the people I care about so you're safe."

"Ouch," he said smiling. Gabe came back in the room and told us we could go. I left without another word and went back to my room to shower and wait until I could meet Aidan.

I waited until nightfall. Once I felt it was safe, I snuck out of my room and headed to Aidan's. "Going somewhere?" Mackenzie said, stepping out of the shadows, and scaring the crap out of me.

"Christ Mackenzie! What are you doing out here?"

"I believe I just asked you that?" she said, thinking she somehow cleverly got me.

I stood there with my arms crossed, not in the mood. "What do you want Mackenzie?"

"I want you to tell me where you are going?"

"I'm going for a walk," I said, hoping she would drop it.

"It's a little late for a midnight stroll, don't you think? Aren't you afraid that whoever is after you is out there somewhere…waiting?"

"Maybe I'll get lucky and he'll take you instead."

She scowled at me before she walked away but not before calling over her shoulder, "Tell Aidan, oops, I mean Mr. Callahan I said hi." I opened my mouth to say something, but then thought it wise not to. There was no way she knew anything. She was just probably taking a guess and hoping to get a reaction out of me to confirm it. I refused to give her the satisfaction of thinking she was right. I waited until I knew for sure she was back inside before I started on my way again.

As Aidan had mention to me earlier, there were more guardians than before which made it harder for me to be discreet. I managed to make it across campus and into the teachers' dorms without an issue. When I opened the door to Aidan's room I was taken back, surprised. He had lit up the entire room with candles, rose petals littered the floor and bed. I closed and locked the door behind me. I spotted Aidan over by the window, closing the curtains. He smiled brightly when he saw me.

"All this for me?" I asked sheepishly.

"You don't like it?" he asked, crossing the room.

"I do, it's just..."

"Hey, no expectations. I just wanted to do something nice. I told you I can wait."

I wrapped my arms around his waist and laid my head on his chest. "How do you always seem to understand?"

He ran his fingers through my hair and then pulled me over to the bed to sit down. "How was your training session today?" he asked.

"Painful," I groaned. "I don't think I'm cut out for this."

"Give it time. You'll get used to it. Gabe's the best and he didn't get that way by doing a few push-ups."

"I know," I said, rubbing my sore shoulders.

"Here, let me," Aidan offered.

I adjusted myself so he could massage my shoulders. "You were right about them doubling the guardians. I had a hard time getting over here. Not to mention the run in I had with Mackenzie."

"I thought you said she moved out of your room?"

"She did. I ran into her outside. She cornered me and wanted to know where I was going."

"You didn't tell her did you?" he asked panicked.

"Of course not," I turned to face him. "You believe me, right?"

"Of course I do," he said, cupping my face. I leaned into him and he coaxed me back on the bed. We just lied there next to each other staring into each other's eyes. I pulled him closer and started to kiss him. It was only a matter of minutes before I felt that extreme desire to be with him. I pulled him even closer to me and tugged on the button on his pants. Then I pulled back so he could take off my shirt. As usual, things started to get hot and heavy, but this time there were no distractions to stop us.

Right before Aidan was about to take off my bra I pulled back. "What is it what's wrong?" he asked.

"You have condoms, right?"

He smiled. "Of course I do." He rolled over and reached into a draw. "There in here somewhere?" he looked for another couple of minutes before he gave up. "I guess I don't," he said, turning back to me.

I sat up and sighed. "I guess another night then."

"Come here," he said, pulling me closer to him. We just lied there and held each other. "You know, I never noticed all of your tattoos before."

"How could you miss them?" I joked.

He traced his finger along the tattoo on my side. "What made you get them? You don't really seem like the tattoo type."

"I was bored," I shrugged. I figured that was the best explanation without getting to detailed and it seemed to work. "And who's to say you have to be a certain type to like tattoos?" He ignored my last question and continued to trace the tattoo on my side. I closed my eyes as my skin started to tingle from the light brush of his fingertips. "You're making it hard to resist you when you keep doing that." He smiled and continued down to the ones on my stomach. That urge was pulsing through me again and I had to pull myself away. "I should go."

"You don't have to," he said, pulling me back, and kissing my neck.

"I do. We can't control ourselves when we're alone." As soon as the words fell out of my mouth something occurred to me. "Did you ever notice that every time we're together we can't keep our hands off each other?"

"What's wrong with that?" he asked as he worked his lips across my chest.

"That's it. I mean that's all we seem to do. I don't ever remember wanting to do anything else. Doesn't that seem weird?"

"Well sometimes when two people care about each other the way we do..." he began as he kissed my neck again.

"But that's just it. Do you really care about me?"

"Ella, what are you talking about?" he said, finally stopping to look at me.

"I don't know. I just never felt this way before. I guess that's why I don't understand it."

"Do you not want to be here?" he asked upset.

"No I do. I do. It's just...never mind."

"Ella, I would never make you do anything you don't want to do. If you want to go you can go."

"I don't want to go," I said, knowing that was the odd part. I just met him and all of a sudden I couldn't pull myself away. He grazed my cheek, causing me to melt. I started to kiss him and fell back into the sex induced coma I felt every time I was with him. "You sure you don't have any condoms? Somewhere else maybe?"

He smiled his most sexy smile and said, "No, but I think I know where I can get some." He got up off the bed and got dressed. "I'll be right back," he said, giving me a quick kiss before he took off.

Not able to sit still, I stood up, and walked around the room checking things out. He had a few pictures around the room of what looked like him and his dad and some with friends. I walked over to his bureau and picked up his cologne, taking a whiff. I spotted a loose picture that had fallen. I bent down to pick it up. When I saw the picture I almost dropped the bottle of cologne. I thought maybe I was imagining it, like my mind was playing tricks on me.

Aidan walked back in to the room and I turned on him. "What is this?" I said, holding out the picture.

"Where did you get that?"

"I found it," I said, annoyed he didn't answer my first question.

"You were snooping?"

"No I wasn't and you still didn't answer my first question," I snapped.

He took the picture from me and ripped it in half. "It's nothing," he said dismissing it.

"It didn't look like nothing."

"Ella, just drop it."

"How can I? I just found a picture of you with your arms around Mackenzie, kissing her!"

"Ella, you're over reacting," he said, looking at me like I was a little kid throwing a hissy fit.

"Explain," I demanded.

"It was a long time ago. It was my last year here as a student and it was visitors' weekend where future students can come and check out the school."

"Let me guess, you offered to give her a private tour," I said, putting my clothes back on.

He stopped me. "Ella, look, it was really stupid. I see that now. There was this party and we were both really drunk and one thing led to another. I didn't know how young she was until after. It was just a one night thing, but to her it meant more."

"Well of course it did," I growled.

"Look," he grabbed my arms. "It was stupid and it happened. I can't change it. It's not my fault she thought there was more to it."

"Really? Because that picture would indicate you led her to

believe there was."

"It was the day after. We had lunch together and I told her it was a one-time thing. She took the picture. She was the one with the crush. I tried to let her down easy, but she wouldn't take no for an answer. After she left things got a little out of hand."

"What do you mean out of hand?" I asked, not liking this scenario.

"She emailed me almost every day. Telling me she loved me and couldn't wait to come back. I tried to convince her it was just a crush and not love. I tried everything I could to convince her to get over me. I stopped emailing her back, changed my number, hoping she'd get the hint. After a month of ignoring her I never heard from her again."

"Until now."

"Ella it was mistake. It's not something I'm proud of. If I could, I'd go back and change it. I would, but what's done is done." He took me in his arms and pressed his forehead to mine. I could feel the heat building up between us again. I was so mad at him I wanted to leave, but when we were this close, all I wanted was him to touch me. He kissed my lips and for a moment I forgot what we were fighting about.

Aidan picked me up and carried me over to the bed. One by one our clothes came off again. "Something's not right," I said a little breathless. He just kept kissing me.

I felt like something was trying to break through a barrier. My mind was all hazy and the more he touched me the harder it was to think straight. Aidan leaned off the bed to get the condom and my head got a little clearer. "Wait, weren't we just arguing?" I asked unsure. My head was still fuzzy.

Aidan looked just as puzzled as I was. I got up off the bed and the more distance I got from him the clearer my head got. "Ella, what's going on?"

"That's what I'd like to know. I think I should go," I said, putting my clothes back on.

"Don't go," he said, reaching for me.

I jumped back. "No. Stay there! Every time you get near me or touch me I can't think straight."

"There's nothing wrong with that. I feel the same way," he smiled.

"Actually, there is something wrong with that. There is something wrong with all of this," I said, heading for the door.

"Ella wait, stop!" He was in front of me in an instant. "I think you should just sit down and we can talk this out."

"No. I want to go." I tried to push past him, but he grabbed me.

"You don't really mean that," he said, his voice all velvety soft, trying to coax me back.

I tried to pull away but he gripped me tighter, pulling me in for a kiss. I turned away but he didn't stop. "Aidan, stop it."

"You know you don't want me to stop."

"Yes I do," I said, trying to push him away again, but he just held on. "Aidan."

"Quit being such a tease," he said, kissing me again. I stomped on his foot so he would let me go, but that move came back to bite me in the ass. He cracked me across the face so hard I flew into the wall and crumbled to the floor. I held my hand up to my cheek and just stared at him wide eyed. He walked over to me and bent down in front of me. "Ella, I'm so sorry. I don't know what came over me. Oh god I'm so sorry," he said, reaching for me.

"Don't touch me," I said, scrambling to get up.

"Ella, please, you have to believe I didn't mean to. I swear. I don't even know what happened." He looked as puzzled as I was. He held his hand out to me again but I slapped it away. Something changed. I felt it. He turned to look at me and his eyes were glowing. I opened my mouth to scream but he had it covered before I even had the chance.

"Relax," he said. "I just want to be with you. I promise I won't hurt you." My brain couldn't form words as the tears began to stream down my face. "Oh, Ella, don't cry," he said, brushing my cheek. I flinched at his touch, making him upset. "Why are you so upset? This is a good thing. This is what we both want." He started to take off my jacket, then shirt. "You are so beautiful." I never thought hearing those words would sound so awful.

"This is not what I want," I said, finding my voice. He ignored me. It was almost like something had come over him making him a completely different person. Every time he would try to kiss me I would turn my head, but he would grab my jaw and force it back. He was strong, but so was I. Just as he was about to tear off my pants I brought up my knee and nailed him in the groin. A move to this day that has proven to not fail me yet. He howled in pain, falling forward. I socked him in the face, knocking him off of me. I scrambled to get up. Grabbing my jacket, I ran out of there as fast as I could.

I ran so hard and so fast I didn't see the person in front of me. I slammed right into them falling down to the cold ground. "What's the matter? You look a little flushed," Mackenzie said, straightening out her jacket.

"For someone who has made it clear I'm a threat to her safety sure is spending a lot time around me," I said, getting up and dusting myself off.

"Please, I was simply out for a stroll," she smiled.

"You seem to have impeccable timing. I find it hard to believe that this was some strange coincidence." I glared at her, knowing she was up to something. "Whatever, I don't have time for this," I said, looking over my shoulder, and walking away as fast as possible.

"What's with the waterworks? Aidan not as good as you thought?"

I stopped and turned around. "Look, whatever game you're playing you can just stop right now."

"Now why would I do that when I'm having so much fun," she laughed. "So how was it? Was it everything you imagined? Did you see fireworks?" I stood there not sure what to say, so she continued. "Did he tell you he cared about you and loved being around you and every time you touched you couldn't seem to stop."

"What did you do?"

She smiled wickedly. "Oh, it was so easy. I knew how easy this would be when I first saw you two together by the fountain."

"What did you do?" I repeated, louder this time.

"I may have cast a little spell," she said with the wave of her hand like it was nothing.

"What kind of spell?" I asked, taking a step closer to her.

"Oh come on now Ella, I know you're not that dumb. You have to have figured it out by now." She looked down at my exposed chest and I quickly zipped up my jacket. In my rush to escape I had left my shirt. "That bad huh?" she said, having no idea what she had done.

"You have any idea what you have done?" I said, getting in her face. "Your stupid little spell almost..." I bit my tongue to keep the tears at bay. "You are such an evil bitch."

"Well, I can't take all the credit. I did have some help. Turns out you're not that easy to bewitch," she said a little bitterly. "We had to crank it up a bit and I have to say I am quite exhausted. So if you don't mind I think I might retire for the night," she said, placing her hand over her mouth and faking a yawn. She smiled, sashaying her way past me.

I grabbed her arm. "Break it. Break the spell now!"

"What's the matter? Was he not that good?" she laughed.

I gripped her arm tighter in a desperate plea. "This isn't funny Mackenzie. I mean it. Break the spell!" I heard a noise from behind me, panic surged through me.

"You already did that."

"What are you talking about?" I said, pulling her away from the door, hearing the sound getting closer.

"The spell breaks after you give it up. Geez, maybe you are as dumb as you look," she said rolling her eyes.

I knew she was mean, but this was beyond cruel. "Well, your stupid spell back fired, badly. So break it now!" She laughed, thinking she had the upper hand in this. I had enough of her comments and her vindictive behavior. She had to be taught a lesson. This time there was no one around to stop me. "You bitch!" I yelled, shoving her to the ground.

"What the hell is wrong with you?" She stood up and brushed herself off and that's when I attacked. We wrestled back and forth on the ground, yelling and screaming. I'm surprised our chaos hadn't caught the attention of the guardians. "Would you get off of me?"

"No! Break the spell Mackenzie!" I yelled, grabbing a big chunk of her hair. She squealed and tried to push me off of her, but I was stronger. "You have to break the spell before it's too late! You have no idea what you created."

My emotional state finally took over and she managed to push me off of her. I flew back, hitting the ground. I sat up, exposing my ripped bra and torn jeans. Mackenzie looked at me, her eyes for the first time apologetic. But before she could open her mouth, the door to the teachers' dorm burst open and a very angry Aidan stepped out into the cold, eyes glowing.

"Mackenzie, break the spell," I said, getting up quickly.

"I...I..." she stumbled.

Aidan turned at the sound of her voice. "You. You did this," he said, going after her.

"Mackenzie, now!" I yelled as I charged Aidan. Fear had my adrenaline pumping, ready to take on anything. I jumped him but he threw me off. I rolled and got right back up. We each took a stance, waiting for the other to strike. "Mackenzie, I need your help here."

"I'm working on it!" she yelped.

Tired of walking in circles, instinct kicked in, and I went for the attack, kicking him in the side of the knee, throwing him off balance. I spun around and kicked him again knocking him to the ground. It took him less than a minute to recover. He pounced on me, whacking us both to the ground and rolling a couple feet. Aidan was quicker and had my arms pinned to my sides. "Ella, why do you have to make me do this? Things could have been great if you would have just cooperated." He exposed his teeth, leaning closer to my neck.

"Mackenzie!" I shrieked.

"Done!" she yelled.

Just as Aidan was about to sink his teeth into my neck he froze. Something flashed in his eyes and he looked at me, scared and quivering beneath him. He fell back and scurried a few feet, looking petrified. He looked at me exposed and frightened. "Ella...what?" He was so confused. "What is going on?"

"You might want to ask your girlfriend over there," I said, motioning to Mackenzie.

"Will someone please explain to me what is going on?" Aidan pleaded.

"Is everything alright over here?" called one of the guardians as he jogged over with two more. "We heard a commotion."

"A little late on that one," Mackenzie said.

The guardian ignored her and looked at Aidan. "Mr. Callahan, I'm sorry. I did not see you there."

"It's okay Rick. I got it. You guys can go back to your patrol."

He nodded respectfully at Aidan. All three of them were about to walk away when Rick spotted me. I quickly tightened my jacket. He took a few steps closer to me. "Miss, are you okay?" I nodded, afraid my voice would betray me.

"Nothing you need to be concerned about," Aidan said. "Just a small fight between classmates. I have it under control."

Rick glared at him from over his shoulder and then turned back to me, eyes worried. "I'm fine," I said, trying to sound convincing. "Just a misunderstanding."

"Are you sure?" he asked softly.

"Yes I'm fine," I said, forcing a weak smile. I didn't know if he believed me, but he didn't ask any more questions. Before he left he gave Aidan a warning look saying, *'I'll be watching you'.*

Once they were gone, Aidan gestured for us to come closer. While I did move in, I still kept my distance. "Now, will someone please explain to me what the hell is going on?" Aidan asked frustrated.

"Are you going to tell him or you going to make me," I said, glaring at Mackenzie. She looked away from me embarrassed, making it clear she wasn't going to confess her dirty deed. "Mackenzie put a spell on us, a lust spell."

He looked back at her eyes wide and slowly filling with rage again. "Why?" he asked.

"It was just a joke. Didn't think you'd go all crazy and what not," she said, acting like this was in no way her fault.

"Leave," he growled at Mackenzie.

"This is a free country you know. I can do what —"

"You've done enough," he spat. "I will deal with you later." For once Mackenzie took the hint and left. Aidan tried to collect himself before he turned and faced me. "Ella I'm…" he broke off when he saw my tattered clothes. Words had lost him, but I could see in his face how sorry he felt for what he had done. He reached for me and I flinched. "Ella…you have to know that wasn't me…it was the spell. These kind of spells…if not careful, can go horribly wrong."

"Yeah, I got that," I said.

"Ella I'm —"

I stopped him. I knew it wasn't his fault, but an apology right now just didn't feel right. "I just can't do this right now." He came after me to stop me. "No," I held up my hands. "I know you're sorry and I know this wasn't you, but I just need some time." He nodded, understanding. I left him there, out in the quad, alone. I buttoned up my coat and walked back to my room feeling embarrassed, betrayed, pissed, and ashamed. If I didn't somehow realize something was off I could have…I shook the thought out of my head. I couldn't believe Mackenzie was that heartless? What the hell did I do to her to piss her off that much? This was just beyond cruel. Something needed to be done, but what? I didn't even want to think about it anymore. I just wanted to put the entire night behind me.

When I got back to my room it was just past one. I changed into my pajamas and climbed into bed. Tomorrow was going to be a long day and I had to get up in a few hours for my training session with Gabe. The only thing I needed right now was rest.

I did not get the good night's rest I so hoped for. I cried for the first hour before I eventually fell asleep. I tossed and turned all night. I had dreams about Aidan and I being together and going all the way – Mackenzie in the background laughing. I also dreamed about Jack coming after me in the maze and my friends calling for my help. When my alarm went off in the morning I felt like I only had about an hour of sleep. I wished so badly I could go back to bed, but I didn't want to piss off Gabe.

I dragged myself out of bed, got dressed, and headed out to the track where Gabe and Roman were already stretching. "You're late," Gabe scolded.

"I'm sorry I –"

"I don't want to hear any excuses. Two extra laps." I opened my mouth to say that's not fair, but quickly closed it when Gabe narrowed his eyes at me.

I was practically dragging my ass around the track. "Ella, pick up the pace!" Gabe yelled, making me cringe. I groaned and tried to jog faster.

Roman ran up next to me. "You know you look like shit," he said.

"Thanks for the observation," I mumbled.

"Maybe if you weren't out sneaking around late at night you wouldn't be so tired."

"What are you talking about?" I said annoyed.

"I saw you Ella. I saw you go into the teachers' dorms last night," he spat accusingly.

"Were you spying on me?"

"I ran into Mackenzie and asked her if you were in your room and she told me you were taking a walk. So I tried to catch up to you and that's when I saw you."

"Not that it's any of your business, but Mackenzie is to blame for this whole thing."

"It's pathetic that you can't even admit it even after you were caught," Roman said, pushing past me. My jaw dropped, the nerve of him, how dare he point fingers when he had no idea what was really going on. And why the hell was he looking for me? I mean really, was he that bored he felt the need to come torture me?

"Ella, I'm not going to tell you again. Pick up the pace or I'm adding laps," Gabe said. I sucked it up and pushed past Roman and finished my laps.

At lunch, I apologized to Dixon for freaking out yesterday and he forgave me. He didn't deserve that and I was glad to make things right. Besides, at the rate I was going, keeping friends might be harder than I thought. I was slowly realizing with all the catching up I had to do, plus the extra training sessions I didn't have time for anything else - including time for friends. I tried to look at it as a good thing. The less time I spent with my new friends meant a possibility of keeping them out of danger.

I did the same thing every day for the next few weeks. Got up, ran, then class, then training again, and then back to my room to do school work. I was in bed by nine and up at five. After our fight, Roman has yet to talk to me. I hadn't seen Mackenzie since she confessed about the spell – no loss there – and I avoided Aidan every chance I got. I still wasn't ready to face him yet. Frankly at this point, I almost just didn't care about anything anymore. I was just trying to get through the semester.

CHAPTER SEVENTEEN

I woke up Saturday morning just in enough time to make breakfast. I found Riley at a small table in the corner and took a seat next to her. "Hey," I said.

"Hey Ella."

"So, I was thinking maybe we could hang out tonight?" I said, feeling like I needed to make up for lost time. It has been over three weeks since I've had the chance to talk or hang out with anyone, especially Riley.

"Oh, can we maybe make plans for next weekend?"

"Sure," I said a little disappointed.

"It's just that Justin asked me to hang out. You know because we didn't really get a chance to last time, but I can cancel if you want?"

"No, don't do that. I'm happy you're going to get another chance. I'll just see what Cameron and Sienna are doing."

Riley looked uncomfortable and I could tell she didn't want to upset me. "Umm, Cameron and Sienna are hanging with us. Cameron's bringing Austin and Sienna's been hanging with Kenny so..."

"So it's a couple's thing. I get it. It's cool."

"You're welcome to join us. We just thought you might feel a little uncomfortable with it being all couples and well, you know, after what happened last time," her voice softened.

"Riley, really, it's okay. We'll just make plans for next weekend," I smiled, reassuring her.

"Next weekend, definitely," she said.

I'd been so busy lately I didn't know what to do now that I actually had some down time. Having time to do nothing left me with...well...time to do nothing. I thought maybe I'd call home but didn't want to alarm my mom. I didn't know if she had heard about

220

the break in at school yet and I didn't want to risk her finding out if she didn't know – although knowing my dad I'm sure he was the first to hear about it.

I ended up spending the weekend in my room working on school work. I thought it would be nice to be ahead instead of behind for once. I decided staying in my room would be best so that way I wouldn't run into Roman, Mackenzie, or Aidan. That was just too many people to avoid so staying put was my best option.

Getting the rest I so desperately needed I was able to get up in time for my training session on Monday which pleased Gabe. He praised me for being on time and said if I kept it up he'd go a little easier on me. I wasn't quite sure if he was messing with me or not, but I decided not to take any chances.

He had us do laps again and sprints. Roman still wasn't speaking to me. I didn't mind. When he did decide to talk to me it was only to insult me or make fun of me so the silence was welcomed.

At lunch I noticed Justin and Kenny had now become additions to our table while Roman had sat alone at a table by himself. I also noticed Reagan and Blake had left our table to sit with the triplets at their new table. Apparently the new seating arrangements were a big to do. Dixon filled me in on all the gossip. Most assumed Roman was sitting by himself because of the so called public break-up between him and Mackenzie. And the whole reason Blake and Reagan were sitting somewhere else was because of Justin and Kenny. I didn't know there was any animosity between them until Dixon informed me that Addyson used to date Justin which ended badly, causing a riff between their friendships when Reagan started dating her.

I was just glad for once the gossip wasn't about me. When I first got here, I was the hot topic of conversation, but just like anything else as soon as there's new gossip it's out with the old and in with the new. I was so happy now that I could just blend into the background unnoticed. But the way my life was I knew at any moment I could be right back in the spotlight.

The rest of the week went by pretty much the same and by Friday there was already a new rumor spreading and the talk of new seating arrangements was already forgotten. I was looking forward to doing something with Riley this weekend until I found out Justin had surprised her with a romantic dinner and everyone else had plans as well. Apparently I had forgotten it was Valentine's Day. That tends to happen when you're anti- love. I should have known my friends would have plans. So once again I was alone. It's funny, when I first got here this is what I wanted, but now it doesn't seem as great as I thought it would be.

By Wednesday I was tired of running. "I don't understand how this is going to help me defend myself against a predator?" I whined to Gabe. "All this is teaching me is to run away."

"And that's exactly why you need to do this," he said.

I stopped. "Wait, so what you're saying is our best defense is to run?"

"Yes. Sometimes you are going to come up against someone that you cannot beat and your only chance of surviving is to run. So let's go. Two more laps."

I rolled my eyes and finished my laps. You would think by now I would have learned to keep my mouth shut, but no, I have this strange uncontrollable urge to keep opening it. Once I was done with my extra laps I met Gabe and Roman in the gym. Today we were finally going to start one on one combat. Gabe had us show him what we learned so far in self-defense. Then he went over some techniques to help us improve on what we had already learned.

"Why do we have to learn self-defense when we have powers?" I complained, tired and out of breath.

"What are you going to do? Heal them to death," Roman smirked.

I glared at him. "I can read minds too," I said proudly.

"Yes, that might seem like an advantage to see your attacker's next move, but what happens when he's stronger than you. He has the strength to keep going while you weaken and tire out, giving him the advantage," Gabe said.

"You just have an answer for everything, don't you," I mumbled to myself thinking no one heard.

"Yes, I do," Gabe said.

Damn it.

Roman smirked again. "What are you smiling about?" I snapped.

"I guess we can't all be as lucky as me. Having a defensive power and the moves to back it up," he said cockily.

"Defensive power, please, what are you going to do? Jump start their car for them," I said laughing.

Roman's face turned bright red with anger. He clenched his fist and then opened his hand making a crackling noise. I saw a spark at the base of his palm and took a step forward, challenging him to go ahead. "That's enough!" Gabe yelled. "You're here to learn how to fight as if you didn't have any powers at all. Some of the best guardians fight with nothing but their own strength. You want to argue who has the better power do it on your own time."

Roman and I bowed our heads at our childish behavior. "Now, Ella, you're going to be on the defensive and Roman take the offensive," Gabe said, getting back to business. I took my defensive pose and waited for Roman to attack. We were pretty evenly matched considering Gabe taught both of us. "Ella, pay better attention. You're letting him get you with moves that you should have no problem blocking," Gabe shouted.

"What's the matter? Afraid you're going to break a nail?" Roman taunted. I scowled at him and concentrated.

"That's good Ella, now faster," Gabe said. "Roman hit harder."

Roman came at me full force, but I kept up with him. I saw an opening and I took it, knocking him on his backside. I smiled and turned around, happy I won. Roman swept his leg out, knocking me down. "And that is why you never turn your back on your opponent," Roman said.

"Good job Roman. Ella, you'll get there. Let's go again."

Pissed off that I let Roman get me, I came at him with everything I had. Neither one of us wanted to let the other win. We kept at it. I was getting tired, but I refused to give up. I could tell Roman was tired too and I felt if I just kept this up he would eventually tire out enough and make a mistake.

I was right. Roman was getting sloppy, and just like I predicted he made a mistake, giving me my opportunity. He swung high leaving his left side open. I struck hard and he curled forward. Then I bent down and swept my leg under him, knocking him on his back. To finish it off and claim my win, I jumped on top of him and pressed my knees down hard on his shoulders. I smiled proudly at my victory until he flipped me over his head and pinned me down.

We were both breathing hard, sweat dripping down our faces. Our eyes locked and for a second I saw a flicker of desperation in Roman's eyes. I felt longing, desire, and then it was gone. "I bet you're enjoying this. I know how you like to spend most of your time on your back," he said harshly.

I pulled my knees up and pushed him off of me. Then I got up and walked away. I had enough of his insults and was not going to put up with this anymore. "Ella, where are you going? We're not done!" Gabe called.

"Well I am!" I yelled.

"What's the matter? Can't take a joke?" Roman spat.

I stopped and turned to face him. "A joke? You think that was funny?"

"I call'em like I see'em." I walked right over to him and shoved him. "You're just going to stand there and let her do that?" Roman complained to Gabe.

Gabe shrugged his shoulders. "Defend yourself," he said.

I came at Roman again. This time he blocked me. "You've got a lot of nerve," I said, still attacking. "You have no right to talk. You dated Mackenzie."

"Yes but I actually cared for her unlike Aidan who preys on naïve little girls. Then after he feeds them his lies and convinces them to sleep with him he dumps them."

"I see Mackenzie was telling lies again."

"It's not lies it's the truth," he yelled, getting in my face. I was back on the defensive now as he came at me. "You're just too dumb to see it. You're just like all the others."

"You know nothing about me!" I growled, throwing punch after punch.

"I know enough. I know you're just as weak and pathetic as they were."

That did it. I did not like being called weak. My body started to get hot as I felt the power surge through me. I flung my hands out as he struck. His fists never made it past my hands. It was like he hit a wall, an invisible barrier. And when he collided with that wall there was a bright flash. Roman flew about ten feet in the air. His body slammed into the wall of the gym, knocking him unconscious.

I stood there staring at my hands with my mouth open not believing what just happened. "Ella!" Gabe called. I was so shocked I hadn't even noticed he was kneeling next to Roman. "Ella, focus, we need you," he said, pulling me out of my daze.

I ran over and bent down next to Roman and placed my hands

on his chest. Nothing happened. "It's not working," I said panicked.

"Ella, concentrate, you can do this," Gabe encouraged.

I closed my eyes and tried again. I could feel the power start to surface and when I opened my eyes I saw my hands were glowing. I quickly pressed them on Roman's chest. His eyes flickered and went wide when he saw me. He quickly sat up as I slowly backed away. "You okay?" Gabe asked Roman. He nodded, but never took his eyes off of me. Gabe helped him up. "I think we can call it quits for today."

"How'd you do that?" Roman asked.

"That's what I'd like to know," Gabe said.

"I...I don't know?" And I didn't. I had no idea how it happened or what I did.

"It was like I hit a wall," Roman said.

Gabe looked at me. "You have no idea how you did it?"

"All I remember is getting really mad and then I felt my body get hot and the power. I felt so much power."

"Yeah, I felt it too," Roman said, rubbing the back of his head.

"Roman, I'm sorry I really didn't –"

He put up a hand to stop me. "It's okay. I know you didn't." I could see in his eyes he felt guilty for what he said and thought he deserved getting body slammed into the wall.

"Ella, do you think you could do it again?" Gabe asked.

"Oh, I don't know?"

"Could you try?"

"I guess?"

"Good. You can try on me then," Gabe said.

"Oh, no, I don't want to hurt you."

He laughed. "I think I can handle it. Besides, you have the power to heal if anything goes wrong."

"That's not encouraging," I sighed.

"Just concentrate. Remember what you learned in your powers class." I never thought those breathing techniques were any good until now. I closed my eyes and tried to focus. Breathing in, and out steadily. "Ready?" Gabe asked.

"Ready," I said.

He came at me and I panicked. I threw my hands up trying to block his moves, but he was faster and stronger. "Ella concentrate!" he yelled.

"I can't," I shouted.

"Yes you can! Do it! Now!" he screamed.

It took everything I had, but I found the power deep down inside me. I concentrated on that, pulling strength from it. I flung my hands out as I had before and watched as Gabe struck the invisible wall, flying backwards, and hitting the floor. He didn't go as far as Roman but it was enough to knock him down. "Gabe, are you okay?"

He stood up laughing. "I'm fine," he said, walking back over to me. "I think you might have proven me wrong," he smiled proudly at me.

"Is this another new power?" I asked.

"I believe so," Gabe said.

"But how is that possible? Most vamps only have two at the most, but never three different types of powers?" Roman said, scratching his head.

"That's because Ella is special. She is going to change everything," Gabe said, smiling again like a proud parent.

Roman just stood there staring at me. "What," I said, starting to feel self-conscious with the way he was staring.

"Nothing," he said, giving me a faint smile.

"Ella, I'd like to work with you on this new power of yours," Gabe said.

"That's great, but can we maybe do that tomorrow?" I asked, feeling run down.

"Of course, I think you guys had enough for today."

I sighed thankful and headed into the girls' locker room to shower. When I stepped outside of the locker room Roman was there pacing back and forth. "Hey," I said surprised.

He stopped when I addressed him. "Okay, so, um…" He ran a nervous hand through his hair. "I'm not sure how to say this so I'm just going to say it." I waited with my arms crossed while he tried to spit it out. "Okay, I know I can be a real dick sometimes."

"No, you?" I said sarcastically.

"Look, I'm trying here," he snapped. He caught himself and took a breath. "Sorry, just be…quiet…till I'm done." I gestured for him to finish, interested in what he had to say.

"So, it's clear I have some anger issues," he gave me a warning look and I bit my tongue. "But I'm working on it. I say a lot of stupid shit and don't realize it until it's too late."

"Is there a point, because I basically knew all of this?"

I knew he was trying really hard not to get upset. "What I'm trying to say is I'm working on it, okay. But you don't make it easy."

"So it's my fault you're an ass?"

"Yes, I mean no, ugh!" he growled frustrated. "I just, I'm sorry, okay? I was out of line. I should have never said those things and I didn't mean them," he said like he sincerely meant it.

"Yes you did." I put my hand up to stop him from protesting. "But I accept your apology," I said. Watching the way he struggled to get it out, I knew it was hard for him to admit that.

"Good, 'cause you know I don't just give these things away," he said, returning to his normal self.

"I think you're just afraid because you know I can kick your ass," I smiled.

"Alright, so that's how it's going to be? How about we see who wins when it's a fair fight," he challenged.

"That was a fair fight," I said defensively.

"It was up until you blasted me into the wall."

He had me there. "Alright, how do you suppose we make it fair?"

"Ask one of the witches to cast a spell to block our powers."

"I don't think Gabe will go for that."

"I think he'll love the idea. Remember he did say we should be able to defend ourselves without using our powers."

"Okay, you're on," I said, shaking his hand, and when I did I felt that same spark I felt when our arms brushed lightly in the library. I could see in his eyes he felt it too.

"Hey Roman," Blake called, breaking us from our spell.

"I should go," I said, quickly turning to leave. I rounded the corner and stopped. I knew I shouldn't, but I was curious. I stood still and listened carefully to their conversation.

"What was that about?" Blake asked.

"Oh, nothing. We were just talking about our training sessions," Roman said.

"I wouldn't mind going a few rounds with her," Blake replied and I had to try hard not to get sick. "Is she as crazy as they say she is?" I scoffed at Blake's comment. It took everything I had not to jump around the corner and show him just how crazy I could be.

"Since when did you care if a chick was crazy or not?"

"True, either way it makes no difference to me. Although I

learned from experience the crazier the chick the better they are in bed."

"Please, the only experience you have is with your mom."

I had to cover my mouth to keep from laughing out loud.

"More like your mom," Blake said.

"Shut up," Roman laughed. "C'mon, let's get some grub."

I hurried down the hall so they wouldn't see me. Then I headed straight for the dining hall because like always, I was starving.

Today our table was filled to capacity. Blake and Reagan had rejoined our table as did Roman. By the time I got there, there were no seats left. "Here," Roman said, pulling a chair from another table.

"Thanks," I said softly. I turned to Dixon and asked quietly, "So how come Reagan and Blake are sitting here again? I thought Reagan and Justin had a falling out?" I knew Dixon was the queen of gossip. If anyone knew anything he definitely did.

He leaned in closely. "Well, from what I heard, Reagan found out that Addyson purposely played him and Justin against each other and used them both just so she could become part of Mackenzie's coven."

"Those three are truly evil," I said, glaring at Mackenzie as her and her 'coven' walked in. As if she knew I was talking about her, she turned toward me, and gave me her best vindictive smile. Clearly she had no remorse for what she did. "She needs to be stopped."

"Who?" Sienna asked.

"Who do you think?" I said.

"Mackenzie," Sienna and Cameron said together.

"You don't want to go up against Mackenzie, trust me," Austin chimed in.

"Yeah, you didn't hear about the last girl who tried to take revenge on them," Blake said.

"What happened to her?" I asked, more out of curiosity than fear.

"Let's just say they never found the body."

I rolled my eyes. "Please, I managed to survive an attack by a crazy vamp. I think I can handle a tiny blond with split ends," I said.

"I wouldn't underestimate her," Reagan said. Part of me knew he was right. I already seen what she could do with that spell she put on Aidan and me. I couldn't even begin to think how truly powerful she really was.

All of a sudden we heard a huge commotion out in the hall. I froze not sure what was going on. There were a few grunts and growls as the doors flew open and a large man tumbled down the steps. Roman got up and stood in front of me defensively, which really pissed me off because clearly he thought I couldn't take care of myself.

"What's going on?" Riley asked, craning her neck to see. I stood up and tried to get a better look at the young man as guardians flew into the surrounding area and attacked him. He was strong and took them out with ease. He picked off each guardian one by one as they came at him.

"Wow, look at him go. He's amazing he's −"

"Oh my god," I said, interrupting Dixon when I caught a glimpse of his profile and stood up. I knew I had to stop this before it was too late.

I tried to get past Roman but he wouldn't budge. "Ella, what are you doing?"

"I need to stop this," I said.

"What are you crazy?" Dean said, blocking my other side. I had no way out.

I knew I would get my ass chewed out for this later but right now it was my only option. "Dean, get out of my way."

"No way," he said standing firm.

"Move or I'll make you move," I growled. He stood there with his arms crossed. "Fine, but don't say I didn't warn you." I tried to shove past him again but he shoved me back. So I attacked. I knocked him to the ground.

"Oh my god!" Sienna shrieked, thinking I've lost it.

"Ella!" Roman yelled, grabbing my arm. I turned on him next but he wasn't as easy to take down as Dean.

"What the hell has gotten into you?" Cameron yelled. "Stop this!"

But I didn't stop. I didn't have time to. I managed to back Roman up enough to make a getaway. I leapt onto a table to get out of his reach and ran full speed across it, leaping from table to table and right into the middle of the scuffle.

"Stop!" I yelled, but no one listened. This time I put some force behind it. "Stop!" I yelled again. My voice boomed and echoed throughout the entire room. There was so much power in it, it silenced everyone and stopped the fighting.

One of the guardians turned to me, eyes wide. "Miss," he began, choking on his words. I looked at him funny. "You need to step away," he said, taking a step back from me like he was scared. I held my head higher, thinking, *"you better move."*

"No, this is just a big misunderstanding," I said, pleading with them. I looked around the room as everyone stared at me a little frightened. *Huh, didn't think I was that intimidating, but okay.*

"What is going on?" Gabe asked, coming into the room.

"Gabe, tell them to back off," I said.

Gabe froze when he saw me, his eyes grew wide, and then he quickly collected himself. "Stand down men," he said.

"But sir —"

"I said stand down!" he yelled. "This child is not a threat."

"With all due respect sir, he just took down half my men."

Gabe looked at them confused. I guess he thought the scuffle was because of me until he noticed the young man to my right. "I would hope so. After all I did train him," Gabe smiled.

The guardians backed off, but remained with strange looks on their faces. I turned to face the person behind all this chaos. "Billy, what are you doing here?" He looked at me funny. Basically he was wearing the same expression as everyone else. "What...do I like have something on my face?"

"Ella, you're glowing," he said.

I looked down and saw a silvery blue light illuminating my skin. "What is it?" I asked.

"I don't know, but it's beautiful," Dixon said, joining us. "Hey Billy."

"Hey Dixon," he said casually.

I could feel everyone's eyes on me. "How do I make it stop?" I asked a little panicked.

"Ella, Billy, you two come with me," Gabe said.

"I'm coming too," Dixon said following us.

The guardians followed and kept close as we walked over to the teachers' dorms while I lit the way.

CHAPTER EIGHTEEN

Gabe took us straight to the teachers' dorms and knocked on one of the doors. Ms. Kraft answered. "Hello Sylvia. I'm sorry to disturb you, but we seem to have a bit of a problem," Gabe said, stepping out of the way.

"Oh dear, Ella, you're glowing," she said.

"Yeah, how do I make it stop?" I asked.

She pulled me inside and over to one of the couches. "Give me your hands." I did as she said. "Now close your eyes, breathe deeply, and imagine yourself letting go."

"Letting go of what exactly?"

"Your anger. Think calm thoughts, and release it."

The first thing I saw was his eyes, deep, dark blues that I always seemed to get lost in. Then came his messy black hair and cocky smile. I put everything together and waited for Tristan to come into focus. Only, it wasn't Tristan who I thought I was picturing. It was Roman. I stiffened at the image. "Ella, you need to relax," I heard Ms. Kraft say.

I let out a breath and tried again, but every time I tried to clear my head Roman would pop in, making me agitated. "Ella, whatever you are holding on to, you need to let it go," Ms. Kraft said, guiding me. "Listen to your heart. Let it lead you to where it belongs."

Not knowing what else to do, I let myself go. I opened my heart and my mind, allowing it to take me to where I belong. At first I got flashes; a sexy smile, twinkling, dark blue eyes, strong hands running through silky, black hair. When the images came into focus again, I opened my eyes. "Roman," I whispered. His name brushed like soft air across my lips.

I looked up to see Dixon's smirking face and I knew he heard me.

I avoided his eyes and turned back to a smiling Ms. Kraft. I looked down to see the glow was gone. I sighed relieved, until I saw the goofy grin on Ms. Kraft's face. "What is it?" I asked.

She pulled me up off the couch and over to a mirror. I now understood why she was looking at me funny. I had another blue streak in my hair. This one was in the same spot as the other just on the opposite side. I sighed. *Great, now I have two.* "I think it's wonderful," Ms. Kraft said.

"Thanks," I said, forcing a smile. I turned back around and noticed Dixon was the only one left. "Where are Gabe and Billy?"

"Gabe took him down to the office. They have some things to sort out. Billy caused quite a stir," Dixon said, still looking at me in awe.

"Ms. Kraft, thank you for helping me out, but do you mind. I'd like to check on my friend."

"Of course, but I would like you to come back. I want to talk to you about this new power."

"How about this weekend?" I asked.

"This weekend will be perfect," she smiled.

I thanked her again and headed down to the office with Dixon. "Why are you looking at me like that?" I asked Dixon.

"You do realize that you were just glowing a few minutes ago, like as in you looked like a divine being," he said in amazement. "It was the freakin' coolest thing I have ever seen."

"To you yes, but to everyone else I'm sure I now qualify as the school freak again," I said, mortified at having to explain to everyone what the hell just happened when I didn't even know.

Dixon stopped and stood in front of me with his hands on my shoulders. "Ella, when are you going to realize that you are an incredibly amazing person? You are original. One of a kind. There is no one else like you and that is what makes you so special and being friends with me definitely helps," he said, giving me a wink. "When you stop caring so much about what everyone else thinks you can get past this whole bullshit of thinking you are a freak."

If I could just convince myself, this would be a whole lot easier. I didn't used to care what people thought and I had no idea why all of sudden I cared now. I stood up straighter. "You're right Dixon," I said.

"Well of course I am," he said, dusting pretend lint off his shoulder. I stifled an eye roll and thanked him for the pep talk and gave him a hug. Then I braced myself before I opened the door to the office.

There was a lot yelling going on inside Aidan's office. I didn't even bother to knock. I just let myself in. "Ella, what are you doing here?" Aidan asked, clearly upset at the interruption.

I stepped forward to address him. "Billy is my friend."

"Well, your friend here caused a lot of issues for us," he said, glaring at Billy.

"I told you. None of this would have happened if they would have just let me in in the first place," Billy said.

"And like the guardians told you at the gate we cannot let you in without proper identification or stating your business of why you are here."

"I did," Billy growled, irritated.

"Regardless, actions must be taken," Aidan said.

"For what?" Billy asked.

Gabe stepped forward. "Surely you can see how this was a misunderstanding and something that can be overlooked."

"You think taking out half the guardians on campus and causing a riot is acceptable? That we're just going to let this go?"

"You are," I said stepping in.

"You are out of line Ella," Aidan snapped, and then quickly recoiled, regretting raising his voice at me.

I tried not to let my irritation show. I held my head high and spoke with a strong voice. "No, I am not. As you said so yourself, Billy has taken out half of the guardians on campus which makes him quite the warrior. Someone like him would make a great asset in assisting the guardians, don't you think?"

"While I do agree with you on that, I still can't just let what happened go. Some of our best men are laid up in the infirmary right now."

I looked over to see Billy smiling, proud of what he had done. "I will take responsibility for that. You can punish me."

"I appreciate you being loyal to your friend, but I cannot and will not do that. I'm sorry but you are going to have to leave the campus immediately." He made a motion for the guardians to take him out.

I stepped in front of them to block them. "You can't make him leave," I said.

"Yes I can," Aidan said, gesturing for the guardians to proceed.

"Wait, he can't!" I yelled. I was grasping at straws trying to come up with a logical explanation of how to keep him here.

"I'm sure it will be fine. Clearly he can take care of himself," Aidan said. He gestured to the other two guardians standing by the door. "Would you please escort him out?"

"No, he's...he's my guardian!" They stopped and Aidan looked at me confused.

"No, Gabe is your guardian," he said, straightening up.

"Yes he is, well was," I started and turned to Gabe pleading with my eyes for him to go along with this. "With everything that Gabe has on his plate right now I thought it would be easier on him if I relieved him of his duty and called Billy."

"Is that true?" he asked Gabe.

"Yes it is. I apologize for the inconvenience. I've been very busy as Ella has mentioned and I'm afraid the date of his arrival had slipped my mind."

Aidan looked us both over. "If that's true then why didn't you just say that instead of trying to break in," Aidan questioned Billy.

"I wanted to see how easy it was to get in here if I was an intruder. As you can see it was far too easy. I think the only one you should be mad at is the idiot who hired those goons." I elbowed Billy letting him know to shut it. His last comment made Aidan narrow his eyes at him indicating he was the idiot.

I spoke up quickly to diffuse the tension. "It is obvious as to why I called Billy to temporarily take Gabe's place, that part is clear. I can assure you from this moment on there will be no more issues...or surprises," I said.

I didn't know if Aidan was buying our story or not, but he sank down in his chair, looking defeated. "Fine, he can stay. There is one slight problem though. The entire guest housing is filled due to the amount of extra guardians we called in."

"That won't be a problem. I no longer have a roommate so he can stay with me in my room," I said.

"That, I cannot allow," Aidan said.

"Billy is my guardian I'm sure once everyone is aware of that it won't be an issue. It only makes sense that he stays with me."

"I can vouch for him," Gabe said. "Billy was a former student of mine and I can assure you he is and will be a perfect gentleman."

Aidan rubbed his head, showing he had enough. "Fine, but this is only temporary until a room becomes available," he said, caving.

We all nodded in agreement. "Are we done?" I asked.

"We're done," Aidan said. The two guardians left with Gabe, Billy, and Dixon. "Ella, can I talk to you for a minute?" I stopped, with my hand on the door. "Can you close the door?" I didn't want to do this now, but I knew sooner or later I would have to. I closed the door and turned to face him.

"I know you probably hate me and I don't blame you. But you have to know that wasn't me."

"I don't hate you." He sighed, relaxing a little. "But I still don't feel like I'm ready yet."

"I understand. I just don't want you to be afraid of me, because that is not who I am."

"I know. I just...I just still need some time."

"Take all the time you need. I just want you to know you can still come to me if you need anything. I don't want you to feel like you can't. I'm still here for you, as your headmaster of course."

"Thank you, Mr. Callahan." With that I left. I wasn't ready, but I knew over time I would be able to forgive him. I knew we were under a spell, but the harsh memory of what could have happened was still too fresh in my mind and I couldn't get past it. Spell or not. I knew the real person at fault and she would pay for what she did. Yes she would pay.

I found Billy at the end of the hall with Dixon waiting for me. "Well, aren't you quite the trouble maker," I said to Billy.

"You know how I like to make an entrance," he smiled, giving me a big, bear hug.

"What are you doing here? I mean, not that I'm not happy to see you, but really?"

"I heard Jack was in the area," he said, his face no longer amused.

"You heard right, but why don't we talk about that later. You must be starving."

"I could eat," he said, rubbing his belly.

"I don't care if you do or don't. Your little show interrupted my dinner and I haven't had a chance to eat and I'm starving."

He laughed, throwing his arm over me. "Well, come on then."

You could hear outside the doors that the dining hall was

bustling with talk of what just happened. But as soon as Billy and I walked back in the crowd fell silent and all eyes were on us. "Is it always like this?" Billy asked.

"Well when you bust through the doors and take on five guardians –"

"Seven," he corrected.

"Sorry, when you take on seven guardians single handedly." He smiled and gave me a small squeeze. "Not to mention the fact that I was glowing when I stopped the fighting."

"That was pretty cool. How'd you do that?"

"I have no idea," I said as we stepped into the food line.

Dixon pulled another chair over for Billy and we all sat down. Everyone just stared at us. "Oh, yeah, guys this is Billy." They all managed a hello or hey there.

"Ella your hair," Cameron said. I half expected her to bitch me out for attacking Dean and Roman, but no, my hair is the first thing she would mention.

"Oh, yeah," I said rolling my eyes. "I have another blue streak." They just stared with astonishment.

"Okay, so I'm just going to say it," Cameron started. "You know you were glowing about twenty minutes ago? And what the hell was with you going all Buffy on Dean and Roman?"

And there it is.

"Um, yeah," was all I said.

She looked at me. "Care to explain?"

"If I understood it myself I would, but I have no idea how it happened," I said, shrugging my shoulders. "And Dean and Roman wouldn't let me go. I did warn them," I added.

"I thought it was really neat," Riley said. "The glowing part not the fighting," she smiled sheepishly.

"Whatever it was, it was powerful. I felt all the energy that was exuding from you," Sienna said.

After a few minutes, everyone stopped gawking at us like we were some science experiment and went back to their dinner. They seemed to understand and accept my explanation of why I hulked out on Dean and Roman, which I was thankful for, allowing me to go back to my dinner.

Billy finished all his food and was now picking off of my plate. "Where's Dean?" I asked. I hadn't seen him since we returned.

"He, uh, said he needed to get some air," Austin said. I didn't need any other explanation. I knew Dean was mad at me for rushing into the fight and knocking him out. He needed time to cool off. I knew to give him time to clear his head and talk to him later.

Always the one to diffuse an awkward situation, Cameron started a different conversation. "So Billy, how do you and Ella know each other?"

He looked at me to explain while he continued to stuff his face. "Billy and I went to school together in Vermont."

"I guess that means you know Dixon as well?"

"Dixon and I were fraternity brothers," Billy said in between bites.

"Dixon, you never told us you were in a fraternity," Sienna said.

"It never came up," he shrugged and then smacked Billy's hand away from his food. He had finished everything on my plate and was now looking for more. Riley noticed his hungry eyes and offered her plate of fries to him. He dug in without a second thought and gave her a mumbled, "thanks."

"Ella, I never would have expected you to be hanging out with fraternity boys," Cameron teased.

"Ella was in our sister sorority," Dixon said, opening his big fat mouth.

"Wait, you were in a sorority?" Cameron's eyes grew big with excitement.

"Okay, well, we need to get going so I can help Billy get situated," I said getting up.

"Wait I want to hear more about the fact that you were in a sorority," Cameron said.

"Sorry got to go." I grabbed Billy and hauled butt out of there.

Once we were out of earshot, Billy turned to me and said, "Care to tell me what that was all about?"

I sighed. "The people here don't know what happened back at Vermont. I know with Jack showing up they're bound to find out eventually, but right now I'm not ready to tell them."

"So, anything else I need to know, for future reference?"

"Billy, we have a lot to talk about," I said as we walked across the campus to my room.

We walked the rest of the way in silence. When we reached my room I unlocked the door and let him in. "So, this is your room," he said, looking around.

"My roommate moved out temporarily so you can have her bed."

"She moved out?" he asked, eyebrows raised.

"Long story, anyway, what was up with the big theatrics?" I asked, sitting down on my bed.

"When I got to the gate and told them I had to see you right away they wouldn't let me. So I found another way in."

"You couldn't use the phone?"

"I was never one for conversation," he smiled.

I caught Billy up on what was going on. I told him about how Jack got on campus, but got away before anyone could catch him. I told him all about my newly developed powers, my new friends, the school and my classes. Turns out Billy had gone to a similar school back home when he was sixteen. That's how he met Gabe. Gabe was a teacher there and had trained Billy to become a guardian when he finished college. This would explain how he was able to take out all those guardians.

Billy then told me all about his adventures tracking Jack up until they brought him here. When he found out Jack was in the area he knew he had to come here and make sure I was safe. "You must be exhausted," I said.

"I am pretty tired," he admitted. "I could also use a shower."

"Do you even have any extra clothes?"

"I did have a bag, but it kind of got confiscated in the scuffle."

"The bathroom is right there," I said, pointing to the door behind him. "Why don't you go ahead and take a shower. Help yourself to anything in there. I'll go see if they have your bag. If not I'm sure I can scrounge up some extra clothes for you."

"Thanks Ella, for everything."

"It's no biggie," I said. I left and headed to the office to see if they had Billy's bag. The secretary told me they had it in the guardian's office down the hall. I walked down the hall and luckily was able to retrieve it without any hassle. I picked up the bag and headed back to my room.

On my way back I ran into Roman who was coming out of the dorms. "Hey," I said, not sure how to approach him. He just glared at me. That was expected, considering. "I just wanted to say I'm sorry.

"Apology not accepted."

"Fine then, be that way." I wasn't going to beg for his forgiveness, besides it was his fault since he got in my way.

"You know how stupid that was?" Roman growled, throwing his arms up in frustration. I looked at him confused. "Of course you don't. You're just some dumb, little girl who likes to play hero," he spat and walked off to the side of the building.

Jaw dropped. I followed him. "Excuse me, I don't know who the hell you think you are but you have no right to talk to me like that. I am so sick of you treating me the way you do when I –"

I didn't even get the chance to finish my sentence. Roman pushed me up against the wall and attacked me...with his lips. I was so shocked I didn't know how to react. When I came to my senses I pushed him away. I narrowed my eyes at him and then slapped him across the face. Then I grabbed him and kissed him back. I think he was the one surprised now. I pulled away. Panicking, I slapped him again and then I took off, leaving him standing there shocked and confused, which was pretty much what I was feeling right now.

I almost dropped Billy's bag in my haste to get away. I was flushed and winded by the time I reached my room. To make matters worse, when I got back, Mackenzie was there. "What are you doing here?" I snapped.

"Not that it's any of your business, but in case you forgot this is still my room too and I just had to get a few things," she said as Billy walked out of the bathroom, wearing only a towel. Mackenzie's eyes widened and she smiled. "Well, I see you traded up."

"You can leave now."

"When you get tired of playing with children you can come find me in room 306," she purred, shaking her behind as she walked out.

"Who was that?" Billy asked.

"My roommate, Mackenzie. Stay away from her. She bites and not in a good way."

He made a face letting me know I didn't have to worry about that. "You found my bag."

"Oh yeah, here," I said, handing it to him and trying not to stare. I could definitely see the appeal Josie had to him. He was very attractive and built, very built. I had a hard time taking my eyes off of him. Billy noticed my staring and cleared his throat. "Oh, I'm sorry," I said embarrassed, and quickly turned around.

"It's okay," he smiled and walked back into the bathroom.

"I'm such an idiot," I said to myself falling down on the bed and burying my face in the pillows. My mind was swimming with images of Roman. I couldn't believe he kissed me. Worse, I couldn't believe I kissed him back. What was I thinking and was Sienna right? Ugh this couldn't be happening. I covered my face with my hands ready to scream.

"Are you okay?" Billy asked, fully clothed.

"Yes," I said sitting up. "I'm gonna change." I grabbed my pajamas out of the drawer, and went into the bathroom to change. Then I turned off the lights and hopped into bed. "Goodnight Billy."

"Goodnight Ella." I turned over on my side and pulled the covers tight. "Hey, Ella?"

"Yeah?"

"I still hear her, Josie. Sometimes I think I even see her. I dream about her all the time."

"I miss her too. I even thought I heard and saw her, but I know it was just my mind playing tricks on me."

"Do you miss him?" he asked. He didn't have to say his name. I knew who he was talking about.

"All the time," I admitted.

"Does the pain ever go away?"

"Eventually, all wounds heal, overtime. When you're ready you'll know," I said, trying to reassure him although I wasn't the best person to give advice about this.

I couldn't sleep. After the mention of Tristan I couldn't get him out of my head. I grabbed my journal and headed into the bathroom so I wouldn't wake Billy. I closed the door and climbed in to the bathtub closing the curtain. I opened up my Journal and let the pen do it's job.

I still love Tristan. There isn't a day that goes by that I don't think about him. Some nights I still cry myself to sleep, but with each passing day it gets a little better. Saying goodbye to him on New Year's was one of the hardest things I ever had to do. Sometimes I wish I never did, but I knew if I didn't I wouldn't be able to move on with my life. I just wish I had the chance to tell him I loved him. I know that's a big part of why it's still hard to let go. When I said goodbye to him I felt like I gave a part of my heart away, turning me cold, and making it hard for me to open my heart to anyone. When I thought I had feelings for Aidan, I thought that maybe that part I lost was finally healing, but it was just a trick - a spell that some evil witch put on me for her own amusement, a spell that had gone horribly wrong. I can't imagine what would have happened if I wasn't able to break through the spell on my own. I don't even want to think about it. I feel betrayed, abused, and used. I feel dirty and stupid. And at the same time I feel bad for Aidan. I know he didn't mean to do what he did, but I still feel...uncertain. I'm not sure how I should act around him, but I know things won't be the same. Mackenzie had made sure to ruin that.

And why?

That was the big question, why? What did she have against me? I've never done anything to her...yet. She's probably just some spoiled child who gets pleasure out of torturing other people for her our entertainment because she has nothing better to do. She will get hers, when the time is right, she won't see it coming.

And then there's Roman. I never saw this coming. I never imagined this outcome. I don't know what to do with him? I honestly wonder if he does have multiple personalities. That would explain a lot. I mean what the hell happened tonight? One minute we were fighting and before I knew it he's kissing me and I'm kissing him back. The worst part of it all is I think I liked it.

In a way I feel like I'm betraying Tristan, but I know he would want me to be happy. Oh who am I kidding? He would want me to pine after him forever, even in death. - jerk.

But that's part of the reason I love him so. What am I worried about anyway. It was just one kiss. He probably thinks I'm crazy. I mean what girl slaps a guy, kisses him, and then slaps him again? It was a onetime only thing. It will never happen again. Really, me and Roman? The thought is just unconceivable, catastrophic even. I mean Roman actually liking me? I liking Roman? That wasn't possible, was it?

Crap, I think I'm in trouble.

I sighed and rested my head back against the cool ceramic of the tub. I laid there for a moment before I started to get a cramp in my neck. I closed my journal and climbed out of the tub and crawled back into bed.

I woke up sometime in the middle of the night. I rolled over to check on Billy, but he wasn't there. I sat up and got out of bed. I thought maybe he was in the bathroom so I knocked on the door, but he wasn't there. I turned around and found Roman sitting on my bed. "Roman, what are you doing here?"

"I'm here for you," he said, getting up off the bed, and walking over to me. He stood in front of me staring in to my eyes. Then he bent down and kissed me and I kissed him back. I ran my fingers through his hair as he wrapped his arms around my waist. I felt that shock again like I had before when we touched. It sent tiny shivers all through my body. He pulled back and smiled at me, but it wasn't Roman anymore it was Tristan.

"But how?" I asked.

"You're dreaming," he said in a strange voice.

"What?"

"Ella, Ella, wake up," Billy said, shaking me gently. I opened my eyes and realized I was still in my bed.

"What happened?"

"I think you were dreaming," he said kindly. "Was it a bad dream?"

"No," I said, not wanting to elaborate.

"You think you'll be okay to go back to sleep? If you need to talk I'm a good listener. Not really good at giving advice but –"

I cupped his hand. "It's okay Billy. Thank you, but I'll be fine," I said, lying back down and hoping I would be.

CHAPTER NINETEEN

I left a note for Billy in the morning telling him that I had a training session with Gabe and would come back to check on him in between my classes. Gabe made us do laps again and said we'd work on my new power later today. I was still weirded out by my dream last night and the kiss that I could barely look at Roman. It helped that he wasn't talking to me at the moment. I mean he kissed me first. He had no right to be mad at me. Okay yes I slapped him, twice, but still that's not the point. He was so frustrating sometimes that he infuriated me. His whole Jekyll and Hyde personality really pissed me off. I just didn't understand it.

In Royal Economics Cameron leaned over close and asked, "So what's the skinny on Billy? Is he like an old flame? Did you guys take advantage of having a private room?" she smiled wagging her eyebrows.

I rolled my eyes. "No, Billy is just a friend."

"He's pretty hot. If I were you I'd definitely take advantage of that."

"Again, he's just a friend."

"Oh god, there's something wrong with him. What is it? Does he have like a third nipple? Impotent? Gay? That's it isn't it he's gay. Why are all the cute ones always gay?" she said, shaking her head.

"No he's not gay or any of those other things. He's great actually."

"Then what's the problem? You're not, like, a lesbian are you? If you are its okay I'm totally cool with it."

"Cameron, I'm not a lesbian," I said, getting tired of this conversation.

"Shoo," she said, wiping her brow. I just shook my head. "Again I ask what the problem is."

"He used to date my best friend Josie until she was killed by the same vamp that's after me," I said. That shut her up for the rest of class.

When class was dismissed, Cameron started the conversation again. "Ella, I'm sorry I didn't know. I feel like such an ass."

"Don't," I said. "You didn't know. No one does. But I think it's time you guys know the truth." I didn't get too detailed, but I told her enough. I explained about Jack and all the things he did to get my powers, including all the people he killed in his efforts.

"Oh, Ella, no wonder you were so freaked."

"Yeah, well, that's how I got sent here. On top of my parents wanting me to learn about who I am they also thought I would be safe here and Jack wouldn't find me."

"You don't have to worry anymore. We won't let anything happen to you. We'll make sure he doesn't get anywhere near you."

"No. You can't. You need to stay away from him. This is why I didn't want to tell anyone. I don't want anyone else to get hurt or worse...killed."

"Ella, don't worry so much. It will give you premature wrinkles."

I laughed. "That's what Josie used to say."

"Smart girl," she smiled. Cameron had convinced me to tell the rest of the group at lunch. I wasn't prepared for this, but she was right. They had the right to know.

I checked on Billy before my next class and found a note from him on my bed. It said he met up with Gabe and was going to spend some time with him and that he would meet up with me at lunch. I was glad he knew someone else here besides Dixon. That way he wouldn't be cooped up in my room all day.

I found Billy at lunch already sitting with everyone else. Roman wasn't there, but that didn't surprise me. I got in line, got my food, and sat down. "Hey guys, Ella has something to tell you," Cameron said, getting right to it before I had the chance to chicken out. I thought she would at least be kind enough to let me eat first but I guess not.

All eyes were on me and I started to get nervous. "Ella, it's okay, you can do it," she smiled, encouraging me. I looked at Dean who was curious as to what was going on and then I turned to Billy who I was pretty sure already had an idea on what I was going to say.

"Go ahead," Billy said, squeezing my hand.

I told them what I had told Cameron. How dangerous Jack was and all the people he and Cadence had killed. I left out the part about Tristan. I just let them know he was a good friend who saved me when Jack and Cadence came after me. They didn't need to know the other stuff. That was private.

"Wow Ella," Sienna said.

"We are definitely going to be here for you no matter what," Riley said.

"See, this is exactly what I didn't want. I don't want you guys involved. I couldn't stand to see any of you get hurt."

"We won't take no for an answer," Sienna said.

"Besides, we have wolves and some kick ass witches on our side," Cameron said confidently. "What's one guy against all of us?"

I smiled weakly. The last thing I wanted was them to get involved, but it was obvious no matter how much I protested they wouldn't take no for an answer. I guess I was kind of glad they didn't run screaming. But I wasn't happy about them volunteering to put themselves in danger. I pushed my cold food around my plate while everyone chatted about all the kick ass powers they had to contribute to take to the fight. If there was one. I planned on not involving them if it came down to that.

On the way to training I did feel like some weight was lifted off my shoulders. I guess telling them wasn't as bad as I thought it would be. Now I wouldn't have to hide my past anymore and that felt good. When I got to the gym I saw Billy was there talking to Gabe. "Hey Billy, you here to watch me kick some ass?" I joked.

He laughed. "Is that a challenge?"

"Come on, let's see what you got," I said, putting my fists up.

"You guys can spar later," Gabe said. "Billy's here to help. Going up against someone different will give you more of a challenge. He's also been able to offer me a lot of good information on Jack. From following him he knows how he moves."

The mention of Jack shattered what little happiness I had left. "I found out from my informant's that he's planning something big. He's rallying up some other rogue vamps to help him with his plan."

I no longer felt good about my friends knowing about Jack and wanting to stand by me. "What does all this mean?" I asked worried.

"That just means we need to be prepared," Gabe said. "These

extra sessions are what are going to help you defend yourself against him when the time comes."

"You don't have to worry Ella. I won't let him get close enough to you to let that happen," Billy said, seeing the fear on my face. Just the thought of going up against him again was terrifying.

"Ella, I want to work with you on your new power and then I'm going to have Billy teach you some new techniques."

When he said you, I looked at the clock and realized Roman was late. Roman was never late. "Where's Roman?" I asked curiously.

"He's going to be taking a break from training," Gabe said like it was no big deal.

"Is everything...okay?" I wondered.

"He informed me his school work was falling behind and he needed to catch up."

"Oh," was all I said.

"Do a few laps. I want to go over a few more things with Billy." I nodded and took off circling the gym. I knew Roman's excuse was a lie. He was amongst the top is his class. He never missed an assignment and I never heard of him getting less than a B- on his tests. There was another reason and I knew that reason was me. "Ella, we're ready," Gabe called.

We started with practicing my new power. Gabe had me focus and try to bring up my shield without him attacking me. After about the hundredth try I managed to do it, but it only lasted about a second. We learned that it took a lot of energy for me to use this new power and I got weaker faster after using it. Gabe suggested that I only use this power as a last defense or if I absolutely had to. After giving me a few minutes to regenerate, Gabe had Billy show me some new techniques and then had me go up against Billy.

"Don't worry Billy. I'll go easy on you," I teased. "Remember, don't hold back on my account."

"I won't," he smiled wickedly and I got a little nervous.

I struck first and Billy countered my attack, but I didn't give up. I fought with everything I had. But against someone like Billy it wasn't enough. He knocked me down on my behind again and again and every time I got right back up.

After my last failed attempt, I didn't bother to get up. I just lie there on the floor and stared at the ceiling, trying to catch my breath. Billy came over and stood above me, smiling. Then he offered me his hand to help me up. "Not bad," he said. "You can definitely hold your own. I was impressed."

"You don't have to flatter me," I said.

"Ella, I've been training for years and the fact that you even kept up with me at all says a lot."

"I was actually taking it easy on you. I didn't want to embarrass you."

"Oh really?" he said.

"Well, ya know," I bumped his shoulder. He bumped me back almost knocking me over. I jumped on him and made him give me a piggyback as we made our way over to Gabe.

"Good job Ella. Alright, now I want you to watch Billy and me," Gabe said. I hopped off Billy's back and sat on the bleachers to watch. I knew Billy was enjoying this, getting a chance to go against his old teacher.

"Come on Billy, kick his ass," I cheered. Gabe narrowed his eyes at me and I laughed. I watched the two of them go at it. It was like watching survival of the fittest. Just when I thought Billy had him, Gabe came back stronger, hitting harder and knocking Billy down. Billy did fairly well for having Gabe as an opponent.

When they were done, Gabe had me spend the rest of the session learning from the mistakes I made. He told me tomorrow we would work on what it would be like to have multiple opponents attack you at once. I was not looking forward to that.

I was definitely sore after tonight's session and couldn't wait to crash. I was so tired I skipped dinner and went straight to bed. Gabe had let me know before I left he was giving me the morning off. He told me I've been working hard and deserved a break. I still had my training session after class – so much for the break – I wasn't going to complain though because now I had an extra day that I could sleep in. I missed those days and longed for when I had them.

I spent the weekend working with Ms. Kraft on my new found glowing power. But no matter what we tried we couldn't figure out what had triggered it. After hours of research and Ms. Kraft trying many different spells and tricks to figure it out, we came up empty. Ms. Kraft said she would do some more research and if she found anything out she would let me know. Now that my weekend was spent, I went back to my room to work on my homework.

"Any progress?" Billy asked.

"No. The most that we could come up with was that I put so much force into my voice when trying to stop the fight that everything kind of just came out," I said shrugging.

"No harm no foul," he said, lying back on the bed.

"What did you do this weekend?"

"I hung out with Dixon for a bit then I hung out with your brother and some of his friends."

"Oh, sorry, I promise I won't leave you alone again," I said, feeling bad for him having to hang with Dean. Nobody should have to suffer through that.

He chuckled. "He's not that bad and you forget I was friends with Tristan."

"Please, like I could forget."

February 25

The following week went as followed; training, classes, training - once again not leaving me with much time to spend with my friends. The only time I got to see them was during class or when we ate. If Billy wasn't helping out with the training sessions I wouldn't see him either. And that's basically how my life went for the next few weeks. Training, classes, training and then my weekends were spent catching up on school work or working with Ms. Kraft. I was starting to feel like a drone. It's not like I didn't appreciate the extra training sessions, I did. They were helping a lot and I was even building some nice muscle from them. I just wish they weren't twice a day every day, but if I was going to take down Jack, I needed to know how.

Roman still has yet to speak a word to me since that night which makes for an awkward hour in spells and casting. At least in history I didn't have to sit next to him which made it a little easier, but in spells and casting it made for *a very uncomfortable silence. Every now and then I would catch him watching me from the corner of his eye and I could tell he wanted to say something, but wouldn't. I know I should say something, but every time I got the courage he would turn to look at me as if he knew. And every time I looked into those deep, dark blue eyes, I lost all my nerve. So I always just sat there, counting down the minutes until class was over.*

Today when I woke up, I felt, strange. I knew something was going to happen that would change my life. I tried not to let this feeling bother me, but it stayed with me. Like an annoying pain in the back of your head that you knew would grow and get worse until you did something about it. I ignored it the best I could and tried to go on with my day.

In spells and casting, I noticed there was something different about Roman. He had a nervous look on his face and would constantly shift his position in his chair like he had an itch he couldn't scratch.

After class, I quickly stuffed my papers in my bag getting ready to leave when, "Ella?" I looked over at Roman. "Can I...talk to you for a minute...in private?" I nodded. That's the best I could do for now. Afraid if I opened my mouth I might say something stupid. He gestured for me to follow him so I did. He led me out of the building and across the quad to the dorms making me start to feel nervous.

"Where are we going?" I finally asked.

"I'd thought we'd go to my room. It's more private," he said, his voice deep.

I froze, not liking the idea. "I have to drop off some books. Do you mind if we just talk in my room?" I asked. For some reason I felt if we were in my room I would have more control over the situation and feel more comfortable.

"Okay," he said, swallowing the lump in his throat. We walked the rest of the way in silence.

When we got to my room, I unlocked the door, and let him in. My eyes widened when I caught sight of one of my bras on the floor from my rush to get ready this morning. I causally, but quickly walked over and kicked it under my bed hoping Roman didn't notice. The smile on his face told me he did. I narrowed my eyes at him and his smile faded. "You wanted to talk?" I said, hoping to get this over with. The longer I stood alone with him the harder it was for me to focus on anything else but his lips.

"Right," he said, clearing his throat, indicating he was nervous. "Do you want to sit down?"

"No. I rather stand," I said, thinking that was safer.

"So um...I wanted to talk to you because I..." he paused, running a shaky hand through his hair. "Well, as you know I took a break from training."

"Because of your schoolwork," I said, testing him.

"Yes, because I was falling behind."

"You're so full of shit," I said before I could stop myself. Now that it was out, I felt the need to let him have it. There was no need to hold anything back. My mouth tended to have a mind of its own anyways. "You could miss your assignments for a month and still have the third highest GPA. So cut the crap and tell the truth. I find it hard to believe this is what you wanted to talk to me about, really?"

He looked up at me eyes glaring. "It is the truth. Yes I have the grades but it's not easy for me to keep them. I have to work a lot harder than everyone else and yes I was falling behind so I needed to take a break. I just wanted you to know so you didn't think –" he broke off not able to finish his sentence, but I already had a feeling of what he was going to say. When I glared at him his expression changed. "And what about you? You come at me wanting the truth when you're the one with all the secrets," he spat.

"Sorry if my personal life is none of your god damn business. And if that's all it was then why did you wait so long to tell me?"

"Because I...I..." he stammered.

"God Roman, just spit it out. Please don't hold back on my account. You never have before," I said, annoyed at him jumping back and forth.

"Fine. It's you. Happy now!" he said, throwing his arms up frustrated.

"Me?" I said, misinterpreting his meaning. "You're the one with all the issues, clearly."

"Wow, you don't get it do you?"

"Why don't you make it real simple and clarify it for me then," I said, needing a real answer I could understand.

He laughed like I was the crazy one. "I've never seen anyone with more problems than you."

I scoffed. How did this conversation get so turned around? "My only problem is you!" I yelled. "I never met anyone who has more personalities than you do. I mean, really Roman. What is it that I've done to you for you to be so angry at me all the time?"

"You're one to talk. You're so hot and cold around me all the time I don't know how to act!" he argued back.

"Well maybe that's because of the way you treat me. One day you're Mr. nice guy and the next you're an asshole! And for no reason. And quit turning this back on me because you're to chicken shit to admit the truth."

"Well maybe if you would stop attacking me all the time," he said.

"I wouldn't have to kick your ass if you weren't such a jerk. Did you ever think it was you," I said, taking a step closer to him, challenging him.

"Well maybe if you didn't drive me crazy all the time," he growled frustrated.

"I drive you crazy?" I laughed. "Seriously, what the hell do you want from me?" I cried, getting in his face. I was so frustrated with this conversation and the fact that it was getting nowhere was making me want to scream.

Roman closed the distance between us in one swift step. His dark blue eyes bored down into mine. "I'll tell you what I want." He grabbed my arms and I flinched. Then he surprised me by kissing me. His lips came crushing down on mine so hard and so fast I lost my breath. He kissed me with such force I thought I was going to pass out. He pulled back gasping. I stood there, panting. "You're not going to hit me again, are you?"

"No," I smiled, grabbing his shirt and pulling him back to me. I slipped my hands up around his neck wanting him to be closer, wanting to feel the power of the kiss. When I kissed him I felt like my body was on fire. There was a passion burning deep down and when he kissed me, I thought I was going to burst into flames.

His tongue glided over my lips. I opened a little wider allowing him access to explore. His tongue slipped inside my mouth and it took all I had to keep standing. His fingers pinched the sides of my hips as he drew me closer to him. I jumped and wrapped my legs around his waist as he glided his hands down to my backside. I ran my fingers through his hair as he kissed me passionately. Roman took a few steps toward the bed and then threw me down, jumping on top of me. My mind was so fuzzy I could barely comprehend what was going on, but I didn't care. All I knew was it felt good and I didn't want it to stop.

Roman slid his hand under my shirt and cupped my breast while he kissed my neck. I pulled him closer, wanting to feel his body on top of mine. I tore off his shirt, needing to feel the heat from his skin. I ran my lips over every inch of his bare chest causing his breath to come heavily. He pushed me down and ripped open my blouse, exposing my chest, making buttons fly everywhere.

I never wanted someone more than I wanted him right now.

He started to kiss me again. My body was burning from his touch. His hand got hot, like really hot. "Ow!" I yelped.

"What is it?" Roman pulled back, concern written all over his face.

"My skin, it feels like it's on fire." He smiled cockily and leaned in to kiss me again. I pushed him back. "No I mean like literally burning," I said, my face pained.

He pulled back and looked at me. Then he quickly removed his hand from my side to reveal a burn mark in the shape of a hand print. "Holy shit, I'm so sorry. I didn't mean to," he said, sincerely sorry and upset. "That's never happened before."

"It's okay. I know you didn't." He leaned over to get a closer look when I heard a key turning in the lock. I panicked and quickly jumped up knocking Roman off of me.

"Hey Billy," I heard someone say, stopping him from continuing to unlock the door.

I grabbed Roman's shirt and quickly shoved him in the bathroom. Then realizing I was still topless, I opened up the closet and threw on a shirt, closing the door just as Billy walked in.

"Oh, hey Ella. Sorry, didn't know you'd be here."

"Don't be sorry. I was just dropping off some books," I said.

"Are you okay? You look a little flushed."

"Me, oh I'm fine. It's just a little warm in here."

His face told me he didn't agree. "Are you feeling well? You're not getting sick are you?" He pressed his hand to my forehead. "Ella, you're burning up. Here, I got some medicine in the bathroom."

"No!" I yelled as he put his hand on the door knob. He turned and looked at me funny. "I just...you're right I'm not feeling well. I think it was something I ate so you probably don't want to go in there, for a little while at least," I said, wanting to kick myself.

I could tell he was trying to keep the disgusted look from his face. "Okay, well, I'll let you rest then."

"Okay," I said, trying not to pass out from embarrassment.

He grabbed a few things and stuffed them in his bag. "Hope you feel better," he said, bolting out of the room.

I dropped my face in my hands, shaking my head. "You can come out now," I told Roman.

"Who was that?" he asked with a scowl on his face. "And why does he have a key to your room?"

"That was Billy and he has a key because he's my guardian," I said.

"Is he that guy that caused the riot in the dining hall?" I nodded. "Why do you have a guardian? Are you like, royalty or something," he joked.

Not wanting to divulge too much information I simply said, "My dad is just a little overprotective."

He mulled over that information for a bit before he asked, "How's your side?" I lifted my shirt just enough to expose the burn mark. "It doesn't look too bad, but you should definitely put something on it."

"I'm not worried about it, besides, I'm a fast healer," I smiled. He still looked at me concerned. "It doesn't hurt. Really I'll be fine." I knew he let it go for the sake of not starting another argument. We both stood there not sure where to go from here.

When he didn't offer up any conversation I decided to speak first. "So, um, what –"

"Okay, I guess I should explain," he said interrupting me.

"That would probably be a good start."

"Right, so I originally wanted to apologize for kissing you like that, the first time," he blushed.

"A little late on the delivery wouldn't you say?"

"Well you're not that easy to talk to you know," he said, narrowing his eyes at me.

"Me? What about you? Every time I approach you I feel like I have to with caution like I'm approaching a wild dog," I said, feeling my anger rise.

"Well maybe that's because −" he stopped and took a breath. "We are getting off track here."

"Right, sorry. What were we talking about?"

"I was trying to apologize for kissing you but then we started arguing and one thing lead to another," he smiled at the memory. I blushed and turned away.

"I don't really know how to explain...that," I said. "I mean one minute we're arguing and the next we're kissing? That's crazy right?"

He grabbed my hand and turned me to face him. He paused for a second to look into my eyes. "Yes and...no," he said, tucking a piece of hair behind my ear, making my whole body shiver. I stepped back out of reach, afraid I might jump him again. I knew he took my reaction as a bad thing. "Look, it's no big deal," he shrugged. "We can just chalk it up to crazy teenage hormones," he winked. "No reason to be awkward around each other wondering how to act."

Right, because that would be different from any other time.

"Exactly, no big deal," I said.

"Good, glad we're on the same page," he said.

"Yeah," I said a little disappointed.

"Okay, I'll see ya," he said, playfully punching me on the arm and taking off, leaving me standing there more clueless than ever. I closed the door behind him and slid down to the floor. *What did I just do?* I slapped myself in the forehead, mentally going over what just happened. I just made out with Roman and liked it, a lot. So much I wanted to run down the hall and drag him back here. Then I thought for a second, was this...was this another spell? No, I shook my head. This was different. I could feel it. The way I felt when I kissed Roman was completely different than when I kissed Aidan. So what the hell did all this mean?

I glanced at the clock and saw I had five minutes before my next class. I didn't have time to deliberate about the Roman debacle now or I'd be late for class. I forced myself to get up, grabbed my books, and hoped I'd make it in time for class.

I couldn't concentrate the rest of the day. I couldn't stop thinking about Roman and his lips. The way they felt on mine, the hunger, the burning. I got called out several times by my teachers for not paying attention and even Riley gave me a few funny looks. I even got my ass kicked in self-defense. I knew Roman was watching which didn't make it any better.

At dinner, Billy told me he told Gabe I wasn't feeling well and that Gabe said I could have today and tomorrow to rest and get better. Even though it was a lie, I was thankful for the time off. I shot Roman a quick glance when he sat down at the end of the table. When he met my gaze, he winked, and smiled at me. I rolled my eyes even though I could feel my cheeks burning. Cameron looked at me with her brows scrunched. Making me think she caught the small exchange between Roman and I. "What?" I asked, feeling uncomfortable under her scrutinizing stare.

She looked back at Roman whose mouth was full of food and talking to his buddies. Then she looked back at me and said, "Nothing." I went back to my dinner as if nothing happened.

Just as I was about to get ready for bed there was a knock on my door. I opened it to discover Roman. Surprised I said, "Hey."

"Hey," he said, standing there. I raised my brows waiting for him to say something else. "I got you something." He reached into his pocket and pulled out a small white tube and handed it to me. I looked at him funny. "It's burn crème."

"Oh," I blushed. "Thank you." Not sure what else to say, I stood there; wondering if there was something else.

"Do you uh...wanna take a walk?" Roman asked nervously.

Surprised by his unexpected invitation, I managed to spit out, "Um, yeah. Just let me grab my coat." I slipped on some shoes and a jacket, then I stepped out of my room, closing and locking the door behind me. He gestured for me to follow him. We walked side by side down the hall and out the back door to the back of the building. I shivered from the cold air, wishing I brought gloves and a scarf, and maybe even a hat or – my thoughts were disrupted when Roman cupped my face and started to kiss me.

Surprised at his abruptness I pulled back. "Sorry," he said.

"I...oh what the hell," I said, grabbing him and kissing him so hard we fell back against the building. He pulled me tighter into him taking pleasure in the kiss. Despite the chill outside I found myself warming up very quickly. I slipped my hands around his waist and up under his shirt making him jump back. "What is it?" I asked worried.

"Your hands are really cold," he laughed.

"Oh, sorry."

"Here." He held out his hands for mine.

I placed my hands on top of his, feeling a tingling sensation, then warmth. "Thank you," I whispered. I slid my hands underneath his shirt again and placed them on his lower back pulling him close to me. We stayed outside for a half hour kissing. I kissed him until I could no longer feel my toes. I pulled back trying to catch my breath. "I think we should head back inside," I said. He looked at me like he did something wrong. "I can't feel my toes anymore," I smiled, letting him know it wasn't him.

"Oh," he said, smiling back at me. He took my hand and led me back into the building.

When we reached my floor, I stopped before entering my hall. "I think this is where we should part ways," I said and he looked at me funny. "It's just...well this is..." I paused looking for the right words not wanting to hurt his feelings. "What are we doing, exactly? I mean, what is this? You ask me to go for a walk and the next thing I know we're kissing again."

He brushed a piece of hair off of my cheek. "I like kissing you," he smiled, giving me a sweet kiss.

"I like kissing you too," I said, returning the kiss.

"Well, since we both like kissing each other, I think we should continue." He slid his hand behind my neck and leaned in.

I pulled back. "As much as I hate to admit that I do enjoy this. If this is something that maybe we decide to keep doing, I just think we should keep it between ourselves," I said, biting my lip, hoping I hadn't offended him.

"Right." He let go of me. The way he said it made me think he didn't agree, but was going along with it. "Makes sense, I just broke up with Mackenzie and well, we're just..." he left the question open for me to answer.

"We're two people who like kissing each other," I said, hoping that was the right answer.

"Yeah, totally. Just two people who find comfort in each other's lips," he smiled cockily. He put a hand on the wall and leaned dangerously close to me. He picked up a small strand of my hair and twirled it around his finger. "You know, if you want, I could come back to your room and help you warm up," he winked.

I pushed him back. "Nice try, but I'm still healing from the last time."

"It was worth a shot," he shrugged. "See you tomorrow," he said, stealing a quick kiss. I pulled him back, wanting it to last a little longer.

"Okay, now you can go."

"But I wasn't done," he smiled, moving in for more.

I heard a door open. "Okay, now you really need to go," I whispered, pushing him back. He stole a few more kisses before I pushed him away, shaking my head.

I felt like I was flying on a cloud. I floated back to my room. Once inside, I changed into my pajamas, and snuggled into my warm bed. It only took a few minutes before I fell into a deep sleep. I woke up in the morning feeling great. I slept through the night peacefully – no nightmares, no tossing and turning, no nothing. It was just a perfect, restful night.

I sat up and stretched my arms above my head smiling. I hopped out of bed and changed for class. "You look like you're feeling better," Billy said as I came out of the bathroom.

"Oh yes, much better," I said, unable to unscrew the smile from my face.

"Well good. I'll be sure to tell Gabe you'll be ready for training tomorrow." My smile faded. I knew Gabe had planned on upping the intensity of my workouts to help prepare me for the battle ahead. Not sure what I dreaded more, the possibility of going up against Jack again or the ass kicking I was going to get from Gabe over the next few weeks. Both were to be debated. At least I had a day off to relax.

I was one of the first to arrive in my history class. I took my normal seat in the back and took out my books. When I looked up I saw Roman. I tried hard to keep the smile from my face. When he saw me, he came right over, and took a seat next to me. "What are you doing?" I asked, looking around even though we were the only two in there.

"Do you have training today?" he asked.

"No," I said nervously. I didn't like the idea of people seeing us together and starting rumors.

I was about to tell him he shouldn't sit here when he said, "Meet me in the library after dinner," he winked. Then he got up and took a seat behind me in the back. I faced forward trying to hide my smile when Mackenzie walked in. She looked at me, then Roman, sticking her nose up at us. I stifled an eye roll and waited for class to begin.

In spells and casting Roman and I were partners so I had to sit by him, which I didn't mind – I think for the first time ever. Once class started, I noticed Roman had inched his way closer. He would casually lean in closer so our arms or legs would touch, giving me a tiny shock every time our skin brushed. The subtlety of it all made me excited, anticipating our meeting later tonight.

In library later that night, Roman and I found a small, dark corner in the back where we proceeded to make out for a very long time. Then we parted ways and went back to our rooms. This became a routine. Roman and I would find a place to get together, share secret glances in class, lunch or dinner, and sneak a soft touch here and there when no one was looking. I had a sneaking suspicion that Cameron thought something was going on so I made sure to be extra careful around her.

I met Roman in the basement. It was one of the few places we could meet without worrying about someone catching us. "How was training today?" he asked.

"Fine," I said, going back to kissing him.

"What are you and Gabe working on?"

"Just some new techniques Billy showed me," I said as I left a trail of kisses down his neck.

"Wait, he's been training with you as well?"

Sensing a change in his tone I asked, "Are you jealous?"

"Jealous of what?"

"Nothing," I rolled my eyes and went back to kissing him.

"What kind of techniques?" he mumbled against my lips.

I sat back and sighed. "What's going on?"

"I don't know. You tell me?" he said.

"I thought we were kissing," I smiled, pulling his lips back to mine.

He turned his head. "Yes, but that's just it. Is this all it is or is there more to it?"

"Less talking more kissing," I said, grabbing the back of his neck and pulling him down on top of me.

"Ella, I'm being serious." He sat back up.

"Roman, just spit it out, because this dance is making me nauseous." I was getting annoyed by the constant interruption.

"Just forget it." He leaned in to kiss me.

This time I was the one to stop. "Do you not enjoy this anymore? Did you want to stop?" I asked a little scared.

"No, I do. I just would like to know where this is going to lead."

"Hey, I never stopped you from copping a feel," I teased.

"That's not what I mean," he said, sitting back.

"Roman, we already talked about this. We're just two people who like kissing each other with the occasional grope," I winked, making him smile and blush. "Nothing more and nothing less. Why complicate things?"

"Yeah, I guess you're right," he said, turning away and looking a little disappointed.

"Did you...want, something more?" I asked softly, afraid of his answer.

"No," he shook his head. "Of course not. C'mon, we can barely tolerate each other," he winked, nudging me playfully. His smile faded and he sighed. "I should go."

"Is something wrong?" I asked worried.

"No, I just have a lot of homework."

"Okay," I said, removing my legs from his lap. "I'll see you tomorrow?"

"Yeah," he said, flashing me a smile. He gave me a quick kiss before he left. I stayed in the basement for a little after he left, contemplating what he was really trying to get at. He never cared how training went before. Did he miss it and that's why he asked? Was he trying to make conversation? Did he no longer like our little arrangement? Was he getting bored? Did he want more? I shook my head and made my way out. I did not like the idea of being in the basement alone.

Just before I was about to ascend the stairs, I heard a noise behind me. I stopped and turned around; walking a few feet back in the direction I just came. I peered all around, looking for the mystery noise while reminding myself not to be scared. "You have some very powerful kick ass powers. You can take on anything that comes at you," I told myself.

When I didn't hear the noise anymore, I decided to stop my investigation and haul ass out of there, my courage now gone. When I rounded the stairs I nearly jumped out of my skin. "I knew it!"

"Christ Cameron, I think I just peed a little."

She stood there with her arms crossed and eyes narrowed. "You lied to me," she said.

"What are you talking about?" I said, trying to walk around her.

She took a step to the left blocking my path. "You and Roman. You two are hooking up aren't you?"

"You have an over active imagination. There's nothing going on between Roman and me."

"Then how come I just saw him leave here not too long ago?" she questioned, thinking she had me.

"I don't know. Why don't you go ask him?" I said with a little bit of attitude, hoping she would drop it.

She leaned closer, getting in my face. "I know there's something going on between you two and I will figure it out."

"Sure Cameron, whatever," I said, wondering why she cared so much. "Are we done with the interrogation now?"

"For now," she said, letting me pass.

The next day in class I noticed Roman was a little distant. I slipped him a note asking if he was okay. He answered – *fine.*

I wrote back asking if he wanted to meet tonight. All he wrote was – *I can't.*

I didn't push, sensing something was off and didn't want to risk making him mad. He didn't show at lunch or dinner and I was beginning to wonder if he was pissed at me from last night.

After a week of him turning me down and ignoring me I decided to confront him. "Did I miss something, because last time I checked we had a pretty sweet deal going? Did you change your mind?" I whispered, while Ms. Kraft let us have some free time.

"Sorry, I've just been busy," he said, not even looking at me.

"So I've noticed," I replied.

He sighed and finally turned to look at me. "Hey, I'm sorry, but I really have been busy. If you want I can stop by tonight. Your room if you want? Mackenzie moved out, right?" Not sure where he was going with this, I nodded. "I'll stop by later." Ms. Kraft dismissed the class and he packed up his things without another word and left.

I was a mess all day waiting for Roman to meet me at my room. It's been a week since we last kissed and my lips were burning for his touch. I also had to come up with an excuse to get Billy out of the room long enough to make an excuse for Roman and I to go somewhere else. He didn't know Billy was staying here and I knew if he found out he would think the worst.

After training, I was so beat it took everything I had to stay awake. I took a shower and changed while Billy was still with Gabe working on some new ideas for my training. In the meantime I decided to work on my homework. Billy had come back to get a quick shower and then told me he was going back to work with Gabe on a few things which I thought would work out perfect. He would be gone before Roman got here and I would have some time.

I jumped at the knock on the door. I told Billy I would get it so he could shower. I opened the door surprised. "Roman, hi."

"Hey," he said. "Did you forget we were meeting tonight?"

"No," I said, stepping out of the room and closing the door. "I just didn't expect you for a little bit yet. Do you want to go for a walk?"

"I thought we could talk here," he said.

Talk, that didn't sound good. I looked over my shoulder. Billy was still in the shower but I still didn't think it would be wise to be in my room so I came up with an excuse. "Riley stopped by and she's in there so..."

"Alright," he nodded, understanding. I stepped away from the door letting him take the lead. "I'll make this quick," he said. I didn't like the sound of that. "I don't think we should meet anymore."

"Oh," I said disappointed. "Was it something I did?"

"No. Like I said before I'm falling behind on my work and I need to keep up my average if I want to stay here," he said, not able to meet me in the eye.

I didn't believe him. "That's the lamest excuse I ever heard," I said hurt.

"What would you rather hear? It's not you it's me, because I thought about that but then I thought I owed you better."

"You're damn right you do. So how about the truth now?" I said, wanting a real explanation why he was acting so weird.

He ran his hands through his hair frustrated. He was about to open his mouth when Billy opened the door, wearing only a towel. Roman was out of sight in a second. "Hey, you okay?" Billy asked. "I thought I heard voices?" He looked at me funny, standing out there alone.

"Yeah, just some kids down the hall," I said.

"You sure you're okay?" he asked, looking worried.

"Yeah, I just have to get something from one of my classmates. I'll be in in a second." He stepped back into the room and closed the door. I knew Roman didn't leave and I knew he saw and heard everything. I could feel him behind me. "I can explain," I said to him.

"Don't bother," he said flatly.

I turned to face him. "Roman look, it's not what you think."

"Guardian, yeah." He turned to leave, but I caught up to him.

"Roman please, wait." He stopped. "He is my guardian and I only lied about him staying in my room because I was afraid of how you would act and clearly I was right."

"Ella, really, I don't care. You don't owe me an explanation. Have fun," he said, turning on his heel.

I grabbed his arm. "Roman please."

"Look, guardian or not you felt the need to lie to me which makes me believe I can't trust you," he said upset. "But why does that not surprise me."

"What the hell is that supposed to mean?"

"Just forget it."

"No, you're not going to start this bullshit again and walk away. This is what I was talking about from the beginning. You're so cryptic all the time, never giving me a real answer."

"I'm over it already," he said, throwing his hands up in the air and taking a few steps backwards before he turned to leave.

"Over what?" I cried frustrated, but he didn't answer me. He kept walking and left me in the hall alone. Frustrated beyond belief, I walked back to my room, and closed and locked the door behind me. Great, I just messed up what little relationship I had with Roman. We were finally getting along for once. We found a common interest. Now it was all gone.

Roman went back to avoiding me and ignoring me in class. I didn't know how to approach him or even how to explain that he would understand. But then I thought, did I really owe him one? I mean we both made it clear that we were just messing around so why was he so upset when he saw Billy. And why was I so upset that he was? I couldn't explain what was going on inside my head, but I knew I was having a hard time concentrating on anything else but Roman.

I decided to throw myself into my training and school work to help keep me distracted. For the most part it worked, but by the end of the week I was beat. Gabe decided to lesson my training sessions. I was picking up quickly and doing such a good job he said I didn't need to meet with him as much anymore. He told me I only had to meet three days a weeks after class – I was ecstatic. Another reason to celebrate, I get to sleep in again, and now have more time with my friends – that was if they didn't forget about me already.

When I first got here, I wasn't worried about making friends much less caring if anyone liked me, but I couldn't be any happier with the group of people I met. They made me see that I could trust people again and that it's okay to be different. They showed me despite how little they knew about me, it didn't matter. They were there for me, ready to stand in the line of fire to protect me because that's what friend's do. I was glad I found a way to open up and let them in because without them, I didn't know where I'd be right now.

At lunch Justin had told us him and his friends were having a party in the basement for St Patty's Day. I told him I was game for the party which made Riley happy considering only minutes ago she was complaining she never got to see me. Riley wasn't one to complain, but I noticed something was on her mind. She had confided in me before that it was easier for her to talk to me than the other girls. I made a mental note to pull her aside later and ask her if she wanted to talk.

Now that the little spare time I had wasn't occupied by sneaking around with Roman I actually could relax with my friends. Dixon caught me up on all the gossip I've been missing. Turns out things didn't work out so well with Sienna and Kenny and now that Reagan and Addyson were done she was back to crushing over him. Dixon kept talking about all the dirty juice when I was distracted. A strange, cold wind blew up my spine and I looked up to see Mackenzie walking in. Her eyes searched the room until she found mine. She smiled, flicked her hair off her shoulder, and had a seat with her friends. Not having to face her every day and having Roman as a distraction, I had forgotten about Mackenzie possibly planning another evil attack on me, but from what Dixon had told me things were pretty quiet with her group. This surprisingly didn't make me feel any better. I had a feeling the next attack was going to be a Trojan horse.

Roman, for the first time in a while sat at our table. I was so surprised by this I didn't know what to do or say. Just the sight of him sent my whole head in a whirlwind. Even though we saw each other every other day in class he acted as though we were strangers. He wouldn't talk to me unless he had to and I never saw him at breakfast, lunch, or dinner, until today. To say I was hurt by his actions, well really I shouldn't be, but I was. I tried not to let it get to me or at least I thought I didn't.

In training I was having a hard time concentrating and Gabe noticed. "Ella focus!" he yelled. I was so distracted I was getting my ass kicked.

I tried to focus but I couldn't. My mind was somewhere else. "Can we stop for today? I'm not in the mood for this," I whined.

"You think your attacker is just going to stop because you don't feel like fighting anymore?" I rolled my eyes. "Now. Again," he said, coming at me full force, knocking me over. "Get up!" I stood back up. He came at me again, backing me up against the wall. I had nowhere to go and he was giving me everything he got and was not holding back. I didn't have the strength anymore and wanted to give up.

"Gabe, I think she's had enough," Billy said, worried he might really hurt me.

"No she hasn't. Now fight back!"

Tired of my back being pushed up against a wall, literally, I drew strength from my powers. Throwing my hands forward, I blasted him across the gym. Gabe stood up a little stunned. "That's better," he said.

"Are we done now," I said annoyed.

"For today," he said, rubbing his back.

I could tell I hurt him and I think that was the only reason he stopped. I left the gym in a huff and Billy chasing after me. "Ella wait!" he yelled, following me into the girls' locker room. "I know you think he's being too hard on you, but he has his reasons."

"When I'm backed up against a wall and —"

"And you think your attacker is just going to let you go?"

"Okay I get it," I groaned, sitting down on the bench to take off my shoes.

"Do you get it though? Do you have any idea how dangerous Jack is?"

"Yes I do," I yelled, getting up. "You think I don't? I'm tired of people telling me how dangerous he is. I know. I fought him. I watched him kill Tristan. I know how strong he is." I bit my lip to keep from crying.

"And that was then and this is now. He too is preparing and getting stronger. Are you ready to face that?" I shook my head unsure. "Ella, this is why Gabe is being so tough on you. This is why he is pushing you to the brink. So you will be able to take on anything."

"I know okay! I'm just tired of everyone depending on me. I just want to have a normal life!"

I nearly lost it when Billy reached for me and wrapped his arms around me. "I know Ella. I know," he said softly, trying to comfort me. "Sometimes we forget how much pressure we put on you and that's not fair. I'll talk to Gabe and tell him to lighten up a bit."

"Thanks Billy," I said as a bunch of giggling girls walked in and stopped dead in their tracks when they saw Billy. I quickly wiped the tears from my cheeks when Billy froze and looked at me. "Yeah, you're in the girls' locker room."

"Oh," he said, quickly making his way out and running into one of the lockers. I laughed as he blushed and finally found his way out. After my minor meltdown, I wasn't in the mood to deal with anyone so I hopped in the shower and then headed back to my room and passed out.

By Thursday I was so ready to party. I needed a day where I could forget my troubles for a while and just hang with my friends. I convinced Billy to come to the party with me and by the time we got there the party was already in full swing. I knew it wasn't exactly a wise idea. But I didn't care. I wanted to forget my troubles and I knew the best way to do that was to drink.

Dean was already half in the bag when we found him and he insisted I needed to do shots to catch up to him. "C'mon Ella we're Irish. Do us proud," he said, handing me a shot. I took it along with several more during the evening. I had a nice buzz going and was having a good time until Roman showed up. When he saw me, he walked straight for me. I froze, feeling apprehensive, but when he reached me, he walked right past me. It was almost like he walked right through me, leaving a cold chill in his wake. I took Dean's shot right out of his hand and swallowed. It burned as it slid down my throat, but I didn't care. I wanted to be anyone but me right now and I felt drinking was the best way to solve that problem.

Thankfully Roman kept himself on the opposite side of the room most of the night. I could still feel his eyes on me which bugged me more than anything. I tried to ignore him the best I could. "I like this Ella," Cameron said as we shook our behinds on the made up dance floor. "I think she needs to come out more often." I laughed, having a good time. I even danced with a few boys Sienna had introduced me to earlier.

I looked over my shoulder and saw that Roman was watching me again. So I purposely pulled one of the boys closer to me as I danced up against him. He wrapped his arms around me tight, grinding his leg in between mine. I glanced over to see Roman's face turning red. I knew he was trying to hide it by talking to Justin, but failed.

Just to piss him off even more, right when he looked over, I grabbed the guy by the face and kissed him. Roman's rage grew. He marched straight for us and pushed the guy. "What the hell dude?" he said, stumbling.

"What is wrong with you?" I said, glaring at Roman. I only wanted to make him jealous not have him pummel the guy. Roman didn't say anything. He just walked away. I turned to Cameron who was glaring at me. "What?" I said annoyed. She just shrugged her shoulders.

"C'mon now," Dean said, joining us and throwing his arms over Cameron and me. "Can't we all just get along?" Dean's happy attitude was infectious. He even got Cameron to smile. "It's a party let's drink!" he cheered, holding up his cup.

"Give me that," I said, taking his beer and chugging it. "Woo!" Dean and a bunch of bystanders nearby cheered.

"This is the old Ella I know and love," Dean said, hanging on me and stumbling. "Look out ladies." He spread out his arms and got ready to completely embarrass himself.

"What is he doing?" Cameron asked, looking horrified.

"Um, he's dancing," I laughed.

"Maybe we should stop him before he completely makes a fool of himself," Cameron suggested.

"Too late," I said, choking back a laugh as I watched him bust out his Michael Jackson moves. "I'm going to walk away now."

I walked over to one of the coolers and reached in to grab

another beer when someone grabbed my wrist, stopping me. "You think that's a good idea?" Roman said.

"What are you, my conscious?" I said, still ticked off from his little pissing contest.

He just glared at me. I tried to pull my hand away but he held on, looking down at my wrist. "Where did you get that watch?"

"It was a gift," I said, tearing my hand away. When I turned to rejoin my friends I found Mackenzie fawning all over Billy.

"I guess you and your guardian are a perfect match after all," Roman said over my shoulder. "Doesn't waste anytime does he? But I guess that doesn't bother you now, does it?" he asked, thinking I would be jealous of Mackenzie flirting with him.

"First off, like I told you before, he is just my guardian. My friend. There is nothing going on between Billy and me. Maybe you're the one who is jealous, watching him over there with Mackenzie."

"I don't care about Mackenzie. She's a free woman. She can do what she wants."

"Than what are you so pissed about? Are you mad because you think I slept with Billy and wouldn't with you?" He narrowed his eyes at me. "That's it isn't it?"

"No, that's not it, but now that you mention it I'm not surprised you admitted it. It must be killing you to watch him flirt with Mackenzie," he said, thinking he had me.

"Okay, one, I didn't admit anything and I'm pretty sure it's Mackenzie that's all over him and not the other way around."

"He doesn't seem to be stopping her."

I turned to face him again. "He's just trying to be nice. Not everyone's an asshole like you," I growled.

"I'm the asshole?" he asked, like I should be ashamed for even considering.

"Yes. You stand there and judge people when you know nothing about them."

"And you'll trust anyone with a dick," he said, getting in my face.

That was the last straw. I was tired of him calling me a slut. I slapped him, hard. And now I was in his face. "You don't know shit about me. So don't talk like you do. And if you ever, insult me like that again I'll —"

"You'll what?" he asked, tempting me.

Dean and Billy had caught our little tiff and came over to see what was going on. "Is there a problem?" Dean asked, standing beside me.

"Why don't you ask your sister? She's the one who hit me," he said, narrowing his eyes at me.

Dean turned to me ready to yell. "Don't even start. This is between me and him," I said, glaring back at Roman.

"No need to worry boys. I'm finished with this conversation," Roman said, walking away.

I grabbed his arm and stopped him. I knew I was going to regret what I was about to say, but all the liquor I had drank was making me not care. "Well I'm not. I'm tired of you calling me names and thinking its okay. You wanna know the truth, well here it is. For your information I'm still a virgin and not that it's any of your business, but I've only been in two serious relationships. And the only reason they ended was because Jack the rogue vampire who's after me killed them. And the reason I know Billy is such a good guy and would never fall for Mackenzie's bullshit is because he used to date my best friend who was also killed by Jack. So go ahead, say something now. I fucking dare you!"

He stood there, with a stunned look on his face. "Ella I'm sorry. I didn't know."

"No you didn't, but now you do," I said, storming out. I had all I could take.

The blast of cold air that hit me was like a slap in the face. I took a sharp inhale of breath before I continued on.

"Ella wait!" Roman called, catching up to me outside.

I stopped and turned on him. "You keep acting like you know me, but you have no idea. You have no idea what I went through or what I have to deal with!" I shouted.

"Then why don't you tell me?" he asked softly.

"Because it's too hard," I cried, no longer able to hold back the tears. "Because I'm tired of losing people I care about. I don't want to do this anymore. I can't do it anymore." I broke down. My knees started to wobble. Roman caught me before I hit the ground. He held me tight and tried to comfort me. I felt so safe and warm in his arms. Too many emotions were trying to take over and I couldn't decipher which ones were right. "I can't do this right now. I have to go," I said, pushing him away and running to my room.

I cried myself to sleep that night.

Jessica Miller

CHAPTER TWENTY

I wanted to skip my classes today, but here that wasn't so easy. I felt like crap. I knew it was from the alcohol and fight with Roman. I wanted so badly to crawl back into bed. I forced myself to get up and in the shower.

I sat in my normal seat in the back of History class and kept to myself. "Ella, can I talk to you?" Roman asked, leaning on my desk.

"Now's not a good time," I said, pulling off my sunglasses.

"Ella I wanna —" he started but Mr. Grant brought the class to order, forcing Roman to have a seat. Unfortunately for me he chose the empty seat next to mine. "Ella, I really want to talk to you about last night," he whispered.

"Not now," I repeated. He didn't seem to care I wasn't interested in what he had to say and proceeded to continue.

"I'm sorry. You were right. I don't know you, but I would like to get the chance if you let me?"

I turned to face him. His dark blue eyes were pleading with me to give him another chance. "Roman I —"

"Miss McCallister, care to tell us what I was just discussing?" Mr. Grant asked me, knowing I wasn't paying attention.

"Umm, I..." I stuttered as the class giggled.

"That's what I thought. I expect you to pay attention," he said annoyed. I glared at Roman pissed that he got me in trouble.

When class was over I grabbed my things in a rush, hoping to get away from Roman. "Ella, please let me explain I —" Roman started before Mr. Grant interrupted.

"Miss McCallister, can I see you for a minute?" Mr. Grant asked, giving me a reprieve from Roman.

"Yes Mr. Grant," I said, standing there nervously, waiting while the rest of the class cleared out.

"I'm going to make myself clear. I don't care what kind of

personal crap you having going on in your life or whatever. When you're in this class you listen. Outside of here I don't care what you do. Got it?"

"Got it," I said, making a bee line for the door. Yikes, mental note not to piss him off again.

On my way out I found Roman waiting for me. I ignored him and kept walking. "Ella," he said, trying to keep up with me. "Ella stop!"

"I'm going to be late." I kept walking.

"I don't care. Will you please stop?" He jumped in front of me. Clearly I wasn't going to get rid of him anytime soon. Not to mention we sat next to each other in our next class.

Not wanting to risk getting in trouble again I paused and said, "Make it quick. I don't want to be late."

"Fine, meet me in the library after lunch," he said.

"Roman no –"

"Look, I have a lot I want to say and like you said we don't have enough time and I'm not going to rush. Library, after lunch." He turned and walked away. I stood in the hall staring at Roman's back a little longer than I should have. I had to run to my next class. I made it just in time. Roman was already seated and leaning back casually in his chair. "What took you so long?" he said, smiling. I just glared at him, placing my bag on the table between us so I could put my head down and not have to look at him.

Thankfully Ms. Kraft hadn't noticed that I was dozing off or I would have found myself in another lecture about the importance of blah, blah, blah.

I knew I was dreaming when I found myself in the school maze. I had no idea why I kept dreaming about this place.

I walked over to the fountain and found a young man sitting there on the edge with his back to me. I approached him slowly, not wanting to startle him. When I was close enough I peered over his shoulder at his reflection in the water. I blinked in surprise at the shimmering white wings I saw in the water. They were the most beautiful thing I have ever seen. I wanted to reach out and touch them, but when I looked at the young man again there was nothing there. As if he felt my presence, he turned around.

"Kyle!" I cried. I threw my arms around him the instant he stood up. "You're here, you're really here," I said smiling, not wanting to let go.

"Yes Ella. I'm really here, but I don't know for how long." I melted at the sweet sound of his voice. "There's something I have to tell you, it's important," he said.

"Can't it wait?" I asked, running a hand over his face, taking in his big brown eyes, his blond, surfer boy hair.

"No. I don't have much time," he said. He pulled back and took a good look at me. "What are you wearing?"

"Oh, this stupid uniform we have to wear –" I stopped when I looked down at my clothes. I was wearing a long, black, strapless gown. I was so distracted when I saw Kyle that I hadn't even noticed. The top of the gown was a tight corset with tiny diamonds down the front. The bottom flared out like a princess gown with more diamonds along the edge. "Oh, what the frig? I have no idea why I am wearing this ridiculous dress."

Kyle tilted my head up to look at him. "You look beautiful," he said smiling. I wrapped my arms around him again. "Ella, I'm sorry, but there's something I came here to tell you."

I managed to tear myself away so I could look at him. "What are you talking about? This doesn't make any sense. Aren't I dreaming?"

"Yes but listen –" His words were cut off by an outcry of pain. He arched backwards, screaming, revealing a dagger through his chest. "Ella..." was his last word as he fell to his knees. Behind him was Jack, smiling, blood covering his hands.

I screamed so loud I woke myself up, startling everyone.

The entire classroom turned around to look at me. I didn't even say anything. I just grabbed my stuff and ran out of class. Roman chased after me, but I didn't stop, I just kept going. When we reached the outside he finally caught up to me and stopped me. "Ella, what happened?"

"Nothing, I have to go," I said, trying to walk away but he wouldn't let go.

"No Ella. I'm not letting you walk away this time. Please let me help you."

"Trust me. I'm doing you a favor." I pulled away and started to walk again.

"I don't care. Whatever it is I don't care. I'll take the risk...for you," he shouted.

I stopped, but I didn't turn around. "Don't...please don't," I said softly.

He was behind me now. He placed his hands on my arms gently and let out a breath. "Ella, please, why won't you talk to me? Why won't you let me in?"

"Because I don't want you to get hurt," I admitted to my own surprise. "Roman you don't want to get involved in this."

He spun me around to face him and placed his hand delicately on my cheek. "Obviously you don't know me very well then," he smiled.

A tear escaped my eye and he brushed it away with his thumb. "I guess you leave me with no other choice then," I sighed, giving in. "Not here though." I thought for a minute. "We can go to my room?"

"Won't Billy be there?"

"No he's helping Gabe out," I said.

When we got to my room, Roman helped himself by sitting on my bed. I instantly jumped over to the other bed and sat down. I ran a shaky hand through my hair. I could feel Roman watching me and I was starting to get uncomfortable. "Before you start, I just want to explain why I've been acting the way I have."

"Roman you don't −"

"Yes I do," he said, interrupting me. "This isn't easy for me, but I have to let you know so you understand why I've been acting so weird." He struggled for a minute while he ran his hands through his hair. I learned this was a trait of his, something he did when he was nervous. "I was jealous," he blurted.

"Excuse me?" I asked, making sure I heard him right.

"Don't make me say it again," he said agitated. I crossed my arms and waited. "Fine, I was jealous, okay?" he said, giving me that, 'Are you happy now' look. He took a breath to calm himself, closing his eyes for a moment before he began again. "From the first day I saw you I knew there was something different about you. I was just too blind to see."

"Roman, what are you getting at here?" I asked, more confused than ever.

"I like you Ella. I did from the first day I saw you. I guess that's why I acted so irrationally. I was still with Mackenzie and it didn't feel right to have feelings for someone else."

I knew what he meant. In a way I felt like I would be betraying Tristan by loving someone else. "And what about after. When you broke up with her?"

"I was confused. After the library," he looked up. Did he feel the shock too? "Then when you kissed me the night of the break in."

"Roman I –"

"The reason doesn't matter. I don't care if you thought you were kissing someone else. All I know is that first kiss changed everything. I wasn't sure what I wanted anymore. So I thought if I got you to hate me it would be easier. But then we started sneaking around, and Billy and the guy at the party..." he trailed off, not wanting to repeat himself again.

"You were jealous," I finished for him, trying to hide my smile.

"I'm sorry for being such a jerk. It was just easier than admitting how I really felt," he said letting out a breath, like a big weight was just lifted off his shoulders. "Now you know the truth."

"Thank you," I said. "I know that wasn't easy for you to admit. I'm not sure what you want from me though?" I asked a little scared.

He looked up at me, his dark blue eyes searching mine. "Nothing. I mean, I just wanted you to know the truth. I don't expect anything in return...except, maybe...a chance to get to know you. The real you."

"I think I can manage that," I said with a small smile. So Roman just admitted he liked me. Where the hell was I supposed to go from there? I didn't know what to say or do. He looked at me expectantly, and I forgot the real reason we came here. I quickly cleared my head and focused.

"So...where do you want me to start?" I asked, wanting to move this along as quickly as possible. When it came to talking about my past I wasn't always quick to jump on that subject.

"You tell me. You don't have to tell me anything you don't feel comfortable with," he said, being the sweet Roman I liked.

"Then we would just sit here in silence," I joked. He got up and sat next to me on the bed. I froze when I felt that shock and then quickly got up. Being close to him made it hard for me to concentrate. I would be lying if I didn't admit I was a little shaken up by his confession. Talk about dropping a bomb.

"Is there something wrong?" he asked, wondering why I was suddenly acting weird.

"No...I just rather stand." I reached up and touched the locket my mom had given me for Christmas. Then I closed my eyes and took a breath. "You sure you want to know all this? You might change your mind about me when I'm done," I joked.

"I'll take my chances," he smiled.

"Okay, so everything started the summer after my senior year of high school," I began. "My boyfriend Kyle and I were on our way to his parent's cabin and there was an accident. Although at the time I didn't know it wasn't really an accident. Kyle died when the SUV burst into flames..." I paused to collect myself before I continued.

Then when I went to college in the fall with my best friend Josie...that's when everything started to fall apart. That's also when I met Jack. He lived down the hall from me in my dorm and was sweet and nice...well, until he tried to kill me."

I gazed out the window and glimpsed at the rays of sun that were shining down. "Josie convinced me to join a sorority. Yeah, I know, me in a sorority," I said, walking over to the window wanting to feel the warmth of the sun. "I'm not the same person I was then." I pressed my hand to the window pane, needing a moment to steady myself.

"I met someone. Someone I thought, well I thought he was the biggest ass when I first met him," I said, smiling at the memory. "Then I fell in love with him, but I never got to tell him." I looked down at his watch I was wearing and ran my thumb over the heart charm. "On the night of the sorority's Halloween party, that's when I lost everything. I found Josie's body in our closet and Billy knocked unconscious. Then when Billy and I tried to get help Jack attacked. I thought Billy was as good as dead. I ran. I ran as far as I could but he still found me. Jack and his girlfriend, Cadence — who just so happened to be the president of the sorority I joined — threatened to kill more people I loved unless I gave them my powers."

Roman got up from the bed and stood next to me by the window. "The funny thing is I didn't even know anything about this stuff until after Jack attacked me. I had no idea about vampires or that I was one or any of this," I said, throwing my hands out. "And I'd never thought I'd lose the people I loved most and for what? For some stupid powers?"

Roman took my hand and squeezed it gently. I looked down at our twined fingers before I looked out the window again. "He saved me. Just before Jack was about to kill me. He gave up his life for mine and for what? What do I have to show him it was worth it? I didn't even get to tell him I loved him." This was the first time I admitted to anyone that I loved Tristan. I still couldn't say his name though. That was too much to say it out loud.

"I'm sure whoever he was he knew you loved him. And from what it sounds like he loved you too. If I was him I would have done the same thing."

"You would risk your life for Mackenzie?" I asked, thinking he was crazy. I mean it was a possibility he saw a side of her no one else did.

"I wasn't talking about Mackenzie," he said, making me flinch.

"Don't say that." I tried to pull my hand away but he held on tight. "Roman, I'm not someone you want to get mixed up with."

"Stop trying to tell me what I do and don't want," he said, his eyes meeting mine. I got lost in the pull of his dark blue eyes. He slowly and hesitantly lifted his hands. They slid across my cheeks like silk as he lifted my chin closer to him. Before our lips had the chance to collide, Billy walked in, interrupting us. I stepped back blushing.

"Oh hey, sorry, didn't know you would be here." Billy took one look at my face and asked, "You okay?" I nodded, not able to form words yet. After last night Roman was currently not on Billy's good side. When Billy came in last night he found me drowning in a tear soaked pillow and spent most of the night talking to me. I could only imagine what was going through his mind right now.

"Good news. There's an open room in guest housing. One of the guardians got called out for duty somewhere else. Now you won't have me crowding you anymore or getting in your way," Billy said.

"Don't be silly. You know I love having you here," I told him while I made some distance between Roman and I.

He shot me a smile as he packed up his stuff. "I'll be out of your hair soon."

"Don't rush," I said, hoping he would take his time. I was a little afraid to be alone with Roman at the moment.

"You know it's a shame you stopped your training sessions. I was hoping we could work together. I heard you got a few moves you could teach me," Billy told Roman, reminding me of how great of a person he was. Despite his current dislike toward Roman he was still always the better man.

"Yeah, I think I might be coming back," Roman said, shooting me a look.

"Great, looking forward to it," Billy replied, grabbing the rest of his stuff from the bathroom. "Well, I think that's everything." He threw his bag over his shoulder and headed to the door. He turned back around before he left. "Not that it's any of my business but aren't you supposed to be in class?"

"Uh, yeah, I kind of fell asleep in class and woke up screaming," I said embarrassed.

"Another nightmare?" Billy asked and I nodded. "You okay? I mean do you need to –"

I shook my head. "Nothing I can't handle," I smiled and gave him a hug, letting him know I would be okay.

"If you want, I don't have to leave. I can still stay with you?"

"No. I'll be fine, besides, you deserve your privacy too."

He gave me another big hug before he left. "If you change your mind just let me know."

"Nah, you snore," I teased.

"Yeah, but not as loud as you." I scoffed and pushed him out the door. He laughed as he walked down the hall. I shook my head closing the door behind him.

"So I take it Billy's not really your guardian."

"No," I said. "Just a really good friend who has been helping me out."

He nodded. "What did he mean when he said another nightmare?" Roman asked.

"After the accident, I started having nightmares about it. They stopped for a little while but then they started up again. Only they're different now."

"Did you ever think maybe they're premonitions and not dreams?"

I sat down on the bed. "No. I never really thought of them like that."

He came over and had a seat next to me. "You want to tell me about them?" he asked softly.

I sighed, knowing I should tell him. I've already gone this far might as well let it all out. "When I first got here it was me in the maze and my friends kept calling for my help. But I couldn't find them and then Jack would show up."

"And today?"

"Today was the worst. Today I found Kyle by the fountain in the middle of the maze. He told me he had something important to tell me, but before he had the chance Jack showed up and killed him, again." I had to look away so I wouldn't cry.

"No wonder you were so freaked." He slipped his hand over mine, giving me a small shock. I had to resist the urge to pull away.

"You still want to hang out with me?" I joked.

"You couldn't get me to leave even if you tried," he smiled. "Ella," his face turned serious. "I'm sorry for the way I've been acting. I've never met anyone like you and well, you kind of threw me for a loop," he blushed.

"I tend to have that effect on people," I laughed. His eyes caught mine and I was afraid he was going to try and kiss me again. I was also scared I might not be able to stop it if he did. I stood up quickly and said, "I think maybe we should at least try to make our other classes."

"Why, we're already here?" he said, lying back on the bed. I rolled my eyes and shoved him. He grabbed me and pulled me down onto the bed, pinning me. "Looks like Gabe shouldn't have taken away those extra practices just yet. You still need some work," he teased.

"Shut up," I said, trying to push him away, but this time he wouldn't let me and I no longer had the strength to stop him. He pressed his lips to mine and I felt that spark. It ignited my entire body filling me up with light. Liking the way his lips felt on mine I kissed him back. He flinched slightly. I think he was half expected me to slap him.

Letting him know that wasn't the case, I ran my fingers through his soft dark curls, enjoying every minute of the kiss. The last time I felt this way when I kissed a boy was when I kissed Tristan and that scared me. Even though I didn't want the kiss to end, it had to. I placed my hand on his chest and lightly pushed him away. It took him a moment before he opened his eyes. I bit my lip to keep from laughing. "Ella, I –"

"Wow, you really get around," Mackenzie said, startling us as she barged into the room. "First Mr. Callahan, then you shack up with that hottie guardian, and now you're even desperate enough to take my hand-me-downs." Roman stood up and from the look on his face I knew he was holding back. "Please, don't let me interrupt," she said smirking.

"Seeing that you moved out, this technically is no longer your room and you cannot just barge in here whenever you feel like it," I snapped.

"Whatever, I just came to get the last of my things," she said, stuffing a few items into a small tote.

"That hairbrush is mine," I told her. She just rolled her eyes.

"Enjoy my sloppy seconds."

"I dumped you, remember?" Roman said, biting back his tongue.

"That's funny, that's not the way I remember it," she said.

I got up and slammed the door in her face, having enough of her. "I'm so glad she moved out. I just hope she stays out."

"I should go," Roman said. He had one of those looks on his face he normally got right before he was about to switch into his alter ego.

"Don't go because Mackenzie's a bitch," I said.

"It's not that...I think you're right. We shouldn't miss the rest of our classes," he said, making his way to the door.

"Did I do something wrong?" I asked, worried that maybe I felt more in that kiss then he did.

"No, no, it's not you..." he stood there looking uncomfortable.

"Was it what Mackenzie said...about Mr. Callahan?" He flinched slightly and I knew that was part of it. "It's not true you know." I felt too ashamed to admit that Mackenzie put a spell on us that almost resulted in the loss of more than just my virginity. I also didn't feel it was any of his business.

"I know...I just..." he looked down and I knew something was bothering him.

"You can tell me? I won't judge. I just told you my crazy life story. I'm sure whatever it is it can't be that bad?"

"You're right. Your life is pretty messed up. I don't think I can hang out with you anymore," he chuckled lightly, teasing.

"Shut up," I said, pushing him playfully. "Why do you hate Mr. Callahan so much anyways?" I asked. I thought maybe if I just said it he would admit it. He got that look on his face and I knew I hit a sore spot. He paced, clearly not wanting to discuss this. "Hey, I told you my back story. I think it's only fair you tell me yours, so spill."

He stopped for a second, clenched and unclenched his fists, and then he took a breath. "He and my sister went to school here together. One night at a party they both got drunk and well, ya know," he said, turning toward the window. "She ended up pregnant and when she told him he said it wasn't his, she was lying, and he wanted nothing to do with her. She had to leave the school and raise the baby on her own."

"Maybe he was right. Is she sure it was his?" I didn't know his sister and there was always that possibility she had secrets of her own. As I learned, everyone does.

"Of course it's his! She was a virgin until she met him," he snapped. "That's what he does Ella. He lures innocent girls and then dumps them when he gets them into bed. He did it with my sister, Mackenzie, and god knows how many others," he said, looking at me wondering if that was what happened, if I was one of those girls.

"Roman, I'm sorry. I wish you would have told me this from the beginning."

"It's not something I just go around telling people. It's not public knowledge," he grunted.

"You don't have to worry about me. I won't tell anyone. I promise," I said, joining him by the window.

"I know," he said softly. I placed my hands delicately on his chest and he looked down at me. I couldn't tell what was going on inside his head. He seemed to have a mix of emotions and then as if a switch went off he suddenly backed away from me. "I have to go. I'll see you at training later." He left without another word and me standing by the window all alone.

"What the hell?" I said to myself. I didn't understand why he got so spooked. Did I have bad breath? I put my hand in front of my mouth to check. Seemed okay to me. I shrugged. Was there something on my face? I checked myself out in the mirror. Besides looking a little paler than normal everything else was fine.

Why the hell did he run out of here like that?

Maybe it was the kiss after all. Maybe I was a bad kisser and he didn't want to experience that disaster again. No, that couldn't be it. I mean, if I was such a bad kisser I'm sure he wouldn't have spent all those nights making out with me in secret. He also just admitted he liked me. Did he change his mind? Was it not what he expected? Maybe he realized being friends with me was more than he bargained for. I sighed and locked my door not wanting to be interrupted. Then I dropped down on my bed and took a nap. I didn't care about missing the rest of my classes and if I got in trouble then oh well. I needed a nap after not sleeping last night and the horrible nightmare I had. Not to mention the disaster that was my so called love life. Just the thought of it gave me a headache.

I slept for about an hour and when I woke up I noticed there was a note that was passed under my door. Curious, I picked it up, and read it out loud.

Meet us in the basement at 3.

I looked over at the clock and it was ten of. The handwriting looked familiar, but I couldn't place whose it was. I let my curiosity get the best of me and headed to the basement. I know. Who's that dumb to go to a basement alone to meet someone who left a note? A note you have no idea who wrote? Yep, I was that person. That would be me.

When I got to the bottom of the steps the door was locked. I scratched my head. Why would they ask me to come to the basement if the door was locked? Out of nowhere, I had a pillowcase thrown over my head and then I was knocked out.

When I came to, I was in another part of the basement. I could smell the dampness. The dust and rusty old pipes told me I was in the very back of the basement. I heard the door open and looked over my shoulder to see who my capture was.

"You've got to be kidding me?" I said when I saw Mackenzie, Addyson, and Madison walk in. "What the hell could I have possibly done now to piss you off enough to result to kidnapping?" I mean seriously, she had officially gone too far. "Does this have anything to do with that stupid spell you put on Mr. Callahan and I, because if you're worried I'm going to tell. I'm not," I said, gritting my teeth.

"Please, I'm so over that," she said, brushing it aside as if it was last year's fashion.

I glared at her. I had yet to begin to pay her back for what she had done. "Is this because of Roman, because that –"

She stopped me. "Just stop guessing. You're so far off. Not everything is about you. God, were you always this conceited?"

"Isn't that the pot calling the kettle black?" She glared at me. "Alright, can we just get to the point and why the hell am I tied to a chair?" I asked, pulling at my restraints.

"We needed you to hear us out and I didn't want you escaping before we said everything we needed to."

"This is ridiculous even for you. If you would have asked nicely I would have listened," I said, twisting my wrists behind me and trying to untie the rope.

"Yes, but this way is more fun," she cooed.

"Let's just get it over with," I said. My wrists were starting to burn from yanking at the tight rope that bound them.

"Come on Mackenzie. Just ask her already," Addyson said nervously.

"Fine," she said rolling her eyes. "We want you to ask Sienna to join our coven."

"Seriously? This is what this is about? Why don't you ask her yourself?" I said, annoyed that they actually had the gall to kidnap me for that. There had to be some catch.

"If it was that easy don't you think we have done that already? You really are dumb."

"Keep it up and I will make you regret this," I threatened.

"Mackenzie, let's just hurry this up," Addyson said as she kept looking over her shoulder anxiously.

"Fine, we need you to convince her to join because we need her power and that dumb bitch Cameron is what kept her away in the first place."

"Wow, and you call me dumb," I laughed. "Why on earth would you think I would help you?"

"Because if you don't, I will tell everyone that I saw you seducing Mr. Callahan and that you two are having an affair."

I couldn't believe she would even use that and spin it around. "You have a lot a nerve. You know that." She was truly heartless. "No one will believe you. The only reason that whole mess happened was because you and the other two stooges started messing around with shit you know nothing about. You're nothing but a bunch of children playing with adult things." I turned to the other girls. "Did she tell you how the spell back fired? How the only reason it broke was because I made her break after Mr. Callahan attacked me." Both girls looked horrified. Clearly Mackenzie failed to mention their goof up.

"Don't listen to her," Mackenzie snapped. "The spell would have worked right if you weren't such a freak!"

I jerked in my chair and something snapped. Addyson and Madison screeched and jumped backwards toward the door. "What are you talking about?" I said, narrowing my eyes at Mackenzie.

"For some reason there's something wrong with you. It took

everything we had to get that spell to affect you and you still somehow broke through it."

I smiled at her, scaring the other girls. "You're going to wish you hadn't done that. Not only am I not going to help you, but when I get free I'm going to –"

"You're going to what? If you lay one hand on me you'll be the one who regrets it," she said, getting in my face. "Now, are you going to help me or not?"

She thought she intimidated me, but she was about to get a reality check. "After all the shit you pulled? I would never help you."

"Fine, have it your way," she said, walking away. "Come on girls."

"You can't just leave me here!"

"Oh, don't worry. Someone will find you eventually and by the time I'm done people will think this was some sick little game you and your boyfriend, Aidan, were playing."

"No one will believe you."

"They don't have to. I know a nifty little spell that will do all the convincing they need," she smiled mischievously, turning to leave.

"Kenzie, she looks really pissed. This was a bad idea. I think we should let her go," Addyson said.

"By all means, go ahead," Mackenzie said. Addyson looked over at me as I struggled to break free from the ropes and then shook her head no.

I was not about to let them leave me down here. Mackenzie reached for the door and when she did I screamed, "NO!" The door slammed shut and all the girls stepped back in surprise. Mackenzie tried for the door but once again it slammed shut.

She yanked and pulled with all her might, but the door wouldn't budge. I could see the frustrated look on Mackenzie's face as she jiggled the handle and nothing happened. I laughed. "You're doing this, aren't you?" she spat. I just shrugged my shoulders. I was as surprised as they were. All I remembered was not wanting to be left down here. I wished the door closed and it did. My guess was that I had another power that I didn't know about. It wasn't too farfetched that I could do it. Xander could move things with his mind so why couldn't I? I never even thought about until now and this was as good a time as any to try.

"Open the door," Mackenzie demanded.

"Untie me first," I bargained.

She walked over to me, getting in my face. "Open. The. Door."

"Not until you untie me," I said. I thought maybe I could undo the ropes the same way I closed the door but that wasn't happening. I was also afraid if I tried too hard to concentrate on the ropes I would lose control of the door and I couldn't risk them leaving without untying me first.

"Open the door!" Mackenzie screamed, ready to throw a hissy fit.

"No wonder you need Sienna. Without her your powers are weak. You're nothing but a pathetic little wannabe witch."

That really pissed her off. She shrieked and raised her hand to slap me, but I was able to bring my shield up and block her. She flew back, smacking her head against one of the pipes. Madison ran over to see if she was okay, but she wasn't responding. Addyson just stood by the door, cowering.

"Untie me," I said. They both looked at me like I was nuts. "Untie me so I can heal her," I tried again. Neither of them made a move. "What other choice do you have? Run and get help? How are you going to explain all this?" It took all of a second for both girls to realize I was right. "Now, untie me!"

Madison ran over and unwrapped my ropes. I rubbed my wrists as I made my way over to Mackenzie. I bent down in front of her and placed my hand on her head. She sat up gasping, looked at me, and then scurried backwards. I stood up and brushed my hands on my jeans. I looked over my shoulder to see Addyson was already gone. I had to let go of the door when Madison untied me so I could concentrate on healing Mackenzie. I still hadn't mastered how to use the powers that I did have let alone knew how to use more than one at time, or even if I could.

Madison was now helping Mackenzie up off the floor. I moved in front of them, blocking their path. Both girls froze. "Pull something like this again and next time I won't save your ass." She nodded. "And now you know just how powerful I am," I said as my last warning before I left.

I didn't even care to see if they got out of the basement okay. They didn't deserve my help. I saved her from internal bleeding only because I was the one who caused it, but that's where my sympathy ended. I grounded my teeth as I walked back to my room covered in dirt, sweat, and who knows what else.

I found Cameron outside my room waiting for me. "Hey, you missed lunch...what happened to you?" she asked, once she got a look at my sweat covered hair and dirty clothes.

"Come in and I'll explain everything," I said, unlocking my door and pushing it open for her to join me. "Can you just give me a minute to wash up?"

"Yeah," she said, wondering what the hell was going on.

I quickly showered, changed into some clean clothes and then joined Cameron sitting down next to her on my bed. I told her everything. I told her about the spell Mackenzie and her group had put on me. I left out the part about him becoming aggressive at the end. That was still too fresh in my head and I didn't think that part was anyone's business. I didn't want to taint his reputation when it wasn't his fault. I knew that now and that wouldn't be fair to him. I just let her know the spell had gone wrong and we almost got horizontal. Then I told her how they kidnapped me and tried to force me to get Sienna to join their coven.

Cameron's mouth hung open so wide I thought I might have to close it for her. "Say something," I said.

"I knew that bitch was crazy, but I never thought. I mean, are you okay?" she asked, looking me over.

"Yes and no. Physically yes. What the hell am I going to do? I can't just sit back and let her get away with this."

"Do you think she'll still spread that rumor about you and Mr. Callahan?

"I don't think she's going to try anything anytime soon. She got a taste of my powers and Madison and Addyson definitely looked scared shitless. I don't think they want to try going up against me again and without them Mackenzie doesn't have enough power."

"She still needs to be stopped," Cameron said.

"Oh absolutely. I let that spell with Mr. Callahan go and that was only because, well, I didn't know what else to do. It was too..." I didn't know how to describe it. Cameron squeezed my hand, understanding that was a sensitive subject and didn't push the issue. "But this whole kidnapping thing and trying to get me to turn my friend over to her, I will not let go," I said, feeling my blood boil.

"Have any ideas?"

"I was hoping you would," I said, biting my lip. "I'm not so good at this whole evil plot thing. I'm normally the one who gets plotted against," I admitted.

"I'm sorry, but my mind is still stuck on the fact that you saw Mr. Callahan naked," she said then quickly apologized. "I'm sorry. That's beside the point."

"Cameron, it's okay. And nothing happened, thankfully." I honestly couldn't blame her. I still can't get the image of his body out of my head.

"Okay, all bad things aside. How was he?"

"Cameron," I scolded.

"Oh, come on. You made out with probably the hottest teacher on campus and I'm not even going to get the details? Was he big?" I laughed out loud, which actually felt good. Before I could tell her she was going to have to use her imagination Dixon knocked on the door.

"Hello, hello," he said, letting himself in.

"Hey Dixon, what's up?"

"You weren't in class so I came to see if everything was okay?"

"Yeah, you know, just had one of my normal freak outs in class. It's starting to become a routine thing."

"Oh, honey," he said sympathetically, putting his arm around me. "You want to talk about it?"

"Thanks, but I'm kind of talked out right now."

"I want to hear more about you and Mr. Callahan," Cameron said, stretching out on the extra bed.

"Cameron!" I narrowed my eyes at her.

"What? You might as well tell Dixon. If Mackenzie follows through with her threat he would have found out anyways. Better to hear it from you."

"Sit, talk, now," he said, giving me a stern look like I was deliberately holding good gossip from him. I had to make him swear on his favorite pair of Dolce and Gabbana sunglasses that he wouldn't breathe a word of this to anyone. He swore to me he wouldn't and even told me he was insulted that I thought otherwise. I knew he wouldn't, but lately learning how to trust people again was an issue.

I told him everything I told Cameron.

"I heard she was evil, but I never thought she was that evil. You poor thing, what are you going to do?"

"Give her a piece of her own medicine," I said.

"So, do you have a plan?" Dixon asked.

"Not yet. I was hoping you guys could help me out?"

"I think we should tell Sienna," Cameron said.

"I don't know. I think the less people that know about this the better," I said.

"While I agree with that. I still think she should know. They did take you to get to her. Plus she's a witch so we could use her."

"Um, Hello?" Dixon said, waving his hand up and down the length of his six foot frame.

"No offense sweetie, but we need someone who's been at this a little longer," Cameron said.

Dixon looked away, picking lint off his pants, trying to pretend he wasn't offended when clearly he was. Cameron opened her mouth but Dixon waved her off. "No, no, it's fine," he said, adjusting his scarf and avoiding eye contact.

I rolled my eyes. "Any ideas?" I asked Cameron. She shook her head no. "Oh, I almost forgot the best part," I said, smacking myself mentally. They both leaned in closely, waiting. "I think I discovered a new power."

"Do tell," Dixon said intrigued.

"Maybe if I show you?" I looked around the room. I spotted my hair brush that Mackenzie tried to steal earlier. I concentrated on that and held my hand out. It flew right into my palm.

Dixon sat up." Very cool." I smiled proud.

"And handy," Cameron said, taking the brush to use on her hair. "Clearly we know they're no match for Ella. So this shouldn't be too hard to come up with a plan, right?"

We all looked at each other and sat there trying to think of something, but kept coming up blank. "I'm sorry, but my mind is stuck on the fact that you and Mr. Callahan were getting your freak on," Dixon said.

"I'm glad to know you are both concerned for my wellbeing," I said, getting up.

Dixon got up and stood next to me. "Ella, I know what you went through was traumatic and trust me when I say we are both more than happy nothing really happened. But you can't let it eat you up inside. Us joking about it is our way of dealing in hopes, that maybe, you will too?"

"I know," I said, knowing I had to get past this.

"So what was it like?" he asked, not wasting time.

"Is that all you guys think about?" They both nodded their heads. "It was good," I shrugged.

"Oh, come on," Dixon said, giving me a dramatic head roll. "You were like this weren't you," he put both his hands on the door and stuck his butt out looking over his shoulder. "Mr. Callahan, no, don't do that, oh no, oh wait yeah, oh no." I laughed so hard I snorted. I pushed Dixon and he wrapped his arms around me, smiling.

"You're one of those girls who pretend to be all innocent, but really you're a naughty little vixen, aren't you."

"Stop it," I said, feeling myself blush. I looked over at the clock and saw it was almost five. "Crap, I have to go. I have training in like ten minutes. We're going to have to come up with an evil plot later." I went into the bathroom to change again.

"Hey, can we come and watch?" Dixon asked.

"Oh, I don't know if Gabe would like that."

"I'm sure he wouldn't mind," Cameron said. I was sure he wouldn't, but I knew I would. Not seeing a way around it, I let them come with to the gym. We ran into Dean and Sienna on the way and they joined us as well.

Just great.

When we got to the gym, Gabe and Billy were already warming up. Gabe looked at his watch as I approached. "I'm not late," I said, running up to him.

He looked over at the bleachers, noticing my friend's piling up. "What's with the audience?"

"I told them it wouldn't be a good idea but they insisted they come."

He nodded and walked over to them. "If you plan on staying then that means you plan to work," he said. "No one comes to my sessions to watch. You have five minutes to change or get out." He stood there with his arms crossed, waiting.

I actually thought they would say no way and leave, but to my surprise they decided to stay. They are in for a world of hurt, I thought, smiling. Dean was the only one who declined, which wasn't a surprise. "Actually Dean, I think you should stay. You could benefit from this. I have seen your handy work first hand and you could use some pointers." Gabe smiled. I laughed knowing exactly what he was referring to – the bar fight. In Dean's defense he was pretty drunk.

"I didn't want to show off, but if you insist," he smiled cockily, heading into the locker room to change.

"Roman you're late, laps now. Ella you can join him while we wait for everyone else to get ready."

Great, why am I being punished too?

Roman and I ran our laps side by side in silence. He didn't even say one word to me. He barely even glanced in my general direction. This was starting to get ridiculous and I wanted to know what happened earlier. "Okay, so what's up?"

"What do you mean?"

"You've been acting weird ever since Mackenzie came into the room and..."

He stopped abruptly and I almost ran into him. "Look, Ella I..." he couldn't even look me in the eye. "I don't know how to say this but –"

"I knew it. I freaked you out," I interrupted.

"No, it's not that..." he finally looked up at me. "It's just that –"

"Ella, Roman, let's go. Finish up," Gabe shouted. I sighed as Roman closed his mouth and turned around to finish his laps. Why did this always happen?

Gabe and Billy split us up into two groups. Roman, Dean, and I went with Billy while the rest joined Gabe. An hour later Gabe let my group rest while we watched his go up against each other. It was interesting to watch and sit on the sidelines. Since Sienna was so delicate and small they paired her up with Cameron, while Dixon went up against Dean. For a skinny boy Dixon was pretty ripped and put Dean to shame. When they were done, Gabe had me spar with Cameron and Roman with Dixon since he basically made a fool of Dean.

I was impressed with how well Cameron was doing. I suggested she start taking some extra training sessions with us, but she said she preferred not to sweat so much. I laughed knowing how she felt, but I was used to it by now. "Alright, Dean and Ella, you two are next," Gabe said as everyone else took a seat.

I smiled big. "I've been waiting for this for a long time."

"Please li'l sis, I don't care how many extra sessions you've had. You still won't be able to beat me," he taunted. I didn't even wait for Gabe to say go. I just attacked catching Dean off guard. "That's not fair. I wasn't ready," he said, backing away.

"Excuses, excuses, just admit you know I'm better than you," I said.

"Never," he shouted, attacking. He hit me in my side and I clenched my stomach, faking I was hurt. "Ella, I'm sorry. Are you okay?"

I turned and socked him in the gut and then knocked him on his back. "Never underestimate the power of a girl," I said, gloating. He grabbed my ankle and pulled me down to the floor. "Hey!" I yelled, kicking him. He slapped my arm and I hit him back.

"Alright you two, enough," Gabe said, sounding like our dad. We both got up and when Gabe wasn't looking, Dean tripped me. I stumbled but quickly caught myself before I fell. I smacked him on the back of the head. This proceeded to turn into another fight that ended with me in a headlock.

"Alright, back to business now. Ella and Billy, show them how it's done."

I smiled big, knowing I no longer had to hold back. Everyone sat on the bleachers watching and cheering us on. After weeks training with Billy and months with Gabe I was able to keep pace with him. I even knocked him down. I put my arms up like Rocky, jumping up and down as my friends cheered. I then noticed Cameron was leaning close to Sienna with her hand covering her ear and whispering something to her.

"Alright, you got me once, but you won't the second time," Billy said, getting up. We went at it again and this time Billy was putting everything he had into it. I almost couldn't keep up with him.

"Ella and Mr. Callahan," Sienna blurted out loud. Shocked, I turned to look at her taking my eyes off of my opponent. This ended with me missing the block on Billy's punch. He hit me square in the eye, knocking me on my behind.

"Ella?" Billy said. When I opened my eyes everyone was standing over me. Billy helped me up. "Are you okay?"

I put my hand up to my eye which was throbbing. "How bad does it look?" I asked, pulling down my hand.

"How about we get you some ice," Cameron suggested. I knew it must be pretty bad.

I looked around the room and noticed someone was missing. "Where is Roman?"

"He was just here a minute ago," Sienna said.

"Yeah, until you opened your big mouth," I thought. I left

everyone in the gym and ran out to find him. "Roman!" I called to him down the hall, but he didn't stop. I sprinted to catch up to him and grabbed his arm to stop him. "Roman, please stop."

"You lied to me," he said, turning on me. "You told me nothing happened between you and Mr. Callahan."

"Nothing did happen," I said.

"Stop lying!" he yelled. "I overheard Cameron tell Sienna everything."

"Did you also hear the part how Mackenzie put a spell on us," I snapped. The look on his face said he didn't. "That's your problem. You only hear what you want to. I don't even know why I thought that maybe you were different. But no, you're just like any other jealous guy." Before I could even react, he took me in his arms and kissed me. I was so caught off guard I almost lost my balance. I had to pull myself away just so I could breathe.

We stood there for a moment, panting and looking into each other's eyes. "Roman I...I'm confused?" I said.

"Confused?"

"Well, I was under the impression you thought when we kissed in my room, it was a mistake and that's why you were acting so weird."

"No," he shook his head smiling. "I was acting so weird because that kiss was amazing." Okay now I was even more confused. "I never felt that way before and I got scared. I wasn't expecting that and I kind of panicked and took off."

"So you still like me?" I asked, wanting to know for sure.

"Very much so," he smiled, caressing my face. I flinched. "Oh, yeah, I forgot. Billy got you pretty good, didn't he?"

"I'm not going to lie, that hurt, a lot. I almost cried," I confessed. "It felt like I got hit with a two by four."

"Ella, you are such a mess," he laughed, guiding me back to the gym. "Why don't you go get changed and I'll go to the nurse's office and get you some ice."

"Thank you," I said, heading into the girls' locker room.

So Roman liked me a lot. And I think I liked him too.

Crap, what have I gotten myself into?

CHAPTER TWENTY-ONE

"Hey are you okay?" Cameron asked as I joined them in the locker room.

"Yeah, I just, um, had to do something quick," I said.

"Cameron told me what Mackenzie did. Ella I'm so sorry. She had asked me before to join, but the spells they do aren't good and I don't want to be involved in that," Sienna said. "And I'm sorry I blurted it out like that." She looked away. Not able to meet my eyes.

"I know we agreed to tell her but it couldn't have waited until later?" I said to Cameron. She just shrugged her shoulders.

"Ella, I promise I won't say anything...well...again," Sienna said smiling guiltily.

"Let's just drop it for now. I'm done talking about it for today."

"How about we get together this weekend and come up with a way to stop her once and for all," Cameron said.

"Sounds perfect," I replied. "Now hurry up and change. I'm starving."

"When are you not?" Sienna said and I threw a towel at her.

After showering – again – and changing, we left for the dining hall together. I found Roman waiting outside for me. I had forgotten he said he was going to get me some ice for my eye. "Oh hey, sorry I took so long," I said to Roman.

"It's okay," he said, handing me the ice pack which surprisingly still cold. I gently placed it over my eye and mumbled thanks.

I found Billy outside the dining hall pacing. "Ella hey, I was looking for you," he said concerned.

"And you decided to look for me outside the dining hall?"

"Well if I knew you would be anywhere it would be here getting food," he laughed.

"Do I really eat that much?" I asked.

"Yes," they all said together.

"How's your eye?" Billy asked, turning serious again.

I pulled the ice pack away and Billy made a face. "That bad?"

"No...no...it's..."

"Just stop," I said, holding up my hand.

"I'm sorry," he said, feeling awful.

"It was my fault. I wasn't paying attention. Don't worry about it. I heal fast."

"It's a shame you can't heal yourself," Dean said, joining us.

"I know. What good is having the power to heal if I can't heal myself," I complained.

"It's good for when you knock my ass into a wall," Roman said, winking at me.

When we sat down at our table Austin automatically informed us of the latest gossip. "Did you guys hear that Mr. Callahan was banging a student?"

I froze.

Sienna and Dixon looked down at their trays. I looked to Cameron next, whose face was as pale as a ghost. Sensing my panic Roman asked, "Who told you that?"

"Who didn't tell me? It's all over campus," he said.

"Does anyone know who it is?" I asked nervously.

"No. All we know is she's a new student with raggedy hair, kind of pathetic, bad skin. Basically a lowly girl who no one would touch," Reagan said.

I gawked. My hair was not raggedy, it may be unruly sometimes, but not raggedy. I still may get the occasional zit, but other than that my skin was flawless and I was not pathetic. Who said that stuff? Cameron leaned in. "Relax Ella, no one knows who it is, but keep looking like that and they'll start getting suspicious," she said.

I turned to her. "I am not a lowly girl," I whispered harshly.

"Yes, I know. But better they think that than realize who it really is."

"True," I thought to myself. I guess I was going to have to grin and bear it. "I can't believe she actually went through with it," Dixon said in a low voice.

Mackenzie and her group walked past our table and she turned to me, smiling. My whole body tensed. It took everything I had not to attack her. "Down girl, you don't want to incriminate yourself," Dixon whispered.

Mackenzie, surprising us all, came over to our table. Addyson and Madison wouldn't even look at me and you could see they had fear in their eyes. "So Dean, now that I lightened my load by getting rid of some excess baggage," she shot Roman a look. "I'm free for the dance next Saturday if you wanted to ask me."

I couldn't believe she had the audacity. I swear, if he says yes there will be nothing stopping me from killing both of them. "As you know, Mackenzie, I'm a wanted man," Dean said, leaning back casually. "Once I narrow it down I'll get back to ya," he winked.

"We all know who you will choose in the end. Don't keep me waiting too long," she purred as she ran her finger down his chest. I slid my chair back ready to get up and say something when Sienna stopped me.

"Ella don't," she said, but only I heard it. I then realized I couldn't move my legs. *"Yes I'm doing that and I will stop when Mackenzie leaves or until you can calm down."* I looked over at Sienna and cursed her. *"I heard that,"* she said.

"So, Ella, will you be going to the dance?" Mackenzie asked. "You know if you can't find a date I hear Mr. Callahan's available. You look like his type," she smirked. If it wasn't for Sienna holding me here I would have ripped each and every strand out of her big, bobble head.

"She already has a date," Roman intervened.

"Oh, really, and who would that be?" Mackenzie asked intrigued.

I sat there silently, waiting for his answer and wondering what the hell he was thinking. Even Dean stopped what he was doing long enough to hear Roman's answer. "Me," he said, surprising everyone.

The shocked expression on Mackenzie's face was enough to make me smile. She quickly recovered and said, "Ella likes things that are old and used." I ignored her jab and turned back to Roman. I stared at him.

"What?" he said.

"Nothing," I said, shaking my head. Dean gave Roman a suspicious look and Cameron glared at me like I was hiding something. I shrugged my shoulders innocently, pretending I had no idea what was going on, which wasn't far from the truth.

After Mackenzie's departure and the shock of Roman's

announcement wore off. I noticed I could no longer feel my legs. "Um, Sienna," I said, gesturing to my legs.

"Oh, sorry," she blushed and let me go. I rubbed my numb legs until the feeling slowly started to return. Roman and I exchanged a few glances from across the table, but neither of us said a word about what happened a few minutes ago. Cameron caught us and made a face saying, *'we will be talking later'*.

Riley and Justin joined us right after Mackenzie's little stage act. "Why does everyone look so tense?" Justin asked, sitting down.

"When you're in the presence of greatness," Dean started but I threw my roll at him before he could finish. We all laughed, diffusing some of the tension.

"I missed you in class today. Where were you?" Riley asked me.

"She was helping me move my stuff to my new room," Billy said and I smiled thankfully at him. Not that I couldn't tell Riley about my dream. I just didn't want the whole world to know.

"What were you guys talking about?" Riley asked as she peeled her orange.

"The dance," Dixon said.

"Are you going?" Riley looked at me anxiously. I didn't know how to answer. I wasn't sure if Roman said he was going with me just to get at Mackenzie or not.

"Of course she's going," Cameron said, elbowing me. I wasn't sure if that was a ploy to get me to admit something, so I just put on a fake smile and nodded. I looked over at Roman. He had his head down and kept quiet. "It sucks we can't leave campus. Now I have to wear something I already own," Cameron whined.

"Sorry," I said, knowing it was my fault that no one was allowed to leave.

"It's not your fault," Cameron said, trying to make me feel better, but we all knew the truth.

"Ella?" Ms. Kraft addressed me. I hadn't even noticed she walked up.

"Yes Ms. Kraft?" I half expected her to yell at me for running out of her class without an explanation.

"Mr. Callahan had asked me to come find you. You are wanted in his office immediately," she said. I was scared this had something to do about the rumor that was floating around. I didn't give myself anytime to deliberate and followed Ms. Kraft to his office.

"Ms. Kraft, do you know what this is about?" I asked her once we were outside.

"No dear, I do not, but I'm sure everything is fine."

She hadn't once mentioned about me leaving class today and I wondered if maybe I should say something. "Ms. Kraft, I'm sorry I ran out of class today. I..."

She stopped and turned to face me. "Ella, I know you have a lot going on and I understand why you were so upset. You don't have to explain anything to me."

"Wait, what do you mean you understand?"

She smiled politely at me. "Ella, I know you had a nightmare."

"But how? Is it because you are a witch?"

"That and I saw you sleeping," she said. I looked away embarrassed and curious as to why she didn't wake me up. "I didn't wake you because the spirits told me you were dreaming and that it was an important dream you needed to have," she explained as if she read my mind.

I looked at her like she was nuts. "Spirits told you?" Seriously, how was I the one that everyone thought was crazy?

She laughed, gesturing for us to continue walking. "Ella, you really need to start doing your homework and pay attention in my class. Remember how I told you that we use the elements to communicate?" I nodded. "Well, they also communicate with us as well."

"Are these spirits, like in ghosts, dead people?"

She laughed again at my stupid question, but didn't make me feel like it was stupid. "Yes dear."

"Can anyone communicate with them?"

She sighed. "Yes and no. The more powerful the person is the greater the connection."

"Oh, so only witches can," I said disappointed.

"It hasn't been proven that only witches can, but it also hasn't been proven anyone else can't either. Like I said, the more powerful the person the better connection," she smiled.

"What about the whole psychic thing? Are they for real or not?"

"Some are, but you must be careful not to be fooled," she warned.

"How can you tell?"

"Ella, this is something that will take some time to discuss. I'd really like to work with you if you don't mind devoting your time?"

I was really curious about learning more, but I was not ready to give up my weekends. Then I remembered I didn't have training everyday anymore and could meet with her after class. "Can we meet on Tuesday? Gabe and I are only training three days a week now so I have Tuesdays and Thursdays free. "

"That will be perfect," she smiled as we reached Mr. Callahan's office.

"Thank you Ms. Kraft," I said, turning to open the door to the office.

"I will see you in class on Monday and I will work this weekend on things to work with you on this Tuesday."

I smiled at her one more time before I stepped inside the office. "Miss McCallister, you may go right in," the secretary said as my stomach started to do flip flops.

I opened the door and almost fell over from shock. "Mom? Dad? What are you guys doing here?"

"Is that anyway to greet your mother?" my mom said, standing up. "Ella, what happened to your eye?" she gasped, noticing the bruise right away.

"Small accident in training. No big deal," I said, brushing it off. I looked at both my parents. "Is everything okay?" I asked worried.

"Of course, why would you think something was wrong?"

"Because you're here," I said. "Why are you here?" I asked suspiciously.

"Can't we come visit our daughter without there being a reason for alarm?" my dad said, kissing me on the cheek.

"With you, no," I said, eyeing him.

He gave me his, *'I'm not in the mood for your smartass mouth'* look and turned back to Mr. Callahan. "I appreciate you filling us in. We will be spending a few hours here before we retire to our hotel."

"We do have some extra rooms available in the guest housing if you would like to stay here. The nearest hotel is an hour and a half away," Aidan said, making me wish I had something to throw at him.

"I guess that would be better than traveling back and forth," my mom said.

"Alright then. We'll stay here. Thank you Aidan. Your kindness is greatly appreciated."

"I can have Gabe show you to one of the empty rooms. It's not the Ritz, but at least it's close," Aidan smiled.

"I'm sure it will be fine," my mom said, flashing her million dollar smile.

Aidan picked up the phone to call Gabe and I turned on my parents. "Okay, for real, why are you here? And don't say it's because you just wanted to see me, because if that were true Dean would be here too."

"We will discuss the why at another time and as for Dean, he will be meeting us later," my dad said.

"Does Dean know you guys are here?" They didn't have to say anything. I already knew the answer. "What the hell?"

"Watch your mouth," my father warned. I stifled an eye roll.

"Gabe will be down in a moment," Aidan said, hanging up the phone. I wish I hadn't had Ms. Kraft renew that spell to block thoughts again. That way I could figure out what was really going on. We had tried to see if I could handle it when it faded the first time, but by my second class I wanted to rip my hair out. So I had asked her to redo the spell. This was one power that was going to take me a while to adjust to.

CHAPTER TWENTY-TWO

After Gabe showed my parents to their room, my mom asked me to introduce her to my teachers while Gabe and my dad talked. I convinced her to let me take her on a tour of the school instead. After the tour I showed her my room. She looked around at everything, judging. I knew she wouldn't out right admit it but I knew she was analyzing the way I had things set up. She was always very particular about where things should go, which is why I made sure to make everything a little more chaotic. "So, what's your roommate like?" she asked. I knew she was trying hard not to move things around.

"Hmm...my roommate...yeah...she's kind of this evil bitch that for some reason has her mind set on destroying me," I smiled. My mom looked at me like I was exaggerating. That was until I let her know it wasn't a joke.

"Did you say something to the headmaster? He seems like a reasonable man. I don't see how this problem couldn't be dealt with rationally."

I could not tell my mom that Aidan was part of her evil plan. "It's not that big of a deal. She moved out of my room about a month ago and since then things have been fine," I said, hoping she couldn't tell I was lying.

She sat down on the bed next to me. "Ella, I know you're hiding something. You can tell me. Whatever it is? I know you think because I'm your mother there are some things you may feel uncomfortable telling me, but I don't want you to feel like that."

"I know," I sighed.

"Have I ever done anything that would make you think you couldn't tell me something? Regardless of what it was?"

I looked at my mom. She was right. She never judged me for all the mistakes I made or for anything I did. She always just listened and gave me the best advice a mom could give. I didn't know if it was because I was holding everything in for so long or I was actually happy to have my mom to talk to, but the second I opened my mouth everything came flying out.

"Okay, so, Mackenzie, my roommate, put a lust spell on me and Mr. Callahan resulting in us not being able to keep our hands off each other and the only way the spell would break was if we slept together. But the spell backfired because apparently my powers are ridiculously strong and I'm hard to bewitch. Then she knocked me out, tied me to a chair, and demanded I make my friend, Sienna, join her coven or she would tell the whole school about me and Mr. Callahan. I refused and she was going to leave me there until I managed to keep the door closed and knock her unconscious making her friends untie me so I could heal her. I still have nightmares, but new ones all the time. I have developed several more powers since I've been here which one resulted in me glowing and I think I'm falling in love with a boy." I stopped there, shocked at my own admission. That last confession came out of nowhere, making me just as surprised as she was.

"Anything else?" she asked nervously. I shook my head no. Her face was expressionless and I started to get nervous. She stood up and started to pace the room. Her mouth would open and then close. She seemed to be at a loss for words. "This Mackenzie girl, she was your roommate?" I nodded. "Where is she now?" I shrugged. She stopped and her face turned bright red. I've never seen my mom this upset. "We're going to find this...this...bitch. Nobody hurts my little baby and gets away with it."

"Whoa...down girl," I said, stopping her before she charged out of the room. "Mackenzie will be dealt with, but on my terms. This is my problem and I can deal with it." She hesitated. "Mom, really. No sense in you getting involved. I'm an adult now and can handle my own problems."

She sunk down on the bed, giving in. I saw a sense of calm come over her as I sat down next to her. She smiled and gently caressed my cheek. "When did you get so grown up?"

"Mom..." I said rolling my eyes.

"Okay, how about we talk about these other things that are bothering you? But first, this guy you're falling in love with. It isn't Mr. Callahan, is it? And when you say you had to have sex with him to break the spell..." she swallowed. "But it didn't work?" She scrunched her face afraid of my answer.

"No, it's not Mr. Callahan. Mr. Callahan..." I paused. "Why yes we did...mess around, the spell was broken before anything went too far."

She let out a sigh of relief. "How was the spell broken then? Most spells must follow through unless the witch herself who casts it breaks it."

"Somehow I managed to see through it. I knew something was off because I only felt so strongly pulled to him when we were around each other. I ran into Mackenzie and she confessed about the spell to gloat and I made her break it."

"And she just let it go? Just like that?" my mom asked, not convinced it was that easy.

"Well, no. Aidan, I mean Mr. Callahan, heard us fighting and when he discovered what was going on he made her break it," I lied. No need for her to worry or get more upset.

"Okay, so let's go back to the whole part about her kidnapping you," she said, her temper rising again.

"Mom, I thought you were going to let that go?" I sighed, not wanting to rehash that memory.

"You're right. You're right," she let out a breath. "Okay, so let's talk about these new powers and you said you glowed?"

I told her all about the new powers we learned I had developed and I even took my hair down to show her my new blue streak. I told her how we weren't sure about the glowing thing yet, but we were working on it. She smiled proudly at me and untangled my hair, pulling it forward. "I don't know why you don't wear your hair down. You should be proud of your blue streaks. It shows just how special you are and that you are destined for greatness."

"Thanks mom. Even though I think you're just saying that because you're my mom."

She hit me playfully on the arm and I laughed, laying my head on her shoulder. "You want to tell me about these nightmares you are having?"

I lifted my head and picked at my thumbs. She placed her hand over mine and I could feel her calming me.

I told her everything.

All the nightmares I had, including the latest one that had me running out of class. I even told her about how I've been seeing and hearing Kyle and Josie. I then told her about my classes and the extra training sessions I was taking with Gabe and how Ms. Kraft was going to spend some extra time with me to help me out.

"It sounds like you have some really good teachers here."

"I do," I smiled.

"So, you want to tell me more about this boy?" she smiled. "I saw some flyers about a dance next weekend. Did he ask you? Are you going?"

"He didn't so much ask me...so I don't really know. " She looked at me confused and I explained to her what happened.

"Do you think he just said that to make her jealous?" I nodded. "Regardless, any boy would be lucky to take you."

"Okay, now I know you're just saying that because you're my mom."

She laughed and hugged me tight. "Oh Ella, when are you going to learn how beautiful and unique you are?"

"I love you mom."

"I love you too honey. How about we go find your brother?"

I knew Dean was most likely hiding in his room. I took my mom downstairs to surprise him. We knocked, but he didn't answer. She was going to announce herself, but I told her not to. Better to surprise him and boy, did we ever. I opened the door and found him entertaining one of his many 'ladies'. "Christ Ella! Knock much?" he yelled.

"We did, but you didn't answer," I said, trying to keep the smile off of my face.

"I didn't answer for a reason. As you can see I'm busy. Now leave!"

My mom took her cue and walked in clearing her throat. The look on Dean's face was priceless. I wish I had a camera. "Hello Dean," she said.

"Hi mom," he managed to choke out. The girl on his bed quickly made her exit. I only noticed who it was when she passed me.

"Madison?" I glared at him.

"What? Keep your friends close and your enemies closer," he smiled.

"That's not exactly what you were doing," I sneered.

"We were studying."

"Let me guess, anatomy?"

"Enough you two," my mom said, looking back and forth between the both of us. "Dean, I have been standing here for five minutes," she scolded.

"Sorry mom," he said, getting up and giving her a hug and kiss.

"I trust you two are getting along?" she asked.

"We were until he starting sleeping with the enemy!"

"I wasn't –"

My mom stopped him. "I know I've asked you kids to be open and honest with me and to feel comfortable to tell me whatever, but can we please keep it PG?" I couldn't help but laugh out loud. "Ella, what is so funny?" she asked.

"Nothing," I said, shaking my head. "Let's go find dad."

Dean and I spent the next two hours in our parent's room catching up on things. My mom told me to leave out all the stuff about Mackenzie and the nightmares. She said some things are better left unsaid. Basically let's just not tell your father. I did tell him about all my new powers and he wanted me to test every single one out on him. I explained to him I was still learning how to control them and figure out how to use them. He let me off the hook for tonight, but told me after talking with Gabe he was so proud of how well I was doing and wanted to see me in action. He said he set something up for tomorrow.

We still hadn't discussed why they were here in the first place, but it was late and I was getting tired. I said goodnight and headed back to my room to change into my pajamas. As soon as I turned off the lights and got under the covers there was a knock on my door. I grumbled and got out of bed to answer it. It was Cameron. She threw her arms around me. "Oh thank god, I thought they found out it was you and sent you away," she said, holding me so tight I couldn't breathe.

"Okay Cameron, you can let go now," I said, gasping.

"Oh, sorry," she said, walking past me, and plopping down on the bed. "Were you sleeping?"

"Not yet," I sighed, so desperate to be sleeping. I sat next to her on the bed. "What's up?"

She gave me the once over. "That's what you sleep in?"

I stood up, annoyed. "Seriously? What the hell is wrong with flannel pajamas?"

"Nothing, if we were living in the 1950's," she quipped.

I rolled my eyes. "Sorry I don't look like I stepped out of a Victoria Secret catalog and just so you know these are very comfortable."

"Alright, chillax," she said, putting her hands up in surrender. "What happened? Why'd they call you into the office?"

"My parents are here. They came for a *'visit'*," I said, using air quotes.

She nodded, understanding. "Well, get changed because we're all meeting in the social room to come up with a plan to take down Mackenzie. But first, you and I are going to have a little chat," she said, pulling me back down on the bed. I rolled my eyes. I was so not in the mood for this. "I know for a fact there's something going on between you and Roman and before you try to deny it, he already told me."

"What exactly did he tell you?" I asked, having a feeling she was lying and using this as a trick to get me to confess.

"You know exactly what he told me," she said, challenging me.

I looked her square in the eye and said, "Nothing," I smiled. "He told you nothing."

"Okay fine. He wouldn't talk either, but I know you're both lying."

"Why do you care so much anyways?"

"Because Roman's a good friend and I don't want to see him get hurt," she admitted.

"But you let him date Mackenzie," I said, questioning her so called loyalty to their friendship.

"First off, that disaster happened way before I could stop it."

"Cameron, I get that you care deeply for Roman as a friend and you don't want to see him get hurt, but you don't have to worry because nothing is going on between us."

"Why not?" she pouted.

"Okay, seriously? You're driving me nuts. First you want me to date him, then get mad when you think something is going on and now you're mad that there's not?" I was so confused I was getting a headache.

She sighed. "Ella, I know he likes you and this is nothing he told me. He didn't have to. I can tell. I just...well...if something would happen, just be careful, he's fragile."

"Okay Cameron, I get it," I said, hoping she would leave it at that.

"You two are totally messing around aren't you?"

"Oh my god!" I laughed. "I'm going to go change," I said, walking into the bathroom and closing the door behind me.

"I'd be totally cool with it if you were. I mean, all I'm asking for is a little detail," she called through the door.

"Give it up already," I yelled back. I didn't have to see her to know she was smiling.

Fully dressed, I followed Cameron to the social room. I was so tired and wanted nothing more than to go back to my room, but I knew this had to be done. When we got there, everyone was already there waiting. I went to the fridge to grab a soda to help wake me up. When I turned around Roman was standing behind me. Startled, I almost dropped my soda. "Sorry," he said. He stood there for a moment, just watching me, making me feel nervous, but in a good way. I could tell he had something to say, but wasn't sure how to say it.

"Ella I...never mind," he said, hanging his head and stepping aside so I could pass.

Confused, I took a step to walk away, but he jumped in front of me. "Wait, I...there's something I wanted to ask you." He ran his hand through his hair indicating he was nervous about what he wanted to ask me. "I went about it the wrong way, but Mackenzie just makes me so mad," he growled.

"She kind of has that effect on people," I joked, hoping to lighten up the situation.

He gave me a faint smile. "Alright, I'm just going to say it. Will you go to the dance with me?" I didn't know what to say. He noticed my odd expression and continued. "I know what I said at dinner and I just said that to shut Mackenzie up, but I really was planning on asking you. I don't want you to think I'm just doing this to get back at her. I really would like to go with you, but it's okay...I'll understand if you say no." He watched me, eyes wide, waiting for my answer. He ran his hand through his hair again.

I thought about making him sweat it out for a little, but when I looked into his eyes, I knew I couldn't. "Yes," I said smiling.

"Yes?" he asked unsure.

"Yes," I repeated.

"Ella, thank you. I really do want to go with you because of you and not well, you know," he babbled and I laughed.

"What?" he said bashfully.

"You're babbling."

"Oh," he said, smiling. Not knowing where to go from here, Roman stood there, still smiling at me, until Cameron came over and cleared her throat. "I'll uh...see you later," Roman stuttered and made a quick exit for the door. I took my cue and made my way over to the couch, plopping down next to Dixon.

"Somebody has a crush," Dixon sang.

I stifled an eye roll. "Dixon, grow up. And I do not," I told him.

"Not you silly, Roman," he said like it should have been obvious. "That boy is seriously head over heels in love with you."

"Dixon, be serious," I said, elbowing him.

"Ella, you need to open your eyes. Has it ever occurred to you that this is not the only social room? You do know that every floor has one."

"Yeah," I said, not knowing where he was going with this.

"Then why would Roman come up here to get a drink when he has access to the same things on his floor?"

"Maybe they didn't have what he wanted," I shrugged.

"No, they definitely didn't," Dixon smiled.

I narrowed my eyes at him and he just shrugged his shoulders. Ready to get to the matter at hand I asked, "Has anyone thought of anything yet?" They all shook their heads no.

"Let's make this quick. I have other things to attend to tonight," Dean whined, coming into the room.

"Wait, what is Dean doing here?" I asked.

"Who else would be better to help you plot an evil plan," Dean smiled.

"Maybe someone who wasn't dipping into the witch's brew," I spat.

"Hey, I'm not picky," he shrugged.

"Obviously," I thought to myself.

"You know, Dean might be on to something here," Cameron said, tapping her chin.

"The only thing he is on is antibiotics from all the skanks he's been with," I said.

Dixon and Sienna tried to cover their laughs. "While that also may be true," Cameron said and Dean glared at her. "What I was getting at was that I think Dean should continue his so called *'relationship'* with Madison."

"What!" I shouted.

"Let me finish," she said. I took a breath and calmed myself while she went on. "I also think he should take Mackenzie to the dance." I opened my mouth to say something, but Cameron stopped me. "Think about it Ella. Dean's the biggest player on campus."

"Hey, I'm a ladies man not a player," Dean complained. I just glared at him. "I can't help it I'm loved," he shrugged. I threw a pillow at him, missing and hitting Cameron instead.

"Like I was saying," she growled, wiping the hair out of her face and looking at us like an annoyed parent. "If we got Dean to secretly date all three, maybe he could use his charm to get some information out of them. We could play them against each other. Let them be the ones to destroy themselves."

"Cameron, that's genius," Dixon said.

"Yeah, but what makes you think they'll so easily give up information about each other, especially to Dean. They do know he's my brother," I said, not totally convinced Cameron's plan was fool proof.

"Have faith li'l sis. I do have my ways," Dean said smiling.

"And I also think Sienna should join their coven," Cameron said, surprising us all.

"No way," I said.

"Yeah Cameron, I don't know about that one," Sienna said.

"Hello, what a better way to find out how to take them down. It's like going behind enemy lines," Cameron said, trying to sway us.

I looked at Sienna. I didn't exactly like this plan, but it was the best thing we could come up with. I told her it was up to her and not to feel obligated to say yes. We would come up with another plan if we had to. "I'll do it," Sienna said proudly.

"Great, so here's what we do," Cameron started. "Dean, don't tell Mackenzie you'll go to the dance with her until the last minute, make her wait. Same with you Sienna, wait a few days before you tell her you'll join her coven." Cameron went over a few more details of the plan. Dean had left, saying he was on his way to start *'carrying out the plan'* as he called it. This was going to take a lot of self-control for me to follow through with this plan. And a lot of Tums to settle my stomach from all the nauseating details I'm sure Dean will provide.

When I knew Dean was gone for sure, I pulled Cameron aside and asked, "So what did you tell Dean to get him here? You didn't tell him about me and Mr. Callahan did you?"

"Relax, I didn't tell him anything," she said, like it was no big deal.

"Then how did you get him to go along with it?" I knew my brother and he didn't do anything out of the goodness of his heart.

She sighed, seeing I wasn't going to let this go. "All I told him was we were making a plan to get back at Mackenzie and asked if he wanted to help."

"That's it?" I asked, having a feeling she was holding out on me.

"Yep, that's it," she said and walked away letting me know she wasn't going divulge any more information. I dropped it, figuring it was probably better off I didn't know. I decided to call it a night. I was exhausted and had to get up early tomorrow. Everyone else stayed to watch a movie while I went back to my room to crash.

When I got there, I found Roman pacing back and forth outside my door. "Um, hey, what's up?" I asked.

"I just wanted to talk to you," he said.

"Is everything okay?" I asked, wondering if maybe he thought asking me to the dance was a mistake.

"Yeah, I just...um..." I could tell he was feeling uneasy, but I was too tired to spend the next twenty minutes waiting for him to try and spit it out.

I opened my door, stepped inside, and turned to face him. "I'm sorry, but can this wait? I'm really tired and I oh −" He leaned forward and kissed me, catching me off guard.

He pulled back smiling. "Sorry, but I've been wanting to do that since dinner."

I was speechless. My lips were tingling and I so wanted to feel his lips on mine again. I grabbed his shirt and pulled him into my room. Then I shut the door and pushed him up against the wall. I stood on my tip toes and pressed my lips to his. They melted with every touch. It was almost magical.

And then it hit me − magic.

I pulled back. "Wait, does this feel weird?"

"No, it feels wonderful," he said dreamily, leaning down to kiss me again.

I pushed him away. "No. What if this is another spell? What if after Mackenzie saw us in here she put the same spell on us she put on Aidan and me?"

He tensed at the mention of Mr. Callahan's name. "I would be able to tell," he said.

"How, you didn't notice last time?"

"That's because I wouldn't let myself," he said almost shamefully.

"But..."

"I can tell when someone is under a spell."

I looked at him confused. "Care to elaborate?"

"I'm half witch. We can usually tell when someone puts a spell on us or someone else, but it's not always easy. That's probably why I didn't realize at first that Mackenzie had put one on you. After you had told me, I remembered I saw the signs, but refused to believe it. I'm sorry Ella. If I wasn't so stubborn..."

"Don't," I said. "It's not your fault. But are you sure that we're okay now? You said so yourself it's not always that easy."

"Yes, but it also takes a very powerful witch to mask it and Mackenzie nor her coven combined have that kind of power. You already proven that you are more powerful than any one we know and cannot be bewitched easily," he smiled, stroking my hair.

"How do I know you didn't cast a spell on me?" I teased. "You just admitted you're half- witch and you're also half-vampire which I'm unsure how that works," I said, getting slightly off track. I shook my head. "You could be more powerful than I am aware of," I said, semi kidding. At first it was a joke, but now that I actually said it, I was a little frightened it could be true.

He smiled, sensing my uneasiness. "I don't need a spell to convince you to be with me."

The slightest touch of his hand on my hip melted away any doubt. "Oh, really, than how do you plan to do it?" I provoked.

"Like this," he said, cupping my face with his hands, leaning down, and kissing me softly. My lips quivered from the soft touch. He pulled back and his hand slid down to my shoulder. My eyes were still closed and I could hear him laughing at me. "Ella, you can open your eyes," he whispered.

I pressed my lips together, savoring the taste of his lips on mine. Then I slowly opened my eyes and looked into his. They were sparkling, tender, and adoring. "I should go," he said, smiling.

"You can stay. I mean you can sleep here. I mean..." I slapped myself in the forehead embarrassed by my ramble. "It's just that with Billy gone, it's lonely, and sometimes scary all by myself. There's the extra bed so..."

"I'll stay."

I let out a sigh of relief. "I have some extra blankets over there in that chest and I'm just going to go into the bathroom to change," I said bashfully. I searched for some pajamas that were not 1950's-ish as Cameron had said. I found some silk pajama pants and a kami. I grabbed them and went into the bathroom to change. I quickly checked myself out in the mirror and saw my swollen black eye. I sighed, knowing there was nothing I could do about it. I brushed my teeth and carefully washed my face, then closed the door behind me.

Roman was lying on my bed in just a t-shirt and boxers. "I like those pajamas better than the granny ones," he said, smiling big.

"Uh, that's my bed. That one is the extra bed," I said, pointing to the one over by the window.

"Wouldn't you feel safer with me right next to you?" I crossed my arms and waited for him to get up. "The bed over there is colder because it's next to the window."

"And you would know how?" I glared. I remember him telling me he never stayed in this room with Mackenzie. Something about her having a no boy policy, which I found hard to believe.

"Look, we can be mature about this. I promise I'll keep my hands to myself. You can even put pillows in between us."

"I might believe that if you weren't in your boxers."

"I always sleep in my boxers," he frowned. "Did you expect me to sleep in my jeans?"

"Whatever," I said, crawling into the opposite side of the bed. He put two pillows in between us. I lied facing the wall. He laid flat on his back and stared up at the ceiling.

"Goodnight Ella."

"Goodnight Roman."

I slept like a baby that night. When I woke up in the morning, the pillows between us were gone, and I had my head on Roman's bare chest and my arm around his waist. I got up quickly and slid over to my side of the bed. "Good morning," Roman said grinning.

"Morning," I said, pushing the hair out of my face. "Umm, what happened to your shirt?"

"I got hot so I took it off."

"And the pillows?"

He shrugged. "When I woke up they were gone."

"How long have you been awake?"

"Not long."

"Why didn't you wake me?"

"You looked so peaceful I didn't want to disturb you."

I got up off the bed and noticed the pillows were on my side of the floor. "Oh," I thought to myself. I looked over at Roman who was still lying comfortably. Okay, so here comes the awkward part. "Well, um, thanks for staying," I stammered.

"We could go to breakfast together, if you want?" he said, standing up. That's when I noticed his ripped body. His six pack abs, the way his boxers hung low on his hips. "Like what you see?" he said, noticing my lingering eyes.

"Shut up," I said, hitting him. He moved closer, pulled me into him, and kissed my lips ever so softly. "What was that for?" I asked breathless.

"Just wanted to know what it was like to wake up next to you in the morning and be able to kiss you."

"And?"

"Eh," he laughed.

"Very funny," I said, pushing him and walking away. He wrapped his arms around my waist and pulled me down on the bed. "Hey!" I yelped, giggling.

He pinned me down and said, "You know, you really should start practicing more. You're losing your touch."

"You ever think I'm letting you pin me?" He smiled big and pressed his lips to mine. I felt comfortable in his arms, safe. I lost track of time the minute his lips connected with mine. The only thing that broke us apart was when Dean sent me a message in my head to meet him and our parents in their room for breakfast.

"I have to go," I whispered as he moved his lips down to my neck.

"It's Saturday, what do you have to do that's so important," he mumbled as he brought his lips back to mine, distracting me. If Dean wasn't shouting in my head to hurry up I never would have left my room.

"Uuuhh," I whined. "I have to go."

"Nooo…"

"Yes I have to. My parents are here."

He stopped dead. "Talk about mood killer."

"I know but you weren't listening."

"Can you blame me," he smiled, nibbling on my neck.

"Okay, okay. Parents, parents, parents," I repeated, trying to get him to stop.

He sighed, pulling back. "How long are they here for?"

"With my parents, who knows?"

"Will I see you later?" he asked with a little desperation in his voice.

"I think I can find some time," I teased. He laughed and gave me a quick peck and then got dressed.

I opened my door and peeked outside to make sure no one was around and then told Roman it was safe for him to leave. He gave me another quick kiss and sweet smile before he left. I felt like I was floating on a cloud. My head was spinning and my body was tingling. All that changed the second Dean started screaming in my head again. Then after he was done it was my dad telling me to get dressed and head to their room.

Ugh! This was so unfair that I couldn't talk back to them. I hated that they could get in my head like that. I quickly changed, washed my face, and brushed my teeth. When I got to their room Dean started whining. "It's about time you got here. I'm starving."

I rolled my eyes and sat down on the couch. "Good morning sweetheart," my mom said, kissing me on the cheek. "You seem in better spirits today." She stepped back and took a good look at me.

"What?" I said, feeling uncomfortable under her stare.

"Nothing," she said smiling brightly. Her smile faded when she looked at my horrible black eye. "I wish there was something we could do about this?" She gently reached up and I flinched. "Sorry honey."

"Why has someone not healed it yet? Surely there are other healers on campus," my dad said.

"Yes, but they are only used for emergencies and this isn't considered one," I shrugged. "It's okay. It doesn't hurt as much as it did and I'm a fast healer. I'm sure it will be gone in a few days." *I hope*, I added to myself. "So what's on the agenda for today?"

"As soon as your father finishes up we're going to head out for brunch," my mom said.

"But we can't leave campus?" Dean shot me a look to shut up.

"Ella, you will be with your father and I and they cannot tell us we can't take our own children off campus," she smiled. I never thought of that.

Dean and I spent all morning and all afternoon with our mom and dad. We had brunch, then my mom and I went shopping while the boys did...well I didn't know what they did, but they weren't bothering us. "Did you decide if you're going to the dance or not?" my mom asked.

"Um, yeah."

"Why didn't you tell me? Do you have a dress yet?"

"I didn't tell you because I didn't think I was going."

"Don't worry honey. You're beautiful and sometimes that can be intimidating to a boy. I'm sure someone will ask you."

"Thanks mom," I rolled my eyes. "I didn't think I was that pathetic."

"No honey, you're not pathetic. You're special."

"Okay just stop. You're not helping."

"Why don't you just ask someone? Didn't you say there was a boy you liked?" This was her way of fishing for information. Trying to subtly slip questions in there I wouldn't normally answer.

"Mom! If you would just please stop I can tell you that I already have a date."

"You do? That's great. Tell me all about him and why you do that we can look for a dress," she gleamed.

"Mom, this isn't like prom. I don't think you need to go all out. Something simple will be fine."

"Isn't this dance to celebrate Ostara?" I shrugged. I had no idea. "Ella, aren't you paying attention? What have you been learning?"

"Sorry, I've been a little distracted with everything else that's going on."

"Honey I know. I'm sorry. I know this can't be easy for you," she said sympathetically.

"I'm dealing."

She pulled me in for a hug. "I think going to this dance will help you get your mind off of things. Take this opportunity to enjoy yourself," she smiled tucking a piece of hair behind my ear. "Now, let's go find you a dress."

We shopped for about an hour and everything she picked out was a ridiculous, puffy gown. "What about this one?" she asked, holding up a black, strapless gown that looked like the one I wore in my last dream.

"Definitely not," I said. I looked through the racks ready to give up when she held up another dress. My eyes lit up when I saw it.

It was perfect.

It was a long, white, strapless dress. It reminded me of the one Reese Witherspoon wore in the movie 'Walk the line'. "Try it on," my mom said. I went into one of the dressing rooms to try the dress on. The fabric felt like silk on my skin and hit just below my ankles. I fell in love with it the moment I put it on. "Well?" I stepped out of the dressing room and my mom gasped.

"You like it?"

"You look beautiful," my dad said. He and Dean had come into the shop while I was in the dressing room. "You look like a princess," he smiled, placing his hands on my shoulders. If I didn't know better I swear it looked as if he was going to cry.

"Dad," I said, rolling my eyes at his comment.

My mom turned to the cashier and said, "We'll take it."

We headed back to the school and I hung up my dress in the closet and then changed. My dad wanted to see the progress I was making with Gabe. I wasn't happy about having to do this on the weekend. The weekends were my time off, but who was I kidding. I should know better than to expect any time off. My life if anything was always changing.

CHAPTER TWENTY-THREE

When I got to the gym, I saw that my dad was wearing gym shorts and a t-shirt. "Uh, Dad, seriously. Aren't you a little old to be wearing shorts?" I heard Dean chuckle under his breath. My dad narrowed his eyes at me not amused.

"You're going to show me what you and Gabe have been working on and then you and I are going to spar," he said.

"Um...you think that's a good idea?"

"What, are you afraid I'm going to hurt you?" I laughed so hard I almost peed in my pants. "That wasn't meant to be funny."

I wiped the tears from my eyes. "Good one Dad. Thanks, I needed that." Gabe just shook his head at me. "What?"

"Let's just get started," Gabe said.

Gabe and I went one on one for a while and then he told me to show them how I use my shield. My dad's eyes went wide with surprise. "Ella that's amazing," he said proudly. I smiled at him, feeling happy about my new power for the first time. "I always knew you would be something special." He hugged me tight before he said, "Okay, now my turn."

"Dad, I still don't know?"

"Don't worry. I'll take it easy on you," he winked.

"Alright old man. You were warned."

"Old man, eh?" He took his stance and got ready. We danced around each other, but neither of us made a move.

"Okay, I'm sorry, but I can't hit you. I feel like I'm setting myself up for a possible future grounding."

My dad laughed. "Oh come on, you know you've been dying to get a few swings in," he said smacking my arm, taunting me.

He was right. I was dying to take a swing at him, but I wouldn't admit it. Not out loud at least. Knowing we would be here forever if I didn't do something, I put on a brave face, and swung. He blocked it with ease. He took his cue and came at me. I gave him everything I had, not holding anything back. I was impressed at how well he could keep up with me. He never got winded or tired out, well, that he showed. I was pretty sure he was dying on the inside.

Not wanting to get showed up by my own father. I came at him full force, knocking his ass on the floor. I held out my hand to help him up. "Not too bad for an old man," I teased.

He held his hand to his back. "I guess I am a little out of practice," he said, slightly limping. I had to cover my mouth to keep from laughing out loud.

"Alright, I think we had enough for today. We have an early flight tomorrow so I think we should retire for the night," my mom said. I think she was more worried about my dad over doing it and didn't want him to end up breaking something. I passed my dad over to my mom and looked at my watch. It was almost ten. We had worked straight through dinner. No wonder my stomach was growling.

"Hey Dad, want me to heal you before you go?" I asked, not able to keep the smile off of my face.

He narrowed his eyes at me. "I am perfectly fine," he said, straightening out his back. I heard several cracks and pops. I knew he was masking how much pain he was in. Men and their stupid pride. I walked with them out of the gym. Dean and my mom managed to get ahead while I lagged behind with my dad. When they rounded a corner my dad held an arm out stopping me. Then he turned to look at me. "Okay, maybe a little healing wouldn't hurt," he said.

"Sure Dad." I had to bite my tongue to keep from laughing.

"Just don't tell your mother."

"It will be our little secret." I healed my dad and he sighed with relief. Then we met back up with my mom and Dean. She gave us a funny look when she saw us, but didn't say anything. I had a feeling she already knew.

Dean and I said goodbye to our mom and dad. They had decided to stay at a hotel tonight to avoid the long drive in the morning. I never did find out why they stopped by for an unexpected visit, but it was pleasant so I couldn't complain.

On the way back to my room I stopped by the social room and grabbed myself some food to munch on. "Hey Ella!"

"Oh, hey Riley. I'm sorry we haven't had a chance to hang out much," I said, realizing I couldn't remember the last time I had spent any time with her.

"It's okay. I know you're really busy with training and stuff."

I remembered a while ago there was something she wanted to talk to me about, but with Billy's arrival and everything else going on I forgot. I deemed myself the worst friend ever. "No it's not okay. I'm such a bad friend. How about just you and me hang out tonight and catch up?"

Her eyes twinkled, indicating she was excited. "That would be great," she said.

"Okay, just give me some time to shower and eat," I said, holding up my bag of chips.

"Ella, is that your dinner?" she asked appalled.

"Yeah, I, uh missed it earlier so..."

"Go take your shower and I will find you some real food to eat," she said, sighing at my lack of nutrition.

"Okay, meet me in my room in like a half hour," I said as I walked out.

When I opened the door to my room I almost dropped my bag of chips when I saw Roman lying on my bed. "What are you doing here?" I asked, thinking I need to remember to start locking my door.

"I'd thought you'd be happy to see me?" he said, getting up, walking over to me, and kissing me.

I pushed him back and looked over my shoulder to see if anyone was out in the hall, then closed the door. "Are you crazy? Someone could have seen that," I said.

"I didn't know this was some big secret?" He crossed his arms and looked like he was ready to transform into one of his many alter egos.

"Relax, that's not what I meant. Well, I mean, what is this exactly? What are we doing?" Roman had already confessed that he liked me but never really expressed interest in pursuing anything.

The expression on his face told me he didn't know either. "Having fun?" he said unsure.

"If that's the case then maybe we should just keep this between us for now." With everything going on I did not want people to think I was some boyfriend stealing whore. I had enough rumors going around about me I didn't need anymore.

Roman stood silently for a moment and I was afraid I offended him. He stepped closer to me and took my hands. "I think I can handle that, for now," he smiled, kissing me again.

"Okay, while I'm glad you're happy. I need a shower."

"Want some company? I could wash your back for you?" he smiled cockily.

I pushed him away. "You need to go." I laughed and headed into the bathroom. I took a quick shower knowing Riley would be here soon. When I got out of the bathroom Roman was lying on my bed. "What are you still doing here?"

"I thought we'd hang out tonight?"

"Sorry, girl bonding with Riley."

"You don't look like the girl bonding type," he smirked.

"Clearly you don't know me very well," I smiled back.

He got up off the bed and put his hands on the doorway of the bathroom blocking my path. "I like this look on you. You should wear a towel more often." I rolled my eyes and pushed him back, but he pulled me closer, placing a gentle hand on my cheek, and staring softly into my eyes. I tilted my head back and let him kiss me.

He ran his hand down my shoulder and across my chest, tugging at my towel. I gave him a light punch to the stomach. "Now you really have to go," I said, making him laugh.

There was a knock on the door. "Ella?"

"Crap, you have to go," I said to Roman.

"What am I going to do? Jump out the window?" I raised my brow. "I was kidding. Look, what's the big deal? I'll just say I stopped by about a project or something." That sounded plausible so I nodded in agreement and told him I would wait in the bathroom until he left. He rolled his eyes and walked out saying hi to Riley and nothing else – so much for our cover story.

Riley walked into the room. "Ella? Are you in here?"

I stepped out of the bathroom. "Yeah, I was just getting out of the shower, sorry."

"Did you know Roman was in here?"

"Yeah, he had to drop something off for a project we're working on." She just made a face and I made it seem like it was nothing. After I changed, Riley surprised me with a couple slices of pizza. "Where did you get this?" I asked, stuffing my face.

"Justin snuck into the kitchen and got it for me."

"In human form or wolf form?" I asked worried, because if he did it in wolf form then how the hell did he carry these besides his mouth? Gross, I shuddered.

"Human form, geez Ella," she said rolling her eyes and I just laughed.

"How are things with you two?"

"Pretty good," she said, taking a piece of pizza for herself. "He asked me to the dance."

"That's great Riley. I hoped he would since you guys are going out."

"It's a given, but still nice to be asked boyfriend or not."

"True." I could tell by the shift in her position there was something else. Something she wanted to talk about, but was unsure how to approach it. "Riley, is there something you wanted to talk to me about?" I asked. She looked down at her over chipped nail polish. "You know you can talk to me about it. Whatever it is."

She picked at the blanket. "I'm scared I might lose Justin," she admitted.

"What do you mean?"

"Well, we've been dating for a bit now and well, we have kissed," she stopped to blush. "I'm worried about the rest of the stuff. I like Justin a lot, but I'm not ready and I'm scared he might get tired of me if I don't, you know, put out," she said, whispering the last two words as if it was unheard of to speak them out loud.

I had to hide my smile. Even though Riley and I were the same age, it's safe to say Riley's upbringing was a little more conservative than mine. "Riley, first off, you never need to be embarrassed about talking about sex, especially with me." She blushed indicating she was. "And second, never let a guy push you to do anything you're not comfortable with. And if he has a problem with it than he's not worth your time."

"I know. I mean I want to do these things, but it's too soon."

"Riley, when you're ready you'll know and as far as Justin goes, I may not know much about him, but from what I do know, he's one of the good guys. I can tell he's crazy about you. And I'm pretty sure he wouldn't jeopardize your relationship by being a douche."

"Yeah, but he dated Addyson. How can I compete with that?" she said, not convinced this relationship was solid enough to survive the lack of nookie.

"Okay one, Addyson is no competition. Rumor is most guys only date her because she puts out." Riley gave me a look saying I wasn't helping. "I know Justin's not that type of guy. Regardless of who he dated before you, that's irrelevant. He's with you now and he's with you for a reason. Have you talked to him about this?" She shook her head no. "Riley, you need to tell him how you feel. I know you're afraid you'll lose him, but if you don't talk to him you might end up doing something you'll regret."

"I know. You're right. It's just hard."

"Riley, I don't think you have to worry about Justin. I have a feeling he's not going anywhere."

"Thanks Ella, you really helped me."

"No problem, that's what I'm here for," I smiled.

"Are...you...going to the dance?" she asked carefully, changing the subject. "I'm only asking because at dinner the other day you didn't seem so sure."

"Yes. I'm going with Roman."

"Don't you and Roman hate each other though?" she asked, confused at my choice of date.

"Yes. No. It's complicated," I said, not ready to give up any more information. "Let's talk about you for once. I'm tired of talking about me all the time."

"I know right? Geez, you act like you have some complicated life or something?" Riley said, trying to keep a straight face, but when I looked at her she fell into a fit of giggles.

"Funny," I said, smacking her.

"Careful, we're not all buffed up warriors like you," she giggled again.

"Shut up,"

"I'm going to start calling you Buffy."

"I'm a vampire not a vampire slayer."

"I'm still going to call you Buffy."

"Okay, enough with me. Do you know what you're going to wear to the dance?"

"Sienna said I could borrow something of hers, but I'll admit I'm scared to see what she has."

"I can help you out if you want? Since we can't leave campus maybe we can order something online."

"No Ella. You guys already did enough for me. I couldn't ask you to do that."

"You don't have to ask and I insist," I said, waving her off and pulling out my laptop. As we searched for the perfect dress for Riley, we talked more about her and Justin and the dance. Once she was finally comfortable with her relationship status, I caught her up on all things me. I told her what Mackenzie did and our plan to take her down. I even told her about my nightmares and how I thought I was hearing and seeing my dead friends. I knew Riley was one of the few people I could trust with my secrets. I even told her all about Tristan and confessed that I think I'm starting to have feelings for Roman.

"Ella, I wish you would have told me this. No wonder you're so tense all the time. It's not good to keep things like this in. You should have been able to talk to someone about this."

"That used to be Josie. And with everything that happened I didn't feel like I could trust anyone."

"I totally don't blame you. I would have been the same way. Honestly I think you're very brave to have gone through what you did. I don't think I could have handled it. I think I would be a wreck still."

"I was. Trust me."

"Well, you have me now and you can definitely trust me. I promise I'm not evil."

I laughed. "I have to agree you're definitely not evil. I have yet to meet an evil being who doesn't swear." She pouted. I bumped her with my shoulder and she started to laugh.

"So, does Roman know you have feelings for him?"

"No, and as far as everyone else is concerned this little thing between us is just between us and now you of course."

"Don't worry. My lips are sealed," she said, pretending to lock her lips with an imaginary lock.

"How about this dress?" I asked, pointing to a knee length yellow one. It was a one shoulder strap with diamonds around the waist and a lighter color skirt.

"I like that," she said with a wide smile.

"That one it is. One dress with express shipping and it should be here by Tuesday."

"Thank you Ella. You have no idea how much I appreciate this."

"It's no problem."

We spent the rest of the night gossiping and by one am we were both ready to pass out. I said goodnight to her and crawled into bed.

Within the hour I felt someone slide into the bed next to me and wrap their arms around me. I knew who it was. I felt that spark as soon as he touched me. "Roman, what are you doing?" I asked groggily.

"I couldn't sleep," he said.

"And you thought you could sneak in here and what?"

"Well, I was just planning on sleeping, but if you have something else in mind?" I didn't have to see his face to know he was smiling. I elbowed him. "Hey," he laughed. "Just go back to sleep. I promise I'll be good. I just needed to be with you." I didn't argue with him. When he was here I felt safe and I didn't dream.

In the morning when I woke up, I was face to face with Roman. I smiled as I watched him sleep. He looked so peaceful and happy. I gently pushed the hair off his face and he stirred slightly. His hand shifted from my lower back down to my behind and I saw his lips twitch. "I thought you were asleep," I whispered.

"I am," he said, pulling me closer and squeezing my backside.

"So you violate people in your sleep?"

He chuckled. "I can't help it. All that working out you've been doing...man your butt is..." I pushed him away and smacked him. "What, that was a compliment?"

"I thought you said you were going to be good?"

"That was last night. It's morning now."

"Oh, I see," I said smiling.

"Come here," he said, pulling me close again. I pressed my forehead to his and placed my hands on his chest while he wrapped his arms around me tight. "I think I might have to move in here. That was the second best night of sleep I've ever had."

"The second?"

"The first was the first night I spent with you."

"You're good," I said, kissing his lips.

"You should be careful. A guy could get use to this."

"So could a girl," I said, sliding my hands around his neck and pulling him closer for a kiss.

"Do you have to be anywhere this morning?"

"Nope, I'm all yours."

We spent the next few hours in bed and not all those hours were spent sleeping. The best thing I loved about Roman was that we could kiss for hours and that was good enough. He never tried to make a move or push me to do anything else. The only breaks we took were when we needed to catch our breaths. We did manage to pull apart and get out of bed, but I believe that was because my stomach was growling so loud Roman couldn't take it anymore. He claimed it was distracting, saying, far be it from him to deprive me of food.

Roman snuck back into my room later that night and it was just like this morning all over again. When things started to get a little hot and heavy we stopped. And when I say hot, I really mean hot. He would heat up and burn me with his hands. He said it was my fault he kept overheating. I took it as a compliment and thought about keeping a bucket of ice next to my bed. I eventually fell asleep in his arms and then we continued where we left off in the morning until we had to get ready for class.

Roman winked at me and gave me a sly smile when he took a seat in the back of our history class. I knew he was watching me the whole class which was very distracting. In spells and casting, when no one was looking, he slipped his hand under the desk and held mine, making me ache for more of his touch. "Ella, are we still on for tomorrow?" I quickly pulled my hand away and caught the slightest bit of a smile on Ms. Kraft's face.

"Yes Ms. Kraft. I'm looking forward to it," I replied.

"Great," she smiled brightly. "I have lots of stuff for us to go over. Just stop by my desk at the end of class." I nodded and she proceeded to walk the classroom. Roman gave me a look of concern, but I shook my head letting him know it was nothing.

After class, Ms. Kraft handed me a pile of papers and books. "Here are some of things I want you to look over for tomorrow." I looked at the huge pile. "Don't worry. I don't expect you to get through all this by tomorrow. Just do what you can." I stuffed the papers in my bag and grabbed the pile of books to drop off at my room.

"Need some help with that?" Roman asked, startling me.

"No. I'm good," I said, looking around, worried that someone might see us.

"Relax," he said, picking up on my nervousness. "Helping you carry your books is not the international sign for hooking up." I rolled my eyes. "I could help you carry your books to your room and while we're there we could…" He reached up to twirl a piece of my hair between his fingers.

I smacked it away, more out of irritation. "Nice try, but no. And on that note, I'm leaving so I'm not late for my next class."

At lunch Roman and I would exchange looks when we thought no one was looking. We both knew what we were thinking – we couldn't wait to get back to my room where we didn't have to hide. At training I had a hard time trying to keep my hands off of Roman. All that fighting and sweating really made me want to rip his clothes off and I could feel he felt the same way. I managed to keep myself under control and took a very cold shower to calm myself down.

By the time I was done I was starving. I quickly inhaled my dinner which caused me to receive strange looks from my friends. "Sorry," I said through a mouthful. "Sometimes I forget there isn't a short supply of food around here." I slowed down so they would stop staring at me. Dean Just shook his head and laughed.

After dinner I went back to my room to wait for Roman. While I waited, I decided to go over the tons of work Ms. Kraft had given me. I only got a partial way through before Roman got there. He sat down on my bed behind me, gently brushing away the hair that fell on my shoulder. He grazed his lips tenderly across my skin. "That's very distracting," I said.

"That's the point," he said, continuing.

"Stop that tickles," I said giggling.

He sighed and rested his chin on my shoulder. "What's that?"

"It's something Ms. Kraft wants me to look over for tomorrow."

"I don't remember this being on the list?" he said, picking up the papers and examining them.

"It's not. I'm meeting with her tomorrow after school. She's going to work personally with me on some things."

"Is anything wrong?" he asked concerned.

"No. I just don't know as much as everyone and she just wanted to help me catch up. Plus all these powers I have, she wants to help me work with those too."

"You want me to come with you? Maybe I could help?"

"Thanks, but this is something I have to try on my own."

"Work on this later," he said, kissing my neck again.

"Roman." He pushed all the papers and books on the floor. "Hey, you better clean that up." He tangled his hand in my hair and pulled me down on the bed. Once his lips hit mine I forgot all about the papers on the floor.

We called it quits before things went too far. Not to mention he still hadn't learned how not to 'overheat'. He cuddled up next to me and when I shivered, he warmed me with his power, careful not to burn me. "What do you tell your roommate when he asks why you haven't been sleeping in your room?" I asked, curious.

"I tell him that I've been shacking up with this really hot chick," he said.

"Shut up," I said, elbowing him playfully. "For real, what do you say?"

"That is what I say," he said seriously.

"No you don't."

"I have a reputation to uphold, you know," he joked.

"Roman," I scolded.

"What? It's no big deal. He doesn't know who and Dean's more than happy to have a room to himself. Now he can entertain his ladies in private."

I turned around and faced him. "Wait, Dean is your roommate? How come I never knew that?"

"You never asked," he said simply.

"You didn't tell him anything else, did you?" I asked frightened.

"You mean like how you giggle when I nibble on your neck?" he said, placing tiny kisses along the side. "Or how you let out a tiny moan every time I do this." He slid his hand along my waist, dangling close to the top of my pants.

"Roman!" I said, hitting him.

He chuckled, pulled his hand back, and let it rest gently on my hip. "I don't understand why we have to be so secretive anyways? I mean, everyone knows we're going to the dance together. Thanks to Mackenzie," he said bitterly.

"I know. I just...I don't know. I need...I need more time to get use to the idea. I mean we said we were just having fun so why tell people?"

Roman's face turned serious. "What if I told you that this wasn't fun for me anymore?" I pulled back and glared at him. "No! That's not what I meant...what I mean is, I enjoy being with you."

"Okay, well that's good?" I didn't understand what he was trying to say.

"Let me try this another way. I treasure the time I spend with you and I dread the time when we're apart. That's not right either," he said, sitting up, and running his hand through his hair. Clearly he had no idea what he was trying to say. He closed his eyes and let out a breath. "I like you Ella, a lot. I don't just want to have fun with you. I want to be with you." He opened his eyes and looked at me. "I love you Ella."

I didn't know what to say. I was almost too shocked to speak. I liked Roman a lot. Hell I even think I loved him too, but I was scared. I was scared to love someone again and lose them. When I didn't say anything he took it as a bad sign. "I should have never said anything...just forget it," he stammered.

"No, Roman, I'm glad you did. I just..."

"It's okay. You don't have to say anything. Let's just go back to sleep," he said, lying back down and pulling the covers up. The look on his face almost broke my heart. I opened my mouth but no words came out, so I just rolled over and let him wrap his arms around me. I couldn't help but feel a twinge of guilt for not confessing to Roman how I really felt about him. The last person I was with I waited too long to tell him how I felt and then I was too late.

"Roman? Are you still awake?"

"Mm hmm," he mumbled.

I didn't know what came over me, but I decided to stop worrying about myself and being selfish. I was going to live in the now and not contemplate about the later. I turned around and faced him. I slipped my hand behind his neck and pulled him closer for a kiss. "You know if you start that again, we'll never get to sleep," he said, running his hand down the back of my thigh and then pulling me on top of him.

I sat up and looked into his dark blue eyes. He smiled and reached up to touch my face. I took his hand and held it in mine. "There's something I have to tell you," I said.

"You're not a man are you?"

"Roman be serious!" He raised a brow and looked at me. I grabbed his hand and put it on my breast. "They're real, okay? Not store bought." He laughed and I threw his hand away.

"I wasn't done testing the merchandise," he said, reaching for my breast.

I grabbed his wrists and pinned them down to the bed. "Roman...stop!"

"Mm...I like when you get mad."

"God, you're such a dick!" I stood up from the bed and started to pace the room. "I'm trying to tell you something and you're making this hard," I said frustrated.

He sat up and swung his legs over the side of the bed. "Ella, I'm sorry. Come here." He lifted his arms out wide. I glared at him. "I promise I'll be good."

I slowly walked over to him and he placed his hands on my hips and looked up at me. I took a deep breath and let it out. "I like you Roman."

He smiled. "I like you too."

"No. I mean, I really like you. I want to be with you."

"I want to be with you too," he smiled and pulled me closer. I pressed my lips to his and pushed him back on the bed. I knew now more than ever I wanted to be with Roman and I wanted him to be my first. I pulled off my tank top. "Ella, what are you doing?"

"Shh..." I said as I nibbled on his neck. I pulled at his t-shirt and he took it off. Then he rolled over on top of me and I tugged at his pants.

"Ella?"

"It's okay. I want to."

"Are you sure? I didn't tell you I love you just so you would sleep with me. You know that, right?"

"Yes," I said, knowing he was telling the truth.

"Okay, good," he said relieved.

When he didn't make a move I asked, "Do you not want to?"

"Oh no! I do!" he said in a rush, making it hard not to laugh.

"Roman, I've never been so sure of anything but this right now." I started to kiss him again and he let me slide off his pants. He kissed me passionately, causing my body to heat up. Then his lips moved down my neck, across my chest, and down my stomach, leaving goose bumps all over my skin. He stopped when he reached the top of my pants, hesitating. I let him know it was okay. He slid them off slowly and then tossed them to the floor. He ran his hands up my legs, making me shiver. When he reached my hips he paused. He was teasing me. I could see the smile on his face. Not able to take it anymore, I grabbed him and pulled his lips to mine.

"Roman," I said in between breaths. "Just remember to go easy on me. I haven't done this before."

"It will be a first for both of us," he whispered.

"Wait, what?" I pulled back.

"Ella, I'm a virgin."

"Yeah right. Seriously Roman you don't have to pretend to make me feel better."

"I'm not pretending. I'm serious Ella."

"But you dated Mackenzie?"

"Nothing happened between us. I didn't care for her like I do for you. It wouldn't have been right."

I pulled him back down on top of me and kissed him like crazy. Before I knew it we were naked. "Do you have any condoms?" I asked.

"Yeah, in my pants pocket," he said, reaching for them.

"So, you just carry one around? In case?"

He started to blush. "Well...I just..."

I laughed. "You're so cute when you stutter." He rolled his eyes and tore open the wrapper.

"You ready?" he asked.

I nodded, biting my lip. "Just try not to burn me."

That was not what I expected. All those movies and books totally glamourize sex and make it seem like losing your virginity is the most magical thing in the world. Like you make love for hours and you see stars and fireworks. I'm here to tell you they are wrong. The only thing I saw was the inside of my eyelids because my eyes were shut the whole time. And it kinda hurt – at first. Not just the initial part, but for also the fact that he kept burning me. It was also kind of awkward both of us being virgins and all. It's not like we read the encyclopedia of sex or anything like that. It was more like kind of feeling your way around, but I guess that was kind of the point.

When we were done – or should I say when he was done – we both laid there on our backs, staring up at the ceiling, not saying anything – basically creating a big bubble of more awkwardness with the silence. "How do you feel?" Roman asked, breaking the silence.

"A little sore," I said honestly.

"Are you still happy we did it?"

I rolled over and ran my hand over his chest. "Of course I am, very happy." Despite the weirdness of it all I was glad it was with Roman.

"You want to do it again?" he asked with a big smile on his face.

"Just...go slow this time. If you keep burning me the way you do I might not have any skin left by the time we're done," I teased.

"Sorry, I'll try to take it easy."

"Alright good, now, give it to me baby," I laughed.

He growled and pounced on me. This time was better than the first. Still not the fireworks explosion I expected, but close. I wasn't worried though. We would have plenty of time to practice.

CHAPTER TWENTY-FOUR

My body was warm and tingly. I felt a small shock when I opened my eyes and saw Roman was watching me sleep. He started to trace his fingers along the tattoo on my back. "You know that the Dragon was the master of all the elements of nature. They are both creators and destroyers. They're also associated with wisdom and longevity. Dragons can be thought to symbolize the ability to see the "big picture" as well as the ability to see far off danger or future circumstances."

"How come you know so much about dragons?"

"I did a research paper on them my senior year of high school," he said, still tracing the dragon tattoo on my back. I closed my eyes and let the shock of his touch tickle my skin. "These flowers remind me of my grandmother's garden," he said, kissing my shoulders.

"Do you know that sometimes when you touch me you shock me?" I asked.

"I'm sorry." He stopped.

"No, I like it. It feels nice," I smiled.

"Really," he said, shocking me so bad I jumped.

"Ow!" I smacked him. "Not like that."

"Sorry," he laughed. "I don't always realize when I'm doing it, but I feel it too."

I laced my fingers with his and rested my head on his chest. "What time is it?"

"Time for you to bring those sexy lips to mine," he said.

I obliged. "How much time do we have before we have to get ready for class?"

"Why can't we skip our classes today?" he whined as he started to nibble on my neck.

"Because we can't," I sighed.

"You think maybe now we can tell people we're together?"

"I'll think about it," I teased as I got out of bed.

"Where are you going?" he asked, pulling me back down to the bed.

"I was going to take a shower."

"Want some company?" he asked with a devilish smile.

"Then we'll be late for class," I said, peeling his hands off of me and heading into the bathroom. After I turned the water on and hopped in the shower I heard the door open and close. "Roman, I told you no." He didn't say anything. All I heard was silence. "Roman?"

"Who's Roman? Is he that hot naked guy on your bed?" A familiar voice asked.

"Whh-oo's there?" I asked scared.

"Gee whiz Ella, you don't even recognize your best friend's voice?"

"Riley?"

"I'm only gone a few months and you replace me with a guy for a best friend," she said appalled.

I slowly pulled the curtain back and popped my head out. My eyes went wide with shock and I closed the curtain. *Okay, I must be dreaming.* This wasn't real. It couldn't be. The shower curtain flew open. "You bet your ass this is real. Now pay attention because what I have to tell you is important."

"Wait, you can read my mind?"

"No, but I know you, and I know what you're thinking," she said, hands on hips.

"You're real? You're really here?" I started to choke up as she nodded. I reached out and poked her to confirm.

"Satisfied? Now as much as I'm enjoying this little reunion we don't have a lot of time. And if I stare at you naked any longer I might turn gay."

"Oh Josie!" I cried, throwing my arms around her.

"Whoa there...um, let's not forget that you're naked and wet and I'm starting to feel a little uncomfortable," she said, handing me a towel.

"Sorry," I said, wrapping myself up. "What? How? Why?" I was so confused. "What are you? Are you like a ghost?" I asked, not understanding any other explanation for it and not to mention she was wearing the dark angel costume she died in.

"I don't have time to explain that right now."

"Wait, can he hear us?" I asked, referring to Roman.

"Doubtful. He was passed out cold when I got here," she said. "So who is he? Because I got to say –"

"Josie," I whispered harshly. "This is not the time."

"Right," she said, her face turning serious again. "I have something very important to tell you."

"Wait, I had a dream like this with Kyle."

"I know."

"You know? So then it was real?"

"Yes and no." I started to rub my temples. None of this was making sense. "I know all this is confusing and I wish I could explain it to you, but I can't. I'm not even supposed to be here right now and that is why I don't have a lot of time. I'm here to tell you what Kyle tried to in your dream."

"So if that was real then Kyle is..."

"Kyle's fine. Trust me he's fine. You have to listen to me," she said, grabbing my shoulders to get my full attention. "Jack is planning to attack, again. At the dance. It's going to be bad Ella. He's planning a massacre." She dropped her arms, allowing the information to soak in.

"Okay, we'll just cancel the dance and warn everyone and maybe they'll close the school?"

"No Ella," she said, shaking her head. "You can't stop it and you can't forewarn anybody."

"Then what's the point of me knowing, of you telling me. Why even bother?"

"So you're prepared. You can't stop it, but you can change it. You can change how it ends."

"How Josie, this makes no sense?"

"I know," she said, taking my hand. "But Ella, you have to understand the only reason I'm here is so you know what's coming. It's not your time yet. You are destined for greatness and we need you here and we need you to survive this."

I wish people would stop telling me I'm destined for greatness.

"But Josie I..."

"Ella, I have to go," she said, hugging me.

"Josie no. I have so many more questions," I said, holding on.

"I know you do, but my time is up. Just remember, the dance is when he will attack."

"Josie wait!" I called as she slowly faded away.

"Nice tats by the way," she said as she faded completely out of view.

My hand lingered in the air where she held it. Hit with the seriousness of the situation, my only response was to sit on the edge of the bathtub, bury my head in my hands, and cry. "Ella?" Roman knocked on the door. When I didn't answer he opened the door and let himself in. "Ella, hey what's wrong?" he asked, bending down in front of me. I wrapped my arms around him and he pulled me onto his lap while I balled my eyes out. "Shh...it's okay." He tried to comfort me by stroking my hair.

"It's up to you Ella. I know you'll figure this out. You'll do what's right." I heard Josie whisper to me. I pulled back. Her voice of encouragement gave me a little bit of strength to hold my head up. I needed to figure this out and sitting here crying was not the answer.

I got up. I turned the water off and went out into my room and threw on some clothes. "Ella, what are you doing?" Roman asked, following me.

"I have to go. I have to go see Gabe and Billy."

"Ella wait," Roman said, reaching for me to stop me. "What's going on?"

"I can't explain it...I just have to go." I turned to leave but he stopped me.

"Wait, I'm going with you," he said, grabbing his clothes.

I opened my mouth to protest but when I saw the look of fear on his face I couldn't. "Hurry," I said. He threw his clothes on in a flash and we were out the door running to the teachers' dorm. I banged hard on Gabe's door and hoped he was there. "Gabe!" I shouted, not caring if I woke anyone else up.

Gabe opened the door disoriented. His normally combed hair was a mess and he had dark circles under his eyes as if he hadn't slept in days. "Ella? What's the matter?" he asked, quickly switching into guardian mode.

"Jack, he's coming," I said.

"Get inside, both of you," Gabe said, letting us in. He gestured for us to have a seat. "What's going on?"

"Where's Billy? I think he should be here too," I said.

"I'll go get him," Roman offered.

"Third door on your right," Gabe told him. As soon as the door closed behind him Gabe turned to me. "Ella, tell me now if there's anything you need to tell me and only me. If you don't want to discuss this in front of Roman let me know and I will make him leave."

"It's okay. This concerns him to."

Roman came rushing back into the room with a half awake Billy. Roman sat down next to me on the couch and laced his fingers with mine. "What's going on? Ella, you look like you saw a ghost," Billy said as he pulled a shirt on over his head.

"I think you might want to sit down," I told Billy. He looked at me muddled and I hated what I had to say next. "I saw Josie."

"In a dream?" Billy asked.

"No. She visited me while I was in the shower."

"Where was I when that happened?" Roman said jokingly. I gave him a look letting him know this wasn't the time.

"You actually saw her, as in her ghost?" Billy's face turned pale.

"I don't know exactly, but she was real and she came to give me a message," I said. I looked up at Billy and he looked like he was about to pass out. I walked over to him and took his hand. "Billy, if this is too much for you I can –"

"No. Go on. I have to hear this," he said. He looked me in the eyes and I could see he was fighting back the tears.

"When you say you saw Josie you mean?" Gabe started.

"I mean she was here in the flesh, so to speak. She said she had message and that was the only reason she was here."

"What did she say?" Billy asked, trying to be strong.

"She told me that Jack was coming and he was planning a massacre."

Gabe and Billy sat down, letting the information soak in. "When?" Gabe asked.

"Saturday. At the dance."

"That doesn't give us a lot of time," Roman said.

Billy tensed and stood up. "I'll be ready."

"We need to alert the school and cancel the dance," Gabe said.

"No, we can't."

"Ella, I know sometimes these dances are important to you young ones."

"Don't patronize me Gabe. This has nothing to do with the stupid dance. Trust me. I already said to Josie about doing that and she told me not to. She told me that we couldn't."

"I don't understand," Billy said.

"Sounds like a trick," Roman chimed in.

"Shut up! She would never!" Billy snapped, coming after Roman.

Gabe stopped him and held him back. "Enough, fighting against each other is not going to help us." Billy backed down. "Ella, I need you to tell me exactly what Josie said and all of it."

"That was just it. It was very vague. All she said was that he was coming and it was going to be bad. She said I couldn't alert anybody and I didn't understand why. All she said was that I wasn't meant to stop it just control it. It's not my time and that's why she had to warn me."

"Anything else?" Billy asked.

"No. She said she wasn't even supposed to be here and that's why she had limited time."

"I think I understand," Gabe said, bowing his head.

"I don't. Will someone please explain it to me," Roman said, standing up. "I'm not on board with just letting my friends get killed."

"I won't let that happen," I said, standing next to him.

"How do you know? You said so yourself he can't be stopped." I opened my mouth to protest, but he didn't give me the chance. "Ella, the last time he was here you could barely move. What makes you think you can stop him now," Roman said angrily.

"I'm stronger now and more powerful," I said, hoping my voice wouldn't deceive me.

"Yes but when face to face with him it's different. You think you can take him on when he's actually in front of you?"

"What are you saying? That I'm just some pathetic, weak, little girl?"

"No. I just don't want you to get in over your head."

"You have no idea what I'm getting myself into. The sacrifices I've made and are still making."

"Ella, this isn't just about you anymore. Others people's lives are at stake too."

"You think I don't know that! Then you don't know me at all. I live everyday with the fear of something happening to my family and friends because of me."

"Ella I —"

"Just go." He didn't budge. "Get out!" I snapped. I was on the verge of a break down. Roman just happened to be the first one to get in the line of fire.

He tightened his jaw before he turned around and left, slamming the door behind him. "Do we need to worry about him telling everyone?" Billy asked.

"I'll talk to him later," Gabe said, then turned to me. "Ella, we're going to need your full focus for the next few hours. Do you think you can pull yourself together?" I nodded my head. "I will excuse you from your classes today."

"But wait, I'm supposed to meet up with Ms. Kraft after school to work on some things."

"You'll have to cancel," Gabe said. "Unless...No...I think she might be helpful."

"You want to involve Ms. Kraft? Can we trust her?"

"Of course, Sylvia will be most useful to us with all her knowledge and use of witchcraft. I will talk to her and ask her to meet with us here later."

"So why do you think Josie said we can't warn anybody?" Billy asked confused.

"Because you can't stop death," Gabe said solemnly. "Everyone has a predetermined time of death."

"That sucks," I said, not liking his answer.

"That is how it works. When it's your time it's your time."

"But how is that fair? Can't we still stop it?" I hated the fact that I knew people could get hurt and there was nothing I could do about it.

"You would just be preventing the inevitable. It will still happen, just in another way. Things happen for a reason Ella. We may not always understand what that reason is, but there is always a purpose."

"It's just not fair. I don't understand why this has to happen?" The more I was learning the more stressed out I was becoming. I couldn't wrap my mind around all this, 'what was meant to be was meant to be' bullshit.

"Because it will open the door for something greater to be achieved."

"Huh?"

"We'll discuss the why later. Let's figure out the how and when and hopefully come up with a plan to stop it."

"I thought you just said we can't stop it?" My head was pounding.

"Let me rephrase that," Gabe said, seeing my confusion. "We can control it just not prevent it." I threw myself back on the couch moaning. None of this was making any sense to me. "Why don't you and Billy go get some breakfast and I will talk to Sylvia?"

On the way down to the dining hall Billy asked, "So...did she ask about me?"

I sighed. "I'm sorry Billy, but no. I'm sure she wanted to but she didn't have a lot of time."

"It's okay," he said disappointed.

"I'm sure she's checking in on you from time to time."

"How did she look?"

"She looked good...happy." He smiled at that and then let it go. I knew he was hurting and he was trying really hard to be strong. I wouldn't blame him if he wanted to hide for a while and just cry. That's what I wanted to do.

We grabbed our food and then headed back to Gabe's. Neither of us wanted to be around people right now. I knew our mood would cause too many questions and I didn't have the strength right now to lie to my friends. By the time we got back to Gabe's room he was already taking action. He was on the phone making calls and starting plans. Billy and I sat quietly eating our breakfast while Gabe did his thing.

"I talked to the other guardians and let them know to be on alert," Gabe said.

"I thought we weren't going to let people know?" I asked.

"I was thinking it over and decided we have to let the guardians know and the teachers. We're not going to alert the students, it would just create panic, but the school has to know. Trust me on this Ella. I'm going to let you know we have a hard fight ahead of us and not just with Jack. I've called a meeting with everyone after classes and suspect they'll want to cancel the dance. We're going to have to convince them not to. I'm also going to pull you from all your classes for the rest of the week so we can train."

"We can't do that. It will raise too much suspicion on why I'm not there."

"She's right Gabe. She needs to go to class and pretend as if everything's normal," Billy said.

I was slowly starting to wish I said nothing at all. Not that I wanted anyone to get hurt, but this was becoming too intense. "So what do we do now?" I asked.

"I still insist on excusing you from your classes at least for today," he said and I agreed. "I want you to go back to your room and change. We're going to train. You need to know how to take out your opponent."

"I already know how to do that."

"No just incapacitate. You need to know how to kill them if necessary," he said gravely.

I never thought there would come a day where I would actually have to kill someone. I didn't think I was ready for that. "Ella?" I looked at Billy. "Don't worry. I won't let it come to that. I'll be with you and I'll finish it," he growled. I placed my hand on his and tried to calm him. Then Gabe told me to hurry up and go change.

When I got back to my room I found Roman standing outside my door. "Whatever you have to say I don't want to hear it," I said, to upset to even deal with him right now.

"Ella, just please hear me out," he pleaded.

"I don't have time for your crap."

"Once again it's all about you," he spat.

I had it.

"You know what, you're right. I'm sorry that some psycho is after me and innocent people are going to get hurt in the process because of me. And I'm sorry that you have your head so far up your ass that you can't see that the world doesn't revolve around you! Now, for the last time, move out of my way!" He took a stand and did not move. "Don't make me physically move you," I hissed under my breath. He opened the door and let himself in. "What are you doing?"

"I'm not leaving until you talk to me," he said, putting his foot down.

"For the last time I don't have time for this."

He grabbed me and I swung, but he blocked it. I tried again, but we were too evenly matched. This would end up taking longer than I had time for. He pinned me up against the wall and I gave in. "Are you ready to listen?" he asked, panting. I didn't even bother to give him the satisfaction of an answer. "Ella, I'm sorry. I panicked and I shouldn't have acted that way. I just...I just don't want to lose you. Not when I finally got you."

"Roman, you're not going to lose me."

"You don't know that for sure. You have no idea what's going to happen."

"No, I don't, but I'm not going down without a fight. I beat him before and I can do it again. I'm stronger now. I have my powers and more powers than anyone even knows about."

"But still..."

"But nothing Roman. I'm not going to just lie down and take it. I'm going to fight," I said with conviction.

"Then I'm going to fight with you and there's nothing you can do or say that will change my mind." I could feel the tears start to well up in my eyes. I looked down, no longer able to look at him. He cupped my chin with his hand and forced me to look him in the eye. Then, he kissed me. That was all it took before all our clothes were off and we were making love.

As I lay there with my head on his chest, I took in this memory, and held it close to my heart. I never wanted to forget this, him. After Tristan, Roman was the first person I opened up my heart to, and now all I wanted to do was make sure nothing happened to him. He was a part of my life now. He made feel...well he just made me feel and that was something I didn't think I would be able to do again. I sighed as I lay there, knowing this moment had to end. "I have to go change before Gabe gets pissed. I was gone for over an hour and I was only supposed to change my clothes," I said.

"Technically you were, but you just didn't put them on yet," Roman joked while he stroked my hair. My phone buzzed and I checked to see who it was. It was a text form Billy saying he stalled Gabe as long as he could by telling him I needed some time to myself, but he couldn't stall him any longer.

"Okay, I really have to go now," I said, getting up and getting dressed. Roman told me he was coming with. I didn't argue.
Before we left, he pulled me aside, taking my hands in his and said, "Hey, can we make a promise that no matter what happens, from now on we'll promise not to argue?"

"Umm..." I stuttered, thinking that was impossible.

"I just don't want to fight with you anymore. Even though I really do enjoy the makeup sex," he smiled.

I rolled my eyes. "I can't promise I won't get mad if you irritate me again..." He gave me his annoyed look. "But I will try my hardest not to let my stubbornness get the best of me."

He leaned down and kissed me. "You are very stubborn, but that's what I love about you."

"Okay, we really have to go now," I said, dragging him out of the room.

We met Gabe and Billy in the gym and thankfully Gabe didn't mention anything about how long it took or ask why Roman was here. Instead he just got right down to business. "We are to meet with the entire faculty at four. We will work here until then," he said.

Gabe pulled out a bag and dumped everything on the floor. Inside were all different types of weapons; everything from daggers, knives, and wooden stakes. I picked up the stake and looked at Gabe. "Really?" I said, thinking what a cliché.

"Yes. One of the ways to kill a full vampire is a stake through the heart," he said.

"And the other?" I asked hesitantly.

"Decapitation or incineration," he said, like it was no big deal. Like this was something people did every day.

"What about us, half-vampires?"

"You can be killed just as any human can."

"Oh," was all I could say.

"Ella, I don't want you to feel overwhelmed. You can do this. I know you can. Now let's start with the small stuff and work our way up."

Billy helped Gabe assemble some dummies and Roman and I stood back and watched as they both demonstrated some moves. After we worked on them for a while we moved onto staking and then decapitation. It was not as easy as it looked and I had a hard time getting the stake to stick or chop the dummies heads off. "It's alright Ella. I don't expect you to get it the first time around. Let's stop here for today and pick up tomorrow. Meet me outside the teachers' lounge at four." I nodded as I headed back to my room to shower. Roman followed me back, but I suggested he shower in his own room. After he whined for about ten minutes he finally gave up and left.

Now alone, all I wanted to do was crash on my bed and sleep for the next few days. Unfortunately that wasn't an option I had. I knew the moment I sat down I wouldn't get back up. I dragged my feet into the bathroom, got undressed, and got in the shower. I let the steam soothe my aching muscles and then thought maybe I should have let Roman shower with me. With him here I could have had him soothe me with his heat. I guess I'll just have to hit him up later for a massage.

As I rinsed the sweat from my face I thought about everything that happened in the last twenty-four hours. It was crazy to think I lost my virginity and woke up to find out I have to face my enemy in a few days and possibly lose some of my friends and I can't even warn them. This all just seemed unfair. Once again I found myself dealt a bad hand. I wish there was a way I could talk to Josie again. Find out some more information and well, just talk to her.

"You know, I'm still waiting to know who that gorgeous guy in your bed was."

I nearly jumped out of my skin at the sound of her voice. "Christ Josie!"

"The one and only," she cooed.

"Please don't tell me you're here to warn me about something else because my plate's full. I can't handle anymore right now."

"No. This problem is all mine," she said sourly. "Finish up and I'll wait for you in your room and explain everything."

I quickly finished my shower and got dressed thinking she might be on another time limit like last time. "You know Josie, you really have impeccable timing. If I didn't know any better I might actually start to believe you are a lesbian, considering you keep popping up when I'm in the shower," I teased.

She rolled her eyes. "Please, if I was a lesbian you would not be my first choice."

"Thanks, I think? So to what do I owe the honor?"

"They found out I was here," she said.

"Who?" I asked. She pointed to the ceiling and looked up. "What are you exactly?"

"Duh, isn't it obvious?" She turned and pointed to the wings of her angel costume.

"Josie, you really expect me to believe you're an angel?"

"You're half-vampire. Why would I being an angel be so

342

unbelievable?"

"Seriously Josie, you really want me to answer that?" She threw a pillow at me. "And what's with the costume?"

"It's kick ass and I thought it was fitting," she smiled.

"Are those real wings?" I asked, reaching for them.

"No. I got temporarily stripped of my wings until they figure out what to do with me."

"Wait...what happened?"

"Like I said, they found out that I came to warn you and I'm not allowed to intervene. But I couldn't let you not know. I couldn't see you hurt."

"So what does this mean?"

"It means I'm stuck here until they decide if they trust me enough to come back."

"So...you're like here to stay?"

"For now," she nodded.

I couldn't help but scream for joy. I leapt up, tackling her and wrapped my arms around her tight. I felt horrible that Josie was being punished, but I was happy to have my friend back even if it might only be temporarily. "Sorry," I said. "I just missed you so much."

"I know. I missed you too. I was able to check in on you from time to time, but that wasn't enough."

"So that was you in the library?"

"Guilty," she smiled.

"You know, because of that stunt you pulled I'm now deemed as the crazy girl."

"It was bound to happen with or without my help," she shrugged.

Too excited to care, I ignored her jab. "I have so much to tell you, but first we have to figure out what to do with you."

"What do you mean?"

"Well, you're not like invisible are you? This isn't like I'm the only one who can see you?"

"Geez Ella, what the hell are they teaching you here? No I'm not invisible. I'm living flesh so to speak."

"So, you're like, human?"

"Yes and no. I still have some of my powers. See, I can do this." She closed her eyes and in a blink she was gone.

"Josie?"

"Boo!" she said from behind me.

I jumped. "Okay. How about you not do that again," I said, clenching my chest. "Now, how am I going to explain you to everyone?"

"Simple. I'm the awesomest person in the world who came back to save your butt."

I stifled an eye roll. "I'll figure something out. How about we get you a change of clothes and grab some food because I'm starving."

"I see some things haven't changed," she giggled. I rummaged through my draws for an outfit she could wear. "Please don't tell me I have to wear one of those god awful uniforms." She cringed at the thought.

"No. I have some jeans and plain shirts you can borrow."

"Ella, what happened to your wardrobe? Once again I'm gone a few months and everything goes to shit. And what's with all the tattoos? I admit they're freakin' hot, but not something –"

"Here," I said, throwing clothes at her and cutting her off. "I'll explain everything later. I promise."

"You better because I still want the dish on that hottie," she winked.

As we got ready to leave, I stopped before I opened the door. "You do know Billy's here and he's going to freak when he sees you?"

"I hope so. I mean, I am his beautiful lost love back from the dead...so to speak," she said, fluffing her hair.

"Don't you think maybe we should warn him first? Maybe prepare him so he doesn't have a coronary?"

"I prefer to go with shock value," she said, pulling me out of the room.

Oh boy. I couldn't wait to see everyone's faces when they saw Josie. This was gonna be interesting.

I held my breath as we approached the doors of the dining hall. "You ready?" I asked Josie.

She took a breath, pushed her shoulders back, and held her head high. "I'm ready."

I took her hand and braced myself as I opened the door. All the students turned to look at us as we descended the stairs. "What's the matter? They never saw an angel before?" Josie joked. "Is it always like this?

"Yes, but that's usually because I'm the topic of conversation."

When we reached our table and Dixon saw who was standing next to me his jaw dropped to the floor. He sat there, rubbing his eyes as if they were playing tricks on him. Josie automatically went up to Dean and ruffled his hair. When he turned around and saw who it was he skidded back in his chair. "What the…"

"What's the matter Dean? You look like you saw a ghost," she giggled.

"H-how?" Dean stuttered.

"Look, long story short, she was an angel until she interfered and she's being…" I tried to find the right word.

"Punished," Josie mumbled.

"Riley, I think I need your glasses," Dixon said, making Josie's head shoot up.

"Dixon? Oh my god!" she shrieked, running over to him.

"I can't believe it? You're real," Dixon said, looking her over. "You surprise us and this is what you decide to wear?" Dixon said with distaste.

"It's Ella's," Josie said, making a face.

"Oh," he said, understanding.

"Hey, I'm right here you know," I complained.

Dixon squeezed Josie tight. Dean just sat there too shocked to speak. "Umm, okay, is anybody else here lost?" Cameron said.

"I'll explain later," I said just as Billy walked into the room. "This is about to get very interesting."

When Josie saw Billy I noticed her eyes were starting to well up with tears. She stepped out in front of me and when Billy looked up and saw her, he stopped dead in his tracks. Josie took a step toward him, but he didn't move. Then slowly, one by one, they each took a step until they were face to face. "Is it you? Is it really you?" Billy asked, lifting his hand to touch her face. Josie nodded unable to speak. Billy's eyes flooded over with tears as he took Josie in his arms.

I felt like we shouldn't be here. It was like we were invading a private moment that should be between only them. Josie pulled back and planted a big fat kiss on his lips. I had to clear my throat to remind them they were still in a crowd of people. "I hate to break up this reunion, but we don't have much time before we have to meet

Gabe and I'm starving. You all know how cranky I get when I don't eat."

"Sorry," Josie giggled as she took Billy's hand.

When we got in line to grab food I asked Billy if he had seen Roman. "He said he'd be here shortly," he told me.

Roman showed up as soon as we sat down. "Everyone, this is Josie, and this is Cameron, Sienna, Riley, Justin, Blake, Reagan, Austin, and Roman."

"Wait, Josie as in the friend who died last year?" Cameron asked.

"In the flesh," Josie said.

"But how is that?"

"Long story, I promise I'll explain later," I said.

"So, you're Roman. I have to admit you look as good with your clothes on as you do off," Josie cooed. Everyone at the table looked at her and then at Roman, wondering what the hell was going on. I had forgotten to tell Josie that my relationship with Roman wasn't public knowledge. I squeezed her thigh hoping she would get the hint and shut up. "What?" she said, looking at me.

"Spying in the boys' locker room again?" Dean said laughing.

"No, Ella's room," she said.

"Josie!" Roman's face paled and I just wanted to crawl under the table and die.

"It must have been when Mackenzie was still living there," Roman said, trying to distract everyone.

"Not it was –"

"Josie shut up," I whispered harshly.

Dean was the only one who caught on. His eyes turned on Roman. "That hot chick you were shacking up with was my sister!" he growled, eyes glowing.

"Oh god," I whispered to myself. Everyone turned to look at Roman and me. Both of us were speechless and looking guilty.

"You're dead meat Ashby," Dean called, jumping out of his seat. Due to Billy's excellent reflexes he was able to stop Dean before he leapt across the table and socked Roman. Even though Dean knew he couldn't get through Billy he still tried.

"Billy, please take Dean out of here so he can cool off," I said.

"It doesn't matter," Dean said, shaking Billy off. "You better sleep with one eye open," he pointed at Roman.

Once Billy took Dean out of sight I grabbed Josie. "We got to go,"

I said, dragging her out. I was no longer able to eat with everyone's eyes on me.

"I guess the cat's out of the bag now," Josie said.

"Josie, this is not the time to joke," I snapped.

"Ella, I'm sorry. I didn't know it was some big secret."

"I know you didn't," I sighed. "But after the first shut up you think you would actually shut up."

"I said I was sorry." She batted her eyes and gave me her sad puppy face.

"I know. It's not all your fault."

"If you want I can help you smooth things over with Dean?"

"I think you've done enough. I don't have time for him right now. We have to meet Gabe."

"I can't wait to see the look on his face," Josie smiled wickedly as I pulled her to the teachers' lounge.

Gabe was waiting for us with Billy outside the lounge. When Gabe saw Josie he basically reacted the same way everyone else did. "I know I know, but we don't have time to explain now because we have a meeting to attend to," I said, hoping to avoid a million questions.

Gabe managed to close his mouth and collect himself. He turned his attention back to me. "Are you ready for this?" he asked. I nodded as he opened the door. Right away I got dirty looks from some of the teachers.

"Mr. Kelly, why are there students here?" asked one of the teachers who I didn't know.

"Because this concerns her too," Gabe said.

"Why does that not surprise me? You've been nothing but trouble since you showed up here," said another teacher. His eyes narrowed in my direction. I glared back. I didn't know this teacher either, but already I didn't like him. He was a skinny, balding man with dirty brown eyes. He talked with a slight British accent and I wondered what classes he taught. Clearly it wasn't mannerisms 101.

"George, I suggest you keep your opinions to yourself for the rest of the meeting," Ms. Kraft said as she walked into the room. "And who is this?" Ms. Kraft asked, looking at Josie. "I don't believe you are a student here?"

"No ma'am. I'm Josie," she said, extending a hand.

Ms. Kraft kindly shook Josie's hand, flinching slightly. "My child," she said, smiling and caressing her face. "You are a true gift to us."

"Sylvia, what nonsense are you babbling and why is this strange girl here?" The dickhead teacher said, clearly not taking Ms. Kraft's advice about keeping his opinion to himself.

"I am not strange," Josie said offended.

"No my dear, what he's simply trying to say is we can sense you are different," Ms. Kraft said, smiling at Josie.

"You know what she is?" Ms. Whitney, the dance teacher asked.

"Of course I do...and you do not?"

"It's impossible!" shouted some short, stubby old man with an overly large nose.

"It is and she is proof," Ms. Kraft said.

"Will someone please care to enlighten the rest of us who do not know?" Aidan said, causing me to just now realize he was even in the room.

Ms. Kraft placed her hands delicately on Josie's shoulders and said proudly, "She is an angel."

There was a collective gasp amongst the teachers.

I leaned in closely to Josie. "No offense, but I don't see what the big deal is?"

"Please, Ella you should know I was always a big deal," she said.

"Why I understand this is an amazing discovery. We have a more important matter at hand to discuss," Gabe said, interrupting their gawking. It wasn't like Josie didn't like the attention. This was just one of those times when it was the kind of attention you didn't want. The kind where after a while the stares became uncomfortable.

CHAPTER TWENTY-FIVE

"Yes Gabe. Why have you called us all here today?" Ms. Kraft asked, turning her attention to him.

"I have recently found out there is a threat on the school," he said.

"What kind of threat?" Aidan asked.

"I was let aware of someone planning an attack," Gabe replied.

All the teachers started shouting at once. "Who? When? Why? How?"

"Everyone needs to calm down and let Gabe explain," Aidan shouted above the noise.

They quieted down enough to let Gabe continue. "The attack is to take place this Saturday during the dance."

"And how did you come about this information?" Mr. Cormac asked.

"I told him," I said.

"And let me guess. It came to you in a dream?" asked the balding British man, mocking me. I believe his name is Mr. Atkins, but I think I'll be referring to him as Baldie from now on.

"No. I told her and it's true," Josie said, standing up for me.

"Please, we're supposed to believe the ramblings of children?" Baldie said.

I was really getting tired of him. "I am not a child," I said angrily, stepping forward. "And you bet your ass this is a valuable threat. The man who plans to attack us, his name is Jack Lennox. He is the same person who broke in here a month ago." That got some attention.

"I've been tracking Jack for months and he has led me here. Through my contacts I have learned he is building an army to help carry out the attack," Billy said, stepping in.

"We should cancel the celebration and send everyone home for their safety," said Ms. Kiel, my art teacher.

"No, you can't," Josie said.

"And we're supposed to listen to you? A fallen angel," said the man with the overly large nose. I will call him honkers.

"What is he talking about? I am not fallen," Josie said, looking from me to Ms. Kraft.

"Then how do you explain you being here? Only the fallen are cast down to be punished," honkers spat. He looked at Josie as if he was disgusted to be in the presence of her.

"Shows what you know. I'm here because I came to warn my friends about the attack," Josie sneered.

"But how are you still here? You should not be allowed to preside here for this long without fore going a punishment or serving some sort of consequence," Honkers said suspiciously.

"You know, you sure do know a lot about this for someone who seems to look their nose down on me," Josie said.

He looked spooked for a second, but quickly recovered. "I'm a teacher. It is my job to have knowledge of such things."

I could tell Josie wasn't buying it, but we didn't have time to argue. "Look," I said, getting frustrated. "Josie came here to warn me and got in trouble for it so now she's here." Baldie went to open his mouth again but I interrupted him. "She is also the perfect person to help us out along with all the information Billy has collected about Jack."

"And how exactly is she going to help us?" Mr. Miller asked, curious.

"Um, hello? Jack killed me. So I think I know a little bit about he works," Josie said annoyed.

"Clearly she would be no use to us. He already killed her once. Who's to say she's not the reason he's coming here," Mr. Hendal, my royal economics teacher shouted.

"No! He's coming because of me! He wants me!" I flipped. Clearly we weren't going to get anywhere.

"What do you suggest we do? Just set all the students up to be slaughtered?" said Ms. Kiel, panicked.

"No. We just need to figure out a plan," I said, trying to calm myself.

"I say we evacuate the school," Honkers shouted.

"And what do we tell the students as to why we have to leave?"

Aidan asked.

"The truth," said Mrs. Bickler, the secretary.

"That would create panic amongst the students and cause chaos. No. I won't do that. We will figure out a way to handle this rationally," Aidan stated.

"I stand by Aidan and Gabe," Mr. Miller said, standing up. "I say we make up an attack plan of our own." Everything was chaos again. The room was split fifty- fifty. One half wanted to stay and defend the school, the others wanted to leave. Honestly, I didn't blame them.

Gabe leaned in closely. "I warned you this could get messy."

"You're telling me," I said.

"People please!" Aidan tried shouting above all the voices. "This is not getting us anywhere."

"This is all your fault! I say we just get rid of her. Problem solved," Honkers said. Gabe stepped forward, puffing his chest. Ms. Kraft placed a gentle hand on his shoulder, calming him.

"Playing the blame game is not going to solve this," Ms. Kraft said.

"Maybe he's right. Maybe I should go," I said, not wanting to cause any more problems.

"No," Mrs. Daniels said. "We are teachers sworn to protect our students. All of them." She looked at me with kind eyes and I silently thanked her.

"I am headmaster and I am calling the shots here," Aidan said.

"Why should we listen to you? You're still a child yourself."

Aidan's eyes started to glow as he stared down Honkers. "I am still your boss and if you don't like it you can leave," he growled. "We stay and defend the school. Gabe you make sure all the guardians are on board and prepared. Call in more if you have to. Mr. Miller, how far have you gotten with the students in their training?"

"You expect the students to fight?" Mrs. Bickler asked appalled.

"No. I expect the students to be able to defend themselves if need be. Isn't that why we're training them in the first place?"

"Yes Aidan. I believe most of my students are prepared enough. I'll even work in some extra time this week with them if I have to," Mr. Miller said.

"I'll help too," Billy said and Mr. Miller nodded his head in approval.

"Then it goes without saying. We stay and we fight," Aidan said, trying to end the meeting, but it was obvious some of the teachers had more to say.

"I don't think you need to be here for this," Ms. Kraft said to Josie and me. "Why don't we head to my classroom and work on the things I wanted to go over with you. That's if you're still up to it."

"Yes I am. Thank you. Gabe, is it okay if I leave?"

"Yes Ella. There's no need for you to be here anymore. You did well," he said, reassuring me, although I didn't think I helped much. Josie and I followed Ms. Kraft to her room while Billy and Gabe stayed behind to fill in those who cared on what they knew about Jack.

"So why don't you tell me what you have learned so far Ella?" Ms. Kraft said. I nervously bit my nails. I hadn't had a chance to look over much. Roman had *'distracted'* me.

"I really didn't get that far," I admitted a little embarrassed. Josie giggled, knowing full well what I was doing instead. I shot her a look to shut up.

"It's fine Ella," Ms. Kraft smiled. "Why don't we start here?" She pulled out one of the flyers for the dance.

"The dance?" I asked confused.

"Do you know what the significance of the dance is?" I shook my head. "The dance is to celebrate the spring equinox or what we call Ostara. As spring reaches its midpoint, night and day stand in perfect balance, with light on the increase. We give thanks to the goddess Eostre. It's a time of renewal and rebirth where we take time to celebrate the new life that surrounds us in nature. Although it is known as a Wiccan holiday, we all celebrate in different ways. We are all thankful for the beautiful things that surround us and this is why we have the dance to acknowledge the earth's wonderful gifts. In the morning before the dance, each student is given a different seed that we plant around campus."

"That is really neat," Josie said and Ms. Kraft smiled.

"Okay, got it. Now, what did you mean the other day when you said the spirits told you not to wake me?"

"Witches are more in tune with nature and all the elements. That is where we pull our strength from, which is why it is so important that we give back to nature to thank them for the gifts they allow us. The more powerful the witch the easier it is for us to communicate with the spirit world. They can see what we can't and sometimes help guide us when we don't even know their doing it."

"So does that mean physics are witches?"

"Not all of them. You have to know how to weed out the fakes."

"That's easy. If they're human than their fake," I said, feeling sure of myself.

"No dear. Even humans can still communicate with the spirit world. You have to be careful because most will pretend they can."

"How can you tell then?"

"You'll know," she smiled. I looked at Josie and she shrugged her shoulders. "Now, how about we work on some spells and your power control?"

We spent the next couple of hours learning different spells that hopefully would be useful in the event of an attack. Mr. Cormac joined us to help me work on how to channel my powers better and control them. By the end of the night I was exhausted and happy to go back to my room and crash.

I had learned a lot from Ms. Kraft and Mr. Cormac today and was getting more confident with controlling my powers. On the way back I asked Josie, "So. Do you like, sleep?"

She rolled her eyes. "No offense Ella, but I don't remember you being this dense," she said.

"Thanks jerk," I said, shoving her. "You know this whole angel thing is new to me. I don't know how it works. Hell, before you, I didn't even know angels existed."

"Ella you're half-vampire. You think you'd be more open to believe there are other creatures out there."

"So, I'm a creature now?"

"You know what I mean," she said, bumping my shoulder.

I laughed. "I'm so glad you're back even though it's only temporary. I hate to sound selfish, but I wish you were here permanently."

"I know. The longer I'm here the longer I want to stay. Who knows they might end up banishing me here forever."

"Would that be so bad?"

"Not as long as you're still here," she smiled as I put my arm around her shoulder.

When we got to my room, I opened the door to find Roman sleeping on my bed. "If I came home to that every night I'd smile too," Josie whispered.

I poked her in her side. "What about Billy?"

"What? We're not exclusive," she shrugged. I shook my head, walked over to Roman and shook him gently.

"Hey," he said, rolling over.

"What are you doing here?" I gasped when I saw his face. "What happened to your eye?"

"I need an excuse to see you?" he said, avoiding my question and leaning in to kiss me. I put up my hand to stop him. "What's wrong?"

"Hi!" Josie said, plopping down on the other bed.

"You're avoiding my question. What happened to your eye? Did Dean do this?"

"Why you think I'm sleeping in here?"

"He kicked you out?"

"Not exactly...I'm hiding from him."

"Awe, you poor baby," I laughed.

"It's not funny," he said.

"It kind of is?" Josie said.

"You stay out of it." I glared at her and she stuck her tongue out at me. "You want me to go talk to him?"

"No. Let him cool off. I'll try again in the morning," he said, getting up.

"Where are you going?" I asked.

"I'm going to stay with Reagan in his room."

"Are you sure?"

"Yeah. I don't want to intrude. You guys need to catch up."

"Let me at least heal your eye," I said, reaching up but he pulled away.

"It's okay. I deserve it."

"No you don't. You did not do anything wrong. Now stop trying to act all proud and just let me heal it."

He gave in and let me heal his eye. I walked him out and gave him a kiss before he left. There was no point in hiding our relationship now. By tomorrow the whole school would be talking about it with all different types of spins on it. I sighed and went back into my room to change and get ready for bed. If I couldn't have Roman with me tonight I was still glad to have Josie.

The exhaustion of the day took its toll and I was out before Josie even came out of the bathroom. Sometime in the middle of the night I felt someone creep into my bed next to me. I rolled over to find Roman curled up against my side. "What are you doing here?" I whispered, not wanting to wake Josie.

"Funny thing," he said. "This cute, little, perky blond popped into my dream and told me you shouldn't be alone tonight." I looked at him funny. "Josie," he clarified. I spied to find she wasn't sleeping in the other bed. "She said she had someone else she needed to see and make up for lost time," he shrugged.

I knew right away Josie was with Billy. I didn't mind and was thankful to have Roman here with me, in my arms. I snuggled closer to him and fell back asleep almost instantly.

In the morning when I woke up, Josie was sleeping in the other bed, and Roman was gone. I quietly hopped in the shower and got ready for class.

"Hey," Josie said groggily, sitting up, and stretching. "Whacha doin'?"

"Getting ready for class. This is a school, remember?"

"Can't you skip your classes?" she whined.

"No, I cannot."

"What the hell am I supposed to do all day?" I looked at her. "No, I am not going to class with you."

"Then what else are you going to do?"

"I'll just hang out with Billy," she winked.

"Nice try, but Billy is going to be busy all day helping Gabe."

"Fine, but I'm not wearing that god awful uniform."

"Suit yourself," I shrugged. "I'm going to get breakfast. If you want to join me you have five minutes to get ready."

"Ugh!" she groaned, laying back down on the bed. I rolled my eyes and finished combing my hair. Josie eventually got dressed and grumpily followed me to the dining hall. After she got some food in her she perked up a bit. "Did you get my delivery last night?" she asked with hopeful eyes.

"If you're referring to the hot Irishman you sent to my room, then yes I did, and thank you," I winked.

"So I guess that means things are okay? I didn't mess things up with you and that guy?"

"His name is Roman and no. We were keeping our relationship a secret and eventually we were going to tell people, but not blurt it out like you did," I said, narrowing my eyes at her.

"I said I was sorry."

"I know I know. We'll talk about it later. We have to go before we're late for class."

When we got to my first class I told Mr. Grant that Josie would be joining us while she was there. He said that while she attended his class he expected her to do all the work all the other students did. She wasn't happy about it, but I told him she would be the perfect student.

We took a seat in the back just as Roman showed up and took a seat next to me. He smiled at me and leaned over to give me a kiss on the cheek. I flinched and he looked at me funny. "Sorry. I guess I'm still getting used to everyone knowing," I said.

A few students whispered and looked our way. "Just ignore them," Roman said.

"Don't worry I'm used to it. You are dating the school freak, remember?"

"Yes, but you are a hot freak," he smiled. I just rolled my eyes. "And we're not the ones they're talking about," he said, looking over at Josie.

"That's because they're all jealous of my beauty," Josie said. We heard a few more students gossiping until Mr. Grant brought the class to attention. Anyone that dared to look at Josie got her icy stare in return. Josie was not one to put up with gossipy little bitches, as she called them.

Ms. Kraft was more than happy to have Josie join class and in powers class I introduced her to Riley. In self-defense Josie spent most of her time hanging all over Billy. She made him show her the moves over and over again saying she was just not getting it. We both knew it was just an excuse for some kind of weird foreplay.

I partnered up with Dean in hopes of talking to him about mine and Roman's relationship. "I don't want to talk about it Ella," he said.

"Well, I do, so you're shit out of luck. What's the big deal anyways? It's not like I've never had a boyfriend before. You liked Kyle and Tristan. Why did you get so mad when you found out I was seeing Roman?"

"Because you are my sister and with the others I didn't have to hear about the things you did."

"That was an accident and I always have to hear about your tryst with all the girls you're with. How is this any different?"

"One, Kyle doesn't count. We grew up together so I knew he wasn't a douche and wouldn't hurt you. And two, I liked Tristan before I knew you started dating him. Then he was just another dick trying to get in your pants."

I tried not to roll my eyes. "And what's wrong with Roman?"

"He's...he's...I don't know. You're my baby sister and he's my roommate."

If this was his argument he was losing miserably. "Look Dean, as much as you and dad still like to think of me as a little girl, I'm not. I'm an adult now and you need to realize that. What I do on my own time is my business and who I spend it with is also my business. Not to mention having Roman as a roommate you should know he's not a bad guy."

"I know but..."

"But nothing. I really like him and he really likes me so get over yourself and go make nice," I said, putting my foot down. Dean knew I was right, but hated to admit it. He knew he overreacted, but he was just being an older, caring brother – I think?

"Fine, but I don't have to like it," he complained.

"What do you have against Roman?"

"I guess I just know how guys think and I..."

"Dean, not all guys are perverted, egotistical, assholes."

"That's what we want you to think, but trust me, we're all thinking the same thing," he said, tapping his head. Clearly I wasn't going to get through to him anytime soon, but he did say he would apologize, which was better than nothing.

Before lunch, Dean apologized to Roman, but told him he was keeping an eye on him and if he ever hurt me he'd kill him. I didn't expect anything less.

Being with Roman openly was still weird to me, but still nice we didn't have to hide it anymore. And of course as soon as Mackenzie caught wind of us being together she pretended to be the victim. She started one of the many rumors that were making the rounds. She claimed I stole Roman from her because I was jealous and put some spell on him so he would like me. I ignored them like I did all the rest. I knew she would get hers soon.

The rest of the day went as followed – students were whispering and gossiping about mine and Roman's so called torrid affair and wondering who the new student was and why she was hanging with me. Josie took in the excitement of being the center of attention, me, not so much. But I did my best to ignore the whispers.

After lunch I was happy to go back to my room and just relax and spend some time with Josie. I caught her up on everything that had happened so far. I told her all about Roman and all my new friends I made here. I also told her about the nightmares and she explained to me that while the last dream I had with Kyle was still a dream, it was also real. It was the only way they could get to me and warn me without them knowing. I still didn't know who they were. Josie said it was better that I didn't. She also said she didn't know how Jack was able to manipulate the dream and when that happened, that's when she made the decision to come and personally warn me. Damn the consequences. I also told her all about Aidan and the evil one, Mackenzie.

"I don't see why you just don't have that Sienna girl or Dixon put a spell on her to give her warts or make her hair fall out," she said.

"Tempting, but no. And after what Ms. Kraft told us, definitely not."

"What, about black magic?"

"Yes. Remember she said that when you create a spell under anger and use it for revenge you can conjure bad magic and darkness. That darkness can consume you and I don't even want to think about the other stuff she said." I shivered at the thought.

"Okay, okay, I get it. Sheesh, enough with bad mental pictures," Josie grumbled. "I still can't believe you almost did it with one of your teachers. I see I must be rubbing off on you," she laughed.

"Josie, I was under a spell," I said rolling my eyes. "And why does everyone seem to keep forgetting the fact the end result of that was him attacking me?"

"A minor detail," she said. "Regardless he's hot. I would actually thank Mackenzie for that one." I threw my pillow at her and she squealed. I continued to catch her up on everything that had happened. It went without saying that she loved the blue streaks and as far as the tattoos went she said she was taking claim for the angel on my hip. She apologized for knowing what I went through after I lost her and Tristan and not being able to be there for me to help me get through it. To let me know she was okay. And she even admitted she was there in the cemetery that day when I visited her grave.

"Josie, you did help me. I knew you were there. I felt you," I smiled, squeezing her hand. Our little bonding moment was interrupted by a knock on the door. "Come in," I called.

"I'm not bothering you, am I?" Riley asked, sticking her head inside.

"No. Of course not. Come in."

She closed the door behind her and stood by the end of the bed clutching a box. I could tell she felt uncomfortable, like she was invading mine and Josie's time together. "What's in the box?" Josie asked.

"Oh, yeah. That's why I stopped by. It was delivered this morning. I think it's the dress."

"Why didn't you tell me earlier?" I asked, pulling her down to sit.

"Well, you were kind of busy and I didn't want to bug you." She looked down at the box and I could tell what she meant was – my best friend is back and I didn't have time for her.

"I'm going to grab a soda, you want?" Josie asked, taking the hint that I needed to talk to Riley. I shook my head no. "Riley?"

"No thank you," she stammered.

"I'll be back," Josie said, jumping off the bed.

Once Josie was gone I turned to Riley. "So what's up?"

"Nothing," she said, looking at the box again.

"Riley, you don't think just because Josie's back that means I don't have time for you?"

"Um, I did kind of think I was just filling in so now that she's back I guess you don't need me anymore."

"Riley, that is not true and you were never a replacement friend. Both of you are my good friends and I will always have time for you. I'm so sorry you feel that way. I wish you would have said something earlier. If I had realized I was making you feel that way I never would have –"

"Ella, it's not your fault. I was being silly."

"Riley, no you weren't. I don't ever want you to think you can't come to me if something is bothering you, okay? Promise me, no matter what. If something is bothering you even if it seems silly, you'll tell me?" She nodded and I gave her a hug. "Now, what are you waiting for? Open the box so we can see the dress."

She smiled brightly and tore off the tape. The dress was even prettier than I remembered. "Go try it on so we know it fits," I said, scooting her into the bathroom.

Josie returned to the room while Riley was changing. "Everything good?" she asked.

"Yeah, it's good," I said as Riley stepped out of the bathroom. "Oh, Riley, it looks great!"

"You think so?" I nodded. "It's a little big at the top though," she said, biting her lip.

"I can fix that," Josie said, jumping up. "We don't all have big boobs like Ella so I know a few tricks to make it seem like you do." I rolled my eyes at her comment.

"Oh. I don't want to stuff," Riley said bashfully.

Josie laughed. "No, not stuff. All you need is a good push up bra and someone who can take the dress in."

"I don't know anyone who can do that?" Riley said, looking at me.

"Now you do," Josie said smiling. "Ella, do you have any pins?"

"Please, you should see all the extra stuff my mom packed. I'm sure if I dig deep enough I'll find a sewing machine," I joked.

The three of us sat around gossiping until Josie and I had to leave for training. I offered for Riley to come with even though I knew Josie thought it was a bad idea. I just hated the thought of not being able to tell my friends what might happen at the dance. Asking Riley to come with and practice with us made me feel better about her knowing a few things to defend herself.

Riley agreed to come with because she said she could use the practice.

When we got to the gym, Roman and Dean were there also. Dean marched straight for me and pulled me to the side. "Why didn't you tell me Ella?" he said angrily. Apparently Gabe and Billy had filled him in on what was going on and felt he should be here too to learn what he could.

"With everything else that was going on I really didn't have a chance to," I said a little annoyed at his attack.

"I think Jack planning an attack on the school is something pretty damn important to have just slipped your mind," he yelled loud enough for Riley to hear.

"What did you say?" Riley asked, joining us. I gave Dean a nasty look for his big mouth then turned to Josie for what to do.

"I'll take this one," Josie said. "Might as well. I'm already in enough trouble for telling you. What else can they do?" She pulled Riley over to the bleachers and sat her down. I followed and sat on the other side of Riley. "Okay, so, the whole reason I'm here is because I came to warn Ella about something and then got caught for doing it. I'm telling you this because I don't want you to be mad at Ella for keeping it from you. I wasn't supposed to tell her and I told her she couldn't tell anyone else so I want you to know it's not her fault."

Riley looked at me. "What's going on?"

Josie continued. "There's going to be an attack on the school."

"What, when?"

"Saturday sometime during the dance," I said.

"Ella, we have to tell Mr. Callahan and make him cancel the dance."

I shook my head. "He knows Riley and we can't cancel the dance."

"Why not?"

"Because I was never supposed to interfere," Josie said softly.

"I don't understand?" Riley said, looking between us.

"I don't really understand it either Riley, but I don't want you to worry. Everything is being taken care of. All of the teachers and the guardians know. I promise I won't let anything happen to you," I said, hoping to somewhat make her feel better.

"But what about Justin, Cameron, Sienna, and all the rest? Do they know? What happens to them?"

I had to bite my lip to keep the tears from falling. "They don't know and we can't tell them. We can't risk this leaking and setting panic amongst the rest of the school."

"They have to know Ella. This is crazy. They have to be warned," she said, getting up and I turned to Josie worried. "I'm sorry Ella, but I have to tell Justin and the rest of them. I won't let them get hurt." She made her way toward the door.

"What do I do?" I asked Josie.

Everyone figured out what was going on and tried to stop Riley. Roman and Billy tried to coax her not to leave. "Compel her," Dean said.

"Are you nuts? I'm not going to do that to my friend."

"Ella, it's the only way," he said.

"He's right Ella. We can't risk this getting out. You have to compel her to forget what she heard," Gabe said.

I turned on Dean. "Why can't you do it? You're the one who opened your big mouth in the first place," I said, narrowing my eyes at him.

"I can't and you know I can't. You're the only one who is strong enough to make it stick," he said, knowing well it was killing me to do this.

"Fine," I said, walking over to Riley. "Riley?" I could feel my hands start to shake. My lip began to quiver. "I can't do this." I walked away, but Dean caught up to me.

"You can do this Ella. I know you can."

"But I never did it before."

"Try it on me first," he suggested.

I looked over his shoulder where Roman was still standing with Billy. "No. I have a better idea. Roman!" He jogged over to us. I put my hands on his shoulders and looked straight into his eyes, concentrating. Once I could feel the power start to rise I said, "Punch Dean in the face."

"What! This is your brilliant idea?" he said, panicked.

I turned to Dean. "Don't move." He stood there frozen in fear and then I turned back to Roman. "Punch him, now." And that's exactly what he did. I got to say it definitely made me feel better.

"I think it's safe to say it worked," Josie said, pushing me back over to Riley.

"Ella, please," Riley begged.

"Riley," I began. I was no longer able to stop the tears. "Riley, I'm sorry. I don't want to do this and you have to know I don't want anyone to get hurt and that this is killing me."

I took a breath as the tears spilled down my cheeks. I felt Josie take my hand and I looked back up at Riley. "Riley, you have to forget everything you just saw and heard. You have to forget about the attack on the school. You came here to work on your self-defense and we were just waiting for Gabe to set everything up." I watched as Riley's eyes glazed over and then she shook her head and looked up at me.

"Ella, why are you crying?" she asked.

"I...uh..."

"She stubbed her toe," Josie said.

"Are you okay?"

"Yeah, I'm fine," I said, turning away, not able to face her anymore and annoyed that was the best answer Josie could come up with. When I reached Dean I had forgotten he was still not able to move. If I had my way I would have let him there all day.

"You really couldn't find another way to test your compulsion," he said, narrowing his eyes and rubbing his jaw.

"Just be glad it was Roman and not Gabe. Besides, you hit him first so it was only fair he got to hit you back."

"Yeah but that was –" I glared at him and he shut up.

As soon as we knew it was safe, and the compulsion had worked, Gabe and Billy started to set up everything. As far as Riley knew she was just here to work on her self-defense. I managed to pull myself together and get to work. I didn't do any better today than I did yesterday. Stabbing someone in the heart or cutting off their head was easier said than done. The dummies were made of rubber, but Gabe had explained it would be just as hard on a vampire. I had to manage to get through all the skin and muscle. I also had to learn to avoid bone when I was going for the heart.

By the end of the session I was worn out – physically and mentally. I even thought about skipping dinner, but I was too hungry. I spent some extra time in the shower. I thought maybe I could wash away the grief, but I knew I was just kidding myself. I didn't say a word at dinner. I didn't even complain about the fact that Mackenzie and her group had joined us. Apparently Dean had told her he would take her to the dance and Sienna agreed to join her coven.

"Ella, are you okay?" Cameron asked.

"Yeah. I just got a lot of homework to do," I said, getting up. Not even bothering to finish my dinner. I wasn't in the mood to socialize and just wanted to be alone.

When I got back to my room, I lay on my bed, and closed my eyes trying to forget that I was me. "Hey, you awake?" Josie asked, coming into the room. I sat up. "I brought you some food. You didn't really eat at dinner so I thought you'd be hungry," she said, sitting next to me and handing me a sandwich.

"Thanks," I mumbled in between bites.

"You wanna talk about it?"

"What's there to say? In two days I'm about to face my enemy who created an army just to get to me. And I know people are going to get hurt. Maybe even my friends and I can't do anything about it."

"But you are Ella. You are doing something about it. By telling the teachers and the guardians you did the right thing. They will protect the school. From what Gabe told me they are the best of the best so we have nothing to worry about. Besides, what did I tell you about worrying so much?"

"That it gives you premature wrinkles," I sighed.

There was a knock on the door. "Hey, can I come in?" Roman asked.

"You can even stay here tonight," Josie said. I looked at her. "I talked to Billy earlier and I'm staying in his room and you should not be alone."

She got up to walk out and I asked, "Aren't you going to take something to sleep in?"

"I don't plan on sleeping," she said, closing the door behind her.

"Are you okay?" Roman asked, sitting next to me on the bed.

I put my sandwich aside and pulled him down on the bed next to me. "Just hold me," I said, wrapping his arms around me.

"That I can do," he smiled.

We laid there for a while in each other's arms. I thought about everything that was about to go down in only two days and then I started to kiss Roman. I wanted to forget and I knew kissing him would help. I guess I came on a little too aggressively because he pulled away. "What's the matter? You don't want to?"

"No, I do. It's just...you're coming on a little too strong."

"I thought you said you like it rough," I teased, nibbling on his ear.

"Okay, that's not fair," he said. I ran my hands up his shirt and across his chest. Then I took off my shirt and kissed him with so much force I accidentally bit his lip. "What's gotten into you?"

"Nothing. I just want to be with you," I said, trying again, but he pushed me back.

"Ella, I want to be with you, but not like this."

"Like what?" I asked annoyed.

"I can tell you're not really into it. It's like you're forcing yourself so you can forget."

"What's wrong with wanting to forget?"

"Ella…"

"Just forget it. Just go," I said, turning away from him. I pulled my knees up to my chest and rested my forehead against them. He reached for my shoulder and I pulled away from his touch. He didn't make a move to leave and I knew I wouldn't be able to get rid of him easily. Not caring anymore, I let the stress of everything hit me and I started to cry.

Roman tried to comfort me, but I resisted. I finally gave in when I felt like the weight of the world was on my shoulders. "I know you're scared and I'd be lying if I said I wasn't scared too," he said, caressing my hair. I pulled back to look at him and gently pressed my lips to his. Then I laid my head on his chest as he held me. "That's the Ella I know and love."

I could feel him take a breath and then exhale. "I love you Ella and I don't care if you love me back, but I want you to know that I do and I mean it."

I pulled back, turned his face to mine, and looked into his dark blue eyes. "I love you too."

"Don't say it because you think you have to."

"Roman look at me…I'm not just saying it because you did. I mean it. I love you."

And I really did.

He smiled, pressing his lips to mine. We laid back on the bed and ended up making love. Afterwards, as I lay my head in the crook of his neck and ran my fingers up and down his chest he said, "So what made you decide to compel me to punch Dean?"

"Really? That's what you're thinking?"

He laughed. "Actually, I was thinking about it earlier, but then I got distracted," he said, rubbing my back.

"I figured it was only fair. Besides, he needed a good punch to the face."

"I guess thank you for the honor."

"You're welcome," I said, reaching up and placing my hand behind his neck as I kissed it. I could feel his pulse start to race and I could hear the blood coursing through his veins. I could feel his blood calling to me. I started to nibble on his neck and I felt my fangs come out.

"Go ahead," he said breathlessly. "It's okay. I want you to." I didn't hesitate as I sank my teeth into his neck. The pull was too strong for me to hold back. The feel of his blood trickling down my throat was so intense and empowering. It felt so good. It was warm and it tickled as it went down. I bit harder, not seeming to be able to get enough. I knew they said you could get into the other person's mind if they let you, but I was too distracted to even try. I couldn't seem to get enough.

"Ella...Ella," Roman said panting.

I managed to pull myself away. "I'm sorry," I said. "I didn't take too much, did I?"

"No," he smiled. His eyes were all glossy. He tangled his hand in my hair and rolled over on top of me, pressing his lips so hard on mine I was gasping for air. I forgot how the endorphins from a bite are so engrossing. I knew how they made the person you bite feel, but I had no idea it was just as intense for the biter.

The weight of his body on mine was crushing me, but at the same time felt incredible. Every time I saw the wound on his neck from where I had bit him, I wanted to sink my teeth right back in. If it wasn't for him distracting me with his hungry kisses I would have. I never felt a rush like this before and I never wanted it to stop.

When the feeling finally wore off, we both laid on our backs panting. "That was..."

"Amazing," I finished for him.

"I only heard about how intense a bite was, but I never imagined it to be like that," he said.

"I'm just glad I was able to stop," I said, reaching for him and pulling him to me.

"I knew you could," he smiled, brushing the hair off of my face.

"But I almost didn't," I said, embarrassed at letting myself get so out of control like that.

"It's always hard your first time. When you first get a taste for it you feel like you don't want to stop. Like you can't seem to get enough."

"Have you ever bitten someone before?" He nodded. "Oh."

"It wasn't like that though. It was different...I mean I still felt the attraction, but not like I felt it with you." He brushed his thumb across my cheek. "I love you," he whispered, kissing my lips.

"I love you too." I looked at his neck that was bruised and covered in dry blood. "Oh my, I didn't realize I bit you that hard."

"I didn't mind," he smiled. "But I should teach you how to close the wound." I looked at him puzzled. "After you drink from someone you run your tongue over the bite so it stops the bleeding and closes the wound. It also helps it look less noticeable. It was partially my fault. I didn't give you the chance," he said.

"Lucky for you this is where my nifty little healing power comes in handy," I said, placing my hand over his bite.

"I knew I was with you for a reason."

"Shut up," I said, snuggling up close to him.

CHAPTER TWENTY-SIX

I woke up in the morning feeling refreshed. The thought of the dance hadn't even crossed my mind until I opened my closet and saw my dress hanging there in the garment bag. I sighed as I stood there staring at it. "What's that?" Roman asked, coming up behind me and wrapping his arms around my waist.

"That's my dress for the dance," I said.

"Can I see it?"

"Nope. You're just going to have to wait."

"You're such a tease," he said, nibbling on my neck.

"Look who's talking. You need to stop. We have to get ready for class."

"Let's just skip it."

"No. Now go away," I said, giving him a little shove.

"Fine," he groaned. He stole a few more kisses before I finally pushed him out the door. "Good morning Josie."

"Yeah, yeah," she grumbled, falling down on the bed.

"I didn't expect you back anytime soon," I said.

"Neither did I, but Gabe busted us and said it wouldn't be appropriate for me to stay in Billy's room blah, blah, blah."

"Since you're up, you can join me for class today."

"Nooo..."she moaned in to the pillow.

"Yes. Now get up and get ready," I said, smacking her on her behind.

"You seem in a better mood. I trust you slept well?"

"Well, I can't say that I actually slept."

"I see I'm definitely rubbing off on you...finally. It's about time you loosened up. If I knew you getting some would get that stick out of your butt I would have tried to get your cherry popped a long time ago."

"Josie!" She just laughed. "Why does everyone think I'm such a prude?"

"Because you are," Josie said, giggling again.

I had found out that we didn't have classes today. The whole day was spent preparing for tomorrow, which meant my day would be spent training and preparing for the attack. While the rest of my friends were helping with preparations for the celebration, Roman, Dean, Josie, and I were sparing with several different guardians in the field outside. We couldn't use the gym due to the fact that's where the dance was being held. Aidan had switch the location from the atrium to the gym, telling us it would be a more secure place for the students in the event of an attack.

It was overwhelmingly warm for late March. To keep us from passing out, Gabe let us have a twenty minute break to relax. As soon as those twenty minutes was up we were right back to work. I was sweating so bad my eyes were burning and I was getting dehydrated, but Gabe kept pushing us. I was surprised he even let us go for lunch. As soon as we got the okay to go eat. I ran. Scared he would change his mind. I didn't even care I was sweaty, stinky, and dirty. All I wanted was that hour to sit down and eat as much as I could.

Shortly after we sat down the rest of our friends started to file in and make themselves comfy. "Geez Ella, ever heard of this thing called a shower?" Cameron said when she got a look at me. Before I could open my mouth she saw Dean, Roman, and Josie looking just as pitiful. "What the hell happened to you guys?"

"Yeah, why do you all look like you were rolling around in the dirt?" Sienna said.

"Training," was all I said.

Everyone was chatting about all the stuff they were going to do and the dance tomorrow. My stomach was churning at the thought of something happening to them. I wanted to tell them to leave and go home where they would be safe, but I couldn't. "I know it's hard to relax, but try not to look so edgy," Roman said, noticing my tension. I squeezed his hand and forced a smile while I finished my lunch.

After lunch, Gabe worked us, hard. This would be the last chance we had to practice like this so he wanted to make sure we got it. He threw as much at us as he could. He had us take on several guardians at once and worked us into the late evening. I was so sore I thought I wouldn't make it back to my room. For once I actually let Roman shower with me, afraid I might drown from how tired I was. I healed him and then made him give me a massage. The heat from his hands helped. He stayed with me as long as he could. He stayed until Josie returned from Billy's room. I said goodnight wishing I didn't have to.

Snuggled tightly into my blankets, I rested comfortably while I waited for sleep to come. "Josie, what's it like, where you were?" I asked, curious.

It took a moment before she answered me. "It was like paradise. Whatever you imagined heaven would be like that's what it is. It's your interpretation of glory, pure happiness. Everything and anything you wanted was at your disposal. All you had to do was close your eyes and wish for it."

"Was...he..." I couldn't bring myself to say his name.

"No, Ella. He wasn't," she said softly.

"Then where?"

"I don't know...when we die, our soul doesn't leave right away. Our spirit lingers and then we move on."

"Why?"

"I don't know. I guess for the people who have unfinished business."

"What about the people who don't move on? What happens to them?"

"They stay here?" she said, not quite sure.

"Does everybody become an angel?"

"No."

"Who determines whether you do or don't?"

"It's not really who it's more like what. It's hard to explain," she yawned. "I'm tired. You mind if we talk about it later?"

"I'm sorry," I said.

"Sorry for what?"

"That you're here. It sounds like that place was perfect."

"It was, but if I can't be there there's no other place I rather be than here with you."

"If I didn't know any better I'd think you were hitting on me," I joked.

"Nah, you're not my type," she laughed. "Now shut up, stop

stressing, and go to sleep," she said, turning away from me.

At breakfast, those who knew what was going down tonight sat silently while everyone else chatted about the day ahead. When we were done we all met Ms. Kraft outside to plant some seeds along the wall. It was a nice day outside despite the mood. The weather was warm, but muggy. They said it was unusually warm for spring in Rhode Island and Sienna said she could sense a storm on the way. I covered my eyes from the glare of the bright sun as I looked up to the sky. Not a cloud in sight. I should be happy for the nice weather, but today my mood was a somber one.

When we were finished with all the outside activities, everyone else went inside to help set up for the dance while the few who had other things to worry about joined Gabe outside on the track to go over the plan and practice what we could. They told us the guardians on campus had tripled for tonight and were on alert. If anything were to go down and security was breached we were to barricade the doors from inside the gym and guardians would surround the students. Aidan told us the gym was the safest place in the whole school. That did not make me feel any better.

"Are you ready for this?" Gabe asked, after our final practice.

"Honestly...no," I said.

"Ella, I have faith in you. I never had a student progress as well as you did. If I had to pick someone to fight by my side in battle I would pick you. I believe in you and you should too."

"So do I," Roman said, taking my hand.

"You're just saying that because you're my boyfriend," I said, giving him a playful nudge.

"I Believe in you," Dean said, catching me off guard. "And so do the rest of your friends. Ella, there is no other person who could handle this better than you. You are one of the strongest people I know. I sometimes envy how brave you are. I know if anybody can get through this you can," he said, squeezing my shoulder.

"Thank you Dean," I said, giving him a hug. "I really appreciate the encouragement, but I think I need some time to myself," I said, looking at Roman. He gave me a soft kiss before I took off. I needed to clear my head and mentally prepare myself. I took a walk along the wall where we had just freshly planted flowers and saplings.

"Hello Ella, how are you feeling?" Ms. Kraft asked, startling me.

I didn't even hear her approach. "Ms. Kraft, I'm sorry. I didn't see you."

"I know. I could tell you were somewhere else," she said, pointing to the pile of dirt I was standing in.

"Oh, I'm such a moron."

"Ella, you are not a moron. You are a young girl who has more on her plate than she should. Come with me." She held out her hand and we walked over to the fountain and had a seat. "I want you to meditate with me."

"I don't know...I don't think I..."

"Yes you can. Just concentrate and close your eyes. Listen to the sounds around you and open up your mind. Breath in and breath out."

At first I didn't think this could possibly work and I knew she felt my skepticism, but she didn't give up. Once I let myself go and tried, I could feel myself start to relax. We sat there for a half hour just meditating. I felt completely at ease until Dean started to call me in my head. I had left my cell phone in my room and Josie was waiting for me. I sighed and opened my eyes. "I have to go," I said.

"Do you feel better?"

"I do. Thank you Ms. Kraft."

"Ella, remember, you are one of a kind, and everything you are is inside of you. I have faith in you and I know you will know what to do when the time comes." I thanked her one last time then headed off to my room to get ready.

"Uh, hello, what the hell took you so long? I had Dean channel you or whatever that thing is he does for like twenty minutes," Josie complained.

"I'm here now. What's up?"

"Duh...we have to get ready and you need to shower, eww," she said, holding her nose. I rolled my eyes and got in the shower.

"Did you find something to wear?" I called from the bathroom.

"Cameron and Sienna let me raid their closets. Not exactly my style, but Sienna said she wouldn't mind if I made some alterations." Sienna's going to find out the hard way that some alterations means say goodbye to your dress.

Josie had picked out a cute, purple, baby doll dress. She took the hem up two inches and took the sleeves off to make it a strapless. She had also added some gems and silk flowers to the dress. "Where did you get that jewelry you're tearing apart?" I asked.

"Don't worry about that," she winked. I didn't bother to ask any more questions. I knew the less I knew the better. After I dried my hair, I packed my purse with weapons. Then I sat down to do my makeup. Josie suggested I curl my hair, which she offered to help me with while I did my makeup. She even made me a double jeweled headband to go with my dress. We pinned different sections of my hair back leaving curls hang around my face and down my shoulders.

I started to get nervous as I got dressed. Once I felt I was ready, I turned to the mirror to check myself out. "Wow Ella, you look like a princess," Josie gleamed.

"Thanks," I sighed.

"Hey. You really do look hot," she said, thinking I was unsure with my appearance. I could have cared less right now. The only thing I was worried about was surviving the night.

"Come on we better go," I said, grabbing my purse. "Can you put this in your bag? I don't have any more room in mine." I handed her my lip-gloss and then went to go meet everyone else in the social room. When we got there Dean was on the couch drinking from a flask. "You really think that's wise?" I scowled.

"It helps me think," he said, almost dropping the flask when he saw me. "Wow."

"What?" I said, feeling uncomfortable under his stare.

"Ella you look...grown up."

"Thanks, I think." I grabbed his flask and took a sip.

"Now, that's not a good idea," he said, taking the flask back.

"You don't look so bad yourself," I said, straightening his tie.

"Please...I'll be the best looking person there."

"Until they see me," Roman announced, coming into the room. When I turned around to face him, his jaw dropped, and he stopped dead in his tracks. I blushed at the way he was staring at me. "Ella you look...beautiful," he stuttered. I walked over and placed a soft kiss on his lips. "How did I get so lucky?"

"I have no idea," I teased. "I have to say you do clean up pretty nice." He raised a brow at me. "Where did you even get this suit?" He had on a dark, navy blue suit that matched his eyes, a white button down shirt that was a nice contrast to his slightly tanned skin, and a light blue tie to match.

"Just something I had lying around," he said, brushing it off like it was nothing. When I looked at him again he leaned in closer and whispered, "It's Deans."

"Oh," I smiled, thinking it looked familiar. "It looks better on you anyways," I winked and gave him another kiss.

"Alright, enough of that," Cameron said as her and the rest of the gang joined us in the room. "Ella...Wow!"

Everyone stopped to stare at me.

"Okay, if you all don't stop staring at me I'm going to go change," I said, feeling uncomfortable under their stares.

"Sorry, you just look amazing. It's almost like you have a glow," Sienna smiled in awe.

"Thank you," I blushed. "I think maybe we should get going."

"I'll meet you guys there. I have to pick up my date," Dean said, taking another swig from his flask.

When we got to the gym I felt like I was back at prom. It definitely was decorated better, but still very prom-ish. There were a few tables with chairs set up here and there. Twinkling lights hanging from the ceiling and wrapped around a few small trees that were set up in different areas of the gym. As I walked through the gym with my friends I got several stares from the students and looks of utter astonishment. "Why is everyone staring me?" I asked.

"Because they're jealous that you're here with someone as handsome as me," Roman said.

"Oh, really?"

He laughed. "Ella, when are you going to realize how beautiful you are and that is why everyone is staring."

"It's true," Austin said. "You look hot." Cameron smacked him and he quickly corrected himself. "I mean not as hot as my baby," he smiled, planting a kiss on her cheek. I couldn't help but laugh.

"Yeah Ella, even I got a stiffy," Dixon said.

I looked at him strange. "I don't know what to say to that," I said.

"Just take it as a compliment," he said, giving me a light pat on my behind. I just shook my head as Roman escorted me to a table.

"You want something to drink, eat?" Roman asked, once we were settled.

"I'm too nervous to eat," I admitted.

"That's a first," Josie said, taking a seat as Billy pulled out a chair for her.

"You look very handsome in a suit Billy. Who would have

guessed?" I said teasingly.

"And you look amazing as well," he said, giving me a small bow.

Roman looked at me concerned. "What is it?" I asked.

"Nothing," he said, shaking his head. "I'm going to go get you some fruit and water." He stood up and headed over to the snack table.

I turned to Sienna and asked her where Reagan was. She ended up mustering up some courage to ask him to the dance. "He said he'd meet me here. There he is now," she said, smiling brightly, causing her cheeks to turn pink.

Roman returned to the table just as Dean and Mackenzie made their entrance. She was wearing a hot pink gown that sparkled from head to toe. Her hair was pulled up into a tight bun on the top of her head. She wore elbow length gloves, with an outrageously large diamond bracelet, necklace, and earrings to match. If I didn't know any better I would think she was auditioning to be a princess, but this is Mackenzie we are talking about. She already thinks she is the queen. The only thing missing is her black crown. They made their way to our table. The look on Mackenzie's face when she saw me was priceless and for the first time tonight made me feel good. She turned to Josie. "Nice dress. I actually have the perfect necklace that would go with that," she said.

"Not anymore," Josie said, giggling with Sienna. Mackenzie just looked at them confused and I now knew where the jewelry came from.

I watched my friends enjoy themselves while they danced and had a good time. I couldn't do that. I was too worried that at any moment I would have to spring into action. A slow song played softly through the speakers. Roman stood up and held his hand out to me. "Dance with me?" I hesitated. "Come on, one dance won't kill you," he winked. I took his hand and he led me to the dance floor. I tried to let myself relax as he held me in his arms.

Once the song was over, I pulled away to go sit back down, but he pulled me back to him smiling and planted a tender kiss on my lips. I melted under his touch. If there was anywhere I wanted to be right now it was here, in Roman's arms.

The dance was over in an hour and so far nothing had happened, which made me nervous. I would look over at Gabe from time to time and he would let me know nothing unusual yet. "Relax Ella. Maybe it might not even happen and we were worried for nothing," Roman said, trying to calm me again.

"Hey, have you guys seen Riley?" Justin asked.

"She was just here a minute ago?" I said. "Maybe she went to the bathroom."

"Don't you guys normally do that in groups?" I looked over at the table and saw everyone else sitting there.

"I'll go check," I said, excusing myself. When I got to the bathroom she wasn't in there. "Maybe I just missed her," I thought and headed back out into the gym. "Sorry Justin, she wasn't in there, but I'm sure she's around here somewhere."

The dance was almost over and we still hadn't found Riley. Now I was worried. I told Gabe the situation and he said not to panic. No students had left the building, but he would go outside and check just to make me feel better. I turned from concerned to alarm as the dance started to let out. Not to mention Jack had yet to attempt to attack. I ran the thought over in my head. Why hadn't he attacked yet? What was he waiting for?

On the way out of the gym I bumped into Justin's friend Kenny. "Hey, Kenny, have you seen Riley?"

"Yeah, I saw her a little bit ago. She was talking to Mackenzie and then she left," he said.

"What do you mean left? Left where?"

He shrugged, having no clue. Great, I could only imagine what happened. I saw Madison and I grabbed her. "Where's Riley?" I demanded. I knew if Mackenzie was up to something she would know.

"Chill freak. I don't know. I don't hang with losers," she said.

I brought my hand up to smack her, but Josie stopped me. "Whoa, down girl. As much as she deserves it it's not going to help us find Riley."

I thought for a moment and then realized the only way I was going to find out was to compel Madison to tell me. I gripped her by the shoulders and stared into her eyes. "Where is Riley?" I asked again.

I saw her eyes glaze over and she opened her mouth to speak. "She's in the tower," she said robotically. I let her go.

She narrowed her eyes at me. "What the hell?" she said

confused.

I pushed her out of my way. "I don't have time for you." I shoved past all the students on their way out of the dance. I looked over to the tower and out of the corner of my eye I saw one of the guardians rush across the grounds. Then I saw two more follow in his direction and over to my right I saw more running in the opposite direction and then I heard a blood curdling scream. "It's starting." I looked around at all the students making their way back to their rooms and the different parties being held. Some were halfway across campus and I knew I couldn't reach them in time.

"Everyone back in the gym, now!" I yelled.

"Ella, the dance is over," Sienna said.

"I know but get back in the gym. Hurry!" I shouted as we heard another scream.

"What's going on?" Cameron asked.

"Just get back in the gym where it's safe," I said, pushing them.

"Ella, what is it?" Roman asked.

"I don't know why I didn't think of it before? I knew something was off when he didn't attack. That's because he was waiting till after the dance. He knew they would be waiting for him to attack during, but not after."

"You're right," he said. "Now! Everyone back inside!"

"Seriously guys, what's going on?"

"Just get in the gym! And make everyone else get back in there too!" I turned to go get Riley.

"Ella, where are you going?" Roman asked.

"I have to go get Riley," I said.

"I'm coming with you."

"No, you have to get everyone back in the gym. I'll be fine. I promise."

"I'll go with her," Justin said, joining the conversation. There were more screams and guardians running everywhere. Students were starting to panic and my friends finally took the hint to get back in the gym.

Roman and Dean wrangled up the straggling students and forced them back inside with the others while Justin and I ran to the tower to find Riley. I was never so glad that Gabe had made me do all that running for training. I sprinted across the grounds, racing to get to the tower.

Of course it had started to rain. Sienna had predicted earlier it would storm and she was right. The rain was coming down so hard it was making it difficult to see, but I managed to make it there with no interference. "Riley!" I called, running up the steps of the tower.

"Ella?"

"Riley where are you?"

"I'm up here," she said. I was surprised that I had beaten Justin here. Considering he was a wolf I thought he could run faster, especially since I was running in heels.

"Riley, oh thank God you're okay," I said, throwing my arms around her. "What are you doing up here?"

"I ran into Mackenzie and she told me Justin wanted to meet me up here and he had a surprise for me."

"Riley, I'm sorry, but it was a prank."

"Why is she so mean?" she said, hurt that she fell for one of her tricks.

"We don't have time to discuss it now. We have to go," I said, pulling her down the steps.

"Ella, what's going on? I heard people screaming and saw guardians running around everywhere."

"I don't have time to explain. We have to get you to safety."

"Where's Justin?"

"He was right behind me. You know, for a wolf he's pretty slow."

"Actually, he's not. Something must have happened," Riley said worried. When we reached the outside I had found out why Justin never made it. He was fighting off threats and he was in wolf form. That is how I made it to the tower unscathed. Justin made sure no one would get to us. I pushed Riley back inside to help Justin fight off the rogue vampires. Once it was clear, I signaled for Riley to come out.

Things were worse than before. The school was on full attack and students were running everywhere trying to find safety. I kept Riley tight to me as I pulled her across campus. Justin stayed close to us and helped fight off any threats. We were half way to the gym when I saw a few students trying to defend themselves against some of Jack's army of rouge vampires and failing. I thought quickly. "Justin, take Riley to the gym. Riley stay close to Justin and don't stop running until you are safely inside. Got it?"

"Yes Ella but –"

"Go!" I yelled, taking off to help the other students. I took on the rouge vamps without even thinking. All I knew is that I had to get them away from these students. I managed to knock out one of them right before I was attacked by another. I fought with everything I had, taking out everyone that came at me. I was blindsided and knocked to the ground. Before I had the chance to recover, my attacker was on top on me, ready to strike. I brought my hands up to block his punch when someone else held my hands down. I braced myself for the pain. The second before his fist was about to make contact with my face he was sent flying into the air and the girl behind me was ripped away by a wolf.

I wiped the rain from my eyes to find a hand held out for me. "I told you I got your back," Billy said, helping me up.

"Thanks," I smiled, relieved. I looked at the students bleeding and cowering on the ground. "We need to get them back inside." I heard a growl and turned to see Riley and Justin hadn't made it back to the gym yet. "Can you get them back inside while I help Riley and Justin?"

"I got this, go," Billy said, waving me off. I ran over to help Justin who was fighting off three vamps on his own while Riley tried to stay out of the way. Once I joined the fray, more of Jack's army appeared. I was struggling with fighting two and trying to keep them from Riley.

My attacker was knocked out from behind. I looked up to see Roman. "Go, take Riley. I'll help Justin," he said. Before I reached Riley, Roman grabbed me, and crushed his lips to mine leaving me breathless. "I love you."

"I love you too." I grabbed Riley and took off running again.

We had a few more close calls. Riley could not run as fast as I could. She was having a hard time keeping up because of her asthma and slipping from the rain. I managed to get her safely to the gym just as I was struck from behind. "Riley, get inside now!" I yelled as I attacked my opponent. She didn't move. "Riley, go now!"

It was hard fighting back. With all the rain, anytime I tried to get a grip on my attacker my hands slipped. Roman and Justin were busy keeping the rest of the vamps away from us so I was on my own with this one. I fought hard, but I was losing.

All of a sudden, time started to slow. I watched confused as my attacker was moving in slow motion. "Ella your shoe," Riley shouted over the screams. I looked back and saw she had her hands up. She was the one slowing time. "Your shoe!" she said again. I took off my shoe and pierced my attacker's heart with it. I knew it wouldn't kill him, but it would take him out of the equation for the moment.

As soon as I hit him, time returned to normal speed.

"Inside now!" I said. I knew she didn't want to go, but Billy and Dean showed up with more students stuffing them into the gym.

"Ella, come on!" Roman called, holding his hand out for me.

I looked back out at the chaos and that's when I saw him.

Jack.

He was standing by the entrance of the maze, staring right at me. That's when I knew how he got in. There were no guardians at the other side of the maze. It was too big and they felt no one could make it through without getting lost. But Jack was fast, smart, and he figured it out.

He smiled when he saw me and turned back to go into the maze. I knew he wanted me to follow him and I knew I had to. I ripped off my other shoe and tossed it to the side. "Ella, where are you going?" Roman called as one of the guardians pushed him into the gym. He tried to fight his way back out but it was hopeless.

I didn't have time to worry. I had to get Jack. Knowing that Roman and my friends were safely inside the gym, I took off. I ran across the grass and into the maze dodging guardians and rogue vampires as they passed. I had no idea how I was going to find him. I had no idea where Gabe was and if Dean and Billy were safely in the gym and I didn't have time to worry about it. I knew they could take care of themselves. I had to get Jack. I had to find him and take him out before I lost all my nerve. No more hiding. No more running. Now was the time to take him down.

I took a deep breath as I entered the maze. I had no idea where to go. I took a moment and closed my eyes. I tried to remember what Ms. Kraft had taught me. I opened myself up to the elements around me and asked them for guidance on where to go. The wind picked up and a breeze rustled the bushes on my left. My gut instinct told me to follow it.

As I walked through the maze following the wind, I slipped a few times on the gravel. One point I thought I twisted my ankle, but I fought through the pain. Halfway through I had decided to take off the headband Josie had made for me. I broke it into pieces and dropped one every so couple of feet. I thought this would help me find my way back out or at least help them find my body if I didn't make it.

CHAPTER TWENTY-SEVEN

I didn't realize how large this maze was. It felt like I was walking forever. Not to mention the rain was making me cold and the dampness was making my muscles ache. I reached a part of the maze where the ground changed from gravel to grass, giving my feet a reprieve from the sharp stones.

When I finally reached the center, I saw it was exactly how it was in my dreams. Soft black pebbles covered the ground, a large fountain stood in the center of a wide open space. And Jack stood by it, with his back to me. I stood there, frozen. Not sure how to approach. Jack lifted his head and turned around. "Ella," he said with a creepy smile. "Oh, how I've missed you." He took a step away from the fountain. "Don't be shy," he said, egging me to come closer.

I walked a few feet away from the archway. I kept my distance and stood across from him. "I hear you've been busy. My spies kept me very well informed," he said.

I narrowed my eyes at him. "What are you talking about?"

"It was so easy. Once I found out where you were, you did all the rest for me. What's the matter? Have a hard time making friends...poor Ella. You're not very well liked here, are you?" I crossed my arms annoyed. "All I had to do was wave a few dollars and they were all too happy to spill about you."

"Figures you'd have to pay someone to talk to you," I quipped.

He just laughed, making me cringe. "Oh, how I missed your clever wit," he said, taking a casual step toward me. "From what I heard, you've been a very bad girl. Flirting with teachers, stealing boyfriends..."

How could he have possibly known all this? Spies he said. He told me he had spies on the inside. I will find them and they will be dealt with. "I'm not really in the mood to exchange words with you so how about we just get to it."

"Very well then. I was hoping to end this cat and mouse game." His eyes glowed and he flew at me, knocking me to the ground. "This is going to be easier than I thought," he grinned.

I picked myself up off the ground. I didn't wait for him to attack again. This time I went after him and I wasn't holding anything back. We fought back and forth. I could tell Jack was surprised at how well I could keep up and at this rate I could probably take him. The only downside was, even if I took him down, I had no weapons to kill him. "I have to say I'm pretty impressed. I see someone wore their big girl panties to the party," he taunted.

I socked him in the jaw. He laughed, spitting blood from his mouth. "You know this is getting tedious. I don't see why you don't just give up. I'm never going to give you my powers and it's pretty clear you can't beat me."

"That's what Tristan said too. Right before I threw his ass into a pole."

That really pissed me off. Jack noticed and took advantage. He had me pinned to the ground and was reaching for my neck. "I'm going to enjoy this even more than I did when I ripped your little blond friend's throat out."

"And I'm going to enjoy watching her rip your heart out," Josie said, coming in from behind the hedge.

Jack's head jerked up in the direction of Josie's voice. "But you're...you're dead," he stammered.

"I may be dead, but I still look good, which is more than I can say for you," she smirked. That was enough of a distraction for me to kick him off of me.

He recovered quickly. "I'll take great pleasure in killing you again," he said, charging for Josie, but she was gone in the blink of an eye. He spun in circles, confused, looking for her everywhere. I started to laugh. He glared at me and started to come after me again.

I was ready. He let his anger get the best of him and I was able to take him down. Once again realizing I didn't have a weapon to finish the job. So I did what I could to knock him unconscious. It wasn't as easy as I thought. We struggled back and forth until I threw him hard enough he cracked his head against the fountain. It wasn't enough to knock him out, but enough to slow him down. I ran up behind him and pushed his head in the water. He only struggled for a moment and then he stopped.

"Ella...Ella," Josie said, tugging at my shoulders. "He's gone. You did it. He's gone." I hadn't realized I was still holding him under the water. I let go and fell back. Josie pulled me away from his body. "It's over Ella. It's finally over."

"Why don't I feel like it is," I said, still staring at Jack.

"Ella! Josie!" Billy called.

"We're in here," Josie said. Billy came rushing in followed by Justin, Dean, and Riley.

"Ella, are you okay?" Dean asked, helping me up.

"Yeah," I said, still stunned. "Where's Roman?"

"Still in the gym. He's safe."

"How did you get out?"

"I was still helping people get inside and when I found Justin he told me you came in here."

"Ella, oh my god, are you alright?" Riley asked, coming up next to me.

"Riley, you shouldn't be here. You should be inside where it's safe."

"I tried but she refused. She insisted on coming with to find you," Justin said, coming out from behind one of the hedges in a t-shirt and jeans. I hadn't even noticed he walked away until now. "I had to change," he said. "It's too cold to stand around naked."

I nodded still in shock. "What's going on out there?"

"Most of Jack's army was apprehended...well those that survived," Billy said. "They're still searching the grounds for stragglers. They're keeping everyone inside until they know it's safe. It shouldn't be much longer."

"What about students?" They looked away not wanting to answer. "How many?" I asked. They didn't answer. "How many?" I demanded.

"So far four dead that they found, too many injured to count," Dean said, being the only one brave enough to answer me. "Come on, let's go." He pulled me away to leave.

Just as we stepped through the archway I stopped and turned around. "Wait, what about..." I ran back over to the fountain. "He's gone!"

"What?" Josie said, running over with everyone else. "What

the...but how?"

"He's not dead," I said, looking around. "Bastard!"

"Ella, let's get out of here," Riley said.

"No! I'm tired of running and hiding. Enough is enough! You hear me!" I screamed. "Come out here and show yourself you coward!" I spun around, screaming in the air.

"Ella, he's gone," Josie said.

"No, he's not. I know he's still here!" I turned around and Jack was behind me, smiling. "Let's finish this," I said.

"Gladly," he replied as five of his flunkies stepped in from behind him. I heard a ripping sound and growling and knew Justin had changed back into his wolf form. "Take care of these other fools, but remember, Ella's mine," he hissed and they all charged.

I saw people flying in every direction.

I didn't have time to worry about anyone else. I was concentrating on Jack.

We danced around each other. I heard a whimper in the corner and so did Jack, but I refused to take my eyes off of him. He smiled and flew to the left and I knew he was going after Riley.

I leapt, but I was too late.

He reached her before I did.

Riley screamed as he held a knife to her neck. "Don't move or I will slit her throat," he warned.

"Let her go. She has nothing to do with this!"

"Oh, but she does. You will give me your powers or she dies!"

Justin was now standing next to me, growling and snarling, ready to attack. "Let. Her. Go." I demanded.

"A trade. You for her," he said.

"Ella, it's a trap. Don't do it!" Josie yelled.

He pinched the knife closer to her neck, piercing the skin. Riley squealed as blood trickled down her neck. "Fine. Let her go first," I said.

"I will when I have you," he countered. I put my hands up in surrender and walked over to him slowly. "But first, a taste," he said, sinking his teeth into Riley's neck.

"No!" I screamed as Justin took off leaping in the air.

Jack threw Riley to the ground and struck Justin in the chest with the knife. He instantly fell, collapsing. Riley crawled over to his side and now Jack had the knife by my throat. "Let them go or I spill her blood and you all can watch her die," Jack yelled. Billy, Dean, and Josie slowly backed away from their attackers. Jack's people retreated behind him. Dean took a step forward. "Eh-uh, I wouldn't do that if I were you," Jack warned.

"Take me instead. We have the same blood," Dean said.

"Yes, but your powers I don't want. They're kind of pathetic, but Ella's...I'm going to enjoy those," Jack said, biting into my neck. I gasped from the pain he was causing me. Everything happened so fast I had no time to react. I was tired, battered, and beaten, and I was losing the strength to fight back. I started to feel woozy, weak. Jack was draining me and there was nothing I could do about it. My eyelids were too heavy to keep open. I vaguely heard voices in the distance; people screaming, loud cracking noises, like bones breaking. Slowly it all started to fade away.

The first thing I saw was his eyes, then his smile. Visions of him were coming to me in flashes. I saw him at the party, where we first officially met, art class, and everything in between, up until the moment he died. I saw Gabe carry me away from him. Then I was hovering over him with my hands on his neck. I flinched. These weren't my memories. Where did they come from?

I felt myself fading away. The visions, no longer my own, were dimming. I held on. I held on to these visions to try and find something. A blond haired girl...Cadence, no... someone else...a man with an accent...an angry man.

Everything was coming so fast and then it was gone. All of it slipping away.

I was so weak I could barely hold my head up. I fought to open my eyes. I saw Dean and Billy trying to rush Jack, but more of his people had appeared from behind us and held them back. I thought I was going to pass out. I heard muffled screams as I watched Jack raise the knife above my heart.

This was it. He was really going to kill me this time.

I saw a bright, white flash, and the next thing I knew I was on the ground. When I looked up and saw his face, I knew I was dead. I knew Jack had killed me.

My vision was blurry and I could barely move. "Kyle...Kyle..." I called out to him. I focused on him. I pulled what little strength I had left to get up. Why was I still so weak? If I was dead I should be able to move. Feel no pain, but my body was screaming in agony. I fought through it.

Dazed, I tried to stand back up, but I wobbled, falling back to my knees. "Ella, stay there," Kyle yelled, but I didn't listen. I managed to get up. I was standing between Jack and Kyle.

"You know, when you kill a person, you expect them to stay dead," Jack said as he wiped blood from his lip.

I looked around confused. My hands were covered in blood. There was a long thin line of it down the front of my dress. Everyone was still here and they were all watching me with wide eyes. I didn't understand what was going on.

I looked at Jack and he smiled. "Good, now you can watch me kill him all over again," Jack said, charging. I somehow managed to stop him. It took everything I had but I stopped him. I brought up my shield, too weak to fight. Jack pounded and kicked, trying to break through it. I found the knife, but I had to let go of my shield to get to it. Jack saw my eyes and we both dove for it. He climbed on top of me trying to pin me. The knife was so close, just within reach of my fingertips, and then it was in my hand. I struck, elbowing Jack in the face. He rolled off of me. I knelt down on top of him, pinning his arms down by his side. I raised my hands above my head ready to end this once and for all. "This is for Tristan."

"He's alive!" Jack screamed, causing me to stop halfway.

"Shut up! You don't talk about him." I backhanded him across the face.

I raised my arms again. "Wait, if you kill me then I can't prove it to you," he said.

"Tristan's dead. I saw him and he was dead," I said, even though I'm not so sure anymore.

"No he's not. After you left I came back and he was still alive."

"You're lying!" I said, holding the knife to his neck.

"I can prove it. In my pocket is a necklace that belongs to him. If you let me go I can show you."

"Ella, no. He's stalling. Don't listen to him," Kyle said.

"No I'm not. It's the truth."

"Then why didn't he come for me? If he was alive he would have come and found me."

"I told him you were dead. That's why he didn't look for you."

"And I'm supposed to believe you just let him go?"

"I didn't at first. I wanted to kill him. He begged me to when I told him you were dead, but he didn't deserve it. He needed to suffer for what he did. I knew his grief would eat at him until there was nothing left but an empty shell. So I let him go," he said.

I shook my head. I needed to know for sure, I needed to see. "Show me the necklace."

"You have to let me go."

I stood up slowly.

I kept the knife close to his chest and let him take the necklace from his pocket. I held out my hand and he laid it in the center. Kyle came over and took the knife from me and put it to Jack's throat.

I looked down at the necklace in the palm of my hand.

It was my grandmother's silver cross.

Tristan had told me he found it the night of the accident and said he was going to keep it as a memento, like a good luck charm. He said he would only take it off and return it to my family if something happened to me. I had forgotten all about it.

I closed my palm around the necklace. I knew it was hers because it was twined in Celtic knots with a small diamond infused in the center, along with her initials on the back. I looked up at Jack and grabbed his shirt. "Where is he?"

"The last I heard he was in Ireland," he said.

I let go.

I couldn't believe it.

Tristan was alive.

"Ella, what is it?" Josie said, rushing up to me.

Dean and Billy had managed to defeat their attacker's and were standing there watching. "He's alive Josie. Tristan is alive." She shook her head at me like I was crazy. "Josie it makes sense. It would explain why you didn't see him. That's because he's alive."

"Ella, I don't know?"

"It's true. I saw him myself," Jack said.

"Josie I know he is. He has to be." Jack took advantage of our distraction and knocked the knife from Kyle then knocked him to the ground. Jack picked up the knife ready to kill Kyle with it when I turned and threw my hands up. "No!" I yelled.

I put all the power I had left into my shield and when Jack hit it, it sent him flying over the hedges and into the darkness of the maze. My body was shaking from the force I used to create such a powerful shield. "Holy shit," Dean said, coming up behind me. I didn't get the chance to respond. I heard Riley crying over in the corner.

"Justin," I said. "Help me up." Kyle and Dean lifted me to my feet and helped carry me over to them. Justin was bleeding pretty badly and I thought he might even be dead.

"Ella, can you help him?" Riley asked, tears streaming down her face.

"I...I can try." I had no idea if it would work. I never healed a wound this big, but I knew I had to try for Riley.

"Ella, I don't think this is a good idea," Dean said. "You're too weak and if try to use any more power...it might kill you."

"I have to at least try. I can't just let him die," I said. Dean knew better than to argue with me when I had my mind set so he let me go. I placed my hand over Justin's chest as Riley ran her fingers through his soft fur. My hand glowed, but at first it didn't do anything. I concentrated harder, pulling the power from within. I could feel it flowing through me as I placed my other hand over his chest.

I saw him take a breath and the wound slowly started to heal. "Ella, it's working!" Riley cheered.

I started to feel really hot and dizzy. "Ella, you don't look so good," Josie said. I ignored her and kept concentrating on pulling the power from within. My hands started to shake and I noticed my whole body was glowing, like it had in the dining hall when I stopped the fight. Justin was turning back into his human form. "Dean, give me your jacket." Josie took Dean's jacket and placed it over Justin's naked body.

"Ella stop, you did enough," Dean said worried. But like always, I didn't listen. "Ella, you're using too much power, stop."

I saw Justin's eyes twitch. He opened them and I smiled, just before I passed out.

CHAPTER TWENTY-EIGHT

I could hear voices all around me, calling my name. I blinked a few times, but every time I opened my eyes my vision was blurry. I could feel my body was weak as I struggled to move. "No Ella, don't move," Kyle whispered in my ear. I felt someone sweep me up off the ground. I was being carried.

I was coming in and out of consciousness as I was carried through the maze. "Can't you just transport her?" I heard Josie say.

"No, she's too weak. Her body won't be able to handle it," Kyle said.

I heard other voices, strange ones. They were all jumbled together, but through the mix I was able to pick out Gabe's. "Ella, what happened, what is wrong?" he asked panicked.

"She drained what little power she had left to heal Justin," Josie said.

"Who is this?" Gabe asked defensively. I knew he had to be talking about Kyle.

"Long story short, he's an angel and a good guy," Josie said.

There was a long pause of silence. "I can vouch for him," Dean said.

"Take her to the infirmary," Gabe said.

"Jack..." I tried to speak, but it was barely a whisper. "Ja-ack," I tried again.

"Wait, she's trying to say something," Josie cried. "Ella, what is it?"

"Jack...find Jack," I managed before I passed out again.

When I came to, I was hooked up to all types of machines. "Kyle?" I said. My voice was raspy and my throat was dry. "Kyle?"

"No Ella, it's me, Roman," he said sadly.

"Roman…" I reached for him and he took my hand.

"Shh, just rest," he whispered. I overheard him talking to one of the nurses and she came over and checked my vitals.

"Hi Ella, I'm nurse Edie. How are you feeling?"

I moved a shaky hand to my throat. "Thirsty," I said scratchy.

"I'll go get you something to drink," she said, leaving the room.

I turned back to Roman. "Where's Dean…and Josie?" I tried to swallow, but my throat was burning.

The nurse returned with a cup of ice chips and pitcher of water. "Here you go sweetie. I'll let the doctor know you're awake and we'll come back in to check on you in a bit."

Roman took the cup of ice chips and went to feed them to me. I ripped the cup from his hands. "I'm not a child. I can do it myself," I snapped.

"It sounds like she's doing okay," I heard Josie giggle and peek her head around the curtain. "You up for some company?" I nodded and she pulled the curtain back to reveal all my friends standing there. Even Justin was there with his arm in a sling.

"I'll be back later," Roman said, getting up and leaving. I wanted to stop him, but I knew I had hurt his feelings and now was not the time.

"I didn't know what you liked, but it's the least I could do, you know…for saving my life," Justin said, handing me a small bag.

I reached in and inside was a box of Oreo cookies. "Is this my treat for doing a good job?" I laughed. He shrugged and cracked a smile. "Thank you. I guess we're even now."

"Something like that," he smiled as I offered him an Oreo.

"What did I miss here?" Cameron asked, sitting on the edge of the bed.

I just shook my head. "How are you feeling?" Riley asked.

"Tired and kind of warn out," I sighed.

"You look good though," Sienna said. "And you have another blue streak," she squeaked. My smile fell. "Oh…you didn't know. It looks great," she smiled perkily.

"Okay guys, that's enough for the night," nurse Edie said coming back in the room.

"But we just got here?" Riley said.

"I know, but Ella needs her rest," she insisted.

I asked Dean and Josie to stay a moment and said goodnight to the rest of my friends. Once everyone else was gone, I automatically started with the questions. "Where's Jack? Did they find him?" Dean turned away from me and looked out the window. I turned to Josie and the look on her face said enough.

"No honey, they didn't," she said.

I clenched my fist tight and that's when I felt it.

The necklace.

It was still in my hand.

I opened my fist back up and held the necklace up. "Tristan," I whispered placing my fist over my heart. "What's the word about Tristan? Did anyone find anything out?"

"Ella...you don't really believe him do you? You know he would have said anything to distract you from killing him."

"Josie it's true. I know it is. He's alive and he's out there somewhere."

"Ella, I just don't want you to get your hopes up...at least until we can find out for sure."

"Dean?" He was quiet the entire time he was there.

"Josie, can I please have a moment alone with my sister?" Dean asked.

"Yeah, I'll be right outside," she said, squeezing my hand.

I turned my attention to Dean who was still staring out the window. "When I heard you had gone in to that maze after Jack," he paused and looked down at his hands on the windowsill. "I thought..." he shook his head. "I thought I might lose you," he admitted.

"Dean, I'm okay. See," I said, waving my hand over myself. "Good as new, well, almost."

He finally turned to face me. "Ella, that's not funny."

"Oh, come on Dean, this is the third time Jack tried to kill me and failed. You think you'd get used to this by now." He gave me his I'm not amused look. "Dean, look, we can sit here and talk about what could have happened or we can be happy at the fact that once again I have proven Jack cannot get me."

"This coming from the girl who only months ago wanted to give up. What's the sudden change?"

"Someone once told me we McCallisters don't give up. We're fighters."

He smiled weakly. "I have to admit when you blasted him into the air like that I thought it was pretty bad ass," he said.

"Why thank you."

"Get some sleep. I'll be back in the morning," he said, kissing me on the forehead and sending Josie back in with the nurse.

"I remember telling you you need your rest," the nurse said, looking at Josie.

"I know, but can't she stay just a little while longer?" I pleaded. She rolled her eyes at me and said she could stay, but only for a little.

Josie sat down on the bed next to me. "So, how are you feeling, really?"

"I'm just so...I don't know. I mean I feel better, stronger, but I just have so many questions."

"I know you do, but I think that should wait until later."

"Josie no. You know I won't be able to rest until I know everything that happened."

She sighed, knowing I was right. "Well I'm not going to lie. The guardians have a big mess to clean up. The school is in disarray and they're currently discussing on what to do. Parents are panicking and threatening to close down the school."

"No, they can't do that. What else did they say?"

"I don't know Ella. That's all I heard."

"So...how mad is Roman?"

"Why would he be mad?"

"I kind of said Kyle's name when I first woke up, not to mention I snapped at him."

"Hmm...I can understand the Kyle thing, but the snapping part I'm sure he'll get over. I mean if he really knew you he would have known better."

"That doesn't help," I said, wondering how the hell I was going to fix that. "Speaking of Kyle...where is he?"

"He had to go back," she said softly.

"Do they know? Is he in trouble?"

"I don't know. We really didn't have time to chat if you know what I mean. He carried you here and then he was gone. I'm sorry. I wish I knew more."

"I know," I said, thinking the same thing. "Alright, now I need you to go pack me a bag and find my passport." I sat up and started to pull the IV out of my arm.

"Whoa, what are you doing?"

"We are getting out of here."

"Ella, you're not a hundred percent yet. I think you need to stay here another day or two."

"I'm not going to lay here hold up in some hospital when I know Tristan is out there somewhere."

"Ella, I really think you need to think this through." She gave me that, *'I'm crazy'* look for believing him.

"Josie, I know you think I'm crazy and you find it hard to believe that he would tell me something like that, but think about it. You said so yourself that you didn't see him."

"Yes but that doesn't mean —"

"I know it's not concrete proof and yes Jack could have stolen the necklace from him, but I saw him. I just didn't believe it at first."

"What do you mean you saw him?"

"When Jack bit me. I thought maybe the spell was broken or he just didn't try to block his mind, but I saw him. I saw exactly what Jack had told me. How he went back and Tristan was alive. I saw Tristan take off the necklace and put it in his pocket, but he missed and it fell and that's how Jack got it. Josie I have to at least try. Even though you won't admit it, I know you love Billy and if the roles were reversed you would want to know. Wouldn't you?"

She looked at me concerned, but I knew I had her. "Okay, fine. I'll give you one week for this little adventure, but then you have to promise me if we find nothing you'll let it go."

I crossed my fingers behind my back and promised. I was not going to give up until I found Tristan. "Okay, so we need to find a way to get out of here."

"I'm going to go back to your room and pack us a bag. Then I'll meet up with you back here in an hour and we'll figure it out from there." She turned to leave but stopped by the door. "By the way, I just wanted to tell you that whole glow thing was pretty cool," she smiled.

After Josie left I got back in bed and waited. That was all I could do for now. I thought about how I was going to explain this to Roman. I didn't think I could. He wouldn't understand and I didn't want to hurt his feelings any more than I already had. I knew Dean was going to be pissed off and Gabe. Oh God Gabe. I hadn't even had the chance to talk to him or see him.

I turned on the little light next to my bed and searched for a piece of paper and pen. I wanted to leave a note for Gabe to explain to him why I had to leave. I sat there going over excuse after excuse, but there was nothing I could say to him that would make this okay. I felt someone behind me and I turned to look. "Kyle."

"Ella," he smiled. I got up and ran into his arms. "I can't stay. I just had to see you one last time before I left," he said, pulling back and looking into my eyes.

"I wish you didn't have to go."

"I know, but I do. I want you to know I love you and I'll be watching over you as long as I can. I also want to tell you how proud I am of you." I squeezed him harder, holding on for as long as I could.

"You were there that night. That night on the balcony when my parents told me what I was. I felt you. I knew it was you," I told him, remembering the way I felt.

"Yes. I was there. I couldn't be there for you in person, but I was there with you in spirit."

"Which is more than I could ask for," I said.

"Before I go, can you do me a favor?"

I looked up at him. "Anything," I said. I owed him more than I could give him.

"Please be more careful and stop running head first into dangerous situations."

"I can't promise, but I'll try."

"Oh how I missed your stubbornness," he said, kissing me on the lips and holding me in his arms one last time before he disappeared. I sighed at the emptiness I felt when he faded away. My arms still hung in the hollow space where he just was. This wasn't fair. I needed more time. I was getting tired of people leaving me.

I had a hard time pulling myself back together after Kyle left. I decided to lie back down until Josie came back to get me. I thought it be wise to get as much rest as I could. I was physically feeling better but I knew I wasn't at full strength yet and we had a long night ahead of us.

"Ella?" Josie whispered, shaking me gently. "Here, I brought you some clothes to change into."

I sat up and saw we had some company. "What's Billy doing

here?"

"I figured we could use some extra muscle and plus who else better to help us find Tristan than his best friend?"

She did have a point. "Alright, give me five minutes."

"Make it quick. We don't have a lot of time."

I headed into the bathroom to change. I took a look at myself in the mirror and wished I didn't. I looked like I hadn't slept in days. I had dark circles under my eyes and my hair was a mess. I also noticed the new blue streak Sienna was talking about. This one was on the top right side. There was no way to hide them now. At this rate if I kept getting them all my hair might turn blue and that would not be cool.

I washed my face and managed to brush my nappy hair back into a ponytail. I came out of the bathroom where Josie and Billy were waiting. "Okay, I'm ready," I said.

Billy stepped out into the hallway first to make sure it was clear. Then we quietly made our way outside. Billy told me he found a way out in the back where the guardians had already canvased the area so there wouldn't be as many there. If we stuck to the shadows we would be okay.

When we got to the wall, I wondered how the hell we were going to get out. I didn't see any entrances or exits. "Umm... how are we going to get out?" I asked, staring at the eight foot gray stone in front of us.

"We're going to climb," Billy said. I looked at him like he was joking, but he clearly wasn't. Billy placed his one foot against the side of the building and the other against the wall. He climbed it with ease like he was Spiderman. When he got to the top he took the backpack off of his back and pulled out a rope. "I'm going to drop this down for you and Josie to use."

I made Josie go first. She looked at the rope, then back at me, and smiled. I blinked and she was on the top of the wall. "That's not fair. I don't have special angel powers," I said.

"Oh Ella, just grab the rope," she said.

I mumbled to myself as I pulled myself up the wall. When I reached the top, Billy packed up the rope and hopped down with no problem. Once again I blinked and Josie was at the bottom. "Okay, how the hell am I supposed to get down?" I complained, feeling like the weak link.

"Jump," Billy said.

"What!"

"I'll catch you."

"You better or I'm going to be really pissed off," I said, praying he didn't miss. I closed my eyes and went for it. Thankfully he caught me.

"Okay, this way," Billy said once my feet were planted safely on the ground.

We walked about a mile through the woods and then headed to the road where there was an SUV parked on the side. "How did you guys manage to get a car?" I asked.

"From me," Cameron said, jumping out of the driver side. I looked at Josie pissed that should would involve anyone else.

"Hey, don't look at me. It wasn't my idea," Josie said.

"Don't get mad at them it was my idea," Cameron intervened. "I went to your room to ask Josie how you really were and I overheard what they were talking about and thought I could offer my services."

"Cameron, I really appreciate it, but I don't want you to get in trouble."

"Please, this is nothing. Besides, you need me. How else are you going to go on this little adventure without my funds?"

"Umm, Cameron, no offense but between Josie and I we have more than enough funds."

"Actually, you don't. Let's not forget that Josie is supposed to be dead and if you use your accounts it will be easy for people to find you and I take it you're not looking to be found."

"Huh, I hadn't thought of that."

"That's where I come in," Cameron smiled.

"Cameron, I can't ask you to do that."

"You're not. I'm volunteering."

"What about school and Austin?"

"School can wait and as far as Austin, I'll deal with him later. You're a friend who needs my help and that's more important."

"Thank you," I said, giving her a hug.

"I hate to break up this little girl bonding moment, but we need to go before someone realizes we're missing," Billy said.

"So where we off to?" Cameron asked.

They all turned to look at me.

"Ireland," I said.

To be continued...

Reborn

Playlist

Chapter one

Pictures of you (Opening sequence) * Alicia Keys - Like you'll never see me again

Sweet dreams are made of this (Ella awakes) * Noah Gunderson - Family

By my side (Josie's grave) * Ryan Dan - Tears of an Angel

Chapter two

Reflections (Journal entry) * Zola Jesus - Skin

I never told you (Xander's talk with Ella) * Daughter - Medicine

Chapter three

All I need is you (Ella dreams of

399

Tristan) * Youth Group – Forever Young

Wishing on a star (Dean's gift to Ella) *

Glee Cast – Silent Night

Chapter four

Bright lights (Walk in snow) * Cary

brothers – O Holy Night

First Love (Danni's confession) * The

Gaslight Anthem – National Anthem

Secrets (Ella's talk with her mom) * Kopecky

Family Band – Change

Chapter five

Best thing I never had (Farewell to

Tristan) * A fine Frenzy – Almost lover

Everything I can't have (Ella's hissy

fit) * Of Monsters and Men – Dirty Paws

Chapter six

Last Friday Night (Playing pool/Dancing) *

Macklemore and Ryan Lewis – Thrift shop

That's not my name (Bar fight) * Fidlar –

White on white

Chapter seven

What Doesn't Kill You (Punishment) * Delta Spirit - Parade

Road to Nowhere (Arrival of School) * The Neighbourhood - Female Robbery

Wish I could (Tour of School) * Pink - Sober

Chapter eight

What doesn't kill you (Ella by the fountain) * Oberhofer - Away From You

Chapter nine

Welcome to the Jungle (Party) * Jay Z Ft. Justin Timberlake - Holy Grail

What you know (Catching up with Dixon) * Radical Face - Glory

Chapter ten

Running up that hill (Walk to Dining hall) * Grouplove - Don't say Oh Well

Happiness is overrated (daydreaming on

the field) * Radical Face - Welcome Home

Chapter Eleven

Feel Again (Talk with Aidan) * Blue Fountain - Eyes on fire

Blurred Lines (Lost in the maze) * Birdy - The District Sleeps Alone Tonight

Chapter twelve

Chapter thirteen

Wake Up (Dream in maze) * Garbage - Control

Resistance (Working on project with Roman) * Morning parade - Speechless (acoustic)

Then he kissed me (Aidan's office) * Sky Ferreira - Obsession

Chapter fourteen

Where are you now (Reflection in mirror) * Cary Brothers - If you were here

Walk the Line (Ride to Mall) * Fort Lean - The Mall

You give me something (Aidan's office) *

Charlie XCX - Stay away

Chapter fifteen

Bad Romance (Dean gives Ella pep talk) * Daughter - Smother

Remain nameless (Library) * Laura Veirs - Little Deschutes

Chapter sixteen

Feeling good (Aidan's room) * Des'ree - Kissing You

I put a spell on you (Fight with Aidan in quad) * Mona - Shoot the Moon

Chapter seventeen

Missed the boat (Time Alone) * Cat Power - Keep on running

Roll away your stone (Roman apologizes to Ella) * Mindy Smith and Mathew Perryman Jones - Anymore of this

Chapter eighteen

Wake me up (Trying to un-glow) * Damien

Rice - The Blowers Daughter

Kiss with a fist (Ella and Roman's kiss) *
Miley Cyrus - Wrecking Ball

Patient love (Journal entry) * Noah
Gunderson - He got away

Chapter nineteen

I'm gonna be (Journal Entry) * Young Summer
- Why try

Set it off (Roman talks with Ella) * Yeah
Yeah Yeah's - Tick

Rain over me (Roman explains) * Olivia
Broadfield - Happening

Time after time (Kissing outside) * Israel
Cannon - Letting Go

This nowhere (Basement) * Wild Belle - Keep
You

True colors (Party) * Icona Pop - I love it

It doesn't mean a thing (Fight) * Aidan
Hawken and Carina Rownd - Walking Blind

Chapter twenty

Who will save your soul (Dream in class)
* Lana Del Ray - Young and Beautiful

Don't let go yet (Confesses to Roman) *
Dave Baxter -Whispers

Roar (Training) * Kardinal ft. Dr Dre & the
Clipse - Set it off

Chapter Twenty-one

Chapter twenty-two

Blow me one last kiss (Afternoon with
mom) * Passenger - Patient Love

Chapter twenty-three

Skinny Love (In the morning with Roman) *
Ed Sheeran - Kiss me

When the night comes (First time) * Ray
Lamontagne - Let it be me

Chapter twenty-four

Wake me up before you go-go (The morning after) * Amy Stroup - Wait for the Morning

Stronger (Fight with Roman) * The Lumineers - Stubborn Love

Timeless (Enter Josie/Billy) * Robyn - Be mine (Acoustic)

Chapter Twenty-five

I want you to (Catching up with Josie) * Marina and the Diamonds - Fear and Loathing

Don't let the sun go down on me (Ella falls apart) * The National - Terrible Love

Chapter twenty-six

Such great heights (Heaven) * The Quiet Kind - Arms and Enemies

It's my party and I'll cry if I want to (Getting ready for the dance) * The Airborne Toxic Event - The kids are ready to die

Young at heart (At the dance) * The Airborne Toxic Event - Timeless

It's all coming back to me now (Ell and Roman's dance) * David Roch - Don't let go yet

From the start (The Attack) * Imagine Dragons - Radioactive

Chapter twenty-seven

Hold on to what you believe (Jack draining Ella) * Ellie Goulding - Dead in the Water

Chapter twenty-eight

Endless love (Kyle says goodbye) *Luke Sital-Singh - Bottled up tight

She holds a key (Leaving) * Talking heads - Road to Nowhere

Jessica Miller

Reborn

Jessica Miller

Reborn

Jessica Miller

Reborn

ABOUT THE AUTHOR

Find out more about Jessica on her blog or visit her other sites.
www.jesslmiller.blogspot.com
www.facebook.com/authorJLMiller
Twitter: Jessica Miller @JLMreadingrocks